# MAYBE MURDER

ASH FITZSIMMONS

# MAYBE MURDER

THE LOST HALLS, BOOK TWO

MAYBE MURDER. Copyright © 2025 by Ash Fitzsimmons.

Print Edition ISBN: 978-1-949861-71-6

Cover design by MiblArt.

www.ashfitzsimmons.com

ASH FITZSIMMONS

# MAYBE MURDER

## THE LOST HALLS, BOOK TWO

MAYBE MURDER. Copyright © 2025 by Ash Fitzsimmons.

Print Edition ISBN: 978-1-949861-71-6

Cover design by MiblArt.

www.ashfitzsimmons.com

# CHAPTER 1

"**O**ops."

I registered Ainnet's voice a millisecond before hot liquid poured all over me and my lunch tray. Jumping in surprise, I leapt from my chair and looked down to see vegetable soup soaking into my clothes and pooling on the tile—and unlike the vegetable soup my mom had always made, this one was thick, meat-free, and tomato-based. The fresh red stain on my white shirt looked only slightly paler than blood.

"What the *hell*?" I yelped, reverting to English on instinct, and turned to find Ainnet standing there with her pack of useless lapdogs, one hand holding her emptied ceramic bowl and the other barely covering her lips in a simulacrum of shock.

"Oh, no," she said in Pactish as the girls behind her tittered, "did that splash you? Clumsy of me. You can clean yourself up, right?"

I hunched my shoulders, trying to process her feigned apology, the growing laughter at her back, and the unpleasant sensation of rapidly cooling soup down my front. She'd caught a clump of my hair as well with her spill, and it hung over my chest like a paint-soaked brush, dripping.

"You did that on purpose," my friend Sage snapped, hurrying around the table as those of my cousins nearest to me and the splash zone scooted out of the way. Sage was four years younger than me, skinny, and small, only a couple inches above five feet tall, but what meat she had on her bones was muscle thanks to the rowing team. Though

Ainnet was considerably taller, she had the typical willowy elven build, and my money would have been on Sage in a fair fight. But add in magic, and my friend, though scrappy, would have lost pretty quickly.

Ainnet rolled her eyes as Sage started wiping the vegetable chunks off of me with her napkin. "Don't tell me the halfwit can't tidy herself." Ainnet paused, smirking, then added, "Of course, seeing as she needs *masking jewelry*, I guess I shouldn't be surprised that she's totally incompetent."

I wasn't incompetent—the fact that I had a private tutor to help me control my potentially violent aeromancy was proof of that—but in general, my talent was weaker than Ainnet's. Though we were both eighteen, Ainnet was a full-blooded elf and the beneficiary of a Pactlands education, whereas I wasn't quite three quarters and had only just begun to learn to manage my abilities. She knew I couldn't yet clean soup out of my clothing for the same reason that I relied on a masking pendant to fix my ears, an illusion that would have come as easily as breathing to her.

"I suppose the halfwits *would* stick together," said Ainnet while I stood there, trying to force my arms to stop trembling. My temper was spiking, my pulse quickening, and my talent, so long bottled up, surged against my restraints. I could have let it loose and blown Ainnet halfway across the dining hall, but that would have started a fight in earnest. Sage and I certainly couldn't take on Ainnet's clique—half a dozen elves, nymphs, and sorcerers—by ourselves, and though I knew my cousins would have tried to help, they were in the same boat I was, minus the aeromancy. It'd have been bad enough if, say, Peter and Uncle Kyle had jumped in, or David, who was my age, but Eugene and Little David had decided to sit by Sage and me that day, and those two were seven and six. The last thing I wanted to do was call home to pass along the news that one of the babies had been concussed.

"Bitch," Sage muttered. Like me, she tended to revert to our mother tongue for profanity.

Ainnet's blue eyes narrowed. "What did you—"

"Hey, ti'Har!" a female voice snapped, and I looked up to find Keef marching toward us from the rowing team's table. A few months my junior, Keef was in the class below Ainnet's, but she'd taken Sage under her wing—and by extension, it seemed, my cousins and me. "Is there some reason you can't fix your own messes?"

Keef gestured, and almost instantly, I was clean and dry.

Ainnet turned to her and folded her arms, using her couple inches over Keef to her advantage. Had those two fought, I'd have put my money on the younger of the pair of blondes, whose rower's physique put Ainnet's to shame. "This doesn't concern you."

"Oh, I think it does. Back off."

She tittered. "Who are you to give *me* orders, ti'Mal?"

"I'll be happy to show you if you press me," Keef replied with a dangerous smile.

By then, Ainnet's girls had clustered around her, while my older cousins had risen from their seats, bowing up for a fight. "I'm fine," I said. "Let it go."

Keef ignored me. "What's your problem?" she asked Ainnet. "Leave Maebe alone. She's not hurting anyone."

Ainnet stared her down for a moment, then tossed her hair. "Of course *you're* not concerned about dishonor. Have you been out to the penal farm lately? How's Daddy faring?"

Keef didn't take the bait. "Don't know, don't care, but if you don't back off, I *will* call my mother and tell her all about this."

Though elven politics were still a muddled mess to me, I'd learned enough to know that while Hall ti'Har outranked Hall ti'Mal, Keef's mother headed her Hall, which gave Keef a bit of social leverage she'd otherwise have lacked. But it wasn't a trump card. Ainnet took a step closer and sneered. "You think Mommy cares about the damn halfwits?"

"*Enough.*"

We all twitched at the deep-voiced command and wheeled around as Swift Eagle, backed by her posse from the melee team, strode up the aisle toward our table.

Though she was only twenty, Swift Eagle was the best player in the school—possibly the best North Lake had seen in the last fifty years, or so I'd heard—and she was the clear shoe-in for captain once the current holder of that position graduated. Even for a troll, she was large, about eight and a half feet tall and probably still growing. Her skin was deep purple, and like most trolls I'd seen, she wore her dark hair as a short mohawk. There was, I'd been cautioned, little superficial difference between the male and female of the species, and their tusks grew in equally sharp. Swift Eagle tended to top hers with sparkly blue rubber caps, a safety measure for melee purposes, but nothing in the sport's regulations compelled her to do anything about her claws. Trolls couldn't cast spells to save their lives, but even the magically gifted underestimated them at their peril.

I'd been confused at first about her name, seeing as there was no family name attached to it. Like most trolls, Swift Eagle had been given an evocative name in Troll- ish—translated, it worked out to "The Sound of a Swift Eagle Dancing on the Summer Wind"—but everyone used the shortened form, and always in its Pactish translation. Trollish was a devil of a language to learn and virtually im- possible to pronounce properly without a troll's vocal cords, so most didn't bother trying. Happily for North Lake's melee team, the captain was *also* a troll, and it came in handy that he and Swift Eagle could shout at each other across the field in a language incomprehensible to many of the other players.

Ainnet held her ground as Swift Eagle drew near. "This is none of your concern—"

"Uh, *yeah*, it is," she snapped. "Keef, stand down."

Wisely, Keef raised her hands in placation and took a step back.

"You're antagonizing her," Swift Eagle continued, pointing to Keef. "*And* Sage. Come on, you're picking on youngers students now? Would you like a fight with the rowing team as well?"

I glanced toward their table and saw the older rowers watching tensely, lunches forgotten.

"They're the ones who—" Ainnet began, but the troll cut her off.

"Came to the defense of Maebe here?" she said, and I flinched as her heavy hand landed on my freshly cleaned shoulder. "You didn't trip, Ainnet. I saw the whole thing, and so did a good number of them," she added, cocking her head behind her at her teammates. "What's the matter with you? The new kids are doing their best."

"They can't even talk properly."

She had a point. While my cousins and I had been given language potions for Pactish and both elven languages, the potion did nothing to disguise our accents. We came from a clannish community in the north Georgia mountains—one with no television and limited access to things like radio—and we sounded like it.

"So?" asked Swift Eagle. "You've got an accent, too."

Ainnet stiffened. "Do not."

"Of course you do. You can pick an elf out of a crowd by sound alone. Anyway," she continued as Ainnet sputtered, "they're *trying*, and they're not hurting anyone. Stop harassing the new kids."

Folding her arms, Ainnet countered, "You're not stuck with a bunch of humans masquerading as trolls, are you? It's insulting."

"For what it's worth, if you want to get technical," I interjected, "I'm almost three-quarters elven, and none of us is less than sixty percent. *Human* is a bit of a stretch."

She wrinkled her nose. "And that makes you even

more pathetic. How can you be *eighteen* and still unable to mask?"

I tensed, but before I could retort, Swift Eagle stepped between us and stared down at Ainnet. "I can't mask. Are you calling me pathetic?" she asked in a low and decidedly dangerous tone.

"No, but—"

"Move on, or I'll get a teacher."

Seeing no help in the melee team, Ainnet chose the wiser path and skulked off with her girls on her heels. I released a long sigh as she flounced away, and Swift Eagle murmured, "You all right, Maebe?"

"Yeah, thanks."

She patted my shoulder again with a hand like an iron skillet and walked off, and a few of the players nodded at us as they headed back toward their usual table.

I wasn't sure what I'd done to earn a modicum of protection from Swift Eagle, but I was grateful. Like my cousins and me, she was a boarding student; her family lived somewhere in the hinterlands, and they sent her to North Lake for academic purposes. That she'd turned out to be an athletic prodigy was incidental. She was confident and extroverted, so when she'd noticed our clump sitting alone in the dining hall during the first week of August, she'd cornered me at dinner one night and asked for the details. I didn't know why she chose me—perhaps it was because I still looked my age, whereas my oldest cousins seemed so much older, even by sorcerer standards—but in any case, she was the first student beyond Sage or Keef to do more than whisper and shoot furtive glances in our presence, and I was grateful for a friendly face, even one with razor tusks.

I'd assumed that Swift Eagle would get her answers and give us the same sort of wide berth that the elven students were employing, but she continued to say hi. Perhaps we weren't exactly *friends*, but Swift Eagle treated me like a person instead of a freak of nature, and that fall, that counted for a lot.

As my cousins settled down to finish their lunch, Sage took her seat, and Keef grabbed her tray and joined us. "You don't have to," I murmured when she pulled up a chair.

She snorted. "No problem." Taking a bite of her salad, she glanced at Sage and asked, "What did you call her?"

"A bitch," Sage replied around a mouthful of bread.

"Bitch?" she said, slowly echoing the unfamiliar word.

"A female dog," I offered. "Also a term for an unpleasant woman. It's not polite."

Keef grinned. "I should hope not." She ate for a moment, then narrowed her eyes at me in thought. "You're being tutored in magic, yes?"

I nodded. "All of us except the babies."

"Mm. So…not to be rude, but when do you suppose they'll teach you to mask?"

"Good question," I mumbled into my soup, and she let the matter drop.


Be careful what you wish for.

Since I was a little kid, I'd dreamed of going to a real school. Not the haphazard lessons in reading and arithmetic taught by a rotating group of parents in one home or another, which seldom flowed between sessions and failed to cater to the entire student body, but rather a school like the ones referenced in the modest library of children's books kept in the community meeting house. In those picture books, neatly groomed boys and girls sat smiling in rows of desks while a teacher, always female and as well dressed as her students, wrote words and calculations on a blackboard. The illustrations made the classroom experience seem like fun for all parties involved.

There were no classrooms or blackboards in East Branch, though we did have a store of old slates to mark up and wipe clean, and our only desks were our laps. Our lessons seldom went for more than a couple hours at a time, as our parents were needed elsewhere—tending the crops, hunting in the mountains around us, chopping wood for our fireplaces and stoves, drawing water. But then, to hear the elders tell it, we needed little from the classroom. Our true education came from helping the rest of the community in the endless chores that kept us warm and fed, which would someday become our responsibility. And so it had been since East Branch's founding, each generation passing to the next the skills necessary for survival.

As a small child, I'd asked my parents why I couldn't go to school, holding open the books to show them what I meant. *Because we'll teach you everything you need to know here*, they'd said at first. Later, when I'd continued to press them, the answer had shifted: *Because it's not safe outside.*

Outside—the world beyond the community's long wooden fence, a place so potentially fraught with peril that I'd visited it exactly once as a kid. People outside the community weren't like us, I was warned, and they wouldn't understand us. That was why my parents taught me to carry a headband, just in case I was confronted with outsiders and needed to hide my flopped-over pointy ears at a moment's notice. The flop was, as far as anyone knew, a defect unique to East Branch, and we didn't need strangers taking notice…especially because those of us born with the flop tended to be born with the touch as well.

Translated from East Branch–speak, magical talent.

Having reached young adulthood, I understood where my parents had been coming from. A weird-looking child who could make books fly across the room or set fires when agitated would be a danger to non-gifted children, and his very existence would undoubtedly draw attention to East Branch. We'd survived as long as we had by keeping the rest of the world away from us, and as far as our elders were concerned, the status quo should be maintained.

But I wasn't satisfied.

Three months after my eighteenth birthday, I ran away from home to seek my fortune outside, hoping for a better life than the one ordained for me. Luckily, the first outsider I encountered after several days of rough camping in the woods was Jane Fortune, the sorcerer dating my wayward cousin, Connor. Since Connor's parents had left East Branch and raised him in nearby Whitford, he knew where I was coming from, but Jane understood the potentialities of the Pactlands.

Within days, my life had been upended. Genetic testing led to a closer look at our old community records, and to everyone's surprise, half the foundational stock of East Branch hadn't been human at all, but rather elves—immortal, magically gifted refugees. Since East Branch had been so insular in the nearly three centuries that followed, those refugees' genes had been mixed and remixed...and they'd proven strong. Hoping to find other communities like East Branch, I underwent an excruciating blood trace procedure, only to discover that most of my elven ancestors were alive and well in New York, far from where they'd abandoned their half-blooded children.

My many-times great-grandfather was, shall we say, less than pleased to meet me, and that was before I accidentally set his office on fire. After all, I was a baby aeromancer, unusually gifted with wind manipulation, and my control over my nascent power wasn't exactly fantastic when I was angry and in pain.

It wasn't my fault that the old fart had chosen to use unsecured candles for ambiance.

But aside from my *delightful* progenitors, the rest of the elven population—as well as a mess of sorcerers, trolls, centaurs, nymphs, and more—had migrated into an artificial pocket world several centuries ago as a way to protect themselves from encroaching humans. To a kid who'd barely left her backwoods farm, the Pactlands was an astounding place, its capital a city of glass skyscrapers beyond my wildest imaginings. Never mind that Beukal was apparently smaller than Atlanta—I had no frame of reference, and it was impossibly sprawling to me. In any case, Atlanta certainly didn't have a system of portals like Beukal's, which connected the city to both the surrounding towns and the real world.

Although we were quasi-elven at East Branch, the fact that the rest of our ancestry was human made quite a few Pactlanders balk. Still, as our community was struggling, the Forum had taken pity and agreed to admit us under supervision. Anyone from East Branch who wanted to get an education—particularly in the use of magic—or to start over away from the compound could give it a go in Beukal.

I'd suspected that our elders wouldn't bite, and I was correct. Of our community of fifty, only twenty-one had accepted the offer, none older than thirty-five—which, to my annoyance, was the age of full majority in the Pactlands. Those who came were all my cousins, probably in multiple ways. Peter Smith and Monica Church moved over with their young children, Eleanor and two-year-old Tobias. Kyle Smith, my maternal uncle and Peter's more distant relation, came as well, as did his wife, Laurel Amos, and their six-year-old, Eugene. The last of the families was Paul Church (Monica's second cousin), Amy Smith (my mother's and Uncle Kyle's first cousin), and baby Winston, who was about Tobias's age. At twenty-five, Justin Church, Monica's little brother, was the last of what I'd have considered the true adults. Of the older children and teenagers, Hannah Church had her brother Paul to look after her. The Amos siblings, Heidi, David, and Marshall, came unaccompanied, as did their first cousins, the Amos twins, Sebastian and Stephanie, and the Black trio, Zoe, Peter, and David…though since the Blacks' mother was Peter Smith's big sister, they weren't entirely on their own. And then there was me—Maebe Amos, only child of a different branch of Amoses.

Our surnames hinted at one of our community's many problems. In East Branch, we said our families were "close." Since I was the twelfth-generation product of only thirty-six ancestors, *close* was ridiculously euphemistic.

Back in July, we'd moved into an empty section of a dormitory at North Lake, a school situated at the northern end of Beukal, far out in District 6. While education was both free and compulsory in the Pactlands, some schools were more desirable than others, and North Lake was among the favorites. Ordinarily, potential students had to take tests for admission and keep their grades at an acceptable level to remain enrolled, but the instructors were excellent and the networking opportunities plentiful. For that reason, North Lake was one of the handful of schools with dorms, built for those students from the farther-flung towns whose parents didn't want to navigate the portals twice a day. As the dorms were consistently under-filled, though, someone on the Forum had persuaded the school to house us.

Our accommodations were nice: three small apartments for the couples with children and singles for the rest of us. Having tested us and found us wanting in all subjects magical and mundane, the school kept us out of most regular classes, instead assigning us tutors by age groups. Every weekday morning began with tutoring at eight. After lunch, we were allowed to briefly join our peers for classes like art and physical education—when, to my increasing discomfort, I got to hang out with Ainnet and her clique— but we split off again for remedial tutoring in magic until dinnertime.

It wasn't quite the school I'd imagined from those long-ago picture books, and my days were now far more regimented than they'd ever been at East Branch…but I *was* learning. True, I was no great prodigy, and sometimes, the weight of my ignorance was almost enough to make me want to slink home, but I tried to stay upbeat around the others.

After all, I'd gotten us into this mess. The least I could do was grin and bear the unpleasant bits.

Ainnet was wrong about us: we weren't idiots, just ignorant, and almost certainly not working with as much magical oomph as the standard elf. After a month and a half of tutoring, none of us could yet mask on our own. As I alone had masking jewelry, the others did what we'd always been taught to do around outsiders and simply hid their ears. Nearly all of us had the telltale flop, so the girls pinned the tops back with cloth headbands, while the boys pulled their hats down low. Our tutors insisted that we didn't need to cover up, but they weren't the ones being teased—and whatever else could be said for my ears, my hearing was excellent. Some kids were curious, some slightly disgusted, and many others were just assholes.

The only outsider who regularly spent time with us was Sage, who, as she'd introduced herself to my cousins, was a freak of a different fashion. The accidental offspring of a sorcerer and a centaur, she'd been dumped unmasked in Whitford as a newborn to hide her mother's infidelity. Sage didn't like to talk about the man who'd raised her until he'd decided to cut his losses and sell her to Jane, but Jane had told me enough that I discouraged the others from prying. She'd only made it into the Pactlands about half a year before we did, and as her education was similarly spotty, she'd joined my tutoring group for remedial work. Unlike most of us, however, Sage had decent control of her growing talent—and since her father was a Forum representative, she was a far less frequent target of teasing. But while she was an outsider by East Branch standards, we'd more or less accepted her as one of our own, and she stuck close to us at lunchtime for the opportunity to slip back into rapid English.

Pactlands schooling began at age five, and our tutors

had divided those of us old enough for lessons into four groups. The youngest was a trio close in age: Eleanor Smith, David Black, and Eugene Smith, Years 2 and 3. Next was the preteens and younger teenagers: Hannah Church, Zoe Black, Marshall Amos, the Amos twins, and Peter Black, Years 7 through 13. My group had started as another trio—Heidi and David Amos and me, Years 14 and 17—but Sage, though younger, had joined us, seeing as she was actually a semester ahead. Last was a group for the three couples and Justin Church, Years 20 through 30. It wasn't perfect, but at least I wasn't sharing a classroom with kids five years my junior *and* senior anymore.

Having been de-souped, I turned back to my math notes with Sage while we had the time. I'd always had a decent understanding of basic arithmetic, which was about as far as East Branch's math classes went—adding and subtracting, multiplying and dividing, fractions and percentages, the things one might need to get by. At North Lake, however, I felt like I was starting at square one. Not only were our tutors teaching us new skills, but the symbols were radically different. Sure, I could read the numbers, thanks to the language potion I'd swigged, but when equations were set out before me, my brain ached.

Math was far from the only subject that threw me. *Everything* was more complex than it had been at East Branch. History spanned more than two centuries and a single plot of land. Geography covered the Pactlands *and* parts of the outside world. Science…well, there was little comparison. And though I could read, I was woefully unequipped to engage in anything like the literary criticism expected from someone my age. Though our tutors were gentle, they pushed us, and the novelty of homework had quickly lost its luster.

But we persevered because the alternative was going home—and what awaited us there? The drafty houses built by our distant forebears and patched every winter? The old trucks we could barely keep running? The fear of hunger every time the rain passed us by or the hunters were chased off someone else's land? Or the new threat, eviction? East Branch barely produced enough to feed itself, so when the county finally came asking for taxes, Connor's family had stepped into the breach. His quiet generosity kept us on our land, but that situation was untenable in the long term. We *had* to be educated, either to find work in Beukal or to give us the rudiments necessary to secure jobs in places like Whitford or nearby Ragged Gap, little mountain towns that might have seemed backward to city folk but were leagues beyond my community. I mean, per Connor, young children in Whitford could easily use computers, whereas I'd never seen one until Jane pulled out her laptop.

We were meant to be East Branch's salvation, but we had a long way to go. So, I finished my sandwich and bent over my math assignment with Sage, plowing through the small problems so that I might someday solve the greater ones facing us.

Thursdays were some of the better days because the only class I shared with the rest of my year was physical education. Our coach divided our time between games and circuits with the weight machines, and while I was still learning the rules to the popular sports in Beukal, I could hold my own when it came to bicep curls. There were certain perks to having been raised a farm girl, and I could outlift every elf, sorcerer, faun, and nymph in my year—and the pair of centaurs, but only for upper-body moves. The gnomes, none taller than my waist, could run circles around us all, but like so much that season, this information had surprised only me. Still, not being dead last at *something* put me in a good mood for our afternoon lessons in magic.

Of all the East Branch kids, I alone had manifested a wild talent, a perk that put me in need of immediate extra training. Sorcerers and elves were occasionally born with wild talents of variable strength—particular facility with fire or water magic, say, or an extreme ability to make plants grow. A few sorcerers could manipulate light to the point that they seemed invisible, some elves could slip through solid objects, and a handful of both could see the past or future. My wild talent, aeromancy, was rare in elves, but an experienced aeromancer could manufacture hurricane-force winds with the twitch of her fingers. Personally, I didn't think it was the most *useful* of bonus abilities, especially since I didn't yet have mine under control, but at least it got me individual tutoring for a few hours a week.

My private teacher was Violet ti'Comros, a sweet elf who looked all of twenty-five but acted much like the mothers back in East Branch. She wore her dark hair in a pixie cut and painted her fingernails purple, and for me, she was both aeromancer and therapist.

"Hey, youngling," she said when I let myself into our practice room, a windowless space devoid of all furnishings but a pair of chairs for safety. She patted the seat of the empty chair in invitation as I dropped my bag by the door. "Come on, let's talk. What happened with Ainnet?"

I sank into my chair. "You saw that?"

"No, but from what I heard, the faculty on duty were holding their breaths for a brawl. What'd she say to you this time?"

"It's what she did. Spilled soup all over me."

"Mm. Burned?"

"No, ma'am. Just…"

"Pissed?" She used the English term, a relic of her time at the Division of Plants and Potions. Both of Violet's parents were agents there, which explained her odd name, but she'd changed careers around her hundredth birthday.

I nodded. "She's such a *jerk*."

"Eh." Violet scooted closer and lowered her voice. "Here's a truth you need to understand, Maebe: Hall ti'Har is old and high-ranking…but Ainnet isn't in the main line.

She's just a cousin, nowhere close to Lady ti'Har. So, while she may strut and put on airs, they're not entirely *warranted*, you see." Sitting back, she added, "Not that any such behavior is particularly warranted. The Hall system these days is largely ceremonial."

"Where does ti'Comros fall?" I asked.

She made a face and wiggled one hand. "Not particularly high. We're an old Hall, too, but we're close to the bottom. Top of the bottom third, perhaps. I mean, we're not ti'Gata or ti'Van, but we're nothing special, and *I'm* certainly not in line for a seat on the Forum."

Halls ti'Van and ti'Gata were huge, but unlike the other Halls, their members weren't all related. Before the Pactlands, the old Halls had been headed by noble families, but when everyone moved in together, the untitled wanted Halls of their own. From what I'd gathered, the bluebloods turned up their noses at the new Halls, while the common folk rolled their eyes and went on about their business. At the other extreme from the new Halls was Hall ti'Dana, whose lord had once been a king. I'd only been around Diriem ti'Dana a handful of times, but he'd never treated me like Ainnet did.

"I just don't understand why Ainnet is such a pain, especially if she's a cousin," I remarked. "I mean, Lord ti'Dana's been kind to us, and if *he* isn't offended to share the air..."

Violet chuckled. "Exactly. What you will learn, my dear, is that it's often those with the most precarious standing who feel the greatest need to belittle others. Your group has the backing of Hall ti'Dana *and* Hall ti'Cren, so...you know, the ti'Har brat should probably watch her tongue. But enough about Ainnet," she said, and grinned. "I'm proud of you for not blowing out the dining hall windows. Let's go over our breathing exercises, shall we?"

Though Violet was gentle, she knew how to push me, and

by dinner, I was ready to call it a night. An early bedtime wasn't in the cards, however, as the research healers were scheduled to come by again that evening, and our dorm parents weren't about to let us sneak off.

Several of the North Lake faculty lived on campus to supervise the boarders, and we'd been given two of them: Chennis ti'Van, one of the librarians, and Dalm Curshin, the junior coach of the rowing team. Both were around ninety, still considered young enough to be fun, but they ensured that we made it to meals, monitored homework, broke up squabbles, and tended to bumps and scrapes. And as both knew enough about humans to appreciate why the adults in our group chafed at the notion that they were considered underage in the Pactlands, they walked a fine line, offering support as needed and even volunteering a bit of babysitting but taking a more hands-off approach. The one time that they insisted on even the parents participating was when the research healers came around, and though we groaned, no one gave them much pushback.

The healers were interested in us as a cohort in part because of our mixed heritage, as there were virtually no elf–human crosses to be studied, but mainly, they came to try to figure us out before we fell apart. While there was decent longevity in our families, our lifespans were pretty firmly in the human camp, as was evidenced by our aging patterns. More immediately important for the healers, the result of our centuries of "close" families was a kaleidoscope of physical problems, most minor but all worth watching. Our floppy ears were a rare but understood elven birth defect known as cifyent, but beyond that, issues varied. Peter, Justin, and Marshall were colorblind, Monica only had about seventy percent of her hearing, Heidi was prone to develop ulcers, and the twins each had twelve fingers and toes, all of them functional. As for me, I had a weakened heart, but whether that was a congenital defect or the result of the awful bloodline potion from the summer, the healers couldn't say. But even for those of us without extra problems, we'd never had much in the way of medical care—certainly nothing like vaccines or teeth cleaning—so the healers had their work cut out for them.

Once I was dismissed, I retreated to my room to finally decompress. I thought about calling my parents, but I wasn't in the mood; I tried to stay upbeat when I spoke to them to put their minds at ease, and I just couldn't muster the energy that night. Instead, I texted Jane since she never seemed horrified when I let down my guard.

*Hey*, I wrote, *Ainnet poured soup on me at lunch. Keef and SE broke it up. I kind of hate A.*

Jane responded almost immediately: *You hurt?*
*No.*

*Good. Want D to make some calls? I'm sure he would.*

While I was tired of Ainnet's shenanigans, I was also eighteen, too old to run and tattle. *No, thanks. Maybe A will get bored.*

Jane's response was difficult for me to interpret, an upside-down smiley face. She followed it up with, *Need a break? Say the word, and I'll take you home for a visit. Promise.*

Home. I missed it more than I cared to admit—my mother's cooking, my lumpy bed, my dad's hugs, the familiar comfort of the woods. The leaves would be beginning to change colors, a sight I longed for in the virtually treeless Pactlands. The apples would be nearing harvest, and in the morning, smoke from the low-burning hearth fires would curl in the frosty wind. I could slip away with Jane on Friday afternoon and be back in time for Monday class...

*Thanks, but I'm fine*, I forced myself to type back to her, then sprawled on my bed and stared at the ceiling.

If the little ones could tough it out, then so could I. My parents didn't need to worry over something as ridiculous as soup.

As I lay there, Chennis knocked at my door. "Maebe, dear? Any questions about your homework?"

Groaning, I pushed myself up and headed for my desk.

# CHAPTER 2

The ringing of my phone woke me in the dark hours, and it took me a moment to understand that I wasn't hearing my alarm. As I'd only owned a phone for a few months, my sleep-addled brain decided that the best way to silence the noise was to paw at the lit screen until I woke sufficiently to register the name of the caller.

"Connor?" I croaked at the phone. "That you?"

My cousin chuckled on the other end. "Did I wake you, mitta?"

"Uh-huh."

"Sorry. I wanted to catch you before school."

He'd caught me before breakfast, but in truth, I didn't mind. Connor had been the strangest of my kin for many years, the only East Branch child raised outside, but his parents had brought him to visit so he could learn to manage his touch. At thirty-one, he was the chief of Whitford's tiny police department, a job he claimed to have acquired by process of elimination, as the runner-up candidate was a German shepherd. Connor had mediated over the summer, driving Jane and Diriem out to East Branch without letting anyone get shot, and since then, he'd taken to calling me every few days to check in.

"What's up?" I asked.

"Well, I was wondering if you would do me a favor," said Connor.

"A favor?"

"Yeah. See, I'm house-sitting for Yacovi this weekend."

I smiled to myself. Yacovi Hewt was Jane's adopted father, a sorcerer in Ragged Gap who masqueraded as an ironworker, farrier, and moonshiner. In truth, most of his business came from growing magical plants and brewing potions, which he exported to the Pactlands. The cop and the part-time distiller might have made an odd couple, but since many of Connor's colleagues at the Ragged Gap PD and the sheriff's office counted themselves among Yacovi's 'shine customers, Connor didn't give him any trouble. Besides, both men loved Jane, so it behooved them to get along.

In the months since Jane had taken a job at the Division of Intelligence, which kept her away from Georgia for days at a time, Yacovi had picked up where she left off with remedial lessons in magic for Connor several nights a week. The old sorcerer knew more about casting than did any of the East Branch elders, and having homeschooled Jane and worked with his share of trainee DPP agents, he was a patient teacher. Connor wasn't yet up to speed with his peers, but unlike me, he could reliably open the fridge from across the kitchen and pour himself a drink.

"Where's Yacovi going?"

"He's actually taking a vacation," Connor replied. "First time in who knows how long. Says he's heading back to the Pactlands to see some of his buddies."

"Good for him," I said through a yawn.

"Right? But he's wary about leaving his house unattended, so I told him I'd stay over for a few days and keep an eye on things."

While I didn't know Ragged Gap well, Jane and Connor had told me it was pretty safe, as small towns went. The odds that anyone would mess with Yacovi's place were slim, particularly as he had a series of wards around the property, magical barriers to keep trespassers out. But Yacovi had suffered a break-in from some sorcerers back in February while he was unjustly imprisoned in Beukal, and I could understand why he might not be eager to lock up and hope for the best.

"Is Jane joining you over the weekend?" I asked.

Connor sucked his teeth. "Unfortunately, no. She's got a training thing with DOI starting Friday afternoon."

"That's not fair."

"That's life, mitta. Anyway, since I'm going to be there all by myself, I was calling to see if you might be willing to hang out with me. Yacovi doesn't have a problem with it."

I didn't have to pry to know that Connor and Jane had talked. The invitation was made too nonchalantly, and the timing was too good. Still, the offer was tempting: a few days out of the dorms, maybe a quick drive out to East Branch to see my family…

"You'd be doing me a massive favor," Connor continued. "If I were to get called out on an emergency over the weekend, at least there'd be someone at the house to look after it. What do you say, huh? I'll throw in pizza."

Curse him, he knew my weakness. I'd never had pizza until I left East Branch, and having been exposed, I couldn't get enough of it.

"Sure, I'll help you out," I said, then paused. "Wait, how am I getting back to Georgia if Jane's working all weekend?"

"She's already made the arrangements," he assured me. "Just pack a bag and be on the front steps at five."

And with my weekend sorted, I rolled over for a couple more precious minutes of sleep.


The day passed uneventfully but for a few mocking glances from Ainnet's group, which was a mercy. After lunch, I hurried back to my room to throw my things in my lone piece of luggage, a faded, repurposed flour sack of considerable vintage, and as soon as I was dismissed from my tutors that afternoon, I told my uncle my plan and made my way outside.

North Lake was a large but fairly contained complex, a gray stone main building five stories tall that was flanked by matching wings to the left and right. The wings bent back from the road as if the school were trying to curve along the portion of the lakeshore behind it. North Lake—the body of water, not the school—was deep enough for boating and decent fishing, but we were situated along a small, shallower portion that seemed to have been pinched from the lake like a ball of dough. Aside from time on the sports fields and the recreation lawn, my life for the last month and a half had been almost entirely contained within the tall stone walls of my new school, and just making it onto the broad front stairs with my bag knotted and slung over my shoulder felt like an exhalation.

I sat on a step and peered down the long driveway toward the main road—a simple task, as the flat, treeless landscape offered no obstacle to my line of sight. Even if I spent the rest of my life in Beukal, I mused, I'd never acclimate to the view. The mountains of home weren't the most impressive, as mountains went—per Jane, they weren't even the biggest in the chain—but they'd wrapped around East Branch like sentinels, forested barriers between us and the dangers of the outside world. Darkness came quickly to our holler, but there was a comfort in the mountains' shadows all the same. Here, with nothing but gently undulating meadows in all directions, I couldn't get past the sensation that I'd been exposed, a deer accustomed to the protective trees and underbrush suddenly confronted with the alien expanse of a golf course.

Connor hadn't specified what my travel arrangements were to be, but I'd anticipated a car. Thus, when a dark-haired woman in a black T-shirt and loose pants suddenly appeared at the foot of the stairs, I yelped and would have stumbled had I not been sitting.

She laughed and raised a hand in greeting. "Hey, Maebe. Sorry, did I startle you?"

Recognition clicked as I caught my breath. Annie Humphries was a friend of Jane's, a DPP agent from Richmond. While I'd never been to Virginia—frankly, I'd

never been much of anywhere—Annie's accent was familiar enough to remind me of home, especially after a day of
lessons in Pactish. At a distance, she seemed human, but
her eyes were a curious amber color and shone like a cat's
in low light, and her ears were subtly pointed like a shorter
version of my own. She'd been human once, Jane had told
me, but that was before she fell in love with Wylan…and
to keep her in the Pactlands legally, he'd brought her into
the Wild Hunt. While Annie wasn't magically talented,
there was no telling what Wylan could do when he put his
mind to it—like, say, change his girlfriend's species. But in
joining the Hunt, Annie *had* picked up a few perks: virtual
immortality, a highly sensitive nose, and the ability to cover
any distance in the blink of an eye as long as she knew
where she was going. "Teleportation," Jane called it.

"Hi, Annie," I said, pulling myself together, and gathered my sack and my purse. Our tutors generally didn't
assign weekend homework, and so I'd left my school bag
by my desk. "Are you my ride?"

"Taxi service," she replied, sweeping one arm toward
an imaginary car. "All aboard!"

"And…you know the way to Yacovi's house?"

"You doubt my mad skills?" she teased. "I've been to
Jane's, Connor's, Yacovi's, *and* Tabitha's, so we have options."

I frowned. "Who's Tabitha?"

"Friend of Jane's, your average neighborhood Wiccan
pharmacist. She's a helpful person to know if you stick
around here—I mean, sometimes, I'd rather have a Ty-
lenol than a pain potion. We're brunch buddies," Annie
explained. "But not this weekend, seeing as Jane's tied up.
Ready to head out?"

Nodding, I scurried down the stairs with my gear.

"Do you not have an overnight bag?" Annie asked,
eyeing my flour sack. "We can nag Connor into taking you
to Walmart…"

"Oh, this is fine."

"Not indefinitely," she replied, but dropped it as she took my free hand. "Hold on tight, okay? Might want to close your eyes. And remind me, do you get motion sickness?"

"Not yet," I told her. "Not like Diriem, anyway."

"Hon, *no one* gets as pukey as he does. I honestly have no idea how he survived the horse-and-carriage days."

Before I could think too hard about what came next, Annie squeezed my hand, and the world went black as the ground disappeared. I almost didn't have time to freak out that I was falling before the earth rose up beneath my feet once more, and I whimpered as I regained my balance.

"Hey, y'all," came Connor's voice from somewhere beyond my screwed-closed eyes, entirely too blasé for what he must have just witnessed. "Right on time. Thanks again, Annie."

Risking a peek, I found that the open yard in front of my school had been replaced by off-white walls decorated with photos of a little girl that must have been Jane. Connor stood in the doorway, leaning against the frame with his arms folded. His brown hair was neat and tidy—a fresh cut, I assumed—and he still wore his dark blue uniform with the gold shield pinned to his chest. His brown eyes crinkled as he grinned at me, his lashes almost girlishly long, though there was nothing feminine about his six-foot frame. Connor wasn't the biggest of my cousins, but he was solid.

"No problem," said Annie, and released me. "So, what's on the agenda for tonight? A little hellraising, some brewskis, cosmic bowling?"

He snorted. "If I dared to go bowling without Tabitha, she'd have my hide."

"True. That woman's scary with a ten-pound ball."

"And busy tonight, so bowling will have to wait." Glancing at me, he continued, "I was thinking pizza, Coke, and a movie. Will that do you?"

"Sure will," I said. "Thanks, Annie."

"Oh, any time," she replied. "And look, I'm just going to be home working on my backlog of incident reports tonight"—Connor winced in sympathy—"so if you *do* somehow end up at the bowling alley, call me, eh?"

My cousin nodded. "Roger that. Does the big guy bowl, too?"

She shrugged. "I've never taken him, but I suspect he could manage. Anyway, if I don't hear from y'all, I'll be back Sunday night to take Maebe to school. Don't get too wasted, now," she joked, winking at me, and vanished.

With a snort, Connor pushed himself upright and came closer to muss my hair. "There will be no getting wasted this weekend, mitta. Let's be clear about that from the get-go."

"What does that even mean?" I asked.

"Getting drunk. Since I can't exactly be a party to underage intox, we'll be sticking to soft drinks."

I scowled at him as I patted my hair flat. "Come on, let me enjoy being an adult again for a couple of days."

"I would, were you legal. The drinking age is twenty-one."

"Huh?"

"Everywhere but East Branch," he allowed. "I don't mean to be a hard-ass, kiddo, but there's the job to consider."

"Fine," I grumped. "You can make it up to me with garlic bread."

"But of course. First, though," he said, reaching over to give my ear a light pinch, "let's switch this, huh?"

Touching my other ear, I realized my Pactlands mask was still in place, kicked myself, and gripped my tiny pendant to change my mask. I checked the result in the hallway mirror: two unremarkably rounded ears, not the reflection I'd become accustomed to of late but still a far better option than their pointed, floppy true form.

"There," said Connor, grinning behind me. "Secret's safe. Now, let's see about dinner."

The only pizza place of note in Ragged Gap was Gino's Pizzeria, the alternative being a questionable selection of slices at one of the gas stations around town, and Connor didn't skimp on the toppings or the dipping sauces. "How do you know you don't like buffalo ranch until you try it?" he asked as I questioned the necessity of so many condiments. "Dip the crust in it. Life-changing, I tell you."

I held the boxes on my lap as we drove to Yacovi's house so they wouldn't go sliding across the back seat of Connor's SUV. The large pizza covered my lap and then some, and I'd stacked the boxes of cheesy garlic sticks and the questionable dessert pizza atop it. Gino's lone dessert option wasn't *bad*, but it was a mess of cinnamon sugar and thick icing, and my East Branch–reared palate cringed at the overly sweet concoction after more than a few bites. Sugar was never something we'd had in abundance growing up.

As we wound our way out of the cluster of buildings that passed for downtown in Ragged Gap and into the more residential neighborhoods, heading toward the mountain that Yacovi called home, I stared out the window with my delicious-smelling leg warmers and watched the trees go by. While I'd been conscious of missing the tall trees and the sharp undulations of the terrain, I hadn't realized just how much I'd craved this view—heck, even in the next valley over from East Branch, riding in a vehicle with a working radio *and* a reliable engine, this felt like home. The commercials in the space between music blocks advertised the same old car dealerships and jewelers and home improvement shops, and for a moment, if I were to have closed my eyes, I could have imagined myself back in my childhood bed, curled up beneath the quilts, listening to my parents' battery-powered radio and the voices of the outside. But so starved was I for the brilliance of fall that I kept my eyes peeled, looking for the first hints of reds and oranges on the dogwoods and sumac as we drove along. Mid-September was still a good month from the leaf peak, but I'd take what I could get.

"You're mighty quiet, mitta," said Connor, speaking over a calm female voice rattling off a litany of horrors one might experience by taking a new drug.

"Just thinking."

"Mm." He propped his elbow by the window and eased to a stop at an intersection. An SUV marked with the Ragged Gap Police Department's insignia rolled across the road, and he and the other driver exchanged brief waves before he pressed on. "That's Jolene Matthews," he offered. "Real sweetheart unless you try to run, and then she drives like she's practicing for 'Dega."

"Huh?"

"Fast driver. Don't know how she manages the curves around here, but she *hugs* them," he explained, a note of admiration in his voice.

"Do you know all the police?" I asked.

"Well, there's not that many of us to know. Whitford and Ragged Gap have tag-teamed on occasion, and everybody knows Sheriff Cain and his crew. We've all traveled to trainings together at one time or another. I mean, you get in a big session with a bunch of Atlanta cops, and those of us from the podunk towns tend to stick together. I've got no beef with Atlanta," he hastily added, "but policing down there is *very* different than it is in this corner of the state. Hell, at least they've got an Interstate. And a real budget," he muttered.

Soon enough, we were climbing Maple Ridge, the narrow road to Yacovi's place. Connor slowed as he neared the turn-off for the long driveway. Unlike Jane's cabin or Connor's home, Yacovi's old farmhouse was situated on a considerable tract of land, including a fenced pasture and a broad slope of trees all the way down the far side of the mountain. He kept a barn on the property, useful for dealing with the horses clients would bring him for shoeing and for storing his smithing tools, and a nondescript little garden shed, which he kept padlocked. When Jane had brought me out to see him just before I left for North Lake, Yacovi had unlocked the shed and triggered a spell to reveal a *huge* greenhouse on the other side of the doors, a space that didn't entirely exist in the real world. I'd run around the back of the shed, looking for a trick, but the shed had been as ordinary as ever unless you stood directly in front of it. One other feature set Yacovi's house apart from the average dwelling in the area. Near the rear of the building, accessible via a hidden door, was a brew room, most of which was used for Yacovi's magical wares. A separate storage area of the brew room was dedicated to his moonshine, however, and once he shut the brew room, no human cop would ever find it.

As we headed up the driveway, Connor said, "Fair warning: don't go wandering off. Yacovi left the wards armed."

I frowned at that. I knew what wards were—even with my subpar skills in magic, I'd learned *that* much—but I couldn't have constructed one if my life depended on it. Wards could be like fences or tripwires, depending on their design, but nothing good ever happened if you crossed them. "Where are the wards?"

"Three layers," my cousin explained as he pulled up to the two-story house with the big front porch. "There's a ward near the edge of the property that makes people really anxious if they trip it—keeps most random hikers away. The next level in leaves you exhausted and makes you throw up, so that *really* deters trespassers. And the third ward wraps around the house, the greenhouse, and the barn."

"What happens if you trip that one?"

He grimaced. "Electrified moat. Now, I don't know if it's strong enough to kill a person, but I don't want to experiment, so don't leave the house without me, okay? Yacovi showed me where the wards run."

"If the property's warded, then how did we drive up here?" I pressed, fearing what might happen once I opened the door.

"The driveway's unwarded right now," he explained. "I'll show you the safe path, and I'll turn the closest one back on once we're inside." Seeing my unease, he patted my shoulder. "Relax, mitta. They're only triggered if you're approaching the house. In case of, like, fire, just run for the road. You won't hurt yourself."

Thus reassured, I let myself out with dinner and followed him up to the porch. "How do you disarm the ward?"

"Eh, concentration and waving my hands at it." He unlocked the door and held it open for me. "Don't ask me for the theory. You probably know more about that than I do."

"They haven't taught us wards yet," I said, sliding past him with the boxes.

"Give it time. And I'm sure you're getting a better education. Jane and Yacovi have been nice enough to teach me some basics, but they tend to focus on practicality over theory." Latching the door behind us, he said, "You'll be running rings around me soon enough, mitta."

I doubted that, but I didn't argue with Connor.

We retreated to the den at the rear of the house and spread the boxes on the low table by the couch, the better to eat while watching TV. Connor and I haggled over the movie for a minute before settling on a comedy—one heavy on the slapstick, he assured me, seeing as I still didn't get so many of the outsiders' jokes—and as I ripped off a chunk of the breadsticks, he settled in beside me and said, "All right, Maebe, what's going on?"

"What do you mean?"

"Jane told me about this Ainnet person. Why am I just now hearing about her, huh?"

I sighed and bit into the cheesy, garlicky goodness. Where had Italian food *been* all my life? "She's just a bitch," I mumbled around the breadstick. "Decided she doesn't like me. But she didn't burn me, so—"

"That doesn't matter. You're being bullied, hon." He paused the movie and put his plate aside. "I had my share, too, okay? Kids are jerks. Sometimes, you can fight them off...and other times, you need to call for reinforcements. Have you told your teachers?"

I shook my head. "It's not *that* bad—"

"Until she pours something scalding on you. Or worse." Connor gave me a look eerily reminiscent of the ones my parents deployed. "If you want to handle this, fine. I get it. But there's no shame in asking for backup, yeah? And what are the others doing about this? Peter and Kyle and the rest?"

"Nothing," I muttered. "David and I are the only ones in Ainnet's year, and she mostly leaves him alone."

"Good for David, but what about *you*?"

"I'm fine."

In truth, things had been a bit strained between my cousins and me ever since we moved to Beukal. I was the catalyst for the whole mess, the runaway who'd gone farther than I'd imagined, and I'd brought the outsiders to us. Beyond that, I was the only one in the bunch with a wild talent, I had the highest percentage of elven genes, and I alone had been given masking jewelry. My cousins weren't unfriendly toward me by any stretch, but there was a sense that I'd somehow become *other* as well.

It probably didn't help matters that I'd been the one to piss off our ancestors. Never mind that my distant great-grandfather and the southern elves' former king, Ivari ti'Ammaas, had thrown me across his office and into the furniture when I'd asked for so much as a loan on behalf of East Branch—I'd heard them quietly debate that someone older or more experienced than I was could have managed a different result. I knew that DOI was keeping an eye on East Branch just in case its founders came around to see what was left of the community, but the fact that I'd been the one to necessitate observation by outsiders didn't exactly endear me to my kinfolk.

Judging by Connor's expression, he didn't believe that I was truly fine, and as he controlled the remote, I gave in and elaborated. "It's not so bad. The soup is the worst she's done so far, and the melee team gave her hell for it. It's just...the whispers, you know? Stares. Ainnet's got a group of friends, and I can tell they're laughing at me, but it's not like they're beating me up."

"Still not great, Maebe."

"I know." With a little sigh, I said, "Don't tell Jane or the others, but sometimes, I think about going home. At least I'm normal there."

"For a given definition of normal." Connor took a bite of pizza and chewed thoughtfully. "If folks around here ever really knew what East Branch is like, they'd treat you the same or worse."

"You think?"

He snorted. "I told you I got bullied, yeah? Mostly because of East Branch. The rumors are *vicious*...and frankly, they're not too far off. I've gotten flak about the place forever. So many banjo jokes."

I suspected I was missing something, but I let it go. "We're not *bad* people, we just don't have much."

"Of anything. Money, education...new blood..." He shook his head, then said, "Doesn't matter tonight. Look, mitta, here's a truth for you: people 'other' what they don't understand. East Branch others the rest of the county, the county others East Branch, and now you've got the Pactlands othering all of us. It's what people do," he said with a shrug. "Now, let's throw teenagers into the mix. Teenagers are assholes—sorry, that's just how it is," he insisted as I started to protest. "No offense. Y'all can't help the hormones, and we've all been there. But y'all are at an age where you're still trying to figure yourselves out, and everyone wants to be on top of the heap, right? Easy way to make yourself look better is to make other people look worse...and I suspect that you and the rest of our cousins make an easy target. Jane said you're not in most of the normal classes."

"Not yet. We're too far behind."

"Okay, so you're in special classes, you look funny, you talk funny, and you probably don't get half the cultural references, movies and music and stuff. You've been dropped in a foreign country, and I do *not* envy you."

"And then there's the species thing," I muttered. "Ainnet's upset because we're not real elves or whatever."

He nodded. "If it helps, just know that the rest of the county would be horrified if they heard about the inbreeding at East Branch. Forget species concerns." He paused briefly. "What I'm trying to say is that I'm sure it's rough at your new school, but it could be rough here, too. East Branch is one investigative journalist away from disaster."

I hesitated, then told him, "A lot of us have something wrong. They've got healers coming in to poke and prod once a week or so."

"Not surprised. It's almost miraculous that we're as healthy as we are."

"The healers think it's the cross-species interaction that's kept us decently strong."

Connor considered that as he ate. "Reasonable, I guess. But think about *this*. We're what, ten, eleven generations from the founders? Jane said *all* of y'all came back more elven than not."

"Yup."

"So, those are the genes that are getting passed, yeah? The pool's getting smaller. What would East Branch look like in another few generations?"

I didn't need a great understanding of science to see the picture Connor was painting.

"Much as I hate to admit it, Diriem may have intervened just in time," he said.

"I don't know that Ainnet is too familiar with the problems at home," I replied. "She just hates me because I'm mixed."

"Doesn't surprise me." Connor ate another bite of pizza and chased it with a swig of Coke straight from the can. "A lot of them can't stand us. Can't stand humans, I mean. And I get where they're coming from," he continued, reaching for the breadsticks, "but it sucks."

"Sucks what?"

He glanced at me strangely, then realized the problem. "It's lousy," he clarified.

Another phrase for my growing list of unknown English vocabulary.

"I mean, I saw how Janie was treated when they thought she was half human. Turns out she's all sorcerer, and *well*, that just changes everything," he said, rolling his eyes. "Then there's Annie—she actually wanted to stick around, and they were ready to wipe her memory and be done with her. And Rose." Chomping into his breadstick, he said, "I've only heard bits and pieces, but apparently, there are folks who think Diriem has irrevocably stained the honor of the Hall by letting her in. That woman's, what, ninety percent elf? *And* farsighted? Shit."

We ate for a moment in silence.

"The point is," Connor murmured, "we can't help who our families are. Not our fault for being born. None of us asked to exist, right?"

"No," I replied. "But Ainnet doesn't have to be such a jerk about things. We're *trying*, but it's…it's so much, all at once, and people are homesick, and…"

"And she's just mean?"

I nodded and sipped my drink.

Connor thought briefly, then smirked over his plate. "There *might* be a particular reason she picks on you."

"What's that?"

"Well…you're kind of the face of East Branch, yeah? You're the one who went to the Forum. Jane said that Diriem told them you're a ti'Ammaas heir."

"Yeah, he mentioned that…"

My cousin chuckled. "I'm not going to pretend to be any expert in the Halls, mitta, but don't you think ti'Ammaas outranks whatever Ainnet's Hall is?"

"Ti'Har. It's old and pretty high up there."

"Okay, big damn deal. Correct me if I'm wrong, but there are only two royal Halls, yeah? Ti'Dana and ti'Ammaas?"

I shrugged. "Guess so."

He leaned toward me and lowered his voice. "This could be a teen girl pissing contest because she's now out-ranked. Adding insult to injury, it's by a half-breed with a weird accent."

"I'm not trying to outrank anyone!" I protested. "I want an education. That's it."

"And I hear you, but having been through school my-self, I'm telling you it's not always that simple." He sat back again and resumed his attack on his pizza. "You can handle this, Maebe—you're a big girl. But if you want backup, tell Jane. I'm guessing that a quiet word from Diriem to whomever heads ti'Har would make Ainnet mind her manners."

With dinner over and the leftover pizza shoved into the refrigerator for Saturday lunch, Connor grabbed my flour sack and led me upstairs to show me the rooming situa-tion. "That's Yacovi's," he said, pointing to a closed door at the far end of the corridor. "I'll be in Jane's room, and you've got the guest bedroom."

Connor dropped my bag atop an antique chair, and I took a look around. The furnishings were simple, just pol-ished pine without any frills or fussiness, but the bed gave nicely beneath my hand. Yacovi hadn't been stingy with the blankets. Between my room and Connor's—well, Jane's—was a bathroom with two sinks and a combination shower/tub, and Connor had already left a plastic bag on the counter with his toothbrush and other necessities. A pair of plush bath towels with coordinating hand towels and washcloths hung from the rail on the glass shower door, and Yacovi had left a nightlight plugged in.

"If you want to hit the hay, be my guest," said Connor. "I don't know what sort of schedule you've been keeping…"

"I'm not tired yet," I replied. "Can we at least finish the movie?" Having never had access to TV as a child, I'd acquired a taste for it during my stay in the Pactlands, and it was refreshing to watch a program in English.

"Sure. Popcorn?"

"Wouldn't say no."

I flopped on the couch again, and Connor soon joined me with a big bowl of popcorn and fresh Cokes. "Here's to staying up past our bedtime," he said, clinking his can against mine, and popped the tab. "And getting a night off from asshole elves."

"I'll drink to that," I said, and grinned at him before I swigged the sweet soda. "Question."

"Shoot."

"Any chance that you could take me home this weekend?" I asked. "Just for a little bit. If you're busy, I understand, but—"

"Sure, mitta," he said, and ruffled my hair. "Tell you what, unless a bomb goes off in Whitford, I'll drive you out tomorrow morning. Sound good?"

"Thanks, Connor," I replied, and smiled as I reached for the popcorn. The phone calls to my parents had been great, but I was badly overdue for a hug.

# CHAPTER 3

**A**round ten that evening, partway into our second movie, I was finally beginning to wind down. Despite the sugar and caffeine, I was full of pizza and snacks, and Yacovi's den was cozy. Twice, I caught myself nodding, but I figured I could hold on a little longer. After all, I reasoned, fighting my fatigue, it wouldn't be fair to leave Connor up by himself, would it?

A rumbling noise drew my attention from the screen.

The den was at the back of the house, at the end of a hallway. From my spot on the couch, I had a clear line of sight to the darkened foyer…and as the noise grew louder, I noticed twin lights drawing nearer.

"Connor," I said, nudging him, and pointed toward the front. "Is that Yacovi?"

"What?" When he paused the movie, the sound of an engine outside was unmistakable. "Let me see…"

As he squished in close to me, a bright flash flared beyond the porch, and the headlights disappeared with a horrible crackling sound.

"Is that…" I muttered.

"The moat," said Connor as a second pair of headlights appeared. "No, that's absolutely not Yacovi. Come with me, *now*."

"Where are we going?" I asked as he turned off the TV and hustled me out of the den.

"Brew room. I can't get us into the greenhouse, so this'll have to do. Get your purse…" He paused at the door of the den, looking back at our leavings. "Shit, forget the cleanup. Let's move."

I'd left my purse on a table in the hallway beside Connor's things: his wallet and phone, the keys to his vehicle, and a black pistol. Shoving everything he could into his pockets, he handed me the gun and said, "Don't point that at me. If anyone comes through the door, shoot first."

"Con—"

"Don't argue with me, Maebe. I've got to concentrate."

A patch of wall near the den seemed boring enough, just an undecorated expanse of off-white plaster, but Connor took up a stance in front of it, exhaled, and began to make a series of complicated gestures. Within seconds, a door appeared—an ordinary door framed with wood like every other door in the house, but one that absolutely had not been there a moment before. Connor turned the knob, and it swung open, revealing nothing but blackness beyond.

"In here," he ordered, almost pushing me through the door, and slammed it behind us.

As my eyes adjusted, I found that the room wasn't entirely dark. Yacovi had left a nightlight plugged in halfway up a wall, the twin of the light in our bathroom, but it didn't reveal much. I groped my way toward it and narrowly missed walking into a workbench.

A blue light flashed off the cabinetry above the nightlight, and when I wheeled around, I found Connor gesturing again as the doorframe glowed. With a final twitch of his hands, the light pulsed brighter and went out.

"Locked," he murmured, making his way toward me with his phone's flashlight on. "The door's gone from the outside."

"I'm scared," I whispered, and gave him his gun back.

"Shh, mitta. If we're quiet, they may miss us."

"Who's *out* there?"

"I don't know, but anyone authorized would have alerted Yacovi. Try not to make any noise, okay?"

The brew room might have been locked, but it wasn't

soundproof, as I couldn't miss the crash when the front door was flung open and slammed into the wall. I heard two voices at first, male and female, judging by the pitch, though they spoke too quietly for me to make out their conversation. A third voice soon sounded behind them, a much louder male voice that practically shouted, "What are you waiting for? Find them!"

"What about—" the woman began.

"He's fine, just soaked. Is there a back door?"

"Um...I'm not sure," she admitted. "Maybe down there..."

"Go. *Now*. Secure it. I don't want to have to play hide and seek on a fucking mountain in the dark."

Footsteps ran down the hall past us but turned before reaching the den. "Yeah, there's a back door," the woman called. "Looks like a mud room."

"You're on it," said the loud man. "I've got the front. Pean, upstairs. Flush them out. There are two here."

"Right," the other man replied, and the staircase groaned as he made his rapid ascent.

That there were three strangers in the house worried me. That they were looking for two people was worse, considering the trail we'd left—our luggage, our snack foods. But what truly concerned me the fact that all three were speaking High Elvish.

Most elves spoke Low Elvish. High Elvish was an older, purer form, but outside of a few ceremonial bits, it was seldom used—it was, I'd learned, a dead language. *Old* elves could generally understand it, especially those who'd grown up before the two languages truly split, and Diriem had ensured that my cousins and I had both tongues before we started school—Low for practical purposes, High because that had been the language of the southern kingdom, those ancestors of ours who'd founded East Branch and sneaked off for greener pastures. But my cousins spoke High Elvish with a distinct accent, the product of our Appalachian rearing. *These* strangers didn't have a trace of Georgia in their vowels, which told me we were in deep trouble.

The elves out there were either our ancestors or their purebooded descendants, those born after the flight from East Branch, and judging by the tones of their voices, they hadn't come to invite us to a family reunion.

"Elves," I whispered to Connor. "Three of them, maybe one more guy in the moat."

"You understand that?" he whispered back.

Of course he was lost—Connor had yet to take a language potion. I started to nod, then realized how futile that would be in the dark. "Yeah, it's High Elvish. They aren't from the Pactlands, and they're looking for two people here."

He softly swore and pulled me deeper into the brew room, putting distance between us and the door. I backed into a stool and almost sent it toppling, but Connor grabbed it before it could hit the ground and righted it. My heart hammering, I used the lab bench as a guide and tried not to breathe loudly.

The elves outside made no effort to be sneaky, however. The ceiling creaked overhead, and then the man sent up to look around—Pean, I thought—called down, "Nothing! I've checked the closets! Maybe they went out a window."

The guy on the front door groaned, but the woman at the rear replied, "Keep looking! If they left, they left in a hurry. There's food in the den here..." Soft footsteps crossed closer to us, and then she said, "The couches are still warm. They either fled out the back or they're hiding."

The one at the front, the apparent leader of the operation, said, "Just did a reverse address on this place. Belongs to a Coby Hewt. Is that one of the surnames they used?"

"No," said the woman. "Hewt? Spell it."

"H-E-W-T," he said in clear English. "Like *newt*."

Footsteps stomped onto the porch, and a third man said, "This isn't the home of one of the damn half-bloods. You think they could manage wards like *that*?"

"Dry off," the loud man told him. "How's the Jeep?"

"Fried," he muttered. "Father's not going to be happy."

"He'll be even less pleased if we don't find them," the loud man snapped. "Hewt…could be a sorcerer."

The woman's voice grew clearer as she left her post at the mudroom. "If this is a sorcerer's house, then there's bound to be hidden storage, yeah? And there are outbuildings here—looks like a barn, maybe."

"Fucking rubes," the wet elf griped. "So, we're looking for two of them *and* a sorcerer now?"

"I only saw the Santa Fe out front," said the guy at the top of the stairs. "Maybe the sorcerer's not home."

Their leader grunted. "All the better. Now, if you were a sorcerer, where would you hide your storage?"

"There *is* a shed in the back," the woman offered.

"Nah. Let's do a ward check. Hewt's probably got it locked up."

"What we *should* have done on the way in," groused the wet elf. "But you think the half-bloods could access warded storage? Doesn't seem likely to me."

"They've got at least one aeromancer," said their leader. "You heard Father. There's no telling what the rest of them can do, and if he says there are two here, then I'm not going home emptyhanded. Culta, can you do it?"

I heard a sigh. "Yeah, sure," said the wet elf.

"Great. Pean, cast it upstairs. They're here *somewhere*."

"What's going on?" Connor whispered.

"Looking for hidden rooms," I quickly whispered back. "Sounds like a spell to detect wards. And I might be wrong, but I think at least two of those guys out there are Ivari's sons."

"Fuck."

A moment later, I felt Connor press his pistol into my hand. "I'm going to call for help," he said, barely breathing into my ear. "If anyone comes through the wall, shoot 'em."

"But—"

"I can't fight off four elves by myself, and neither can you. Stay behind the lab bench."

While I knew how to handle a gun, I'd never shot a *person* before, and the notion left my stomach in knots. Still, Connor was right—if they made it into the brew room, surprise would be our only advantage. Swallowing my fear, I leaned on the bench with the gun raised, listening to the voices outside.

Behind me, Connor had made a call, as I heard his quiet murmuring. "I'm sorry to bother you, but we're in trouble. Bunch of elves just broke in…three or four at least, I'm not sure. Maebe and I are locked in Yacovi's brew room, but they're looking for us…" He paused as the person on the other end responded, then said, "Yeah, I'll send you one. Can you get past the wards?"

He'd called Annie, I realized distantly, but the conversation on the other side of the wall was more pressing.

"Got something, Danirri," said Culta. "Look, there on the wall. See the traces?"

Rapid footsteps neared. "Well, now, isn't that a pretty piece of work?" said their leader—Danirri, I assumed. "What do you suppose Hewt's hiding in there, hmm?"

"Why is there even a sorcerer here?" Culta asked. "I thought they all fled."

"A few pass through," said the woman. "I've seen a handful over the years. This one seems rather well established, but this town *is* fairly isolated, so perhaps he feels safe here."

"Fool," said Danirri. "Tella, get Pean down here. This might take some work."

"Just because you're bad at wards doesn't mean everyone is," Culta said. "Stand back."

A flash behind me briefly lit the brew room—a reference picture for Annie, I assumed.

Suddenly, the ward around the hidden door glowed red like fire. "What does that mean?" I whispered, risking a glance back at Connor as he put his phone away.

"Don't know, but that ain't good," he replied, and took his gun from me again. "Stay behind me, mitta."

He didn't have to tell me twice. I slipped behind Connor, gripping my purse and trying not to puke. If they broke through—and the intensifying red lights suggested that was a strong possibility—then what could I do? Connor might only take one down before the others went on the attack. I was tense enough that I could feel my talent itching to break free, but what use was that? I could blow them across the hallway—*ooh*, scary. Surely there was something dangerous in the cabinets around the brew room, but I didn't know the first thing about potions, and tossing random bottles at the elves didn't seem like the best plan.

"Almost…" Culta grunted beyond the flaring ward. "Just another minute, this lock is tricky…"

A hand landed on my shoulder, and I bit back a scream as I wheeled around and found Annie standing there. "Gotcha," she said, and Connor lowered his gun. "Shit, what *is* that?"

"The ward on the door is about to go down," I replied. "Can we—"

"Yup. Hold on." She gripped my hand, then grabbed Connor's, and as the red light blinked out, the world went black.

I hadn't braced myself well for landing, and so I stumbled and went to my knees on arrival. Instead of the hard floor of the brew room, I found something thick and furry beneath me—a bearskin rug, deep brown and wide enough to sleep on, though the retention of the massive paws and head made the pelt less than attractive as bedding.

"Sorry, hon, you okay?" asked Annie, helping me to my feet. "Everything accounted for?"

All I'd carried with me was my purse, and I nodded as I straightened myself out.

We'd arrived in a high-ceilinged room of timber and stone, a space lit by lanterns suspended from the rafters and by the glow of a warm blaze in the oversized hearth. Throughout the room were scattered clumps of chairs, benches, and couches, most ornamented with leather, and a variety of rugs, some woven, others hides. Between the arched windows lining the wall were hung weapons— swords and shields, mostly, though there were a few bows and one devilish-looking battle-axe with a wicked blade. Whatever else might be said for the décor, the space had a decidedly masculine feel.

And we weren't alone. Turning in their seats and rising for a better view were at least two dozen men, all tall and solidly built, dressed in lace-up homespun shirts and slim-cut dark pants tucked into boots. The laces were a necessity, as the rack of antlers each man sported would have made pull-on shirts an impossibility. Amber eyes glinted as they caught the light—predators' eyes, I distantly thought, shrinking in their sudden gaze.

This had to be the Hunt's lodge. Annie had brought me once before, right after I set Ivari's office on fire with my uncontrolled winds, and the Huntsmen I'd met that day had been kind. But dealing with them singly or in twos or threes was one thing—finding myself at the center of their group focus set off warning bells in an ancient part of my brain.

Beside me, Connor steadied himself and looked around, calmly staring back at our observers, then glanced at Annie. "The in-laws?" he murmured.

"Uh-huh. It's all right," she said in Pactish, raising her voice to address the room. "They're with me—"

"Annie?" called a deep voice from beyond the doorway, and the men turned as another jogged in, one similarly built to them but with a more impressive rack and an inexplicable aura of authority. "*There* you are! I heard you left in a rush…" He paused, taking in the three of us, and folded his arms as he asked in accented English, "Were you planning to holster that, Connor?"

My cousin aimed his pistol at the floor. "Would if I could. Holster's back in my car, and only an idiot sticks a loaded gun in his pants."

"Fair." He spread his empty hands, a gesture of placation. "What's going on?"

I noticed the other men watching bemusedly and suspected the conversation had turned incomprehensible for most of the room.

Recognition finally broke through my disorienting panic. The newcomer was Wylan, Annie's husband. I'd seen him only once, when I went to the Forum. I didn't know much about the Hunt—few in the Pactlands did, apparently—but I did know that Wylan was their leader, nearly indestructible and a massive source of power. But he was devoted to Annie, and Annie hung out with Jane, so perhaps by some sort of transitive property, our appearance didn't seem to irk him.

Connor rubbed his free hand over his face. "Sorry to drop in—"

"It's no trouble. You're afraid—I can smell it," he said. "Are you hurt? Is Jane?"

"Jane's at a work function," Annie offered. "These two were house-sitting for her dad, and then Connor called and said some elves had broken in. They'd holed up in the brew room."

"That lock failed," Connor muttered, and weakly laughed. "*Shit*. If you'd come any later..."

"Why don't you sit down?" Wylan offered in a tone that made it clear that wasn't a suggestion. "Derat, get some whiskey, would you?"

"Oh, I...I'm fine," Connor began, but Wylan shook his head.

"That tremor in your hand says otherwise. Let's put the gun on that table, that's a good man," he coaxed as Annie showed Connor to a chair. "Sit. Breathe."

"I'm just keyed up," he protested.

"Obviously." Turning to me, Wylan asked, "Elves?"

"Uh-huh. And they were speaking High Elvish, so they're probably not from the Pactlands. Our *other* kin," I explained, trying to grab my racing thoughts and corral them into order. "They said, um...shoot..."

"Take your time," Wylan soothed.

I twitched as I felt something bump the back of my legs, then saw that one of the other Huntsmen had scooted a chair up behind me. Plopping down on the leather cushion, I looked up at Wylan and took a deep breath. "They said they were searching for two half-bloods, and they knew we were there...I mean, they didn't know it was *us*, but they knew there were two half-bloods on the premises. I think some of them might be Ivari's children."

"Any idea of their plans?"

"Kidnapping, maybe. They said they didn't want to leave emptyhanded."

Wylan and Connor shared a look. "Might have intended something worse," said Connor, "but I couldn't understand them."

"Then it's a good thing you called...ah, thank you," he said as the Huntsman I remembered as Derat returned with a glass bottle half-full of amber liquid and a pair of cups. Wylan poured, and Derat passed the cups to Connor and me with an insistent nod.

I sniffed mine—I wasn't overly fond of alcohol, especially not the hard stuff—but Connor slugged his back and grimaced.

"That's it," said Wylan, clapping him on the shoulder, then looked around the room and switched to Pactish. "Who wants to run to Georgia and chase down some elves?"

"We're hunting?" one asked with a bit more enthusiasm than I'd have liked.

"Retrieving," he clarified. "Non-lethal if possible. We're not riding for prey—we're looking for home invaders. Anyone interested?"

Despite the lesser outing, about a dozen stood, pulling weapons off the walls, and Annie smirked at Wylan. "You're going to need a lift, bub."

He sighed. "Please don't get hit."

"You worry too much." She vanished, then reappeared seconds later, strapping a gun holster around her waist. "All right, let's do this. Connor, Maebe," she continued, switching languages again, "y'all hang tight. We'll be back."

"Wait…" Connor began, but the pack quickly linked hands and blinked out of sight.

"Don't worry," said Derat, pulling up an empty chair. "They're just measly elves—my brothers have brought down more difficult prey. Refill?" he offered, cocking the bottle.

Connor took him up on it but sipped that time. "You speak English?"

"Only recently. Wylan thought it would be wise to have another speaker besides himself and Annie, and…well, *he* doesn't need a potion to pass someone a language." He paused, giving Connor a once-over, then asked, "Jane's boyfriend, yes?"

He chuckled into his drink. "My reputation precedes me?"

"I suspected you'd have to be, since you were at her father's home. Breathe, youngling. It's over."

A long sip was Connor's answer to that. "Do I really smell scared?" he asked, giving his underarm a quick sniff.

"Somewhat," said Derat. "It's nothing you'd notice—elf, human, whatever you are, you have a terrible sense of smell. I mean no insult," he quickly clarified. "You can't help it. But yes, there's a distinct combination of scents that speaks of fear."

"Great," Connor mumbled. "That's just fantastic."

"It's no reason for embarrassment," Derat replied. "I overheard part of what you two were saying—you were prepared to fight *how* many elves?"

"Four," I told him. "We were hiding in the brew room,

and they were forcing the door, and Connor had his gun…"

His eyebrows rose toward his antlers. "Boy," he murmured, leaning closer to Connor, "unless you're far better trained in magic than Maebe is—"

"Nope," Connor interrupted.

"As I suspected. You were planning to fight four elves with *that?*" he asked, pointing to the pistol. "With *her* as backup? If you weren't frightened at that prospect, I'd call you a fool." He waited while Connor drained his second glass, then said, "Annie gives me precious little of the gossip. Are you and Jane a serious couple?"

"I, uh…" Connor began, but paused and eyed Derat silently.

The Huntsman grinned. "You think I give a damn about Pact policies on fraternization?"

"I don't know, do you?"

"No, and neither does Wylan. Be at ease," he said, sitting back in his chair. "If Annie brought you here, then you're his guests, end of discussion. No harm will come to you in this place."

"Um…thanks. Good to know." Connor squinted at the fireplace as if seeing it for the first time, then looked past me at the long hall. "Dumb question, but where, uh—"

"Technically, the Pactlands, but that's not precisely accurate. This is a space unto itself, accessible only to the Hunt. Our father built it when we came over, and Wylan has seen no need to open it up, so…" Derat shrugged. "Apparently, you can walk out of here and straight into the Pactlands—Annie did it—but you can't find it again unless you know the way. Another?" he asked, raising the bottle.

"Better not, but thanks."

"As you like. Seriously," Derat told us, "don't worry. Wylan and our brothers will see to your rogue elves, and I assume someone will alert the Division of Laws."

"We should probably call Yacovi…" I began.

"Wait until morning," Derat counseled. "Sit here for

now, make yourselves comfortable. I suspect we can find a couple of extra beds tonight, and once the others return, we'll make the arrangements, eh? Are you hungry?"

The thought of eating left me a little queasy, but before I could ask Derat for a cup of water, I heard a muffled ringing from within my purse and hastily dug out my phone. MOM & DAD, announced the screen, and I tapped the button, surprised but grateful for the late call. Perhaps Connor had told them I'd be coming over that weekend.

"Hi," I said, trying to inject a touch of peppiness into my voice. "How's it—"

"Maebe? Honey, is that you?"

She spoke in a terrified whisper I'd never heard. "*Mom?* Mom, are you okay? What's wrong?"

"It's on fire, everything's on fire—"

"What's on fire? Mama?" I demanded, squeezing my phone as I heard a distant scream coming from her end.

"East Branch! There's outsiders here, strangers, they came in the dark…"

"From Whitford? Police? Not police?"

Connor ripped the phone from my hand and triggered the speaker. "Denise, it's Connor. What's going on?"

"Connor?" She sounded panicked. "You're with Maebe?"

"We're safe," he assured her. "What's this about a fire?"

Another scream—a closer one—cut through the night before Mom could answer. "Outsiders," she whispered. "They're everywhere. I'm hiding in the horse barn. Jason, I don't know where Jason is, he just told me to run…"

My blood froze.

"You keep quiet, now," Connor said. "Okay? Stay on the line, Denise. I'm going to call for help…" He stood and pulled his phone from his pocket, then handed me mine and tapped through his contacts. "Mark? Hi," he said a moment later, running his hand through his hair in agitation. "I've got a report of fire and possible arsonists out at

East Branch. Can you...thanks. I'm out of the county. On my way back."

"It's going to be all right, Mama," I murmured into my phone. "Connor's sending people to help."

"Okay," she managed, her voice small and shaky. "How long?"

"I don't know, but you stay where you are. We're going to find Dad," I said with far more confidence than I felt. Looking at Derat, who watched with concern, I asked, "Can you get us to East Branch?"

He shook his head. "I'm sorry, but I don't know the way."

*Why* had Annie left? Those stupid elves at Yacovi's house didn't matter. If I could just get to my mom...

"Connor, call Annie," I said as he hung up. "We need to get over there—"

Before he could say a word, I heard my mother cry, "No! Please, no, don't hurt me. You can have whatever you want—"

Her plea ended in a pained scream.

"Mom! *Mama*!" I yelled at the phone. "Answer me! Mom, are you there?"

But all I heard was a beep as the call was disconnected.

# CHAPTER 4

**B**y the time Annie and Wylan reappeared, both smiling in satisfaction, I was beside myself and frantically pacing before the fireplace. Connor wasn't in much better condition, but he was able to tell them about the phone call I'd received with a modicum of coherence, so he had one on me that night.

If the Hunt really could smell fear, I must have stunk.

"Can you get us to East Branch?" Connor asked, having already loaded his pockets and collected his gun.

Wylan looked to Annie, who shook her head. "Not directly. I've never been out there…"

My cousin groaned and smacked his forehead. "Of course. *Fuck*."

"But it's close to Whitford, right? I know the way to your house."

He brightened. "Oh! Yes, that…yeah, that works. My ride's at Yacovi's, but I left my Explorer at home. Let's go," he said, and grabbed Annie's wrist.

She took my hand. "Hon?"

"I'm in," said Wylan, gripping her shoulder, and with that, the world went black once more.


**C**onnor had two vehicles, his personal SUV and one marked as property of the Whitford Police Department. I hadn't fully appreciated the capabilities of the latter until Connor jumped in, flipped on the blue lights and siren, and threw the Explorer into reverse.

Beside him, having masked, Wylan clung to the door as Connor tore down the dark road out of his neighborhood. "Going a little fast, aren't you?" Annie yelled from the back seat beside me, leaning toward the Plexiglas barrier. "Are you not worried about deer?"

"Nope," Connor said, barely slowing around a curve. In the trunk behind us, the bags holding his hunting rifle and shotgun rattled as they slid into the sides. "What happened at Yacovi's?"

"We caught them in the brew room," said Wylan. "They were ransacking the place, throwing open the cabinets and closets in search of you. It wasn't difficult to subdue them."

"Alive?"

"Yeah, just unconscious. They should have nasty headaches in the morning," he added without the faintest trace of guilt. "Three male, one female. The idiots put up a fight."

"I mean, decently trained elves are pretty formidable, aren't they?" Connor asked.

"Sure," said Wylan, "against ordinary opponents. But the Hunt has killed more than its share of their kind without taking losses, so you tell me. And I think you're correct about them not being from the Pactlands," he continued, bracing himself as Connor whipped around a corner. "If they were, they'd have recognized us. Instead, they seemed perplexed."

"Oh?"

"Yup," said Annie. "A whole lot of, 'What the fuck is *that*?' and then they started shooting. Couple good hits to the head, and they went down hard."

"We bound them, and I told the others to deliver them to DOL," Wylan continued.

"Probably the best place for them, but there's a problem: DOL doesn't have jurisdiction here," Connor pointed out. "The B&E happened in Ragged Gap."

"B&E?" Wylan echoed.

"Breaking and entering," he clarified. "Maybe attempted kidnapping, too."

*Or attempted murder*, I thought, but kept that to myself.

"Had they broken into, say, Jane's house, then we'd be out of luck," Annie replied, "but DPP considers brew rooms and greenhouses here to be under their jurisdiction. The greenhouses especially, since they don't fully exist in this world, but a brew room like Yacovi's is a regulated space subject to Pact oversight. If DPP claims it, then Laws will prosecute crimes that occur there."

Connor braked hard as a deer bounded across the road in front of us, then swore and floored the Explorer again. "Well, I don't think Ragged Gap or the county are going to fight them for jurisdiction over those four. What about East Branch?"

"What about it?" Annie asked.

"If those elves' buddies have been setting fires at East Branch, will DOL step in? I can't bring down elves by myself, my team sure can't, and I *know* the deputies can't manage it."

"That'd be a question for Laws," she replied. "Let's just see what we're up against first."

"Not to add stress," said Wylan, "but there was one hell of a stream around Yacovi's house when we arrived, and a vehicle was half-submerged near the door. Is that, uh, normal?"

"No. Electrified moat. They tripped his ward," Connor muttered. "I think I can reset it, but—"

"Priorities," Annie interjected. "No one's going to go for a swim in the lethal lazy river tonight."

We said little else, letting Connor concentrate as he raced out of Whitford and into the county, but as we neared home, my heart leapt into my throat. When the split-rail fence that demarcated the boundary of our land came into view, I could already see the unnatural orange glow back in the trees—a forest fire.

East Branch was burning.

We screeched to a halt behind a cluster of vehicles, most topped with strobing lights. I recognized the sheriff's SUVs and a pair of fire engines, and a smaller, more heavily armored truck was driving through the open gate, spraying water to either side as the flames licked at the trees along the dirt road home. Connor had barely slammed his SUV into park before he'd unbuckled and jumped out, leaving Wylan to free Annie and me from the rear.

As my cousin started to weave through the press toward the road, a middle-aged man stepped into his path and caught him in a bear hug. "No, son," I heard him say as Connor struggled to free himself. "*No.* You ain't going in there."

"I've gotta—"

"Nothing's going in but the wildland engine. Running after it like that is suicide."

"Mark—"

"No, Connor. Absolutely not. And if I have to put you in the back of my car for your own safety, I will." He glanced at me as I hurried toward them, and his brows knit. "You one of the East Branchers, honey?"

I nodded, trying not to sob.

He sighed. "I'm sorry, sweetheart. Can't let you in there. It's not safe." Turning his attention back to Connor, who still seemed tense enough to bolt, he said, "There's a chopper coming in with water, and we've got engines trying to drive the perimeter to keep this thing contained."

"My *family* is in there," Connor insisted. "Her mom called, there was screaming, she was hiding from someone—"

"And we're going to go in after them as soon as we can," Mark—the sheriff, I assumed—promised Connor. "But there's not a damn bit of good that we can do dead, and neither can you. I *know*," he said slowly, holding Connor's stare, "but son, killing yourself isn't going to help them."

Connor growled, but he surrendered to the point that

Mark felt comfortable releasing him and motioned one of the deputies closer. "Wilson, you know Chief Willow, yeah? Keep him posted. I've got to coordinate with the firefighters."

As the sheriff walked away, the deputy said, "Why don't y'all come this way, sir? The EMTs just pitched a tent, and there's coffee—"

"I can't sit," he said, stepping away, and marched off toward the woods.

"Chief!" Wilson called after him. "You can't go in there!"

"I can walk the fucking fence!" Connor snapped, and started down the road, peering into the eerily lit trees for signs of life, or possibly a path through the encroaching flames. The woods crackled as they burned, and though I heard a distant, panicked neighing from the horse barn, I strained my ears in vain for cries for help.

The only break we caught that night was that the breeze was minimal and blowing the smoke away from us. As I walked with Connor, conscious of Wylan close behind, Annie jogged up and said, "We're far enough from the mob. Let's get Diriem in on this."

Connor squinted at her. "What's *he* going to do? He's not a pyromancer—"

"You're right, but he might know something," she said with undue patience. "Come on, huddle up."

"Wait—Keef's big sister is a pyro, right?" I asked, struck by the idea. "I could call her...or not. Shit, I don't think I have her number..."

"Yeah, Fell's a pyro," said Annie, pulling out her phone, "but she can't just do her thing out here. Too many normies around."

Connor and I gathered close to her as Wylan continued down the fence, and Annie dialed. As the call connected, she switched on the speaker and held the phone flat in her palm near her chin. "Hey, sorry," she began, sticking to English, "but we've got a problem in Georgia. I'm here with Connor and Maebe."

Despite the hour, Diriem didn't seem to have gone to bed yet, as his voice lacked the frogginess of a sudden wakeup. "Oh? What's happened?"

Connor leaned in, and though I could see how agitated he truly was, he kept his tone calm and matter-of-fact. "East Branch is on fire. Suspected arson, potential fatalities, but I don't know because the sheriff won't let me in the main gate."

"The fire's *bad*," Annie added. "I don't think it'd be safe to run through the woods…uh…"

"Annie?" Diriem asked sharply as she fell silent. "Annie, are you all right?"

Looking down the fence line, I could see the reason for her sudden speechlessness. Wylan stood in the shadows, almost hidden from view behind a large oak tree, with one hand held out in front of him, slowly closing into a fist. The glow of the fire dimmed as the flames began to snuff themselves out, and within seconds, Wylan was standing at the point of a fire-free wedge about fifty feet in radius.

"*Annie*," Diriem insisted. "Can you hear me?"

"Uh…yeah," she managed, and passed the phone to Connor. "Here, fill him in. I've got to go."

As she jogged off toward her husband, Connor asked Diriem, "Does Wylan have any sort of, um, *fire* powers?"

"In all honesty, I have no idea of the true extent of his abilities, but they're considerable. Why?"

"I think he's putting out the fire."

"*Ah.* With…how many humans in the vicinity?"

He glanced over his shoulder toward the cluster of lit vehicles and the pop-up tent at the gate. "I'd say at least a couple dozen, but they're preoccupied."

In the other direction, Annie was gesturing toward the emergency personnel, and though I couldn't hear their conversation, a sudden rumbling of thunder and the smell of ozone told me that Wylan had switched firefighting tactics.

"Bottom line," said Connor, "this isn't an accidental fire. Maebe and I were attacked tonight—"

"*What?* Where?"

That took my cousin aback. "You're surprised?"

"I'm not *omniscient*," Diriem protested. "What happened?"

"I was supposed to be house-sitting for Jane's dad, and Maebe's with me for the weekend, and…" He paused briefly to put his thoughts in order. "Shortly after ten, four elves showed up at the house. First vehicle tripped the ward, and that gave us time to get into the brew room."

"Elves?" he repeated.

"Yeah. I never saw them, but Maebe said they were speaking High Elvish, and after Annie extracted us, she and Wylan went back with, uh…the boys. Found all four, subdued them, apparently dropped them off at DOL."

"I'll check in. But why were they at Yacovi—"

"They knew there were two of us in the house," I blurted. "I don't know how. Maybe Ivari did his own blood trace or something. And I think two of them are Ivari's sons, but I'm not sure. We were listening through the wall—"

"We'll get to the bottom of this," said Diriem. "And…" He sighed deeply. "You think the two are linked, the home invasion and the fire."

"My mom called me. She was scared, and there was screaming, and then…she was begging someone not to hurt her, and that's the last I heard," I said, fighting my useless tears. "If they knew we were at Yacovi's house, don't you think they could have hit East Branch, too?"

"Without question." A soft groan came through the phone. "I've had flashes of fire for the last few days. No wonder."

"And you didn't think to tell us?" Connor demanded.

"There was nothing clearly tying it to you! Just…fire in the dark, the smell of burning wood, ashes…very brief, very jumbled. I wasn't able to lock in on it, and I'm so sorry, but mine isn't a perfect talent."

"I thought your people were keeping an eye on East Branch."

"They have been, and I swear to you, if we'd understood the warning, I'd have sent word. But..." He cursed under his breath. "You need to get out of there. Whoever your arsonists are, they're sure to miss their friends when no one comes back from Yacovi's place, and if anyone tries another blood trace..."

"We're exposed," Connor finished, and nodded curtly as Annie returned. Lightning crackled overhead, and suddenly, the clouds—which hadn't been there moments before—opened into a deluge.

"Is it storming?" Diriem asked.

"I told Wylan to be more subtle," said Annie, retrieving her phone from Connor. "This could be a gully-washer, but it should help."

We were already soaked, and Connor shook his head. "Rain chance this weekend was ten percent."

"Then aren't we lucky?" Annie replied. "Assuming this works, what's the road situation inside the compound?"

"Dirt and rutted to hell and back. It'll be washed out, and if there's trees across it—"

"You don't need to be anywhere near East Branch right now," Diriem interrupted. "Annie, can you get them out of there?"

"Where?" she asked.

"Somewhere in the Pactlands would be a decent start, and if you wouldn't mind overnight guests..."

"Of course not. Let's go," she said, nudging Connor back toward the gate.

"What about Wylan?" I asked.

"He'll come home when he's finished."

Annie hung up and guided us to Connor's Explorer. As we squelched toward the action, we found many of the deputies and the sheriff clustered under the EMTs' tent. "I'm getting these two out of here," Annie announced.

"Unless you need them…"

"No, that's a good idea. Y'all go," said Mark, shooing us on. "Connor, I'll call as soon as I have an update, okay? Try to get some rest."

I climbed into the back of Connor's vehicle, shivering, and Annie took the vacated front seat beside him. "Come on," she coaxed. "There's nothing more you can do tonight."

"I can help—"

"Unless they're still looking for us," I said. "You heard Diriem."

"She's got a point," said Annie. "Let's go back to your house. We'll leave from there."

Reluctantly, Connor started toward Whitford, driving at a much less dangerous speed that time. As he neared the town line, he stiffened behind the wheel. "Shit, Yacovi's ward—"

Annie gripped his shoulder. "Not your problem. Once y'all are safe at the lodge, I'll get Jane to come with me and reset it."

"But she's tied up with a work thing all weekend—"

"It's *fine*," Annie insisted. "Under control."

It wasn't, though. Not at all. But the hour was late, I was shaking with cold and nerves, and at that moment, Annie's seemed like the voice of reason.

"I'd better call Janie," said Connor.

"You let me handle that. Just drive," said Annie, and he obeyed.


The Hunt's lodge was massive, and Annie had no trouble locating a pair of adjoining bedrooms in an out-of-the-way corner of the building for Connor and me. "It's late, and you're exhausted," she said when she arrived with spare toiletries and toothbrushes from her own stash. "Get a hot bath and go to bed. Y'all need it."

Connor, who'd poked his head into my room as Annie

made her deliveries, started to protest. "I've got to take care of Yacovi's place, and when Mark calls—"

"I've already spoken to Jane, and she's handling the ward. *And* the cleanup," Annie assured him. "She's going to fill in her dad, so don't worry. As for East Branch, there's not a damn thing you can do until the fire's out, and I suspect that sheriff of yours won't be calling until he's surveyed the area. So *rest*," she said, and surprised him with a hug. "I'm sorry," she murmured, giving him a long squeeze. "I know your mind must be spinning right now, and if you want something to help you sleep, I've got a potion stash from work. Or there's the whiskey option," she joked, releasing him. "Yacovi's donated a couple bottles of moonshine if that's more your taste, but personally, I'd suggest downing a cup of something decaf and going horizontal."

"I can't drug myself tonight," Connor mumbled. "In case…"

"Small dose?"

"No, thanks. Maebe, now—"

"Nope," I said, shaking my head. "My parents are in trouble, and if the sheriff lets us in—"

"Honey, you're not going to be of any use if you're dead on your feet," Annie gently chided, but she didn't press the issue of the potion. "I'll leave you to it, then. You've got my number, so call if you need anything. And make yourselves at home," she added as she stepped out of my room. "The giant fireplace in the kitchen is a little much, but there's an induction burner on the counter with a teakettle on it, so go right ahead. Oh, hang on." She vanished but reappeared seconds later with two flat black discs in her hands. "Chargers," she explained, passing them out. "There's a distinct lack of outlets in this place. Just put your phone on top, and it'll do the rest." Covering a yawn, Annie asked, "Anything else I can do for y'all?"

"Thank Wylan for the rain, if I don't see him first," Connor replied. "But, uh…we may have a problem."

Her eyebrows rose. "Another one?"

"Yeah. If those guys were able to track us to Yacovi's house, then what's to stop them from tracking us here?"

"How would..." Annie frowned, then chuckled wearily. "Sorry, I shouldn't laugh. This is your first time in the Pactlands, isn't it?"

"Uh-huh."

"Okay. Just understand that the Hunt's weird corner of the Pactlands is terra incognito to everyone else. Even if your little buddies took a bloodline potion *and* managed to sneak their way through a portal, they still wouldn't find us. You'd show up on the map as smack dab in the middle of a whole lot of nothing. Bottom line, as long as you're here, you're safe. Promise," she said, holding my gaze, then vanished.

Connor and I regarded the place where she'd been standing, and then he tapped his charger against his free hand. "Do you think this building is really so big that it's impractical to walk from place to place, or do you think Annie does that just because she can?"

"Wouldn't you?" I replied.

"If I could, I'd be at the center of East Branch right now," he said, and returned to his room.

I'd set up my phone to charge and brushed my teeth, but despite the hour, I couldn't sleep. My pajamas and other clothes were back at Yacovi's, and though the wide bed was soft and quite comfortable, I couldn't still my thoughts or silence my mother's screams.

This wasn't right. We should have been back at the gate, waiting for the fire to die. No, it wasn't safe to run in there with a wildfire burning all around us, but East Branch never had visitors—no one but Connor and his parents before him. When our families saw those county vehicles moving in with their flashing lights and filled with armed outsiders, they'd panic. We *needed* to be there to make introductions and help keep the peace, to assure the elders that these outsiders had only come to help.

What if Mark, the man who'd held my cousin back from the fire and called him "son," ended up on the wrong end of a rifle? After the night they must have had at East Branch, my dad would shoot first and sort things out later.

*If he's still alive...*

I tried to silence that voice with a brisk shake of my head, as if I could dislodge its hooks from my brain. Dad was fine. Mom was fine, just scared. Maybe the person who'd found her in the barn was a kind soul from Whitford, someone who'd seen the smoke or the telltale glow in the night and rushed over to help.

*Then why didn't she call you back?*

Maybe the barn had caught fire. Maybe a horse had stepped on the phone. Mom could have forgotten it in the commotion. Surely our families had been hard at work, filling buckets at the well and running to the creek for more. Even the eldest of the elders would have pitched in with the community on the line. And the crops...

Oh, no, the *crops*.

The summer's harvest would have come in—peaches, pears, peppers, early potatoes—but the apples were peaking. Had the fire consumed the old orchard? The barns? What about the stores of canning jars, had they survived?

If the woods burned, there'd be few animals to hunt. No meat, no fruit or vegetables, and the creek wasn't productive enough to let the community subsist on fish alone.

They'd starve.

More awake than ever, I hurried into the hall and rapped on Connor's door. When he opened it, I saw that he hadn't been sleeping, either; the lights were on, and while his bed looked a little rumpled, he hadn't bothered turning it down. "You okay, mitta?" he murmured, stepping back to let me in.

"No, I just thought of something," I said, and waited for him to close the door. "What if all the food burned?"

Connor's face remained tired but blank. "What do you mean?"

"If the fire got the barns, the orchard, the fields...I mean, maybe the canned stuff survived in the cellars, but if they lost the harvest, and the deer don't come around, they're not going to have enough to eat. I don't want to be a beggar, but do you think Diriem and Teolm might help? You know they can stretch any food they get..." I paused as I thought of another issue. "And the *medicines*. What if those are all gone?" While East Branch always purchased a few storebought remedies, bottles of aspirin and antiseptic cream, so many of the poultices and salves of my childhood were homemade, produced from ingredients grown or foraged. "Jane still has plants in storage, right? For her soaps and things? Do you think she'd sell us some?"

He stared at me for a long moment as I wrung my hands, then said, "Maebe, sit down." I perched on the edge of his bed, and he knelt in front of me. "I need you to understand that there's a strong chance that many...maybe most...of them didn't make it."

The voice in my head tried to push to the fore again, but I shoved it back. "They could have gone to the creek. They'd be safe there."

"You heard your mom, mitta."

"That might have been an outsider come to help," I insisted, willing the scenario I'd cobbled together to make sense. "Of course she'd have been scared. Or...maybe it was Whitford people all along, you know? Campers. What if they had a fire that got out of control? If there were strangers at East Branch *and* a fire, people would be running..."

The look of resignation in his dark eyes made my heart clench.

"If Ivari sent a team after the two of us," Connor said softly, "then why on earth would he have overlooked the others at East Branch? That's the motherlode."

I shook my head. "He probably just wants me. I'm the one who messed up his office—"

"I could be wrong. I hope to God I am. But if you put

the pieces together—"

"They might be fine!"

"It's…possible," he allowed. "But if they're not…"

"Don't say that," I whispered as my eyes blurred.

Connor took my hands and squeezed. "If they're not," he repeated, "then you're going to have to be strong. We all will."

I didn't want to consider that possibility. My parents, my grandparents, Uncle Joel…Alan and Helen Black and their kids, Candice and Mason, Connor's only remaining close kin…all of the elders, the parents who'd packed us off to Beukal in search of something better…little Joseph, the twins' baby brother, only seven…

If they were dead by Ivari's doing, then I was to blame. I was the one who'd run off, who'd gone home with Jane, who'd traveled to the Pactlands and revealed our secrets to Diriem. I was the one who'd sought out Ivari for help but only made matters worse. How long had it been since he'd paid his half-blooded descendants any mind before I came crashing into his life?

If East Branch had been wiped off the map, then my kin's blood was on my hands.

# CHAPTER 5

Saturday dawned pink in a sky of high, streaky clouds, which I knew because I watched the whole thing happen from the lodge's wide porch.

Had I not been exhausted and sick to my stomach, it'd have made a lovely setting. Unlike most of the Pactlands, the Hunt's hidden enclave was somehow able to support a forest of tall pines and hardwoods, which had already burst into their full fall colors. The air was crisp but not freezing, and I'd found a wooden rocking chair where I could wait out the night.

At least Connor wasn't alone. Shortly after I'd pulled myself together and left his room, Annie had arrived with Jane, who'd apparently blown off her training session with Diriem's blessing. While Jane had dealt with Connor, Annie had coaxed me downstairs for a mug of warm milk, which she'd doctored with vanilla and honey. Theoretically, it'd make me drowsy, but it had been no match for my nerves, and so I'd grabbed a woolen blanket from atop a chest in one of the sitting rooms and retreated to the porch, where hopefully no one would notice if I needed to scream for a bit.

Or, more worryingly, if my talent got away from me. I could feel it roiling beneath the surface, searching for an outlet, and so I focused on the steady motion of the chair to calm myself. If Wylan could create a thunderstorm, then I suspected he could repair a window, but I didn't want to risk it.

The sun was up, illuminating the mist that hung over

the grassy expanse between the lodge and the encircling woods, when the door creaked and Connor emerged. "Hey, mitta," he said, watching me rock. "*There* you are. Been out here all night?"

"A while," I allowed, pulling my borrowed blanket more tightly around me. "Where's Jane?"

"Finally dozed off. I didn't want to bother her, so…" He shrugged, then pointed to the empty rocker beside me. "That seat taken?"

"Now it is."

He plopped down next to me with a groan. "Did you get any sleep?"

"No, you?"

"Negative. Just…waiting." Pushing back, he set his chair in motion and stared out at the low-lying fog. "I hate this."

"Me, too," I murmured.

We rocked in silence for a moment, lost in our own thoughts, and then the door opened again. "Long night?" asked Wylan, joining us.

Connor nodded, and as I looked closer in the strengthening light, I noticed the shadows beneath his eyes. "Had better."

"I'm sure." He leaned against the railing and folded his muscular arms. "And I'm sorry. Whatever's happened to East Branch, I'm sorry for your loss. Watching your home burn…"

"If Annie didn't pass the message, thank you for the rain," said Connor. "I have no idea how you did that…"

Wylan chuckled. "It's not easy to explain, especially before breakfast, but you're certainly welcome. Annie said just smothering the fire would be a bad idea, so…best I could do with an audience."

"You did a hell of a lot more than I did last night."

His antlers dipped as he cocked his head and arched an eyebrow. "We're working with *slightly* different tools, Connor."

"Yeah, well, remind me not to piss you off, big guy."

"If you could continue to refrain from shooting me, that'd be great. Those bullets actually do sting, you know." Straightening, he asked, "Anyone hungry? Breakfast should be up in a few minutes if you're interested…"

A shrill melody from Connor's pocket cut Wylan short, and Connor rose to pull his phone free. "Sheriff," he muttered, and took the call on speaker mode. "Willow."

"It's Mark," came the reply. He sounded about as tired as we did. "Where are you, Connor?"

"My girlfriend's place," he fibbed.

"Good. That's…good. You're not alone?"

"Uh, no."

*That* was an understatement.

"Is the fire out?" Connor asked. "Have y'all been in?"

"Fire's mostly out," the sheriff slowly replied. "Got some hot spots, of course, but there's a team working on those. That storm last night was a godsend, I'll tell you. Probably saved the mountain from going up. My daughter's got one of those drone camera thingies, and she put it up a few minutes ago. Looks like all the burned acreage is confined to the East Branch property."

"So…how is it?" He hesitated, then asked, "Survivors?"

Mark's initial reply was a long, slow exhalation.

"None yet," he murmured. "I'm so sorry, son. I…shit," he muttered. "I know those are your people out there. We're still looking—most of the buildings have collapsed, and it's possible someone's trapped underneath the rubble, but…"

I gripped the arms of my chair as a rushing sound filled my ears. The world went gray for a moment, and then I registered pressure on my wrists and looked up to find Wylan leaning over me. "Breathe," he whispered. "In. Out. Follow along, Maebe."

Connor's hand trembled as he clutched his phone, but he kept his voice steady. "How many bodies do you have so far?"

"Let me check..." Papers rustled on the other end, and the sheriff replied, "Twenty-eight."

"That's all of them. Some of the kids have scattered, but..." My cousin paused to take a deep breath. "There were twenty-eight living on the property."

The slight morning breeze began to pick up as I reeled. Twenty-eight dead. No survivors.

My mother's scream would be the last thing I ever heard from her...

"Maebe," said Wylan, pinning me to the chair, "look at me."

I stared up into his odd amber eyes, my chest heaving as my heart raced.

"You've got to breathe. Focus on your breathing..."

"You're going to need someone to come ID them, right?" Connor asked. "Has the coroner been out yet? Where are they going, Atlanta?"

"Coroner's on the scene and making preliminary assessments," said Mark, "but I'm going to be honest with you: unless these folks have dental records I don't know about, you may have trouble putting names on bodies."

Connor closed his eyes and rubbed his face. "That bad?"

The wind around us began to blow in earnest, knocking over a few wooden staves someone had left propped against the side of the lodge.

"I've seen my share of fire deaths," the sheriff replied, "and this one burned *hot*. Fire investigator is on his way, but if this was natural, I'll eat my hat. Place is probably drenched in accelerants, and the rain won't have washed away all traces. We'll figure it out."

"But...the bodies?"

Mark groaned. "Charred pretty badly. Most of them aren't fully intact, and a number of them were practically cremated. But a couple of the more complete skulls show signs of trauma," he added. "Bullet wounds, maybe. It'll take a while to go through the scene, but—"

"You think they were shot?"

"I think it'd have been a mercy if they were," he murmured. "I'll give you a call once we've got the bodies transported. If you want to try to identify them for me, that'd be great, but I'm afraid we may be left with best guesses and process of elimination. Any chance that you could get me data on the residents? Names, ages, any identifying characteristics?"

"If you're looking for someone with a pacemaker or an artificial knee, you won't find one. But yeah, I can make a list."

"I'd appreciate that…Connor, I'm sorry, there's a weird distortion on the line…"

That was probably the wind, which howled around the lodge and shook the trees. Wylan held his post, trying to coax me down, and sweat dripped from his forehead.

"Sorry, Mark," said Connor. "I'll be there soon—"

"No. Don't come."

"Excuse me?"

"Make a list for me, if you will, and I'll let you know when you can view the bodies," said the sheriff, "but I don't want you meddling in this investigation."

Connor jumped out of his chair. "*Mark*! I—"

"This is my case," he said firmly. "East Branch is county. Let us handle it."

"But—"

"You're a fine officer, son, and I respect you. I hope you know that. But you've lost people, and you can't be impartial right now. This is a massive scene, and I need clear heads."

"Mark," Connor protested, turning his back to the wind, "I can help. *Let me help*. That's my family—"

"Exactly," the sheriff interrupted. "You may not be a direct victim in this case, but you're pretty damn close. I swear, Connor, I'm going to keep you informed, but I need you to trust me and stay out of my crime scene. Lean on Jane," he said, his voice softening. "She's a sweet girl, yeah? You don't need to be alone right now. And, uh…those folks with you last night?"

"Friends of Jane's," he mumbled. "Plus my little cousin."

"Jesus. Do *not* let that kid see the bodies. Just…believe me, there's nothing here you want to show her."

"I'll keep an eye on her," said Connor. "But Mark—"

"Stay put. I'll call when I need you, and I've already touched base with your team, so you don't have to tell Whitford the news." He sighed again. "Son, you have my deepest sympathies. Take care of yourself, okay?"

By the time Connor got off the phone, he could barely stand against the force of the wind, and he joined Wylan. "*Maebe*," he snapped, and grabbed my chin. "Stop it. Pull yourself together."

"I can't…" I whimpered, crumbling.

"You can, and you will. *Now*."

As my eyes filmed, Connor reached past Wylan's arms and hugged me. "It hurts," he said in my ear. "I know it hurts, mitta. But this ain't helping."

"Mama," I sobbed. "Daddy…"

"We will mourn them later. All of them. But we've got to do right by them first," he insisted. "And we can't find the bastards responsible until you calm down."

Slowly, the wind began to abate, and within minutes, my fit had passed. Wylan released me and retreated a few steps, and weeping, I stared out at the yard…and the half-dozen downed trees on the perimeter. "I'm sorry," I began.

"It's all right," Wylan replied, wiping his sweaty face on his shirt. "That is…*quite* a talent you've got."

"Did you dampen it?" Connor asked.

He grimaced. "Tried to counter it. I figured you didn't want to be blown off the porch on top of everything else." He opened the door and said, "Come on, you need to eat. You've got a day ahead of you."

"I don't think I can eat right now…"

"*Try*," said Wylan, and judging by Connor's rapid acquiescence, his brain was blaring the same warnings mine was at the note in Wylan's voice.

The two Huntsmen on kitchen duty filled the house with the tantalizing aroma of well-cured bacon, but I could barely stomach the thought of downing a bite. Still, I sat at the long wooden table where Wylan suggested, and by the time one of the other brothers brought a pair of double-sized ceramic mugs and a whole pot of coffee, Annie and Jane had joined us. I stared into space, absently rubbing my arms and trying to drive the sound of my mother's final screams from my mind, while Connor filled them in on the news from home. Jane sat beside him on the bench with one arm around his shoulders, but Connor held his composure, though his gaze seemed distant.

As he finished, Annie pulled her phone from the pocket of her navy bathrobe. "We need to tell Diriem."

"Shouldn't he fucking know already?" Connor muttered into his mug.

Jane and Annie shared a look, and Jane took the lead. "He's got a team of agents who can see into the past," she murmured. "You know what Ganti's capable of, right?"

"Unless Ganti can rewind time—"

"We can't change what happened, but maybe they can tell you who's responsible."

"I've already got a pretty good idea of that," said Connor, "and there's not a goddamn thing Mark can do to bring them in."

She held her temper. "You're right. I…*seriously* doubt the sheriff is going be any help if this is Ivari's doing. So, let's coordinate with DOI. Find out what really happened and where the perpetrators are now. I mean, it's possible that they took hostages from East Branch."

Connor shook his head. "Twenty-eight corpses, Janie.

That's everyone."

"*If* they're real corpses. You think a gang of elves couldn't throw together some convincing fake bones?" Shrugging in the face of his incredulity, she said, "All I'm hearing is that we've got a lot of nothing from the team on the ground. Let's call the cavalry."

"And if DOI can find them," said Wylan, grabbing a spot on the bench beside Annie, "then perhaps we can kill them for you."

Annie turned to her husband, her mouth a tight line. "Babe."

"What?"

"As a member of a Pact agency, I'd like to remind you that we can't just kill people who get on our nerves. No matter how much fun it would be." Poking him in the arm, she added, "And *you* have certain standards to maintain as a Forum rep. Okay?"

Wylan shot her an impressively convincing set of puppy eyes.

"Oh, my God," she muttered, and reached for the coffee. "You've got to take up fishing, I swear."

"And we're putting the cart way before the horse," Jane cut in, "since we don't have confirmation of the culprits or their whereabouts yet. So, what do you say?" she asked Connor. "Let Diriem help."

"Fine," he grumbled, and sipped his breakfast.

While Annie doctored her coffee, Jane did the honors, leaving the phone on the tabletop for ease. Diriem answered on the second ring. "You're with him?" he asked in Pactish.

"Of course," she replied in English. "And I've got Maebe, Annie, and Wylan here as well. You're on speaker."

He followed her linguistic lead. "Any news from Georgia?"

"Sheriff won't let me onto the property," said Connor, "but from what he told me, it sounds like almost total destruction and twenty-eight bodies." Leaning toward the phone, he said, "You didn't see this coming. Help me make it right."

"We don't have confirmation that they're all actually dead," Jane added. "I mean, likely? Yes. But we can't rule out the possibility that some of the bodies are fake. Hostages."

Diriem cleared his throat. "No sign of a ransom demand, I take it."

"None that I know of," said Connor.

"Very well. Still, let's not rule them dead before we have better evidence. Does anyone have pictures of the people back at East Branch? Photographs?"

I scooted close to the table. "I do. On my phone. We took pictures with it before we left in case people started…missing…"

Annie hugged me from the side, and I quickly turned my face into her plush robe as I teared up.

"That's…very helpful," said Diriem. "Maebe, could you send those to Rose and me, please? Annie, Jane, you have her number, yes?"

"Sure do," said Jane, and gave me a little smile as I raised my face.

"Send the pictures. I'll wake her and ask her to start searching," he said, "and I'll call Ganti. He's meant to be off today, but he'll understand."

Jane frowned. "What about—"

"No. I'm putting my best on this. Assuming it's Ivari's doing, we don't know how many of them are protected from farsight—"

"What's your gut telling you?" Connor cut in.

Diriem hesitated before answering. "This isn't farsight talking, merely experience."

"Yeah?"

"Ivari isn't a pyromancer—*that* I know. It's rare in elves to begin with, and I don't recall any notorious pyros out of the south. But that doesn't mean they can't control fire."

"This one burned too hot for a basic forest fire," said

Connor.

"Which makes me even more confident that there's magic behind it. And..." He paused, then slowly sighed. "Ivari had to have used a bloodline trace. That's the only way he'd have known where you and Maebe were."

"Can one of those traces show people in the Pact-lands?"

"If properly calibrated, yes. Does he know how? Unclear. But as of right now, whoever the mastermind is behind the fire is coming up four people short. It's possible that he noticed and took hostages to secure their return..."

Connor met my stare, then said, "But it's not likely."

"Best not to draw conclusions without data," said Diriem, dodging the question. "Send the pictures, and let's start searching."

As Jane hung up, I rose to retrace my steps to my room, but before I could leave the table, another phone began to ring. With a grunt, Wylan rose and pulled one out—somehow, his leather leggings came equipped with pockets—then glanced at the screen and winced as he took the call. "Good morning, Director..." he began in Pactish.

Annie snorted. "Ten to one that's DOL."

"Sorry about the drop-off," he continued. "Had a situation, and it worsened. Have you spoken with Diriem?" He listened for a moment, sipping his coffee. "I've got both victims here, so if you'd like an accounting..."

As Wylan turned on the speaker, I heard a childlike female voice on the other end, slightly croaking with the hour. "You've got Yacovi? Who else was there, Jane?"

"Maebe Amos," Wylan replied, glancing at me. "Have you heard of—"

"*Her*? We've met. What was she doing with Yacovi?"

My slow gears finally turned, and I recognized the speaker as Kabno Erenani, the diminutive director of the Division of Laws.

Wylan looked at Jane and Connor, then shrugged.

"What's going on?" Connor whispered, unable to follow the conversation. "Who's that?"

Jane squeezed his hand and whispered back, "Let me handle it," then leaned toward the phone and switched to Pactish. "Director, it's Jane."

"*Oh*. Good morning—"

"Dad and I weren't there. He's visiting his buddies, and my...boyfriend was watching the house with Maebe."

Kabno paused. "Boyfriend?"

"One of Maebe's cousins."

"I...huh. I see..."

Jane was taking a risk. None of us from East Branch had Pactlands citizenship yet, and so what Jane and Connor had going on was almost certainly illegal. Hell, Connor hadn't even undergone genetic testing.

"He's talented," Jane told Kabno. "I've taught him some, and Dad's been working with him. I'd have pushed harder for him to come over with Maebe's group, but he's the chief of police in the town next to East Branch, and since he's the community's lone guy on the outside, he's been looking after them."

"But he's...informed?" she asked.

"DOI is very much aware of him."

"Mm. Police, you say?"

"Yes, ma'am."

"Is he listening?"

Jane glanced at Connor, then back at the phone. "He's here, but he doesn't speak Pactish, so..."

"Not a problem," she replied, switching into accented English. "Young man?"

With a nudge from Jane, Connor cleared his throat. "Uh, yes? Hi, um..."

"You're law enforcement?"

"In Whitford, ma'am. Sorry, who—"

"Director, this is Connor Willow, Whitford PD," Jane cut in. "Con, this is Director Erenani from Laws."

"*Oh*," Connor replied, eyes widening. "You've got our little friends in custody, I take it."

"Friday-night drop-offs of unconscious elves with no ID from a pack of Huntsmen who leave with *no* explanation are my absolute favorite," she deadpanned. "Currently, I've got four neutralized but *very* vocal inmates in isolated cells, all of whom are making frequent references to *Miranda*."

Connor smirked. "You've heard of it?"

"We have sufficient dealings outside to pick up something of local law," she said. "We took their fingerprints while they were unconscious, and they're not in any of our databases...and since they've been yelling exclusively in English, I'm thinking these are—"

"Ivari's crew," he finished. "Maebe thinks two of them are his kids."

"Interesting. Enlighten me—what would Ivari ti'Ammaas want with Mr. Hewt?"

"He's not after Yacovi," said Connor. "Last night, someone set East Branch on fire, and we've got twenty-eight corpses this morning—"

"Oh, heavens," she murmured.

"Yeah. And since those four in your custody somehow knew there were two more of us at Yacovi's house—"

"They're connected. Oh...I'm *terribly* sorry, that's..."

"More than half our family," he said, his voice calm but his knuckles white from his grip on his coffee mug. "The sheriff won't let me anywhere near East Branch right now and...well, frankly, I can't blame him, but just sitting here...wherever this is...ain't getting it done. You want a hand with your houseguests?"

"You have an idea?" asked Kabno.

"Yeah. Figure out which one's the most likely to crack, and let me take a shot at him. They're disoriented, they don't know where they are. I could work with that."

She thought for a moment, then said, "Under these...unusual circumstances, I suppose a little interagency cooperation would be beneficial. How soon can you be here, Chief?"

"Uh…" He glanced around our huddle, then said, "That's a question for Annie, I think."

"I can have you there in a matter of seconds," Annie said. "Do you want to, like, shower first?"

"It wouldn't be a bad idea," Jane added. "And I brought your stuff from Dad's. Is there anything you need from home? Probably not a great idea for you to be wandering around over there until we're sure Ivari isn't lying in wait with a blood trace…"

"Could you grab my uniform? There's a clean one on the back of the bedroom door," said Connor. "Not the dress one, just the standard gear."

"Uh…sure," she replied. "If Annie doesn't mind."

Annie shrugged. "No biggie. Go bathe, Connor—and Maebe, you, too. It can't hurt."

"They haven't eaten yet," Wylan began as we stood.

"I've got a stash of granola bars," she said, and shooed us on our way as she angled herself closer to the phone. "Director, where do you want him?"


About forty-five minutes later, we landed in the middle of the lobby of the DOL tower in downtown Beukal, a glass spire that rose thirty stories above the street and quite a few below. The lobby was still impressive on my repeat visit, a high-ceilinged space with white marble walls and floor that echoed at the slightest noise. It being Saturday morning, the lobby was fairly quiet, the visitor benches unoccupied. The only person to notice our arrival was the attendant at the wooden desk a few yards away, who seemed cramped even behind the generously proportioned piece of furniture.

"Morning, Little Fox," said Annie as she released us, and raised a hand to the green troll on duty.

He nodded at her but peered at the rest of our group: Connor in his work clothes, me in my slouchy weekend pants and oversized sweater, and Jane, who was presumably sporting Friday's ensemble again. "Agent Humphries, Agent Fortune? Is there something on the schedule that I've missed?"

"Probably not, but the boss is expecting us," Annie explained. "Would you please let her know?"

Jane led us over to a bench against the wall, but we didn't have to wait long. When one of the elevators at the far end of the lobby opened with a chime, the director marched out, speedwalking toward us, her robe flapping in her wake. Despite the hour and the weekend, she looked far more presentable than any of us did, well-dressed and with her white hair pulled back in an elegant chignon.

She was also barely more than three feet tall, with a youthful but almost ageless face and pale blue eyes, and Jane had warned Connor before we left the lodge so that he wouldn't be taken aback by her appearance. While I had yet to see a trained gnome in action, I'd gathered from watching the ones in my year that they were remarkably strong and fast, and I certainly didn't want *this* one on our bad side.

"Right on time," the director said in English. "And Annie, once again, I do appreciate that we're maintaining the fiction that the scanners are any impediment to you."

Annie grinned. "Yes, ma'am. My director prefers when I mind my manners."

"I'm sure he does. Jane, Maebe," she said, nodding to us both, then paused and considered Connor. "Chief Willow, I presume."

"Connor, ma'am," he replied, stooping slightly to shake her tiny hand.

"Kabno. Shall we?" Without waiting, she turned on her heel, heading back toward the elevators. As Annie disappeared, Kabno called over her shoulder, "Maebe, I didn't know you were part of this mess."

"Maebe doesn't need to be alone right now," said Jane as we hurried after her. "And she was there last night, too…"

"Of course." She stretched to push the up button by the elevators, then turned to me. "My condolences, youngling. Is there nowhere you'd rather be? Really, I won't take offense."

*Home* was on the tip of my tongue, but I bit it back. "No, ma'am."

"Very well." The doors opened, and she stepped inside and scanned her badge at the panel below the floor buttons. "I've had one of the four moved into an interrogation room upstairs on six. You two can sit with me and watch while Connor warms him up."

Connor barely cracked a smile. "I'm working with an audience, huh?"

"Standard protocol. Do you not monitor interrogations?"

"Not often live. That's what the camera's for. I've got two officers and a dog on my team—Whitford's pretty tiny, and we tend to be stretched thin."

"I see. Well, no pressure," she replied, and reached up to pat his arm. "This isn't a critique situation."

He nodded. "Any parameters I need to consider before I go in there?"

"I mean, don't kill him if you can avoid it. You should be safe enough," she added. "He's dampened, and he'll be tethered to the desk."

"Dampened…meaning he's not going to shoot lasers at me the minute I walk in there?"

She chuckled as the elevator came to a stop. "Precisely, though I've yet to see an elf manage *lasers*. But if, for some reason, he gets feisty…" She shrugged and stepped out. "You look like a healthy fellow. I'm not overly concerned." Glancing back at him as she walked, she remarked, "Didn't really get the elven build, did you?"

"I wouldn't know, ma'am," said Connor.

"They tend to be wirier. Tall and lean—they don't bulk well. But since I *sincerely* doubt that the one you're about to interrogate has seen the inside of a gymnasium in quite some time…you know, if you two end up squaring off, I like your odds. This way."

# CHAPTER 6

The viewing room was cozier than I'd anticipated, a space large enough for two rows of padded chairs in various sizes and a big floor mat near the door. Facing the chairs was a pane of glass stretching almost the length and width of the wall, which Kabno assured me was one-way: we could see in, but the people in the adjoining interview room couldn't see out. Our room was also soundproofed by means both mechanical and magical, so a microphone in the ceiling of the interview room piped in the conversation.

The elf next door looked disoriented, and judging by his overall disheveled appearance, no one at DOL had yet offered him a shower. His blond hair hung limply over his shoulders, while his eyes—true green, not Ivari's green-brown—seemed shadowed as they darted around the room. He wore a navy pullover sweater and dark, slim-cut jeans, and clearly, he wasn't going to win any heavyweight championships. While he was thin, what I could see of him seemed soft, not lean and chiseled. His right arm was connected to the desk by a set of steel handcuffs, and his fingers twitched against the wood as he waited.

I wondered which one he was. Not Danirri, surely. The guy in front of me seemed more like prey than predator.

"Here we go," murmured Kabno as the door opened and Connor, armed with a notepad and pen, stepped into the interview room. "Let's see how he fares."

The elf straightened in his chair, and Connor nodded. "Good morning," he said, laying on the drawl a little thickly, I thought. "How're we doing?"

"Been better," the other man snapped, and I tried to place his voice. "Someone knocked me out, and I woke up in here. I want my lawyer, *now*."

"Easy," Connor murmured, and pulled out the chair opposite his. "This ain't an interview yet. This is just me getting some basic information." Turning to a clean page in his notepad, he clicked open his pen and asked, "Name?"

"Nathan Rush."

"Mr. Rush," said Connor, writing that down. "Got any ID on you?"

"No," he mumbled.

"Mm. And I'm guessing you ain't from Georgia, right?"

He nodded. "The City."

Connor chuckled. "In my neck of the woods, that means Atlanta, *maybe* Chattanooga. I assume you mean somewhere a little further afield."

"New York. You want a borough, Officer?"

"Chief, actually," he replied calmly. "Connor Willow, Whitford PD. Now, you were picked up in Ragged Gap, but since this has been one *hell* of a night for everyone around here, I thought I'd pitch in. Most of the action's been out at East Branch. You know anything about that?"

The elf who called himself Nathan remained silent.

"What a mess," Connor said, and grunted as he shook his head. "County's out there, my people, Ragged Gap PD, fire department…hell, I'm sure the GBI will be involved before it's all said and done. Fucking nightmare."

"What happened?" Nathan asked. Though he sounded almost bored, I noticed how he leaned toward my cousin.

He whistled low. "Bloodbath, that's what."

Nathan stilled, but before he could neutralize his expression, I saw his flash of surprise.

"God help them," Connor continued. "I think at last count, there were twenty-eight dead. Burned beyond recognition, I heard. Not my show—East Branch is county land—but folks in the area are pretty close-knit. Something like that..." He shuddered and lowered his voice. "I wasn't on the scene when they finally got the fire under control enough to go in and look for survivors, and you know, that's probably a good thing. There are just some images you never get out of your mind's eye, and I've already seen my share of shit in this line of work. But let's get back to you, Mr. Rush," he said, tapping his pen against the pad. "You and your three friends were picked up for burglary."

"Burglary!" Nathan echoed. "We didn't steal anything!"

"You didn't have to," Connor replied. "You entered a dwelling house with the intent to commit a felony therein. That's first-degree burglary in Georgia, friend. Felony."

"This is all a misunderstanding," he insisted. "Really, Offi—*Chief*, sorry. Just a mistake. We didn't hurt that house."

"I hear you, but this is the kind of thing the DA's going to have to sort out."

With a groan, Nathan lowered his head and ran his free left hand through his hair in agitation.

And then he froze.

I watched as his fingers backtracked and prodded the tip of his ear, and judging by his sudden look of horror, he'd just realized he wasn't masked.

Connor regarded him impassively. "Something on your mind, Mr. Rush?"

"I...I, uh..." he stuttered, "I need to call my lawyer. Please."

"Let me give you a little intel," Connor replied, and leaned closer. "You ain't in Kansas anymore, Dorothy, and I ain't Auntie Em. Whatever fancy New York lawyer you've got on retainer isn't going to do you a *lick* of good today."

By then, Nathan had blanched to a sickly color. "Is this a black site?"

He snorted. "You think I'm CIA?"

"Are you?"

"No, and if this is a black site, it's news to me. I really am with the Whitford PD," he said, and rose enough from his chair to pull his wallet from his pants pocket. "Here," he said, flipping it open to reveal the badge inside. "You can take a look."

Nathan squinted at it, then nodded curtly and sat back. "So…what's going on? Where am I?"

"I'll be straight with you if you'll be straight with me."

He arched an eyebrow.

"Why don't I go first?" Folding his arms on the table, Connor said, "You and your accomplices were rounded up last night inside the home of Coby Hewt off Maple Ridge in Ragged Gap, Georgia. Mr. Hewt goes by Coby outside the Pactlands. Technically, he's Yacovi Hewt, and he's a licensed grower and brewer. Approved by the Division of Plants and Potions. He actually used to run the agency greenhouse, but that's not important now," he said almost conversationally. "Now, DPP doesn't claim jurisdiction over *most* parts of Georgia, but there's a hitch, see? Mr. Hewt's home is a licensed facility, and as such, DPP will prosecute certain crimes that occur on the premises. Y'all tripped his outside wards on the property, and then you broke into his brew room."

Nathan tried to raise his hands but only got the cuffed right a couple inches off the table and settled for the left. "Whoa, now. Look, we weren't trying to break into a….a secure installation or whatever. This has nothing to do with the, uh…"

"The Pactlands?" Connor offered. "That's the translation I always hear, anyway. I don't speak Pactish."

"Ah. Probably explains why no one's been talking to me," he muttered.

"Oh, no, there are some here fluent in English— they've been figuring out what to do with y'all, I guess. From what I've gathered, they take stunts like yours seriously. There's a lot of expensive potions and shit in there, you know? Restricted stuff. And one of y'all broke right through the lock Mr. Hewt put on that room."

"It was a mistake—"

"No, it wasn't," Connor insisted, holding Nathan's stare. "Because my cousin and I were hiding in there. I don't speak any variety of Elvish, but the kid's fluent, and I got the play by play. So, don't sit there and lie to my face," he said, his voice dropping toward a growl. "Like I said, it's been one hell of a night."

Nathan swallowed hard. "You…"

"Hi," he muttered, barely smirking.

The elf's gaze flicked toward Connor's chest and his name bar. "*Willow.* You're a ti'Catama, then?"

"That's what they tell me. 'Of willows,' right?"

He swore softly in High Elvish.

"So," Connor said, propping his head on his fist, "did you and your little buddies come after us to have a friendly chat? Because from where I'm sitting, it looks an *awful* lot like y'all came in there with the intent to kill us."

"No…*no,*" Nathan protested, shaking his head. "We weren't trying to kill you. My father just wanted to talk—"

"Your father's Ivari ti'Ammaas?"

"Yeah," he said, speeding up as he warmed to his subject. "He told us to bring you two to him so that he could talk with all of you at once…"

Nathan's voice faded as he made the connection.

"Out at East Branch, right?" Connor rubbed his dark stubble. "What was Daddy talking with, a flamethrower?"

"I…I mean…" Nathan struggled briefly, his eyes darting around the room, then managed to focus on Connor again. "He didn't say anything about killing you. Not to me, anyway. I'm not exactly one of Father's favorites, see? I…I'm good at locks. Puzzles. Comes in handy sometimes, and we didn't know quite what you're capable of, so—"

"You *really* thought he sent four of you to kidnap us for a chat? About *what?*"

"How you've been threatening to expose us!"

Connor sat up, scowling. "Excuse me?"

"Don't play dumb," Nathan scoffed. "I know all about that girl who broke into our building last summer, the one who threatened Father."

"And how did she threaten him, exactly?"

"She demanded half the firm's funds, or else she'd expose us. Father told her no, so she tried to burn him alive. He told us all about it."

The two stared each other down for a long moment, Connor silently watching, Nathan shrinking under his scrutiny.

"Maebe didn't do anything like that," my cousin finally murmured. "She asked for *help*—if not a donation, then a loan. That kid probably can't even get a fast-food job, but she was willing to take on the debt if Ivari would help East Branch."

"A…loan?" Nathan echoed uncertainly.

"Yeah. Because the folks at East Branch are—*were*—a bunch of dirt farmers. No savings, no cushion for the hard years. There wasn't even plumbing on the property, and the only electricity came from generators. I'm talking about poverty," he said, barely blinking. "The kind where parents go hungry some winters so there's enough food for the kids. That was East Branch. Folks left it alone for a long time, but of late, the tax assessor's been collecting. I didn't grow up on the property, and I actually have an income, so I've been helping as much as I can to keep them from being evicted. Again, we're talking subsistence farmers with minimal education, no money, and no prospects outside the community…and most of them have weird ears. Some can do a bit of magic. Not enough to get by."

"But Father…he said…"

"Maebe wouldn't have exposed y'all any more than she'd have gone to the press about the oddities of East Branch. Your father threatened her and threw her across the room, and she's a baby aeromancer without a great handle on her talent," he said as Nathan's eyes widened.

"Lost control and blew over some lit candles. That was an accident."

Well, mostly, but I wasn't going to quibble with Connor right then.

"But I'm pretty sure that what happened out at East Branch last night wasn't accidental," Connor continued, and pulled out his phone. "A wildfire out of nowhere, hot enough to cremate. The sheriff's a friend of mine," he said as he scrolled. "Wouldn't let me on the property, but he gave me the summary this morning. Bottom line is that unless the rest of your folks kidnapped those people and left decoy corpses behind, I've lost twenty-eight family members in the last twelve hours."

"I…" Nathan croaked, then cleared his throat and tried again. "I don't know anything about that. Honestly."

"Mm. Well, while you're here, I've got to go break the news to the ones y'all *didn't* murder that they've all been orphaned. There's a few my age in that group, but we're talking about a mess of kids. And here." Flipping his phone around, he showed Nathan the screen. "The little boy in the middle? That's Joseph Amos. He's seven. Got older twin siblings, and it looks like they don't have parents or a baby brother anymore."

Nathan's lips moved silently as he considered the picture.

"Those people with him are his grandparents, John and Helen. I assume they're dead now, too. Couples of farmers who never hurt anyone."

His gaze rose from the screen. "*Amos*, you said?"

"Mm-hmm. Corruption of ti'Ammaas, but you probably figured that out, yeah? Of course, we've been intermarrying for so long that most of us are likely related to all the founders. Maebe are I are in that boat…though if you look at the community records, her grandfather was Ivari's heir. Eldest of the eldest, if somewhat human."

It hit me then that with my grandparents and my parents gone, *I* had become Ivari's nearest heir. Nothing like pinning a target to my chest.

"So, what I'm getting at," said Connor, pointing to his phone, "is that the kid here, the one who probably doesn't even have enough of a body left to bury...that's your blood, man. Distant, sure, but at least one of his ancestors was a half sibling of yours. And you're telling me Ivari wanted to *talk* to us?"

Before Nathan could answer him, Connor's phone beeped, and he turned it around to read the message. "Goddamn," he whispered, and looked at Nathan again. "Told you my crew's helping out at East Branch, right? Well, one of them just sent me this."

Connor flipped his phone again, too quickly for me to see, but Nathan got an eyeful of the transmitted picture. "*Ugh*," he grunted, recoiling as far as he could, "that—"

"My guy thinks it's a child, judging by the size. That's probably Joseph."

Nathan's eyes widened, and he clapped his free hand over his mouth. Without warning, he leaned to the side and was sick all over the tile floor.

"What'd you give him, anyway?" Jane muttered as he continued to vomit.

"The dampening potion, and then a short-term sedative to knock him out before bringing him up here," Kabno replied. "Nothing that would ordinarily trigger nausea." She watched him heave for a moment, then said, "I think we chose wisely in picking that one."

"Oh?"

"Yeah. If he's reacting that strongly to a charred corpse, then something tells me he doesn't have the stomach for mass murder. Might be telling the truth," she added, swinging her feet above the floor. Kabno's chair gave her an excellent view of the interrogation, but it left her looking like a child.

Connor stepped out of the room briefly, returning with a cup and a wad of paper towels as Nathan caught his breath. "Saw a kitchenette next door," he said, passing

Nathan the cup. "Here, it's just tap water."

He sipped gingerly, as if he feared an encore performance, but his stomach apparently calmed, and he wiped off his face. "Sorry," he mumbled, "I…"

"Don't think you meant to do that. I've never met anyone who *liked* to puke," said Connor. "You all right?"

He nodded weakly, then gestured at the floor and scowled. "What did you do to me?"

"*I* didn't do a damn thing, but someone here gave you a potion to dampen your talent. It's temporary," he assured Nathan, whose eyes had widened to saucers, "but that's why you're not masked right now."

"Huh." He gestured toward the vomit once more for good measure, then grunted. "I was going to clean that up, but could you…"

"Afraid that's out of my skill set," Connor began, just as Jane started whispering. An instant later, as the mess vanished, Connor glanced at Nathan and shrugged. "Guess the cleanup's automatic around here. I've never had a magically enhanced interview room."

"Lucky us," he muttered. "Would you, um…would you put that picture away, please?"

"Sure." My cousin darkened his phone and slid it back to his side of the desk. "You see why I have reason to doubt your story about grabbing us for a chat?"

"I know how it must look, but I swear to you, I swear on anything you like, that I didn't know what was going to happen at East Branch."

"What *do* you know?" Connor asked, picking up his pen.

Nathan hesitated. "Not much, evidently."

"Well, that's probably more than I know, so why don't we start there?" When Nathan didn't immediately answer him, Connor murmured, "Look, it's your dad, I get it. I'd have done anything for mine."

"Did he, uh…was he…"

"At East Branch? No." As Nathan's tense shoulders

slumped, Connor explained, "My old man died nine years ago. Colon cancer. Caught it too late to do much about it. And my mom only lasted three months longer—heart attack. Honestly, I think she didn't want to hang around without him," he said with a small, sad smile. "I've been on my own for a while. But like I said, there's a bunch of kids I've got to face today, and not a damn one of them got to say goodbye. Maebe's parents were the only ones with their own phone, and her mother called her during the attack. Last thing we heard from her was begging and screaming."

Nathan shuddered.

"So, while I understand you wanting to be loyal to your dad," Connor continued, "it looks like he was involved in that massacre last night. Loyalty's great, but only to a point." Leaning across the desk, he said, "Help me, Mr. ti'Ammaas. What do you know?"

Neither spoke, and Connor sat back in his chair, waiting. After a time, the elf heaved a long sigh and rubbed his temple. "It's ti'Pul, actually."

Connor's brow knit. "Come again?"

"My two elder siblings got Father's Hall. I was given our mother's. She's the lady of Hall ti'Pul, so it made sense that she got an heir as well, I suppose. Doesn't really matter," he added with a shrug. "The Halls haven't existed as such in centuries. I use 'Rush' for almost everything these days."

"I see." Nodding, Connor made a few notes. "And I'm guessing they didn't name you Nathan, right?"

"Naculta. Culta," he offered.

"Culta," he echoed, adding that to his pad.

So *that* was Culta, I mused, the one who'd been tasked with breaking into the brew room. Chained to the desk, he didn't look half as scary as I'd imagined him to be when I was hiding in the dark with a gun in my trembling hand.

"New York native?" Connor asked.

He nodded. "Born and raised."

"DOB?"

"April 3, 1859."

Connor paused, then muttered, "That still takes some getting used to," as he wrote it down.

Nathan—Culta, rather—snorted. "I'm not *that* old."

"Man, you predate the Civil War."

"Barely," he protested. "Why is that strange to you?"

"Because," said Connor, lowering his pen, "I didn't know I was anything but human until, oh…June? Been about three months, but it's still sinking in."

Culta's eyebrows shot up. "How did you not *know*? I mean, you look human, but…"

"Actually, not always." He tapped the rounded top of one of his ears. "Surgery. Since the folks around East Branch don't know about that…what do you call it…cifyent?"

"Ooh."

"Yeah, well, it's pretty common with us. I don't know who among y'all is carrying the genes, but they're *strong*. Anyway, I was the first East Branch baby born in an actual hospital, and my parents looked normal, but I came out a little freaky. Doctors chalked it up to a weird birth defect and fixed the problem. So…we had the cifyent, minor magical abilities, and a few loan words from High Elvish, but no one understood what it all *meant* until last summer. Early community records were kept in a script no one could read, and we quietly blamed the quirks on good, old-fashioned inbreeding. But one of the things we *didn't* get was immortality, and now I'm chatting with a guy who remembers freaking Reconstruction, and…"

"I had no idea," said Culta. "Father never mentioned *any* of this."

"He probably wasn't aware. The impression I got from the folks who met him was that he wasn't interested in knowing our side of the family." He cocked his head, then said, "Just curious, but what *did* they tell y'all about East Branch? Before this nonsense about Maebe blackmailing you."

Culta made a face. "Frankly, not much. They told us about how the Halls were slaughtered, and then the survivors made their way west and eventually settled in England for a time. None of the old ones like discussing it. The story told to the kids as they come up is that the survivors moved to the colonies, then eventually settled in New York. I was probably in my fifties before I learned any details about their time in England or their early days on this continent..." He paused. "Assuming we *are* still currently in North America."

"Best I can tell you is it's complicated."

"Fair," he replied, shrugging. "But as I was saying, they don't talk about what happened. It's a sore subject. I got the gist from my sister."

Connor smirked. "By 'what happened,' you mean..."

"The events that led to the establishment of a half-blooded community, yes. I'm not trying to cause offense," he hastily added, "but—"

"No, no, I get it. The folks here don't have much use for humans, either."

"Personally, I don't bear them ill will," Culta insisted. "If I had no talent, I'd probably fear it, too. I've spent my whole life among humans, and by and large, they're decent. The firm employs a number of them—low-level positions, sure, but they're on the payroll. That said, you've got to understand that my parents' generation lost *everything* to humans. Land, people, their families...both of my parents' first families were slaughtered. I mean, imagine going from relative security and control of a kingdom thousands strong to *eighteen* homeless refugees, all in the space of a decade. What they did to survive in England..."

"Sleeping with the enemy," Connor finished.

"Bingo. So, while I know my parents had half-blooded children at one point, I don't know anything about them, nor would I ask. I think the survivors have tried to forget that time."

Kabno tucked her legs up onto her chair. "Your boy's being rather chatty, isn't he?"

"I don't know," said Jane. "I've never seen Con work—"

"Oh, I'm not complaining, dear." She faintly smiled at the window. "The subject was demanding counsel, and now he's talking."

"Is that…legal?"

Her smile turned more pointed. "*Here*, yes. If Mr. ti'Pul doesn't wish to answer questions, all he need do is keep his mouth closed. The Tribunal will appoint counsel for him later if he wants it."

Meanwhile, Connor had been scrolling through his phone. "Are you curious?" he asked Culta, squinting at the screen.

Culta frowned. "About…"

"Your half siblings."

I watched his face work as he considered the question. After a moment, he said, "Yes, actually."

"Well, I made myself a copy of the East Branch records, so you're in luck. Need some more water?"

"Please."

Again, Connor stepped out of the interrogation room, then returned with two cups and settled in with his phone while Culta sipped. "All right, here we are. Ivari had four children. John died unmarried, Henry would have been Ivari's heir, then there was Ella, and finally Mary, who started the recordkeeping. Thanks, Mary," he muttered. "And your mother is…"

"Farral ti'Pul," Culta replied, watching him intently.

"Farral…let's see…okay, yeah. She married a Smith, and they had Jacob and Sarah."

"All deceased, I assume."

"Yeah. The last of the bunch was Mary, and she lived…shit, a hundred thirty years. *That* ain't normal. Died in 1836, so they all predeceased you." He glanced up and studied Culta's expression. "You okay?"

"It's...strange," he mumbled. "I knew about my parents' children from before the kingdom fell, and I heard they'd had others after, but...*six*. Born and gone, and I was none the wiser." Putting his cup aside, he regarded Connor in silence for a time, then quietly asked, "You...you come from one of their lines?"

Connor consulted his phone again and chuckled. "Five of them, actually. John Amos never had children."

Again, Culta stared at Connor as if trying to solve a riddle, then shook his head. "You really are kin."

"Yeah. And so was everyone out at East Branch, I reckon. I think you'd be hard-pressed to find anyone in the community without a Smith or an Amos in the family."

"Joseph," he mumbled.

He nodded. "Denise and Joel Smith were still there—brother and sister. Their mama was an Amos, as I recall. And Denise was Maebe's mother, so her folks are another Amos–Smith pairing. My dad's mother was an Amos," he continued, "but she's been gone for a while. And one of my great-grandmothers was a Smith," he said, looking to the ceiling, "but I don't know the details offhand. Anyway, there were plenty of people on that property with obvious ties to your parents. *Were* being the operative word."

Culta said nothing as he finished his second cup of water, and Connor let the silence stretch between them. When he could stall no longer, Culta put the empty cup aside and faced Connor, his mouth tight. "I'm sorry, catha."

While my cousin didn't speak High Elvish, that word had persisted at East Branch, albeit in modified form. *Mitta* and *catta*, informal terms for a younger female or male relative, respectively. There was no good term to describe Connor's connection to Culta—half great-nephew many times removed and several times over?—but *catha* was a catch-all, and Connor's slight nod told me he understood.

"Then help me," Connor murmured.

With a little sigh, Culta said, "I can't tell you with absolute certainty that I know exactly who was at East Branch, but I *can* tell you who caravanned down alongside my crew. For this to make real sense, though, you need to know something about the players in the firm. Now, I'm on the outside—Father thinks I'm a fuckup, and I just maintain the website. But I can give you some names."

As Kabno quietly applauded, Connor tapped his pen against the table. "Hit me."

# CHAPTER 7

**"H**ey, kid."

Connor, who'd propped his elbows on Kabno's conference room table and seemed to be half asleep with his head in his hands, looked up as a green-skinned, blue-haired nymph in a dark brown sweater and khakis approached. "Heard you might be in need of a pick-me-up," the nymph said, and smiled grimly as they handed Connor a small vial of pale purple liquid.

My cousin frowned at the gift. "I take it this isn't espresso."

"Better," said the nymph, chuckling, and pulled out the chair beside him. "Well, in every respect but taste. You're going to want a *small* sip. Trust me."

Before Connor could ask questions, Jane walked in with her dad. "Hey, Liogh," she said, waving to the nymph. "When'd you get here?"

"A few minutes ago. The director mentioned that this one's been up all night, so I thought a little Happy Juice might be in order."

Yacovi snorted. "Don't drink the whole thing, Con. That's several doses, not a shot."

Connor eyed the vial with deep suspicion, but fatigue won out over caution, and he uncorked it and took a quick sip. "*Ugh*," he gasped on swallowing, and shook his head as he grimaced. "What the hell—"

"Mayonnaise and sauerkraut, right?" said Yacovi.

"Jesus, *yes*. What did I just drink?"

"Eh, you don't want an ingredient list just now, boy,"

he replied. "But you should be feeling a little perkier…"

Connor scrubbed his tongue against the back of his hand, then paused to take stock. "Well…yeah," he admitted, his eyes brighter.

"Good." With that, Yacovi stooped and gave him a brief but firm hug. "Glad you're okay, son," he murmured. "I'm so sorry…"

"Appreciated," said Connor, patting Yacovi's back as the two separated. "And I don't mean to be picky, but is there any chance of a chaser?"

"Here," said a deep female voice from across the room, and a troll in a gauzy floral blouse—also green in complexion, but quite a bit larger than the nymph—stepped out from the adjoining kitchenette with a pair of cans in her fists. "Catch," she added, underhanding one toward Connor.

He grabbed it and glanced at the Pactish label. "Uh…"

"It's orange seltzer, hon," Jane murmured, taking the empty chair on his free side. "Harmless."

Though I was groggy from the catnap I'd snagged on a cot following the morning's interrogation—Kabno's orders—I recognized the automatic use of English and wondered how much forewarning the director had given to the other attendees of the meeting she'd called. She allowed me to sit in—I was there already, and I did have firsthand knowledge of the night's events—but as I understood it, my role was to be quiet unless needed and let the agencies figure out what was to be done with the elves in the basement.

Fortunately for me, as Annie had been ferrying and co-ordinating all morning, she'd invited herself to sit in, and no one tried to show her the door. She and I had pulled up chairs along the wall, leaving the table free for the incoming participants, and she filled me in as they took their places.

"The nymph by Connor is Liogh Birrid," she said, leaning toward me. "They're a detective, and they liaise with

DPP, so that's presumably why Kabno wanted them here. Either that or because they've had experience in your neck of the woods. Or maybe Yacovi requested them—those two are buddies going back to Yacovi's agency days," she explained. "And the sorcerer who just walked in, the black woman with the short afro? That's Liogh's boss, Enva Orafer."

I nodded as she sat beside her colleague.

"The troll down there at the end is Gentle Breeze," Annie continued. "Interdiction chief at DPP—she's my boss right under the director, who—"

"Sorry to cut short your vacation, Yacovi," said a brown-haired elf in Pactish as he walked into the room. Like Kabno, he'd opted for a formal robe, but his pants were definitely dark denim. To my eye, he looked to be a few years younger than Connor, though I strongly suspected that wasn't true. "Is your house all right?"

"Seems to be," Yacovi replied in kind, and pointed to Annie. "Got a lift home to check out the place, and Janie cleaned it up nicely for me last night, so we're in business. Nothing stolen, as far as I can tell." Giving the elf a once-over as he sat, Yacovi smirked. "Come on, Teme, it's Saturday. Surely you've got something casual in the closet."

"Habit," said the elf, and glanced at Connor. "And this is our...visitor?"

"This is my little girl's boyfriend, so be nice."

"*Dad*," Jane groaned.

While Connor couldn't understand them, he noticed the direction of their stares and lifted his can in halfhearted salute. "Morning."

"Looks like you've had better ones," the elf replied, switching languages. "Could you use something stronger than water?"

"He's had Happy Juice, sir," said Liogh.

"Mm. Are we sure it's working?"

"This is an improvement," Connor muttered, and sipped. "No offense, but that shit's *nasty*."

"Oh, don't worry, we can agree on that."

Yacovi reached past Jane to pat Connor's shoulder. "Con, this is Pateme ti'Tam. Heads DPP. Teme, Connor Willow."

"Whitford PD," Connor offered. "For what it's worth."

"Pleasure, though the circumstances are regrettable," said Pateme. "My condolences to you and your…cousin?" he asked, glancing my way.

"Close enough," I told him.

He didn't ask me to explain, for which I was grateful. A trip through the tangled East Branch family trees was more than my exhausted mind could handle that day.

As Pateme and Yacovi chatted, two women in casual clothes walked in together, and Annie whispered, "DOL counsel. Those are the government lawyers. Counselors, they're called here."

One of them—a middle-aged sorcerer, judging by the gray streaks in her brown bob—pulled up a chair and fished a water bottle from her bag. The other, a relatively short blonde centaur sporting a pink zip-up hoodie and coordinating leg warmers, dragged a black mat up to the table, made space beside her colleague, and settled in.

"Those are the two who prosecuted Inade ti'Cren and his minions for murder and everything else in the book," Annie told me. "Remari Houn is the sorcerer, and the centaur's Cennis Paf. From what I've heard, they get stuck with complex cases."

While I had no experience with lawyers, the pair didn't seem overly intimidating, though both were already organizing their notepads and pens on the table.

A petite, dark-haired faun in a long blue cardigan hurried in, clutching a paper cup of coffee. "Sorry, *sorry*," she muttered, looking around the table. "Am I late?"

"Not yet," said Pateme, patting the chair beside him.

She hopped up, then noticed Annie. "Humphries?"

"Transport, ma'am," Annie replied.

"*Ah.*"

To me, Annie murmured, "Syvin Deop. Chief Deputy at DPP. Looks like Pateme doesn't want to have to repeat himself."

Last to arrive were Diriem and Rose, neither of whom had bothered with anything approaching business attire. Diriem seemed weary, while Rose rubbed her head as she sat, then smiled gratefully as Gentle Breeze pointed to the coffeemaker in the corner of the room and arched an eyebrow in query.

Once Rose was provisioned, Liogh shut the door, and Kabno cleared her throat for silence. "Thank you for coming in on short notice," she said, and folded her hands on the table. "We have a *situation*, and I'd like everyone to be on the same page before we proceed…oh, uh…sorry," she muttered, switching to English. "Can everyone understand me?"

The rest of the room nodded, though the counselors seemed bemused.

"We have a guest," she said, gesturing to Connor. "And since he did a fine job with one of our inmates this morning, I'll let him summarize. Chief?"

The eyes of the table turned to Connor, who glanced at his notepad before speaking. "Thank y'all for bearing with me," he said, looking around at his audience. "The alternative is my high school Spanish, and that would be disastrous, so…"

"Donde está la biblioteca?" Rose quipped.

"That's about the extent of it, yeah." Smiling slightly to himself, he looked at his notes again before focusing on the counselors. "Ladies, y'all are counsel for Laws, right?"

"That's us," Cennis replied as her tail flicked and settled.

"All right. The problem we've got here…well, *one* of them…is that this is jurisdictionally messy, and parts are presumably quite a bit beyond your reach, but you're going to want the full picture of what's going on. Y'all've heard of East Branch?"

They nodded. "The quasi-elven community, yes?" asked Remari.

"Exactly. My family's from East Branch. I'm a townie, more or less. Cop," he explained. "Yacovi here's been nice enough to work with me on my, uh…unimpressive talent, shall we say?"

Yacovi waved him off. "You're better than you give yourself credit for, kid."

"Yeah, yeah," Connor muttered. "Here's the situation in brief," he told the counselors. "I was house-sitting for Yacovi last night with Maebe over there"—he nodded in my direction—"and four elves broke in. They're all in custody here now, and one of them has been pretty talkative today. Naculta ti'Pul, alias Nathan Rush. I think you could work a deal with him and get him to turn state's evidence, but this is your show," he added, raising his palms as if to ward off protestations. "Not trying to tell y'all how to do your job."

The pair shared a look. "Breaking into a grower's home…that's our purview," said Remari. "Did they steal anything?"

"No, but they did manage to unlock the brew room."

Her smile wasn't kind. "Even better. How'd they get outside the Pactlands?"

"See, that's the thing," said Connor. "They don't live here. This is Ivari ti'Ammaas's crew."

"*Ooh.*" She leaned back in her chair and turned to her colleague. "Foreign nationals breaking into restricted spaces *outside*, then arrested and brought into the Pactlands…"

"Two of them are Ivari's sons," Connor added, "so if y'all still consider him a head of state…"

Cennis made a face. "Why did my Saturday just turn into a final exam, huh?"

"Okay, you have my attention," said Remari, leaning past her to get a better look at Connor. "Chief, was it?"

"Sorry, uh…Connor. Hi."

"Remari. Now, *why* would those elves break into a grower's home? How'd they find him?"

"They weren't looking for Yacovi—they were after Maebe and me." Pausing, he sipped his water, then blew out a long breath. "A lot of this comes from ti'Pul, so it may not be entirely accurate, but I didn't get the feeling that he was trying to pull a fast one."

The counselors nodded, and Cennis said, "We're listening."

"Then I'll start at the top. Ma'am, if I forget something, jump on in," he added, glancing at Kabno, then scanned his notes. "Right. So...around about the time the Pactlands was made, the southern elven kingdom fell. Eighteen survivors banded together. They got by for a couple centuries, migrated into England, then intermarried with some villagers out of desperation. They and their half-blooded children immigrated to Georgia...and then they ran away from their kids and grandkids. One discovered a conscience about the mess, and Ivari killed him for it, so they were down to seventeen by the time they settled in New York."

I thought of the way he'd looked at me, my impossibly distant grandfather, with those cold green-brown eyes.

*Had I known before now that they lingered, I'd have corrected the problem.*

"They've been growing their numbers ever since," said Connor. "Ti'Pul says there's a little over a hundred of them, by his count. There might be more except they're running into the problem East Branch has faced all this time: they're hitting cousin marriages."

A few people winced at that, and I spoke up. "One of the healers who's been studying us says we're in pretty good shape, all things considered. She thinks the mixed genes at the start helped."

"She's probably correct," said Pateme. "All of the southern survivors were titled, yes? Their pool was small to begin with." Rubbing his chin, he asked Connor, "Any incidents of cifyent? I understand that's been an issue for East Branch…"

"He didn't say, and I didn't ask," Connor replied. "Anyway, they've been keeping to themselves all this time. There's a brokerage firm they own, Rush and Sons. Almost all of them work there in some capacity, and they live in apartments under the building. Ti'Pul says it's like a warren. There's been talk of branching out into other apartments, but apparently, Ivari likes to keep his people close." Again, he stalled as he drank. "Last summer, Diriem and Maebe accidentally tracked them down. They visited, and it didn't go well."

"Understatement," Diriem muttered.

"Since then, Ivari's been telling his people that East Branch is trying to blackmail them—if they don't give us half the firm, we'll go public and…I don't know, tell the *Times* there's an office building full of elves in Manhattan. Sounds ludicrous to *me*, but he's got them riled up."

"When did you learn of this?" asked Cennis.

Connor grimaced. "Today. I've never spoken to any of them before now. But, uh…"

He paused, and though he seemed outwardly calm, I could see he was clenching his jaw.

"I'm sorry," he murmured. "It was a long night, and it's been a long day already…"

"Take your time," Cennis told him. "How did they get from New York to…um…"

"Georgia?" He flipped through his notes and tapped a page. "On Wednesday, a group of them started driving down. Per ti'Pul, it's about fourteen hours on the road, so they split the trip and pulled into Helen on Thursday afternoon. Helen's a town south of us that, uh…well, it really ly wants to be somewhere in Bavaria, but that's neither here nor there," he explained. "I guess, after a couple centuries, Ivari's folks couldn't remember exactly where they left East Branch—it's not like the compound is on any maps."

"Who came down, exactly?" asked Liogh. "Do you have a number? Names?"

He nodded. "Ti'Pul gave me a list by vehicle. Car one was Ivari, his eldest living son, Danirri ti'Ammaas, Paril ti'Tola, and Ylen ti'Elta. Those last two are a couple. Second car was Caven ti'Elta—that's Ylen's little brother—his son Pean, Hemell ti'Vanil, and Calinna ti'Elta, who's Hemell's wife and Paril and Ylen's daughter."

"Should I be making a diagram?" asked Remari.

Connor snorted. "Halfway there. Third car was Onnen ti'Vanil—Hemell's aunt—Laluria ti'Gol, her daughter, and a younger couple, Liffa ti'Gol and Tella ti'Fin. And then you've got ti'Pul in the last car with three of his nephews, Pacul, Kentha, and Mirin. All ti'Ammasses."

"Those are Halls I've not heard mentioned in a very long time," said Pateme, and looked toward Diriem. "Beyond Ivari, I couldn't tell you who was heading them at the Pact…"

Diriem, who'd settled in with a cup of coffee, stared into the distance and sipped. "Paril headed ti'Tola, and Ylen headed ti'Elta. That's three of the eighteen."

"Anyway," Connor continued, "they got a couple of big rental cabins and split up. Ti'Pul wasn't entirely clear on the details, and this is way over my head, but on Friday afternoon, Ivari…he drank this bloodline potion. Is that what y'all call it?"

Pateme nodded. "Old recipe. It's quite effective but painful."

That, I could attest to. My experience with the bloodline potion the previous summer had knocked me out for a few hours and left me aching.

"Ti'Pul says that the elder ti'Elta woman cast some sort of spell after Ivari downed it, and she managed to produce a map of the region. Their cluster showed up, but then there was a big cluster at East Branch, plus Maebe and me in Ragged Gap. They caravanned north, and Ivari sent Danirri, Pean, and Tella to Ragged Gap to pick us up. Allegedly. Ti'Pul was sent along in a separate Jeep so they'd have room to transport us. He says their instructions were to grab us and take us out to East Branch to rendezvous with the others so that Ivari could talk to the whole community at once. Reason with us," he said with a sarcastic smile.

"Obviously, that didn't work," said Remari.

"Right. Maebe and I locked ourselves in the brew room, and Annie got us out of there," he said, nodding to her. "The Hunt picked the four of them up and dropped them here."

"Lucky us," Remari replied, smirking. "What about the rest?"

Connor paused, then turned to Rose. "Anything?"

Slowly, she shook her head. "I'm sorry," she murmured. "They're not being blocked—I know what that feels like. They're gone, Connor. I wish I had better news..."

"Ganti's investigating now," Diriem added.

My cousin's shoulders slumped, and I felt sick. Unless Rose was badly mistaken, my last hope for my parents' and grandparents' survival had just been shredded.

"Well," said Connor, and roughly cleared his throat. "Thanks for trying. Appreciate it. But..."

He stared at his notes for a moment, and I suspected he was doing his utmost to maintain his composure.

"Best information, then," he finally continued, "is that we've got twenty-eight dead at East Branch. Sheriff's team found the corpses, all pretty badly burned. He thinks we may not be able to identify them...and since no one out there would have had dental records, he's probably right. I made it to the scene last night. *Bad* fire on the property. It's wooded...or it was," he muttered. "My team's been helping out, and they've fed me a little info this morning, but the sheriff won't let me anywhere near the site."

Enva nodded vehemently. "*Good.*"

"You say that," he replied with a hint of annoyance,

"but how do you think one rural sheriff is going to apprehend a dozen fucking elves? He'll never ID the perps, much less haul them in. Mark Cain's a good man and a damn fine cop, but he ain't up to this, even *if* he could be convinced that we're looking at magical arson and murder or whatever."

The detective shrugged. "I mean, they *might* have used guns. If this site is remote…"

"They might have," Connor allowed. "But I think we heard Maebe's mother die over the phone, and I didn't hear anything like a gunshot."

At that, her dark eyes widened. "*We?* What we?"

He pointed to me. "Denise called in the middle of it all. She was hiding, and someone found her."

Enva turned to me, aghast, then looked at Kabno. "Has anyone set up therapists yet, ma'am?"

"Regrettably, no. It's been a long morning," the director replied. "And there's the matter of the other children at North Lake, who have yet to be informed of any of this."

She swore softly. "How many?"

"Twenty," I said. It felt like my voice was coming from a distance, from someone else's throat, as my mind refused to focus. "Plus me."

"We'll coordinate with the school," said Kabno, and folded her hands on the table. "So, that's the situation. The children brought in over the summer have been orphaned and left homeless, we've got a rogue group of elves on the outside, and we're holding four for burglary. My thought is that we can prosecute the break-in with the intent to kidnap."

"Not intended murder?" asked Remari.

She shook her head. "Our informant swears he had no knowledge of the planned murder, and while I tend to believe him, I'll defer to Agent ti'Van once he gets his bearings," she said, glancing at Diriem. "It's possible the other three knew of the plan, but we have yet to press them. I think sorting out their counsel would be wise."

The counselors conferred briefly. "Agreed," said Remari. "Prosecuting foreign nationals...that's going to be delicate, but I think we can make this stick."

"What about East Branch?" asked Connor.

Cennis grimaced. "*That*, I'm afraid, is out of our jurisdiction. There's no hook for us—foreign nationals murdering foreign nationals outside? If your family had citizenship, that would be a different matter, but from what I understand..."

"They didn't," said Connor. "None of us do, right?" he asked me.

"No," I mumbled, berating myself. If I'd pushed harder, if I'd been more convincing, if I'd persuaded my parents and grandparents to give the Pactlands a try...

*If. If. If.*

"Their status is...novel," said Diriem. "Teolm and I are superintending the ones here, if that would help."

The counselors were unpersuaded. "Unfortunately, no," said Remari. "There's nothing we can legally do about East Branch. You have my sympathy, for what good that does," she added, glancing at Connor and me, and Cennis nodded vigorously. "Truly, I...I *am* sorry. If they'd been murdered here, we'd have had grounds. But I just don't see a way that Laws can take that to the Tribunal."

Connor's head dipped. "I understand, and thank y'all anyway. If there's anything I can do to help with the four downstairs..."

"You've done enough for now," Kabno said gently. "More than enough. Your sheriff is right—this shouldn't be your case." As he scowled down the table, she continued, "I am not suggesting that you're incapable, Connor. You've performed admirably. But looking beyond the fact that you're a victim here, this isn't your first investigation, is it?"

"No, ma'am," he grumbled.

"So, you understand what a case like this will entail. How intimately familiar the team working it will need to become with every last facet. Even if we can't prosecute Lord ti'Ammaas and his accomplices for East Branch, I'm willing to fight to bring that information before a judge to explain the events at Yacovi's house. And that means my people *will* be hacking into the files of whichever investigative agencies outside have the necessary photographs and reports."

Connor's eyebrows rose. "Excuse me?"

"Wouldn't be the first time, won't be the last," she replied. "Now, considering what you've already told me about the scene and the state of the deceased, this is a case that'll be difficult enough when the victims are mere strangers. But youngling, look me in the eye and tell me you want to remember your family as charred corpses."

"I want to help," he insisted.

"Torturing yourself won't bring them back. We'll keep you informed, I swear it. And should my colleagues at DPP send their own people, I'm sure they'd do likewise," she said, looking at Pateme.

"Of course," he said. "I don't think it's in anyone's best interest to shut you out...Detective?"

"Chief," Kabno corrected him.

"My apologies. You know the terrain and the players better than anyone at this table, and that's a resource we shouldn't ignore," he continued, focusing on Connor. "But Kabno's right. You'd be called as a witness in any case we brought, and while I understand the decision to have you work on a suspect, it'd be best if that didn't happen again. I'm not telling you how to manage your shop," he added to Kabno, "but I've had my share of judges look askance at investigations in which the agents were too close to the subject matter."

"Oh, I agree, but the risk was worth taking this morning," she replied.

"If you say so." Turning to Diriem, he asked, "What's to be done with him in the meantime? If they're using the bloodline potion, I don't know of a way to block it.

Yacovi, am I overlooking something?"

The sorcerer grunted. "Not unless a miracle came out of the greenhouse after my tenure. That potion's pretty damn *effective*."

"As I thought. So, is the boy safe if he leaves?" Pateme pressed Diriem.

Absently, he ran a hand through his loose red hair. "I don't have any clear insight."

"Then let's not be foolish," Syvin interjected. "He stays. Surely someone here can make the arrangements, yes?"

"Connor's welcome with us," said Annie. When Syvin turned to her and gave her a tight-lipped look, she shrugged. "*I'm* not going to tell Wylan that he can't have houseguests."

"And I appreciate y'all, Annie," said Connor, going to his feet, "but first things first. Where's this North Lake place, anyway?"

"I can get you there," she offered, standing in turn. "Maebe? Ready?"

"Hold on, now," said Kabno, "we can send someone to break the news—"

He shook his head and said, "No, ma'am." As Annie took his hand, he added, "This is a family matter. Let's go."

Saturdays were typically lazy in the East Branch end of the dorm. Since we were kept separate for most of our lessons, few of us had begun to forge anything approaching friendships with the other students, and so we stuck around our common rooms, playing games and watching the nearly miraculous televisions. Dalm and Chennis often joined us, refereeing when the young ones argued, suggesting movies, and volunteering assistance if anyone felt the need to tackle the weekend's homework early.

Thus, I wasn't surprised when I opened the door to the

largest of our common spaces and found a dozen people sprawled on the couches and hunched over game tables. Chennis, who'd been playing with Winston and Tobias, the toddlers, looked up at the sound of the door and stiffened. "Maebe? You're back early…" Her voice faded as Jane, Connor, and Annie trooped in behind me. "Oh, sorry, I didn't know we were expecting guests…"

"We weren't," I mumbled. "Um…could you get everybody in here, please?"

Frowning, Chennis rose from the play mats where the boys had been knocking over block towers, and their parents moved in to claim them. "What's going on?" Peter started, picking up Tobias, then noticed Connor near the door and switched into the more familiar tongue. "*Connor?*" he called. "What the heck are you doing here, catta?"

"Are you going back to school?" asked Monica, joining her husband and son. "Plenty of room."

"Not exactly," Connor replied, and clutched his hat, watching as the rest of our cousins trickled in.

I stood close to him, trying to gauge the mood. People seemed relaxed, perplexed but pleased to see us, and my guts clenched.

Soon, all twenty of my peers had clustered around us. *Twenty-two*, the little voice in my mind insisted. Twenty-two, that was it. Less than half of East Branch remained…

Connor took a step forward and cleared his throat, still gripping his hat as if he were clinging to a rope above a chasm. "Hi," he said, his voice low and gravelly. "I…I don't know how to tell you this…"

When he paused, Jane rubbed his shoulder in silent support.

"What's wrong?" asked Uncle Kyle, who was Connor's age and the second oldest of us in the dorm. "Is it the county again?"

"Is someone sick?" Amy queried.

"A death?" Peter guessed.

Connor met my eyes briefly, then sighed and faced our

kin. "Last night...East Branch was attacked."

"Who's responsible?" Uncle Kyle pressed over the sudden babble of voices. "Do we need to go home and help?"

"You're dressed for work, ain't you?" said Laurel, squinting at Connor's uniform. "Does that mean you got them?"

He lifted a hand and waited until the room quieted—all but the toddlers, who'd escaped their parents to run back to the far more interesting blocks. "We don't have firm proof just yet, but all signs point to Ivari ti'Ammaas as the mastermind."

"*Him*?" asked Peter. "Why? What'd he do?"

"He...well, to be blunt, it looks like he came down to tie off the loose ends. Maebe and I were together in Ragged Gap, and he sent a group after us. We barely got out in time," he explained, and cocked his thumb toward Annie. "Owe this lady our lives."

The older ones caught Connor's message almost immediately. "And East Branch?" asked Uncle Kyle.

"They were overwhelmed. There was a massive fire..."

Connor fell silent again, but Peter stepped in. "How many were hurt?"

He swallowed hard before answering. "No survivors."

I don't know who screamed first, but in seconds, the room had exploded into a cacophony of shouting and wailing. A few of my cousins staggered to chairs, while others simply went to their knees.

And then, above it all, I heard David's voice: "Maebe killed them!"

"She did not," Connor barked, pointing at David. "Stop that shit."

"She did!" he insisted, glowering at me. "If she hadn't run away—"

"That's enough—"

"He's right," Peter interrupted, and wheeled on us. "This is *y'all's* fault," he snapped, glaring at Connor and me. "You're the ones who brought the outsiders in. *You* let them know where we were."

"I didn't mean to," I began, but Peter was having none of it.

"You ran away!" he shouted, moving closer to me. "Couldn't be satisfied, could you? Nothing was good enough for precious little Maebe, huh? So, are you satisfied now? Got what you wanted?"

"I didn't *want* this!"

"You broke every damn rule," he said, grabbing the front of my shirt. "Exposed us. And now my parents are dead? Your parents? The elders?"

"Joseph," said Stephanie, swiping at her nose. "He was still with Mom and Dad…"

Peter turned to her briefly, then looked back at me with fire in his eyes. "You're telling me we've all been orphaned overnight," he said through gritted teeth. "Is that right?"

"This isn't on Maebe—" Connor tried.

"It's on you, too!" he said, wheeling on Connor. "You were supposed to protect us! If you weren't going to live with us, then at least you could keep the outsiders away! And what'd you do? Brought them right on in!"

Glancing around the crowd, I saw no one poised to disagree with Peter.

"East Branch was a mess," Connor told him, holding his ground. "All I've tried to do is help."

"It was *home*," Peter spat. "Is there anything left?"

"Not according to my people," he murmured. "The attackers were thorough—"

His thought ended in a grunt as Peter hauled off and punched him in the stomach. Connor doubled over but quickly recovered and raised his arms to protect his face. Before he could retaliate, however, Dalm stepped between them. "Boys, that's enough," the sorcerer said in his accented English, holding the two apart with a wave of force from either palm. "We don't need blood…"

"What *blood*?" said Peter with a disgusted sneer. "*That's* none of mine."

Connor glared at him. "You think I'm enjoying this, idiot? I'm trying my best to get to the bottom of this mess, and all you're doing is throwing blame around."

"Because we wouldn't be here if not for you two traitors," he retorted. "We'd still have a home. Families. A future. Everything y'all've stolen from us."

My talent pressed against its bonds, aching to break free and sweep the crowd away, but I forced it down. "We're going to find them," I said. "*All* of them. We'll make them pay—"

"Until you can bring our families back, you're no kin of mine," said Peter. Retreating a pace from the wall Dalm had erected, he shook his head and turned away, wrapping an arm around his weeping wife. "Get out of here."

Before I could protest, Jane gripped my shoulder. "Come on, hon," she murmured. "Let's give them some space."

Stunned and too tired to argue, I let Annie take my hand, and my cousins' tears and recriminations vanished into blackness.

# CHAPTER 8

Alone in my room at the Hunt's lodge that afternoon, safely hidden behind my locked door, I buried my face in the pillows and screamed.

Once I stopped moving and allowed myself to fully feel, my sorrow and despair were all-consuming. In less than a day's time, I'd lost more than half my family, the people I'd loved and looked up to, the elders with their wisdom born of experience, the parents who'd raised me...

Gone. All gone.

And it was my fault.

We had no home now because I'd run away from East Branch. We'd lost our parents and grandparents, aunts and uncles, siblings and cousins, because I'd been so determined to find something *better* than the life into which I'd been born. How brazen I'd been! How eager to slough off the well-founded warnings and embrace an unknown outside. What were math lessons and art classes and even my aeromancy tutorials next to the lessons of the family who'd loved me and tried to mold me into a responsible young woman, someone who would do her part for the community and see that it lived on?

Blind. I'd been so damn *blind*. Blinded by the wondrous potentials, the shiny possibilities, the twinkling glimmers of magic...

Why did I ever imagine that Ivari would be happy to see me? If I'd only stopped and thought about it, considered the implications of our ancestors' departure...

If I'd used the sense I was born with, we might have made this work—half the community in the Pactlands, half at home, and Ivari none the wiser. But no, I had to alert him to our existence, and the promised protection from DOI was nothing more than empty words.

Because of me, East Branch was ash and bone.

My cousins were right to cast me out. Though I hadn't meant them ill, I'd destroyed everything. And Connor— he'd only brought outsiders to East Branch because I'd poked my nose into places it never belonged. He was suffering for my stupid mistakes.

I told myself I had no right to cry. This was my doing. A girl could snivel over her missteps, but a woman owned her failures, and whatever the school administrators might think, I *was* a grown woman. Since I'd created this disaster, it was only right that I try to fix it.

But *how*? Unless my teachers were holding out on me, magic couldn't restore the dead.

That left the next-best option—a poor alternative, but the only one I had. One way or another, if it took me the rest of my miserable, useless life, I'd find Ivari and the rest, and I'd have my vengeance.

Or, more likely, I'd die trying, as there was no way I could take them on by myself. But that would be all right, wouldn't it? Twenty-eight people were dead because of me. If I met a quick and messy end, perhaps that would go a ways toward evening the scales.

As I thought through my next steps, the wind that had been whistling around my room began to quiet, soon dying down to a breeze. I concentrated until I felt the power retract into myself, and as my heart slowed and my eyes dried, the room grew still.

It was then that I heard the muffled sobs coming from the next room and the indistinct murmuring of a female voice, and I realized Connor had slipped away to break down in private. Guilt-stricken once more and feeling like I'd been eavesdropping, I let myself out into the corridor, straightened my clothes, and started toward the staircase, hoping to find my way to the porch again.

Neither my cousin nor I had much of an appetite when dinnertime rolled around, despite the impressive spread from the kitchen. Whatever else could be said for the Hunt, the men could *cook*, and under ordinary conditions, the smells of rosemary-roasted chicken and herbed root vegetables would have set my mouth watering. Annie tucked in, and even Jane downed a modest portion, but I pushed my dinner around my plate, and Connor seemed to ignore his in favor of the beer he nursed. I knew he'd taken an afternoon nap—Annie had the antidote for Happy Juice on hand, and Jane told me that he'd been out almost before the needle left his arm—but his sleep hadn't refreshed him, and his puffy eyes hinted at his come-apart.

While the men around us ate and carried on a dozen boisterous conversations, and one of Wylan's many brothers started to offer Connor another beer, Jane's phone rang. "It's Diriem," she said, glancing at the screen, and took the call as she rose from her seat. "Just a moment, let me get somewhere quiet," she told him, looking around the long dining room for an exit. Going to his feet, Wylan pointed to one of the doors, and he and Annie led the way down a short hall and into a library. As we gathered around, Jane put her phone on speaker mode and dropped it onto a leather-padded table. "Sorry about that," she said.

"Meals are seldom quiet around here," Wylan added.

Diriem grunted. "Can't say I'm surprised. Are Maebe and Connor—"

"Here," I interrupted, sliding closer to the table. "We're here."

"Good. I've got Ganti with me, so I'll defer to the expert."

Ganti ti'Van, Jane had explained to me before dinner, was the best past-oriented farseer at DOI. He'd started at the agency when he was forty and had been there ever since, some hundred-seventy-odd years. While he'd had nothing to do with East Branch to that point, he *did* have a vague familiarity with the area, thanks to his work on Jane's case a few months prior.

"Good evening," a male voice croaked in passable if accented English. "Sorry, uh…"

"Disoriented?" Jane asked.

"You don't know the half of it," he muttered. "Connor?"

"Hey," said my cousin, pressing nearer to the phone.

"Not that this does any good, but I'm terribly sorry for your loss."

Connor hesitated, then asked, "That bad, huh?"

"Well, it could have been worse, but I've certainly seen better. And the photos I was given, those came from…"

"Me," I told him. "Uh, Maebe."

"Maebe," he echoed. "You lost people as well?"

Though my throat tightened, I'd run out of tears for the moment. "Yes, sir."

He sighed. "Again, my condolences. I suspect you two are in no mood for the recap—"

"Hit me," Connor insisted. "Laws has a cooperating suspect who says the brains behind it was Ivari ti'Ammaas. Can you confirm?"

Ganti chuckled mirthlessly. "I wish. Everyone at East Branch who wasn't being slaughtered last night was protected."

"Protected?" asked Connor, scowling. "From what?"

"From me and my ilk. Prying eyes," he explained. "I'm not certain of the precise mechanics of the system they're using, but it has almost the same effect as the blinding potion that Gerem Aniap took. Remember? I could see everyone in his family directly, but because he was protected—"

"*Right.*" He nodded. "So, if you couldn't see them, then how do you know what happened at East Branch?"

"Here's the trick," said Ganti. "I can't see any of the protected individuals, and when I focused on them, they seemed dead to me, but I know they were there because I was able to hop around the unprotected residents. If I'm focusing on someone, then I can see events play out around him…and when a large blob of nothingness comes into view, that has to be a person protected from farsight. Since I've yet to encounter a human who was blocked from me like that, it's safe to say we're dealing with magically talented attackers. If the cooperating suspect is pointing to Ivari, I have no reason to doubt him."

"But they killed everyone?" Connor asked. "They didn't take hostages or anything?"

Though he paused before answering, Ganti said, "No, they took no hostages. If it's any comfort, they were quick. I say it could have been worse because I don't believe your people suffered great pain—I know there was a massive fire, but I didn't see anyone die that way."

"You saw them die?" I murmured.

"Unfortunately, that's a fair portion of my assignments," he replied. "I traced every individual in the photos you sent me and stayed with each until their deaths. Many seem to have died from head shots—whether magical or from firearms, I couldn't tell you, but that's a fairly clean death."

His clinical description sat at odds with my fresh memory of my mother's screams, but I didn't argue with him.

"Could you see the attackers' vehicles?" asked Connor.

"No," said Ganti, "and I suspect they parked outside the burn zone. Once the last of the victims was dead, I lost my view. But while I can't swear that Ivari was involved, I imagine it's likely. I mean, who else would know how to find East Branch and decide to wipe it out?"

"No one comes to mind." Connor released a long, slow breath, but though his jaw clenched, his voice remained steady. "Thank you for looking. I…I'm sure that wasn't easy."

"Of course. It's what we do. Not my first mass murder, and they're never easy, so don't worry about that."

"Yeah, well, I've worked exactly one murder investigation. Whitford's not a hotbed of homicide." He propped his elbows on the table and rested his head in his hands. "What do I do? Any tips?"

"My understanding was that the sheriff had barred you from the scene," said Diriem, returning to the phone.

"He did, but what's *he* going to do? Mark can't solve this case, so if I'm going to get anything approaching justice for my family, I'll have to do this myself."

"You have a plan?" Diriem asked uncertainly.

"Maybe the kernel of a plan. Here's what I'm thinking: we wait a few days, let those assholes get back to New York, and then maybe Annie could drop me off outside their building. You remember the way, yeah?" he asked her.

Annie nodded. "Uh…sure, but that sounds an awful lot like suicide, bud."

"And what if they don't go back?" I pointed out. "Since four of them are at Laws…"

"This is just a suggestion," said Diriem, "but before you embark on a doomed one-man quest—"

"Going to end that badly, huh?" Connor interrupted.

"I mean, I haven't seen it play out, but common sense suggests Annie's right about your chances."

"Okay," he huffed, "so where am I supposed to get backup? You heard the lawyers—y'all don't have jurisdiction. I can't exactly load my folks into a van and head to New York, which leaves…what, put a gun in Maebe's hands and hope for the best?"

"I can shoot straight," I protested.

"We may not have jurisdiction," Diriem replied as Jane wrapped her arm around my shoulders, "but that doesn't mean we can't offer assistance."

Connor raised his head. "Really?"

"Perhaps. I can't authorize it on my own, and neither can Kabno or Pateme, but if the Forum could be convinced…"

"Or my brothers and I might be of use," Wylan offered. "No need to deal with the Forum."

"Babe," Annie murmured, "there are *laws*."

"Suggestions," he whispered, and she rolled her eyes.

Diriem pointedly coughed. "For everyone's sake, it would be best if we went about this through the proper channels. Having the Hunt on board from the start would certainly be a good thing, so that's three votes. I can work on our trio, and I've got open lines of communication to most of the other representatives. A little pre-session massaging seldom hurts."

Connor nodded along, though his brow knit. "So…you're going to get support for this, then ask the Forum to vote on it?"

"No. *You* are going to ask. Or Maebe, if you two prefer," he continued, "but I believe it would have a greater impact coming from you due to your position."

My cousin made a face, then leaned closer to the phone. "You should probably know that I'm not a great public speaker. I'll do my best, but—"

"I'll work with you. No one's throwing you to the wolves without preparation. But before we do anything else, you need a language potion…and you should take a leave of absence from work."

"In case Ivari's still around, right?" he said.

"That, and this potion is never pleasant. Try to rest tonight," said Diriem. "I assume the Hunt is hosting."

"They're safe here," Wylan told him. "They should stay."

"True, but it'll be simpler to monitor Connor tomorrow from Viratta. Annie, may I impose?"

"Sure," she said. "Maebe's welcome to stay here while Connor convalesces…"

"A kind offer," he replied, "but it's time for Maebe to

return to school."

Wincing, I said, "I don't know. My cousins hate me right now, and—"

"That *is* farsight speaking," he firmly interjected. "So, take your rest tonight."

Going back to North Lake was the last thing I wanted to do just then. I *wanted* to team up with Connor to take down Ivari...but instead, I muttered, "Okay," and resigned myself to the plan.

I'd never heard that tone of voice from Diriem, and it wasn't one that encouraged discussion.

When I climbed into bed that evening, I imagined that I'd be facing a repeat of the previous sleepless night—I certainly didn't *feel* tired. But my apparent energy was simply the façade over a bone-deep weariness of fear and grief, and the next thing I knew after my head hit the pillows was the sound of my phone ringing, a wakeup call from Jane inviting me to breakfast. To my surprise, I rediscovered my appetite as I smelled the platters of roasted meat and fresh bread, and Wylan nodded in approval as I went back for seconds.

While Connor seemed refreshed that morning, he ate little, finally explaining to our hosts, "Nerves. I've never had more than a pain potion or that crap they gave me yesterday."

"Ah," said Wylan, sharing a look with Annie. "It's not *painful*, just...potentially unpleasant."

"You've taken this, huh?"

"Got my English from her," he said, cocking his head toward his wife. "Honestly, there are worse potions to be had, but if I were you, I wouldn't make any plans for the next few days."

Connor sipped his coffee, about the only thing on the table that appeared to tempt him. "How much worse are we talking?"

Annie jumped in. "Part of agency training, particularly at DPP, involves taking a number of potions so you're familiar with the effects. There's a fun one that renders you invisible. Great for about forty-five minutes, and then you have the worst nausea of your life because half the ingredients are toxic. I puked *violently* when I came off that one."

"So did I," Wylan admitted. "It has its uses, sure, but the side effects...no, thank you." He hesitated, then said, "I...might be able to let you bypass the potion. Give you Pactish directly."

Connor frowned at him. "How?"

"You want me to explain how my powers work?" he asked dubiously.

"I mean, it might be nice..."

Wylan shrugged. "I'm still figuring it all out, and that's the best I can offer. It wouldn't be *complete* experimentation with you, now..."

But Connor shook his head. "Thanks, man, but let's go with the option that won't leave me with a tail." He paused. "There's no chance of that, is there?"

"Oh, no, nothing like that," Annie breezily replied. "Think a rough flu."

If they'd intended that as a reassuring pep talk, it didn't work particularly well, as Connor was quiet and clung to the strap of his duffel bag, which Jane had repacked and brought over from Yacovi's place. Similarly equipped with my flour-sack luggage, I caught my breath in the foyer of Diriem's enormous house, a high-ceilinged space between the front doors and the wide staircase with stone and plaster walls, arched windows, a crystal chandelier, and polished oak floors—a space that might have comfortably accommodated my family's home. That Diriem was wealthy beyond my imagining was no secret, but then again, he *was* royalty.

"The hell?" Connor murmured, turning to take it all in. "Where are—"

"Told you," said Jane, patting his shoulder. "It's a little much."

"A *little*?" He craned his neck to examine the chandelier. "Holy shit."

A moment after our arrival, a middle-aged sorcerer came striding in from the direction of the kitchen, his dark formal robe immaculate despite the early hour. "Good morning," he said in Pactish.

"Hi, Scel," said Annie, raising a hand. "Sorry, I checked the weather, and I didn't want to land outside today."

Glancing behind me, I was surprised to register raindrops on the windows. It seldom rained in the Pactlands, and the staccato sound on the glass suggested a downpour.

The house manager grinned. "If he were bothered, he'd have locked this place down. Jane, you're staying with us, I trust."

She nodded and wrapped her arm around Connor's. "Someone needs to hang out with this guy."

"The patient?"

"Exactly."

A brief flash of distaste flickered in Scel's expression. "Can he understand any of this?"

"Doubtful."

"Mm. In that case, have any of you warned him about this potion?"

Jane and Annie gave Scel vague assurances that they'd done so, but I suspected neither had gone into detail. My own experience had been miserable, a few days of fever, chills, and vomiting, and I didn't want to spook Connor.

Scel nodded. "Well, I was told to have two rooms prepared, and there's plenty to eat if you're in the mood for breakfast. You might tell your friend as much, though just in case, I'd suggest not going into this with a full stomach."

"That would be my advice as well," said Diriem, joining us from a hallway. He'd left off the robe that morning in favor of an oddly ordinary pair of khakis and a thin blue sweater, and his hair, usually neatly pulled back, was stuck in a careless low ponytail. Judging by his appearance, I suspected that he'd had little sleep. In one hand, he held a glass vial nearly full of a too-familiar purple-brown liquid. "This one's fresh," he told us, switching to English, presumably for Connor's benefit. "I pulled it from our stockroom last night. Ready to get on with it?"

"Good morning to you, too," quipped Annie.

He gave her a look and a quick grimace. "Aren't you a ray of sunshine? And what's Maebe doing here?" he asked, glancing my way. "I thought I was clear about returning her to North Lake."

"Moral support," said Jane. "Let's get Connor situated, eh? A few minutes won't make a difference to Maebe's academic career."

"Very well. Follow me."

We trooped after Diriem up the stairs and into the southern wing, where Jane and I had slept during the summer. Two rooms at the end of the hallway stood waiting with their doors open, and he gestured to the first. "All yours, Connor."

My cousin, still unusually quiet, stepped inside and paused by the wide bed as he took in the space: the vase of late-season flowers on the table by the windows, the low fire burning in the fireplace beneath the hanging television, the exquisitely soft leather sofa waiting against the wall for company. Pointing to a silver tray of potion vials by the flower vase, he asked, "What are those for?"

"Potential side effects," Diriem replied. "We'll give you a minute to make yourself comfortable—whatever you want to sleep in. Jane, let me show you to your room."

The rest of us slipped into the adjacent guest room, and Annie closed the door as Jane dropped her bag on the luggage rack. "You're going to approve my vacation for this, right?" Jane asked Diriem.

He smirked. "We'll call this sick leave. Though if you

need a break and *want* to go to work…"

"I'm not leaving Con. Besides, my ride's still at the office."

"Want a loaner? The Lotus, perhaps?" he asked, and grinned at her scowl. "Seriously, if you want to take it out—"

"I'd be too nervous to enjoy it, and again, not leaving him," Jane replied, thumbing one hand toward the wall between their rooms. "Be honest with me: do you think the Forum will get on board?"

Diriem hesitated before answering her. "I believe I've seen the path most likely to give us a good result."

"That's not an answer."

He shrugged.

Sighing, she folded her arms and tightened her mouth. "Really, boss? We're playing this game?"

"It's no game. These are details that don't leave the ninth floor for now." When her face didn't soften, he said, "Jane, I want the best outcome for East Branch. I had every available future farseer work overnight to look at the possibilities, and we have a plan that I'm not at liberty to discuss with you. Understood?"

At that, Jane and Annie shared a look.

"Oz the Great and Powerful?" said Annie.

Jane snorted.

"I'll thank Connor for the nickname once he's able to get out bed again," said Diriem, shaking his head. "How much longer will he need to change clothes, anyway?"

"Why don't you go ahead and prep the potion?" Jane suggested. "I didn't mention the secret ingredient."

*That* was saliva. The potion worked on a donor system: the donor called a language or languages to mind and spat into the vial, which determined what the drinker would receive. While it worked fantastically well, the process was admittedly gross.

Diriem did the honors and muttered the spell necessary to trigger the potion's effects, and after a short wait, he rapped on Connor's door and cracked it open. "Ready?"

Connor, who'd thrown on a T-shirt and dark sweatpants, sat uneasily on the edge of the bed, which he'd turned down in anticipation of the events to come. "Ready as I'm going to be," he replied. "Question: if I get sick and can't make it to the bathroom, where should I aim? I don't vacation anywhere much nicer than the Holiday Inn, and this is, like, *fancy*…"

"Ahead of you," he said, stepping into the bathroom, and retrieved a plastic bowl from beneath the sink. "Why don't you cover up? The chills often come quickly." As Connor took a second to tuck himself in, Diriem said, "You've had pain potions from Yacovi, yes? Those are pleasant to drink. This one is rather different." He passed the vial, which was now glowing pink, to Connor. "It's thick, and the taste is off-putting—"

"Like tuna and strawberries," said Jane.

"That's fairly close," Diriem allowed. "So, my advice to you is to hold your nose and shoot it. I've got a chaser ready," he added, retrieving a can of flavored seltzer from behind the line of potion bottles on the table.

Connor eyed the potion. "So…I drink this crap, and I'll be able to speak Pactish?"

"And Low Elvish, and what I know of High Elvish, which is considerable. But it takes about a week to full effect, so don't be concerned if you're not immediately fluent." Sitting at the foot of the bed with the seltzer, he said, "I've been through this mess more times than I care to remember. It's not fun, but it's far better than intensive linguistic study, yeah?"

"Guess so…" he mumbled.

"I'll be right here," Jane promised him. "Whatever you need."

Thus reassured, Connor popped the cap off the vial and met my eyes. "For East Branch," he said, then pinched his nose shut and slammed the potion back. Once it was down, he stuck out his tongue, gagging. "Aw, *shit*, that's gross…"

And without another word, he slumped backward, narrowly missing the headboard as he passed out.

Diriem handed Jane the can and retrieved the empty vial from the rug where Connor had dropped it. "Lucky," he murmured, adjusting the blankets.

"How is that *lucky*?" I cried. "He—"

"Is probably going to sleep through the worst of it. That's the best way to react to this potion. Happened to Rosie, but most of us aren't so fortunate." Turning to Jane, Diriem said, "I doubt we see him again for two days, at least. Want the remote for the television?"

As Jane flipped through the channels and drank the opened seltzer, Diriem ushered Annie and me back down to the foyer. "I realize this isn't what you'd prefer," he said to me as I picked up my bag, "but you need to trust me."

Shouldering my flour sack, I replied, "You didn't hear what they told us yesterday when Connor broke the news."

"I know enough. This isn't going to be easy, Maebe, and I won't lie and tell you otherwise, but…some matters need to run their course."

I sighed. "Will you or Jane at least let me know that Connor's okay?"

"Of course. And Maebe?" he said while Annie took my hand.

"Sir?"

"Without going into specifics, I suspect that I'll be seeing you." Tucking his hands into his pockets, he added, "Until we meet again, be careful, youngling."

# CHAPTER 9

Having learned the way to the dorms, Annie dropped me off in the hallway just outside our corner of the building. "Are you going to be okay?" she asked, squeezing my hands. "I heard Diriem, but if you aren't ready and want to come home with me…"

"I'll be fine," I told her with all the confidence I could fake. "They might be upset, but they're not going to beat me."

My performance hadn't been as convincing as I'd hoped, as Annie held on a moment longer, searching my eyes. Finally, as she released me, she said, "Get your phone out. You're putting my number in before I leave you."

"Oh, I don't want to be a bother—"

"You're not, hon." She sent me a text, and then, satisfied that I had her information, she said, "If it gets to be too much, just call. You've got an exit route, all right? It's not like we're hurting for beds, and Wylan doesn't mind in the slightest."

With a last hug for good measure, she departed, and I braced myself to return to my mourning family.

I let myself in, then listened. Low voices murmured from behind the closed door of the main common room, but I couldn't hear a TV or any of the usual signs of weekend play. Even the toddlers' voices had stilled, though I suspected they were either sleeping or out of the dorm. While part of me longed to clear the air, another part insisted this wasn't the time to make the attempt, and so I slunk off to my room to unpack in peace.

If anyone heard my return, they didn't come to investigate. I tidied up and stowed my bag away, then turned to my books. Friday classes felt like an eternity in the past, and I was hard-pressed to recall anything we'd discussed with our tutors. While I had no weekend assignments, I figured it couldn't hurt to review the lessons, if for no other reason than to distract me from my grief. In the stillness of my familiar room, having rested and eaten, and without agents and counselors and directors talking around me, I began to process the enormity of our loss—not only my shock and sorrow, but the more practical ramifications.

As far as I knew, East Branch was gone, scourged from the earth by fire. The plot of land that had been our family's stronghold for generations was a home no longer. Connor had shown me only a few of the photos slipped to him by the Whitford team and his friends with the Ragged Gap police and the sheriff's office, and though the scenes were almost unrecognizable, if I studied them long enough, I could pick out the places in the alien landscape of blackened stumps and rubble where homes and barns and sheds had stood. If we left the Pactlands that day, we'd have no shelter at East Branch—and that was *if* the sheriff allowed us back on the property. Part of me wasn't sure how he had the authority to keep us away, but I wasn't in the mood for a fight.

For the twenty-one of us at North Lake, then, we had no home to return to. Connor had a house, but it was nowhere big enough for all of us, even if we squeezed. Since it was only mid-September, if we left immediately, we might have time to erect decent cabins before winter set in…but we had no food, no money, and nothing left to sell. Plus, since the eyes of the outsiders were surely now on East Branch, we'd probably receive visits from folks concerned about our lack of electricity and plumbing, especially with the little ones to consider.

Would the county seize East Branch? We had a deed— a *very* old deed—with the other records in the meeting house, but if the pictures I'd seen were accurate, the meeting house was ash. The community's genealogical record book, the one Mary Amos had started and DOI had repaired, was gone, though the information lived on digitally. But what about the deed? If we couldn't prove that we owned the property, would it be taken from us? The fence torn down, the trees cleared, the land subdivided into tracts for new homes? What about the cemetery, where everyone but our latest dead had been laid to rest? Would the headstones be carted away, the graves exhumed, and the land sold to outsiders who'd never know its significance? Even if Connor paid the taxes again, would that be enough?

And just behind my churning thoughts, my mother's final screams echoed in my mind.

After a time, I noticed a draft and realized the wind was my own doing.

*Just like everything else, right, Maebe?*

Concentrating, I pushed my emotions down and let the air still. Surely I'd made enough messes without sending a tornado ripping through the dorms.

Around noon, I risked leaving my room, then steeled myself and cracked open the door to the main common area. The TV was on, albeit softly, and the babies were staring raptly at the screen. Their parents and the others present sat in small groups, talking quietly or simply being together in their silent grief. A few looked my way when the door squealed open, then averted their eyes without a word.

Seeing no friendly faces, I looked for someone my age and spotted David sitting in the corner at a small table with his little brother, Marshall. A board game was laid out between them, but their movements appeared to be mechanical, their minds elsewhere. Not ideal, I decided, but maybe I could get traction with David.

I approached the table and waited for them to

acknowledge me, but neither so much as glanced in my direction. "Hi," I murmured, stopping a couple feet from them. "Little bit of good news. There's a plan in the works to get Connor some help from the Forum to go after Ivari."

They ignored me.

"David? Marshall? I know you can hear me," I said, but I might as well have been a statue for all the good that did.

I sighed. "I'm sorry, okay? I am *so* sorry. If there were something I could do to bring them back, I'd do it. I swear to you, I'd do anything. Connor wants to hunt down Ivari, and I'll help him—"

"Just shut up, Maebe," David snapped, finally looking up from the game. "No one wants to see or hear you right now, so why don't you get out of our faces?"

My power seemed to press against the inside of skin, looking for a seam, but I held it in check. "You think I wanted any of this?"

"You're the one who ran off and told every outsider you met about us. You broke every damn rule. And now look where we are—"

"You were the first to volunteer to come here to school with me," I protested.

"And I was a fool," he said bitterly. "But the blame is yours."

Before I could argue further with him, a hand gripped my shoulder, and I jumped and spun around to find that their older sister, Heidi, had come up behind me. "Leave them alone," she said, her tone gentle enough but firm. "Now's not the time."

"Heidi—"

"This is not a place for you," she said, and nodded toward the door. "Go on."

With everyone in the room either pointedly ignoring me or telling me to get out, I took the hint and retreated behind my bedroom door, where at least no one would yell at me. Flopping onto my bed, I lifted my phone off its nightstand charger and stared at the screen. I wanted to call *someone*, to speak with a person who didn't loathe me...but Annie was for emergencies, Jane was preoccupied with Connor, and my parents would never answer my calls again.

Fighting down my useless tears, I rolled over toward the wall, hugging my phone, and drifted off into fitful sleep.

Late Sunday afternoon, I awoke to a rapid knock on my door. "Coming," I croaked, sloughing off my blanket, and stumbled out of bed. My empty stomach complained, and my sluggish brain struggled to determine the hour—the light outside my window suggested that sunset was drawing near, but exactly how long I'd been asleep, I couldn't say.

Expecting to find one of our dorm parents in the hall, I was surprised to see Sage instead. "Hey," I said, stepping aside in invitation. "What are you doing here?"

"Jane called," she replied, and hugged me. I wrapped my arms around her in turn, grateful for the touch, and clung to my friend until she patted my back and released me. "I got Dad to drive me out here," she explained, and closed the door. "How are you?"

"Been better," I said, and gestured toward my desk chair as I sank onto my rumpled bed. "Half our family's dead, our home is gone, and everyone here blames me. And Connor," I allowed, "but largely me."

"Right, because *that* makes sense," she said as she sat. "Are your parents okay?"

I shook my head.

"Oh, *Maebe*," she said softly, and bit her lip. "I'm so sorry..."

"I am, too, but that won't bring them back. All we can do now is try to find the people responsible."

"So, who would want to destroy East Branch? Jane

wouldn't give me any details."

"Well, the ones who came after Connor and me were fluent in High Elvish, so want to guess?" I asked with a smirk.

Her face twisted. "Seriously? You think—"

"Laws has four in custody, and one talked to Connor. He points the finger right back at Ivari."

"But...you're *kin*."

"Not as far as he's concerned," I muttered, and ran my fingers through my hair as I groaned. "They're right, Sage—this is my fault. If I hadn't gone in search of him and...you know, set his damn office on fire, then he'd never have known East Branch was still around. God, I'm so *stupid*..."

"You're not," said Sage, quickly rising to join me on the bed. "You thought the best of him, and he didn't live up to it. You couldn't have known how he'd react. Heck, if the farseers didn't know, then why are you kicking yourself?"

"Should have used some common sense. He had Diriem's parents murdered, did you know that?"

Sage grimaced. "No...but if that's the case, then why did Diriem help you track him down?"

"I don't know. Guess he hoped Ivari had changed with time. But Ivari and the others clearly abandoned their kids, so why would I have ever thought they'd be pleased to see me?"

She rubbed my back as I closed my eyes and massaged my temples. "And DOI didn't know he'd come after East Branch?"

"Diriem was surprised," I replied. "He said he'd have some of his people look in on East Branch, but I guess they didn't see it coming, either." I paused, thinking back over my conversations with him. "But he *has* been seeing fire. Didn't fully understand it. He told me he saw it in connection with me last summer—he thought I'd shake out to be a pyromancer."

"Not particularly helpful, that."

"Nope. Anyway, none of the farseers can see my ancestors or their other kin because they protect themselves. Ivari had a ring, so maybe they all use them. One of the farseers tried today, but he couldn't crack through the protection on any of the folks who attacked East Branch."

"*Shit.* If y'all had been protected—"

"Wouldn't have mattered. Ivari used a bloodline potion, the same thing I used to find him. That's how he knew to send people after Connor and me in Ragged Gap. And if they don't go straight back to New York, that's probably going to be how we find them again."

Frowning, Sage said, "I thought that potion hurts."

"Oh, it's awful, but if it means we get justice for my mom and dad and the others…" I shrugged. "Worth it, don't you think?"

"I don't think your family would want you to hurt yourself."

"Perhaps not the dead ones. The ones here either ignore me or yell."

"Want to spend the night with me?" she offered. "I talked to Dad on the way over, and he's fine with it. We've got plenty of room."

"Sweet of you," I replied, "but Diriem said I need to be here right now." With that, I pushed myself off my bed and straightened my clothes. "Sticking around for dinner?"

Sage was amenable to eating at school, and the dining hall staff didn't bat an eye when we went through the food line together. We settled at the end of our usual table, but to my dismay, my cousins chose another table and pretended I wasn't there. I caught the eyes of Chennis and Dalm as the dorm parents emerged from the food line, but all they could give me that night were helpless looks.


I had no desire to go to class Monday morning, especially as my cousins continued to shun me at breakfast, but I packed my bag and headed off toward our tutorials, hoping the freeze-out would thaw as they day progressed. But as I neared my usual room, one of the teachers stopped me and pointed to the larger room where my eldest cousins met. "You'll all be in here today," he said, offering a small smile. "Don't worry about your joint classes—you've been excused."

Bemused, I walked in and found a pair of strangers arranging chairs in a circle. "Good morning," said one, a violet-skinned nymph. "Come in, dear. Take a seat wherever you like."

While I couldn't guess the nymph's gender, the other was clearly a male sorcerer, middle-aged and beginning to gray. He nodded as I chose a chair, then welcomed the others with his partner as they trickled in. Unsurprisingly to me, I soon found myself with an empty chair on either side.

Once the stragglers had arrived and seated themselves, the nymph closed the door. "Thank you for coming. I'm Urem Gennid, and this is Banni Defen," they said, gesturing to the sorcerer, who raised a hand. "We're therapists who work with North Lake students."

"In light of what happened over the weekend," said Banni, "the administration thought this might be more useful to you than your ordinary lessons would be." He took a seat and waited until Urem had joined him, then clasped his hands and looked around our rough circle. "Now, I suspect group therapy isn't something most of you have experienced, so let's go through a few ground rules. You can be honest in here, but try to be considerate of others. There are no wrong feelings, only better and worse ways of expressing them. Urem and I are here to help—to facilitate, ask questions, whatever you need." He cleared his throat and sat forward. "Would anyone like to speak first? Say what's on your mind?"

"Yeah, I would," said Peter, leaning past Monica to glare at me. "You've got a lot of nerve showing your face."

"Get her out of here," David added.

"Hold on, wait," said Urem, raising their hands for quiet. "What do you have against—"

"She's to blame," Peter told them. "The blood's on her hands. And since she's the reason my wife and I lost all four of our parents and my sister—"

"And our parents," Davd interrupted, pointing to Heidi and Marshall.

"And ours," Stephanie piped up while Sebastian nodded. "Plus our little brother."

The rest of the circle began to grumble, but before the therapists could fully lose control, I stood and gathered my bag. "I'm going, all right?" I said over the mutterings, and headed for the door.

"Wait, dear," Urem called after me, "you don't need to—"

"Yeah, I do," I said, glancing back at them, then let myself out.

Sage and our usual tutor were surprised when I let myself into our room, having foregone the day's planned lessons in favor of independent reading and a movie, but when I explained that I wasn't a helpful addition to the therapy circle, I was allowed to stay.

That afternoon, I sat down for lunch alone with Sage, occasionally glancing at the long tables where my cousins had migrated but trying to focus on my food, only to jump when a tray landed on the table beside Sage with a bang and a clatter of cutlery. Looking up, I found Keef sliding into the empty chair, her blonde hair plaited into a pair of tied-back braids and an unusual intensity in her brown eyes. "*What* is going on?" she demanded as her butt hit the seat. "I've heard all sorts of rumors today, and I even sent a message to Fell, but she won't tell me anything."

Keef's older sister, the pyromancer, was a trainee agent at DOL. Given her junior status in the agency, I wouldn't have been surprised had she known nothing about the situation…but on the other hand, she was friends with Annie and Wylan.

"Short version," I said, pushing potato chunks around my plate, "someone killed everybody at East Branch on Friday night and burned down the compound—"

"*Maebe!*" she cried, aghast.

"Yeah," I mumbled. "And it was probably Ivari's doing. I mean, he had a team, but it sounds like he was the mastermind."

Keef's brow knit. "Ivari…"

"Ti'Ammaas. That beckim." Just thinking of him made my buried talent stir, and I forced it down.

"Huh?"

I caught myself and winced. Most elves—at least those in the Pactlands—didn't speak High Elvish, and they certainly didn't have a working knowledge of the few words bastardized into East Branch's dialect. "Um…asshole, I guess."

"Got it. But why would he do that to you? You're his—"

"Problem." I stabbed a potato and chewed, collecting my thoughts. "Embarrassment at the very least. He's had other kids since leaving Georgia, but if you go by the inheritance rules—"

"The East Branch descendants would have primacy," Keef finished. "Ooh."

"Me, now, specifically, since he murdered my dad and my granddad. But there's more to it," I continued, giving up on my lunch, which went down about as well as sawdust. "Apparently, the survivors of the southern kingdom still have some trauma about that time they got together with the other half of my ancestors, and I suppose they'd rather not be reminded of what they did."

Her face screwed up. "They took human partners. It's not like they were sleeping with…I don't know, dogs or something."

Sage quietly snorted.

"What?"

"Look, I hear you," she said to Keef, "but speaking as a member of the multi-species club…this stuff's kind of complicated."

"Fair," Keef allowed. "And people are stupid. But back to East Branch—Laws is going to find Ivari, right?" she asked me.

I shook my head. "No jurisdiction. My cousin plans to ask for help, but I sat in when Laws met with DPP and DOI, and the counselors said they couldn't do anything."

She swore and took a bite of her sandwich.

"And all the remaining East Branchers blame Maebe," said Sage while Keef chewed. "Which is why we've got lots of space to sprawl today."

I cut my eyes around the dining hall, but no one else seemed eager to join us. "Hey, Keef?"

"Mm?"

"Keep this quiet, all right? I don't mind telling you and Sage, but I really don't want to have to go through this with the whole school."

"Sure." Eyeing my picked-at lunch, she asked, "Not going to eat?"

If I forced another bite down, I thought I'd puke. I was weary and heartsick, and whenever the sound dropped, I heard my mother screaming, an endless echo of fear and pain.

"Not hungry," I told her, which wasn't precisely a lie, and pushed my tray away.

I spent Monday night alone behind my bedroom door, reading and listening to music on my school-issued computer to distract myself. If the group therapy had done any good, I certainly couldn't say, as my pariah status continued within our corner of the dorm.

We returned to our usual tutoring sessions Tuesday morning, but since I'd eaten alone at breakfast, I wasn't surprised when Heidi and David didn't say a word to me. Sage, trying to bridge the gap, greeted them and expressed her condolences, and they were civil enough to her, but they didn't so much as glance in my direction. Our tutor seemed to have been briefed, as she didn't ask why my cousins were sitting so far away from me or try to force us to work together.

Lunchtime came as a welcome relief from the awkward silence and the lessons I barely absorbed, and I grabbed seats at the end of a table with Sage while the rest of East Branch spread out along the next table over. "I'm sorry," said Sage as she stirred her casserole, a rice-based dish heavy on the beans and greens and flavored with spices far beyond the few I knew from home. "I'm trying."

"This ain't on you," I said, reaching across the table to grip her free hand. "I appreciate it, but you're not going to make them come around. If Connor and I can get Ivari, then maybe…"

"This isn't your fault," she insisted.

"Isn't it? I'm not exactly blameless," I muttered, and lifted my fork.

Sage rolled her eyes and took a bite. "Change of topic: I've got some good news."

I was willing to be distracted. "Yeah?"

"Talked to Keef before I left yesterday, and she says the rowing team is willing to give me a tryout," she announced, grinning. "We all know I might not be strong enough yet, but if I show promise, then they'll let me come to workouts until I'm ready to practice with them."

"That's fantastic!" I said. "Your dad doesn't mind?"

"No, he's all for it. And what's even better, you know Dacce? She's nineteen, so her parents still pick her up from practice."

"Don't think I've met her…"

"Well, her mom is one of Dad's assistants," Sage continued, "and *she* told him that if I make the team and he gets stuck in meetings or whatever, she wouldn't mind giving me a ride."

"Perfect." I couldn't help but smile back at her; Sage's happiness was almost infectious. "Which one is Dacce?" I asked, turning toward the table where the rowers had con-gregated…only to see Ainnet and her friends marching our way. Hastily, I stared back at my lunch, but the damage was done.

"Hey, halfwit!" Ainnet called as they neared. "I see the rest of the freaks kicked you out, eh?"

My shoulders hunched, but Sage shot to her feet. "Leave us alone," she ordered. "Not now, Ainnet."

The older girl waved her off. "I wasn't talking to *you*, midget. Mind your manners." As Sage fumed, Ainnet stopped beside my chair and cleared her throat. "Look at me when I address you, halfwit."

My talent strained against its bonds, eager to break free, but I forced myself to keep eating.

"*Hey*." She grabbed my shoulder hard enough to make me flinch, and I glared up at her. "That's better. So," she said, releasing me to fold her arms, "I heard you got half your freak family killed."

I clenched my teeth and tried counting to calm myself, but after the last few days, my control was stretched to its limits, and my anger was rapidly approaching a boil. "My family was murdered Friday night," I ground out. "My parents, my grandparents. We're all in mourning," I con-tinued, pointing to the table where my cousins sat and were turning to watch. "So, knock it off, okay? You want to pick on me? Do it another time. Have some damn de-cency."

"You heard her," said Sage. "Go away—"

Her command ended in a yelp as, with a flick of her fingers, Ainnet casually flung her off her feet and sent her skidding down the aisle. "Sage!" I cried as she bumped into a pile of backpacks and came to a stop, groaning. As the students at that table jumped up to help her, I kicked over my chair and got in Ainnet's pretty face…or close, as she had a solid three inches on me. "What is your damn *problem?*" I yelled.

"You," she snapped back at me, and smirked as I reddened. "Do you know what I heard? Rumor says that old Lord ti'Ammaas cleaned up his mess."

"You have no idea—"

"Don't you understand that no one wants you?" she continued over me. "Not out there, and certainly not here. If you freaks hadn't tried to insert yourselves where you're not welcome, then I suppose you'd still have your precious little farm, wouldn't you?" Taking a step back, she tsked in mock sympathy. "Poor Maebe lost her mommy and daddy. Why don't you do us all a favor and join them?"

At that, one of the nymphs in Ainnet's clique stiffened, clearly unsettled. "Hey, Ainnet, there's no need for—"

"Shut up," she said, wheeling on her underling, then turned back to me. "What do you have to live for, anyway? It looks like even the other freaks don't want you," she said, cutting her eyes to the East Branch table. "Come on, you can barely use magic. Can't even mask," she said with a sneer, grabbing my delicate gold pendant. "*Pathetic.*"

Before I could stop her, Ainnet gave the necklace a hard yank, and the chain snapped. She stepped back, my pendant in her fist, and chuckled. "That's more like it."

I didn't have to touch my head to know that my mask had fallen away—the feeling of my flopped-over ears was all too familiar, as they shifted with every move I made.

While I was still reckoning with what Ainnet had just done, she reached over and gave one of my ears a hard flick. "They're even weirder up close, aren't they? Oh, well, at least now you look like the rest of the freaks—"

The sudden stinging in my ear broke the weakening hold I had on my temper, but I didn't lash out with my talent. My budding aeromancy was no match for Ainnet's training in magic, and we both knew it. Instead, I used the skills I'd cultivated at home, techniques I'd learned from my protective parents and occasionally deployed when one of the other children picked a fight. See, while I wasn't great with magic, I *was* an East Branch girl, toughened by farm chores and hunting...and for all her big talk, Ainnet was soft.

I grabbed her wrist and twisted almost hard enough to snap bone.

She screamed in pain and struggled to free herself, but I didn't give her the chance. Before she could blast me halfway across the dining hall, I threw her to the unforgiving floor, sat on her chest, and started beating the ever-loving shit out of her face.

I suppose no one ever taught Ainnet to throw a punch, as she did little but writhe beneath me and try in vain to get her hands up to protect herself. She didn't even attempt to use magic against me, but then again, she had to be hurting. A part of me seemed to detach itself and float somewhere over my shoulder, watching as I, furious and howling, slammed my fists into her eye sockets, her nose, her mouth. My knuckles were quickly bloodied—with her blood or mine, I couldn't say, though I suspect it was a mix—and by the time a pair of arms like steel bands hauled me off her, still flailing to get in another blow, I'd broken Ainnet's nose and knocked out several of her teeth.

"Let me go!" I screamed, too overcome to realize that English wasn't my best option for communication just then. "Fuck you, let me *go*!"

"*Maebe*," came a deep voice in my ears, and the arms around me tightened as they held me off the floor. "Calm down. It's over."

I continued to kick at my captor until my vision cleared enough to recognize Sage standing nearby. "It's okay," she said, almost yelling to get through to me over my angry screams. "Maebe, you've got to focus."

Finally, I registered a breeze against my skin and glanced toward the windows...all of which had exploded outward.

Groaning, I stopped resisting and sagged against the

thick arms keeping me aloft...purple arms, I noticed, and recognized the voice behind me as Swift Eagle's.

As teachers rushed toward us, I muttered in Pactish, "Sorry."

"It's all right," the troll soothed. "I'm going to put you down now. Breathe."

I did as she instructed, and though she let me stand again, she kept a meaty hand on my shoulder.

The teachers converged on Ainnet, who wailed on the ground, and pushed her frightened friends aside to tend to her. I watched as one teacher ran off to fetch a healer, but as I mused that I might need to have my fists checked as well, another teacher rounded on me. "*What* is the meaning of this?" he demanded. "You could have killed—"

"She was provoked, sir," Sage interrupted, and didn't flinch when he turned his narrowed eyes on her.

"She tried to kill Ainnet!" one of her lieutenants yelled. "We all saw it! She came out of nowhere—"

The teacher lifted a hand to silence her, then looked up at Swift Eagle. "Did you see it?"

"Yes, sir," she said, her voice almost seeming to rumble with our proximity. "I was eating with the team and saw it happen."

Glancing in the direction of her nod, I noticed that the melee team was on their feet, meals forgotten. Then again, all dining seemed to have ceased around the room, whether because of the fight or because I'd managed to break the windows open.

"Ainnet started it," Swift Eagle continued, then released me and shouldered her way through the ring of teachers and squatted. When she stood, she held my broken masking pendant, which she showed him. "This is Maebe's. Ainnet pulled it off her."

The teacher looked from the crying elf on the floor to me with my red-streaked fists, then rubbed the back of his neck in thought. "Don't move," he told me, and turned his attention to Ainnet.

I was still standing in the aisle, trembling a little as my hands throbbed, when Ainnet was escorted out of the dining hall to visit the healers' suite, half a dozen teachers and her anxious friends in tow. My interrogator handed me my necklace, then asked, "Are any of your fingers broken?"

I flexed them experimentally. "Don't think so. They're going to swell, but I think they're okay."

"Good." Pointing toward another exit, he said, "Head office. Now."

# CHAPTER 10

The principal of North Lake was Keddi Mafatta, a centaur built like a slightly undersized draft horse. My grandpa, who'd looked after East Branch's handful of horses, would have described her as "bay," as her equine parts were ruddy brown but she had black hair and a matching tail. Like most centaurs I'd seen, she wore clothing only over what I privately thought of as her human half—it was, I'd been warned, *highly* offensive to refer to a centaur as half-anything. Her cream-colored robe, a light wool for the changing season, split at the back to drape over her front legs, and I watched it swish from my chair as she paced between her desk and me.

I'd have given almost anything for a robe at that moment, even a sleeveless one like Ms. Mafatta's. Though her office was warm, I continued to shake, and my hands were beginning to hurt in earnest.

"Look," she said, making the turn at the wall, "between you and me, Ainnet ti'Har is a little shit, but she's a well-connected little shit. Generally, I don't give a damn about elven politics unless they affect this school. This is one of those times—Hall ti'Har has been sending children here for decades. They're *generous* donors." She paused in her circuit to give me a disapproving look. "What Ainnet said was uncalled for, but Maebe, was it worth breaking her face?"

"She's been awful to us since the day we met," I protested. "Me in particular. I've tried being nice to her, ignoring her, telling her off…nothing works. She hates my guts and doesn't make a secret of it."

"Not that it's right, but you're going to find that attitude here," Ms. Mafatta replied. "In the Pactlands, I mean, not specifically North Lake. I understand your group is in a difficult position, but you must have anticipated that you wouldn't be welcomed with open arms."

As the principal resumed her pacing, I mumbled, "Sorry about the windows."

"We can fix windows. It's Ainnet's face I'm concerned about. However, since half the melee team and a number of other students insist that Ainnet provoked you, I suppose I can't be too harsh."

My guts clenched. "What do you mean, ma'am?"

"Well...I suspect Ainnet's parents will be calling for your expulsion, but under the circumstances, I believe a week's suspension will suffice."

This being my first exposure to organized schooling, I was somewhat uncertain of all the rules and terminology. "What does that mean? I stay in the dorm and don't go to class?"

"Not quite. It means you need to find alternate accommodations for the duration of the suspension," she explained. "Off school premises." Breaking from her walk, she settled onto the thick mat behind her desk and folded her hands on her blotter. "You'll need to call someone to take you off the property."

I stared back at her, my jaw sagging, then pulled myself together and fought the urge to redo her windows as well. "You...you *do* know my family was murdered a few days ago, right? And my community burned down?"

She nodded, her mouth a grim line. "You have my sympathy, dear—"

"Where would you like me to go? I can pitch a tent on the lawn, but I don't have anyone to pick me up."

Her face softened, and I thought I caught a brief flash of regret in her eyes. "This isn't ideal, I know, but I saw what you did to Ainnet. I can't allow that to go unpunished, Maebe. A week's suspension is a slap on the wrist. Now, do you need to borrow a phone?"

"Got one," I muttered, digging in my purse with my swelling fingers.

"Good. Why don't you use the conference room next door? I'll give you some privacy."

I carried my things out of the principal's office and dropped them by the conference room table, then settled into a leather swivel chair nicer than any piece of furniture in my parents' home and ran through my options. Connor was out of commission. Annie would probably take my call, but the Hunt had done enough, and I didn't want to put her to more trouble on account of my temper. Jane was with Connor…but if he was still sleeping…

Before I could lose my nerve, I called Jane's number.

She answered on the second ring. "Hey, Maebe. How's it going?"

"Not so good," I told her, fighting my tightening throat. "I, um…I got into a fight with Ainnet—"

"Again?"

"A real fight," I clarified. "And I won, but now I'm suspended for a week, and the principal says I can't stay here, and I don't know who to call—"

"Whoa, *whoa*," she said, cutting me short as I ramped up. "Are you okay?"

"Yeah, just sore hands."

"All right. Stay where you are," she said in a no-nonsense tone. "I'm going to break the news to Diriem, and then one of us will come get you. Worst-case scenario, I'm sure you could stay with my dad."

I thanked her and returned to Ms. Mafatta to let her know my ride was on the way. "That's good," she said, then pointed toward the conference room. "Why don't you stay in there, hmm?"

"Um…sure," I said, "but can I go to the dorm and pack?"

"No. Your suspension has begun, and you aren't going

back into the rest of the school for the next week."

I could have argued with her. My possessions might have been on school property, but they were *mine*, and she could have sent someone to get them for me. Instead, I mumbled my assent and returned to the conference room to await my fate, hoping that Yacovi had a spare toothbrush.


Nearly an hour later, I heard the front door of the administration building slam open and poked my head into the hallway to find Diriem storming toward the principal's office, robe flapping in his wake. Noticing me, he said, "I'll be right there," then rapped sharply on Ms. Mafatta's door and waited.

A few seconds later, she opened the door. "Yes—*oh*," she said, surprised. "Uh...Lord ti'Dana?"

"Maebe's coming with me," he said without greeting her, then motioned for me to join them. "Show me your hands," he ordered as I approached.

I held them out, and he carefully prodded my tacky knuckles. In the commotion, I hadn't been offered a sink, and so my fingers remained smeared with blood.

"These are swollen," he said, "and they'll be worse without treatment. Are you in pain?"

"A little, sir."

He raised his eyes to Ms. Mafatta's. "Has this child seen a healer since the incident?"

The principal looked like she'd just remembered a meeting on the other side of the school. "Um, no, not yet, but the other student's injuries—"

"I trust you have more than one healer here." It wasn't a question.

"Well, yes," she admitted.

"A bathroom, perhaps? A damn ice pack?" When Ms. Mafatta continued to stammer, he stared at her and said in a low voice, "*If* I deign to return Maebe to your care, then you and I will discuss minimum standards for the treatment of her and her kin. Is that understood?"

She nodded, then gestured toward a door down the hall. "Maebe, if you want to wash your hands—"

"Come on," said Diriem, and steered me out of the building without another word.

He'd parked his car near the front stairs, a black sedan that didn't look especially flashy to me. A gesture unlocked it, and he pointed to the front passenger door as he walked around to the driver's side. I slid in and buckled up without a word, slumping low in the black leather seat as if I could make him forget my presence if I scrunched sufficiently. While Diriem hadn't yelled, I could almost feel his anger like heat radiating from a fireplace, and so I kept my mouth shut and my injured hands in my lap.

He started the car and released a long, slow breath as he gripped the steering wheel, a calming technique Violet had taught me to hold back my power when all I wanted was to release a whirlwind. After a moment, he put the car in drive and started off, but he didn't speak to me until we left the school grounds. "I'm sorry for the delay, Maebe."

"It's okay," I mumbled. "I'm really sorry about—"

"Stop," he said, and my mouth snapped shut. "I was delayed because I wanted to know what actually happened before walking in, and it took Ganti a few minutes to focus. Fortunately, all of you are wide open, and he found the incident."

A degree of tension began to slip from my shoulders. "So…he saw—"

"Everything. But then he wanted to push back further, having concluded that the two of you share a *history*, and he wasn't wrong." Diriem paused at an intersection and turned to me. "Tell me about your issues with the ti'Har girl."

"It's no big deal—"

"Ganti said she told you to kill yourself today. Truth?" I nodded, and he sighed as he drove on. "That doesn't come out of nowhere—that's an escalation. What have your teachers been doing to improve relations between you girls, hmm?"

"Not much," I admitted. "I try to ignore her."

"Which hasn't worked, I see. Well, if the people charged with student safety haven't recognized the problem by now, then I suspect your little brawl will have brought the matter to their attention."

Again, I said, "I'm sorry."

Diriem grunted as he pulled onto a divided street.

"You're mad, and I didn't mean to drag you into this—"

"I'm not angry with you," he interrupted, keeping his eyes on the road. "Your principal is another matter. You shouldn't have been suspended."

Having not anticipated support, I paused before responding. "I mean, they said I broke her nose, and she was a mess…"

"As far as I'm concerned, you finished what she started. And if she's too stupid to use magic in the middle of a damn fistfight, then she needs remedial tutoring." Pulling up to a light, he glanced at me and smirked. "Incidentally, Ganti said your form is good but that you'll need something for the pain. If you *want* to toughen up your knuckles, now, he boxes, and he knows a good gym."

"Uh…thanks." I looked down at my hands, which had begun to turn colors below the dried red splotches.

"You've never had a fight like that before, have you?" he murmured.

"No, sir. I tussled some as a kid, but it was mostly in fun, you know? Or an argument over something stupid, and one of us would cry uncle pretty quickly or our folks would separate us. That…" Try as I did, I couldn't recall a clear stream of events between Ainnet ripping off my pendant and Swift Eagle pulling me away, just a series of impressions. "I would've kept hitting her," I said softly. "If they'd let me, I'd have beat her to a pulp."

"Mm. Not ideal, but at least you didn't fling her through a window."

"I broke those, too."

He chuckled. "And *there's* the aeromancer."

"I didn't even know it!" I protested. "I just saw red, and when I calmed down…"

"They should be grateful you're not a pyro."

"I guess," I mumbled. Having had a moment to reflect on the fight, I did feel somewhat guilty for how badly I'd pummeled Ainnet, but I couldn't bring myself to take the full blame. "Um…Diriem?"

"Yes?" he asked as the light turned blue.

"Was that why you wanted me to go back to school?"

He hesitated before answering. "No, not exactly."

"Then did I mess things up?"

"No."

"Okay. Good." I nibbled my lip, then asked, "Where should I go while I'm suspended? Jane mentioned that her dad might let me stay—"

"You're coming home with me," he replied. "I suspect Connor will want to see you once he wakes, anyway." Passing a delivery truck, he said, "In all honesty, I think I have sufficient pull to get your suspension revoked."

"Ms. Mafatta said—"

"She answers to the board of trustees, and I know most of them *quite* well. But really, do you think it's a good idea to be in the dorm right now?"

Recalling my cousins' glares, I shook my head and shrank into my seat. "This is all my fault," I muttered.

Diriem let me stew for a moment as he drove deeper into the capital. "You know," he finally said, "sometimes, one must make decisions without knowing how they'll play out."

"Not *you*."

"Please," he scoffed, waving one hand. "I make plenty of decisions day to day without giving them full analysis because otherwise, I'd do nothing but trance. And even when our full team investigates a future issue, the best we end up with is probabilities. Some are pretty damn *strong* probabilities, mind you, but nothing's ever absolutely certain, and that's a truth that young farseers ignore to their peril. But I digress. You made a series of decisions last summer, and you did what you thought was best for yourself and your community using the data available to you."

"Exposing East Branch wasn't my decision to make," I said, picking at the dried blood on my index finger.

"Perhaps not, but…" He hesitated briefly, then said, "These things happen, Maebe. Sometimes, you're forced to make a choice. Deep down, you know that someone older and wiser should make the decision, not you, but it's in your hands. You thought you were doing right by your family. Not to be cruel," he continued, "but the infrastructure and amenities of East Branch were primitive. You tried to show them a better way, and you reached out to a man who, by all rights, should have assisted you."

"He abandoned us," I said, resisting the urge to pick further, as I didn't want to be dropping blood scrapings onto the clean floor mat. "I should have known better. When he turned up alive…"

"You hoped for the best from him, and so did I. It can't be helped that Ivari hasn't changed." Pulling up at another red light, Diriem said, "I've been in your position, youngling…or one somewhat akin to it."

"Oh?" I replied, frowning.

He nodded. "Ivari had my parents assassinated when I was fairly young. Not as young as you," he admitted, "but for an elf, especially one faced with a throne, I was still a boy in the eyes of some of the other lords and ladies."

"*How* old?"

"In my hundred-twenties, but really, you and I are working with different time scales," he said, accelerating as the light changed. "Anyway, overnight, I lost the people who I was convinced knew what they were doing. I found myself with a handful of advisors, the farsight I was still mastering, and constant threats from both Ivari and the humans living around our territories. And eighty-five years later, based on the strength of visions I *desperately* hoped I was interpreting correctly, I convinced thousands of people to abandon the homeland we'd fought for and our people had died to defend. I asked them to trust me and start over in a place I wasn't even sure would last a year— the sorcerers who maintain the stability of the Pactlands are seldom bored," he explained. "Talk about ways to give yourself an ulcer, eh?"

"But you were *right*," I pointed out. "You saw what was coming and saved them."

He chuckled softly. "Ah, but I didn't *know* that. As I said, farsight shows potentials…and like all wild talents, it grows stronger with age. I trusted myself, it was terrifying, and I'm damn lucky that it worked." He moved over to allow a gnome on an oversized motorcycle to speed by, then looked at me again. "What happened Friday night is not solely on you, Maebe, and I'm telling you as a farseer that you were right to have pushed East Branch as you did."

"How? How was I *possibly* right? They died!"

Diriem said nothing in immediate reply, but he pulled off the road into a little lot, then parked the car and shifted in his seat to better face me. "For those of us who see the future, there are certain matters we simply cannot discuss outside the walls of DOI. Even speaking of possibilities to the wrong individuals can lead to actions that make the path deviate from the best of our future options. Understand?"

"I think so…"

"That applies to East Branch as well, though there's one area now safe to discuss." He paused and slightly frowned, gathering his thoughts, then said, "I told you that I was surprised you were an aeromancer because I'd seen so many impressions of fire around you, yes?"

"Yeah," I mumbled, thinking of the leaping flames in

the trees.

"Some of those impressions with fire also had impressions of dark, wooded places," Diriem continued. "Looking at those early visions of you in hindsight, I see now that I was getting flashes of you in Ivari's office and of you standing near the East Branch fire—not a pyromancer, just wrapped up in events."

That did nothing to lighten the heaviness of my guilt.

"But I told you we'd be monitoring East Branch, and whatever you may think about our failings, we *have* been seeing visions. Nothing particularly clear, but one vision has been coming through regularly: law enforcement and media outside the fence."

"That's right," I said. "As to law enforcement, at least. There were a bunch of folks on the scene Friday."

"No, it's a different scene," said Diriem. "Because in this version, East Branch isn't on fire. The police are trying to force the residents to come outside, and they're resisting orders. A massive standoff. There's gunfire."

I stared at him, trying to process that.

"Time was running out for East Branch," he murmured. "If Ivari hadn't come for them first, then the county would have acted...I think. Might have been state agents, but honestly, I'm not great at telling them apart."

"Why didn't you say anything?" I demanded.

"I *couldn't*. That was one possibility, and though it was growing stronger, we were seeking alternatives that wouldn't end in violence. Unfortunately, Ivari stepped in, and that explains the fire visions." Diriem's mouth tightened as he looked back at me. "Even if I'd been able to warn them of the threat, you and I know that your elders would never have willingly evacuated. East Branch was doomed, no matter what we did. I see that now."

But I pressed him. "If the standoff had come to pass instead, what would have happened to them?"

He shrugged. "I can't say with any specificity, nor can I tell you how many would have survived the standoff. Farsight's useless now on the question because that future was averted."

"Would my parents have lived?"

"I'm sorry, dear, I don't know. But what you need to understand now is that because you and Connor made the decisions you made, half of your family survived."

"*Half*," I echoed.

"Yes. And sometimes, half is the best you can do." With that, he started the car again and set off toward a neighborhood I didn't recognize.

"Where are we going?" I asked.

"I thought you might like to have your pendant fixed."

"Uh...*yeah*," I said, brightening for an instant before reality set in. "But what will it cost? I don't have much, and I don't want to ask Connor—"

"I've already spoken with Teolm," he soothed. "We're expected. And here," he added, flicking his fingers toward my hands. The crusted blood vanished, revealing the discoloration and swelling below, and he grimaced as he cut his eyes away from the road for a quick peek. "Pendant first, then a healing potion, I should think. And something to numb the pain."


Having never had occasion to venture into District 4, I was surprised by the unplaceable feeling of *wealth*. It wasn't that the buildings were plated with gold or strung with diamonds, but rather smaller tells. The cars parked along the impeccably clean streets were sleek and shiny, and though I didn't recognize most of them, I'd learned enough to pick out the Mercedes, BMW, and Chanifar logos—expensive imports and domestic models. The brick and stone buildings seemed almost harmonious in their design, as if the architects had taken care to make later additions blend with their neighbors. While the few trees were typical Pactlands dwarfs, they'd been planted in well-tended grassy plots, a few of which actually bore flowers—

not impossible to grow in that inhospitable soil, but not a cheap endeavor. Nothing appeared to be out of place, and even the signage was tastefully minimalistic.

The draw of the district, past the expensive apartment buildings, was a five-block row of the sort of fancy stores I'd never dreamed of exploring. We got enough odd looks just walking into the hardware store in Whitford, so I suspected I might be tossed to the pristine sidewalk if I dared to poke my head into the shops of elaborate robes and fine dishes and magical notions. But Diriem apparently had no such qualms, as he pulled up in front of a gray stone building with square glass windows, each of which displayed a selection of necklaces, bracelets, and rings. Above the entrance, TI'CREN DESIGNS was spelled out in brass Pactish characters.

Diriem escorted me inside, and I dragged my feet as I took in the long glass cases full of jewels and precious metals, which glittered in the glow of the recessed lamps. The dark paneling around the showroom drew even more focus to the merchandise, while the thick carpeting muffled the footsteps of the few customers browsing. Hastily pulling my hair over my ears in an ineffective attempt to hide my deformity, I scanned the room in vain for Teolm. He wasn't present, but people began to notice us, and I caught quick whispers as they tried to sneakily stare.

"This way," said Diriem, steering me with a firm hand on my back toward a tall wooden desk. A clerk—a sorcerer, I noticed, somewhat surprised—nodded as we approached, then murmured, "Good afternoon, Lord ti'Dana. I understand you have a repair?"

"Hopefully one not overly taxing," he replied, and patted my shoulder. "Maebe, let this young man see your pendant."

I passed it over the desk, and he peered at the damage.

"Teolm speaks well of you, Egam," said Diriem as the sorcerer pulled out a magnifying glass—a necessary tool, as the pendant was the size of my pinkie nail. "He believed this wouldn't offer much of a challenge."

Egam grinned, but he didn't answer until he'd completed his close inspection. "Lord ti'Cren is overly generous, but this time, he's right. The pendant itself is unharmed—all it needs is a new chain and a little massaging on the bail."

"The what?" I asked.

He leaned over the desk, pendant in hand, and pointed to the golden bit from which it usually hung. "That's called a bail. It looks like yours has been slightly deformed, but I can have that back in shape in no time. What happened, if I may ask?"

"Classmate ripped it off," I mumbled.

"Well, tell your classmates to keep their grubby hands to themselves. Gold is softer than you might expect. Ten minutes, if that's all right," he added, turning to Diriem. "I'll get this polished up, too."

While we waited, I drifted slowly down the counters, admiring the sparkling jewelry within: necklaces heavy with colored stones, rings designed to wrap around fingers like delicate metal vines, a single display of stud and hoop earrings in various sizes. "For fauns," Diriem whispered when he caught me examining the earrings. "The males pierce their ears. Nice to see that Teolm's branching out—his father would never have sold those."

"Doesn't like earrings?"

"Didn't want fauns around." He rolled his eyes. "Even before his criminal empire days, Inade was always a...*difficult* man."

Soon, Egam brought my pendant to me, now hanging from a new, slightly thicker chain. "Just in case," he said with a wink. "May I?"

As soon as he'd clasped it around my neck, I gripped the pendant to trigger it and breathed a sigh of relief as I felt my familiar mask coalesce. I reached up to check my ears, then tucked my hair back and smiled at him. "Thank you. It's perfect."

"Of course." To Diriem, he said, "If the boss didn't mention it, there's no charge."

"And I appreciate that. Still..."

I saw that he'd palmed a folded bill before shaking Egam's hand, and the jeweler nodded in acknowledgement.

Back in the car, as Diriem pulled into traffic, he said, "I have a few matters to tend to in the office, so you'll need to come with me for a time. Not all day, and I realize this isn't thrilling—"

"Oh, I don't mind," I replied, touching my pendant for reassurance that it was still there. "Thanks again for getting this fixed."

"Certainly."

"It's weird how quickly I've gotten used to having my mask. *Any* mask, really," I continued as I leaned back against the leather seat. "I worked out a different one for home."

He chuckled. "I should hope so. And you can experiment, you realize—I've known agents who put on a different face every time they go outside. Easy way to tell whether you'll like a haircut, yes?"

"I guess so. But it's only been a few weeks, and I almost feel...I don't know, like I'm undressed without it. When Ainnet left me exposed today..."

I didn't finish my thought, but Diriem seemed to understand. "There's no harm in masking, Maebe. *Many* people do it for purely aesthetic reasons—remove an unsightly mole, shave off a little fat, change eye color. *You*, now, you've been warned all your life to keep your ears hidden, and I suspect it's somewhat freeing to not have to worry about that."

Nodding, I replied, "It's not that I'm ashamed to look in the mirror or anything, but...you know, when people call you a halfwit already, you don't want to give them more ammunition."

The sound of a ringing phone interrupted us, and the

screen on the console indicated an incoming call. "Right on time," Diriem muttered, and took it without bothering to pull over. "Good afternoon, Nadull," he said, slipping into Low Elvish. "You're well?"

"*I* am, but one of my little cousins is not," the voice on the other end replied. Definitely female, I thought, and highly displeased. "Ainnet. There's been an *incident*, Diriem."

"Oh?"

"At North Lake. The poor dear's a fourteenth year, a darling girl, and she was *savagely* beaten by one of the half-breeds today."

His expression remained still as he headed out of District 4. "Indeed?"

"Yes. That…*animal* broke her nose and blackened both her eyes. She may have other facial fractures—her parents have her with a team of healers, and I haven't heard the latest, but I do know she'll need dental work. They sent me a picture, and it's just heartbreaking—she was always such a pretty child. Anyway, the school's suspended the half-breed for a week, but Ainnet's parents want more, and frankly, I agree. I know you've been, uh…superintending the half-breeds with Teolm—"

"Do you know why Maebe fought her today?" he interrupted.

Nadull—who, I suspected, was Lady ti'Har—hesitated before answering him. "Um…well…I haven't received a full accounting, but Ainnet's parents say she was ambushed. I take it you've been informed of this, then?"

"I was alerted," Diriem replied, "and before I leapt to judgment about the situation, I had one of my best review the footage, so to speak."

"You mean—"

"Sometimes, it's quite handy to have a team of farseers in the building. He looked back to see what actually happened, and then he searched for past interactions between the girls. Would you like a fuller picture?"

Some of the indignation left Nadull's voice as she said, "I suppose I'd better hear it."

"Very well. Your precious little cousin is the leader of the top female clique in her year, and she hasn't maintained that position through sheer kindness, shall we say?"

"Ainnet's parents said she was popular—"

"She's a bully, and she's been ruthlessly antagonizing the East Branchers since school began. Maebe has been a particular target, perhaps because they're of an age, or perhaps because Maebe's tried to talk back to her. I won't presume to know Ainnet's mind. In any case, today, she suggested that Maebe should kill herself, and then she broke the child's masking pendant and mocked her. Were you aware that most of the East Branchers exhibit cifyent?"

"I…yes…"

"Hence the pendant," said Diriem. "Now, it's unfortunate that Maebe snapped as she did, but to be fair, the child lost her parents and half her community on Friday night."

"Come again?" she said, audibly surprised.

"Murdered, and their homes were burned to the ground. It's still under investigation," he said—an understatement, I thought—"but I'm sure you can understand why emotions are running high for the survivors. Most were orphaned."

She swore under her breath. "I wasn't aware. That's…heavens," she muttered. "Humans found them?"

"I'm afraid I can say no more on the matter, or my counterpart at Laws will come for me. But the news *has* been spreading at North Lake, and Ainnet mocked Maebe for it today. Incidentally, she touched Maebe first."

Nadull said nothing for a moment, and then I heard a deep sigh on the other end of the line. "You're *certain* about Ainnet's behavior?"

"I trust my people," Diriem replied. "And if you don't, you should know that I've also been receiving occasional reports from Mirrik Voln."

"The representative?" she asked, bemused.

"His daughter also attends North Lake, and her accounts match my agent's. Darling Ainnet has been needlessly cruel for weeks. So, if I were you, I would tell her parents to stand down. Escalating this matter would end poorly for their daughter, I fear."

She grunted. "Aren't we above threats, Diriem?"

"This isn't a threat, merely me showing you my plans. See, if they make a move to have Maebe more severely punished, then Mirrik and I will see that dear little Ainnet is expelled. I have a suitable case for the board, and I *know* there are other students who will speak against her if given the chance."

"Very well," she huffed, "I'll pass the message. But honestly, why go to the trouble? I realize the half-breeds are in a difficult position, but…well, just *look* at them! Uneducated, inbred, defective at best…"

Diriem reached across the cupholders to grip my shoulder before my frayed control could unravel. "They're still our people, Nadull. Abandoned and ill done-by. If you had anything to do with them, you'd see the potential there. Maebe's an aeromancer, you know. It's a wonder she didn't fling Ainnet into a wall or worse."

"Quite," she said dryly.

"With that in mind, you might want to have a word with Ainnet as well," he told her. "Leave the East Branchers alone. Yes?"

"I'll…make her aware," she replied, and ended the call.

Diriem smirked and shook his head, then slowed and turned toward the guardhouse at the fence around the windowless DOI tower. "I try not to make a habit of throwing my weight around," he said, pulling up to greet the guard, "but sometimes, it does come in handy. And you didn't hear that call, understood?"

"What call?" I replied, and smiled to myself as we drove into the garage.

# CHAPTER 11

While I wasn't feeling fantastic about my actions after my talk with Diriem—in retrospect, I supposed I didn't have to beat Ainnet to a pulp to make my point—he'd reassured me sufficiently that I didn't feel quite so low as a snake in a wagon rut. If nothing else, I had a place to lay my head for the next week, and though I hadn't been able to bring more with me than my purse and a few books in my school bag, a bed was a solid start.

But despite his afternoon meetings, Diriem looked after me. A call to the agency healers produced a pair of potions to help with my injuries, and shortly after I downed them, a tan-skinned nymph with a black bob and pretty dark eyes rapped on the door of Diriem's office. The nymph wore a blue robe over a gray shirt and dress trousers, giving me no indication of their gender. "Yes, sir?" they asked, and reached up to touch the black bulb nestled in their long, pointed ear. "I heard you were looking for me."

Diriem beckoned the nymph inside. "Keyne, this is Maebe Amos," he said, nodding to me as I huddled on his navy leather couch. "Maebe, this is Keyne Benanae, one of our assistants."

The nymph—*she*, judging by her surname—smiled gently at me. "Hello, there. I'm terribly sorry about…well."

"Thanks," I mumbled.

"Maebe will be staying with me for a time," Diriem told Keyne, "and unfortunately, she wasn't able to pack before we departed. I hate to impose, but if your schedule allows it—"

"Oh, I'll take the youngling shopping," she interrupted, waving away his request, and before I could turn around twice, she'd whisked me onto the elevator, armed with Diriem's bank card.

What might have been a quick trip turned into a multi-hour event after Keyne noticed my bruised knuckles and started asking questions. Since my lunch had been inter-rupted, our first stop *clearly* had to be a little café near DOI that made amazing potato dumplings in a savory sauce. After we'd eaten, she took me into District 3—"Cute shops, and not as exorbitantly priced as the ones in Dis-trict 4," she explained as she parked in front of a block of boutiques. "Who in their right mind would pay five hun-dred marks for a *blouse*, I ask you?"

I didn't have a great concept of either finances or fash-ion, so I let Keyne take the lead. She fussed over me, pull-ing items from racks and hustling me off to try them, and by the time she was satisfied, I'd acquired three pairs of pants, five shirts, a somewhat impractical flouncy green dress, new underthings, silky pajamas, and three pairs of shoes—and then we moved on to a drugstore for toilet-ries. "I'm sure the Director has extra shampoo," she said, perusing the brightly colored bottles on offer as I clutched the shopping basket, "but there's no telling what kind. What do you normally use, Maebe?"

"Um…soap?"

Keyne stared at me, aghast.

"Liquid soap?"

"Oh, *child*. No."

I left the shop lugging a pair of bags full of bottles, tubes, and brushes covering everything from dental needs to the pimple trying to break through at the tip of my nose. At least I'd been able to avoid the aisle of "feminine hygiene" products; I had no need at the moment, and Keyne had apologetically murmured that she was unable to help me in that department. "I mean, I know the *basics*," she'd said, eyeing the merchandise, "but we're built just differently enough that I'm unfamiliar with the *details*. Doesn't sound like fun, though."

"Not exactly," I'd concurred, hurrying after her toward a display of hair brushes. On top of everything else that day, I wasn't eager to explore the intricacies of nymph biology.

We returned to Diriem's office laden with shopping bags, but he just chuckled as Keyne returned his card. "Success?" he asked.

"Well, the poor girl's got a comb now," Keyne replied.

"And a few other things, I trust." Grinning, he thanked her, then shouldered his satchel, took half the bags, and led me out again.

Scel met us as we came in from the mansion's multistory garage. "I've put you in the room next to Connor's and Jane's," he told me, taking my purchases from Diriem against his boss's protestations. "This way."

As I followed him up the massive staircase, I asked, "Is Connor awake yet?"

"No," said Scel, "but Jane's with him. I'm sure we'll know in short order once he comes around."

The guest room to which Scel showed me was every bit as nice as my cousin's, and I unpacked my things and showered before Scel returned to collect me for dinner. Ranarma, his nephew, had made a fantastic meal, but there was no sign of Jane or Connor as I settled in with Diriem, Rose, and her fiancé, Yven. With my stomach full and the pain potion still working, I was considering sneaking off to bed as Ranarma brought out tea, but Yven leaned across the table and waggled his pale eyebrows. "Last time you were here, you didn't get the greenhouse tour."

"Babe," Rose intervened, "she's tired…"

But Yven seemed excited at the prospect of showing me around, and as Diriem and Rose shared a look, I followed him out into his happy place.

That Diriem had his own greenhouse, a glass-walled

space larger than my parents' home, was testament to his wealth; that the plants within were lush and productive was testament to Yven's skill, a connection to the outside world, and the importation of *many* bags of enriched potting soil and fertilizer. While Ranarma had started a garden to supplement the produce he purchased, Yven had been given free rein of the space once he and Rose moved in— and with them had come Yven's expansive orchid collection. I'd seen many of the plants in their apartment, but he'd trellised a healthy vanilla orchid by one wall and begun filling his part of the greenhouse with flowers. Yven wasn't a floramancer like Jane's dad, but he *was* a DPP agent, and so he'd improved upon Ranarma's efforts. The greenhouse, humid as an August day before a thunderstorm, sported neat rows of raised beds, planters, and enormous pots for fifteen-foot fruit trees, and Yven showed it all off. Even the seedlings beneath their bright glow lamps merited a brief lecture.

In all honesty, I didn't mind. As a farm girl, I knew how to plant and tend to crops, so I wasn't a complete novice when it came to gardening. But for Yven, horticulture was a passion, and he ushered me from pot to pot like an excited kid, eager to tell me all about the specimens within. After an hour and a half, Rose walked in to cut short the festivities, insisting that I needed rest, and the two of them saw me back to my room, Yven offering to complete the tour whenever I had the time.

I collapsed into my remarkably soft bed that night, weary in ways I couldn't articulate, and dreamed of impossible flowers blooming in an endless jungle.

Wednesday morning, I woke shortly after sunrise from the deepest sleep I'd had in days. I staggered to the bathroom, then carefully brushed my teeth. My sore, swollen fingers weren't as badly injured as they could have been, but they still protested when I gripped my new toothbrush.

Puffy-eyed but with slightly fresher breath, I peeked into the quiet hallway, then slipped two rooms down to check on Connor. To my surprise, the door was cracked open, and when I looked inside, I saw him sitting up, Jane perched on the edge of the bed beside him. I hurriedly let myself in, then knocked on the wall to announce myself. "Hi!" I called, waving from the doorway. "You're awake!"

"Just now," said Jane, motioning me closer. "Hey, hon. Did you get some rest?"

"Yep. Did you?"

She pointed to the couch. "Off and on. But this one's conscious again," she said, squeezing Connor's hand, then stood and released him. "I'm going to let Diriem know and get you something to drink," she murmured. "Are you hungry? Hurting? Nauseated?"

"I'm...okay," Connor croaked. "Uh...could probably eat. Water would be nice."

"On it." Jane bent over to kiss his forehead before taking her leave. "Maebe, stay with Con, okay? I'll be right back."

"I'm fine," he groggily protested. "Don't need a babysitter..." His eyes focused on me as I sat by his feet, and his sleep-addled brain began to catch up. "Mitta?"

"Hey, there," I said.

"What're you doing here? I thought you were going back to school," he asked through a wide yawn.

"I did, back on Sunday. Right after you passed out."

He grunted. "What day is it?"

"Wednesday."

"Shit." Rubbing his stubble, he asked, "I've been asleep for three freaking days?"

"Uh-huh. You were gone almost as soon as you drank that potion. Feeling okay?"

Connor paused, taking stock, and blinked blearily. "Yeah, I think so. Bit of a sleep hangover, but I'm not sick or anything." He peered at me more closely. "Wait, why aren't you at school?"

"Suspended," I muttered.

"For *what*?"

I folded my arms, hiding my discolored hands. "Got in a fight."

"A bad fight?"

"Rearranged her face."

His eyes widened. "Whose? That bitch who's been giving you a hard time?"

I nodded.

To my surprise, Connor grinned. "Atta girl. Okay, give me the play by play."

As I wrapped up my recollection of events, Jane returned with a tall glass of water in her hand and Diriem two steps behind her. "Good morning," he said as Jane hurried to Connor's bedside. "Nice to see you awake again."

"Does this mean the bucket's unnecessary?" Connor asked, pointing to the plastic bowl by his bed.

"Should be." As my cousin drank, he leaned against the wall and said, "I've asked Canna to make a house call. Let her clear you, and then we'll see about the next steps."

"I feel fine," said Connor between long sips.

"Glad to hear it, but let's allow the healer to be the judge of that."

He rolled his eyes but didn't argue. Instead, turning to Jane, he asked, "How are things at home? Any news?"

"Not much," she replied. "I've been watching your phone—and pretending to be you once or twice—but folks are leaving you alone. There was a piece or two about it online. No new leads that I've seen, but we weren't expecting any, were we?"

"No. How about your dad? Has he gone home yet?"

"Nope." Cutting her eyes to Diriem, she said, "DOI hasn't cleared it yet. It's possible that some of Ivari's people are still lurking in the area."

"We aren't certain," Diriem added, "but to be safe—"

"No, no, absolutely," said Connor.

"So, Dad's staying with his friends here," Jane continued, "and for now, Tabitha's doing drive-bys of Dad's
place and yours to look for strangers. No break-ins yet."

Connor frowned. "Y'all think they can find my house
without me there?"

"Probably not, but no one wants to take the chance
right now."

"And since we have eyes on the ground, we may as well
use them," said Diriem. "This was Tabitha's idea, incidentally. Generous of her."

Jane looked at him again, smirking. "Now, see, aren't
you glad y'all didn't wipe her memory?"

"I suppose so," he allowed with a faint smile, then
asked Connor, "How are you feeling? Any pain?"

"No," said Connor, who seemed to perk as he hydrated. "Actually…any chance of breakfast? I think my stomach just woke up."

"Of course. That can be arranged…but are we thinking
gruel and toast or—"

"*Gruel?*"

"It's easy on a weak stomach. Why, have you never had
it?"

Jane and Connor mirrored each other's slightly disgusted expression. "It's not a thing in our neck of the woods,"
she explained. "How hungry are you, Con?"

"Uh…horse, roughly," he replied.

"Okay. I'll go tell Ranarma," she said. "Why don't you
get a shower?"

"Yeah, that might make me feel a little closer to human," he concurred, then paused and laughed weakly.
"That doesn't really work anymore, does it?"

"You're fine," she said, and kissed him properly. "Ooh,
brush your teeth, too."

"Aw, cut me some slack!" Connor jokingly protested as
she headed out. Shaking his head, he eased himself to his
feet, steadying himself with a hand on the nightstand until
his balance was secure. "All right, I think I can manage,"

he said, glancing at Diriem and me. "I'm not feeling faint or anything."

Diriem nodded. "Then we'll let you be. But as you mentioned feeling closer to human, there's one other matter we should address before Canna gets here."

"What's that?"

"It would be...*helpful*...if you had a blood test prior to your Forum appearance."

The two men held each other's stare for a moment, and Connor blinked first. "Okay," he muttered. "Fine. Whatever it takes to get justice for East Branch."

"Very good. Come along, Maebe," he said, nudging me toward the door. "Connor doesn't need an audience."

Canna Nerin didn't answer to Diriem. She worked as a healer at Laws, so ultimately, Kabno was her boss. But she was also Jane's cousin—well, first cousin once removed, technically—and since her husband was Yven's longtime buddy, she'd become Diriem's pick for tending to...*interesting* cases, especially after she'd been slipped a language potion for English. Plus, as Annie had been sneaking Canna out to Georgia for months to brunch with her, Jane, Tabitha, and Rose, she was well acquainted with Connor and unlikely to make his rough introduction to the Pactlands any worse.

She rang the bell as we were finishing our late breakfast, and a moment later, Scel showed her in, carrying a black object about half the size of the mansion's microwave in the crook of his arm. "Really, I can get that," I heard her protest in Pactish as they came down the hallway toward the dining room. "It's not heavy."

"Not a problem," Scel told her, then entered and deposited the item on a clear potion of the table.

Behind him appeared Canna, a tall, dark-haired woman with soft green eyes that crinkled even with her consternation. "I've carried my gear everywhere, Mr. Curain," she said, adjusting the black bag hanging from her shoulder. "No need to put yourself out."

"As you like," he replied. "Coffee?"

"Please," she said with a sigh. Her purple healer's coat swished around her thighs as she turned to us. "Lord ti'Dana," she began, and nodded curtly. "Have Rose and Yven gone?"

"He had a morning meeting, and they carpooled," he explained, then gestured to an empty chair. "Have a seat. You've eaten?"

She grinned and pulled out the proffered chair. "More or less. When you're getting four children out the door, you grab what you can get. I'm fine," she hastily added before he could call one of the Curains back. "Coffee's great. Now, how's the patient?" she asked Connor, switching to English.

"Eh." He raised one hand and wiggled it. "Still a little groggy…"

"Well, you did just take one hell of a nap. And congratulations—that's the *best* reaction to the language potion. I puke for two days every time I down one."

Connor chuckled. "You've done this more than once?"

She started counting off on her fingers. "Native Pactish speaker, but I've had potions for Trollish, Nymphic, Gnomic…actually managed to get Faunish and Low Elvish in one…"

"Good God," he muttered.

"Not a great time. Most centaurs and nagas prefer Pactish, fortunately, and there are so few sirens that I've been able to avoid that one…oh, and *this*," she said. "So, five times, and believe me, it doesn't get any better."

"You can speak *Trollish*?" I interrupted.

Canna made a face. "I can *understand* Trollish. Speaking it is another matter. But in my line of work, considering the diversity in the agency, you've got to have fluency in case someone comes in missing a limb and reverts to his mother tongue. Oh, thank you so much," she said, briefly slipping back into Pactish as Ranarma hurried out of the kitchen with a steaming mug in his hands.

"Cappuccino, yes?" he asked, placing it in front of her.

"You're a good man," she said, and took a long sip, then rose and carried her drink back down the table to the place where she'd left her things. "Before we get started, let's deal with our little brawler," she said, rummaging through her bag. "Sore, Maebe?"

"I'm fine—" I began.

"Your hands are swollen and slightly green. Another healing potion won't hurt." She deposited a vial in front of me and waited until I'd slugged it back, then recapped it and tucked it away. "Good girl. Now, Connor," she said, slipping into the empty chair beside him, "go ahead and turn your seat my way. Let's take a look at your vitals…"

She checked his pulse and temperature, made him follow a light with his eyes, and asked a few orientation questions, then smiled tensely. "No immediate concerns. Bloodwork's next—and this shouldn't hurt. I'm quite good at finding stubborn veins."

Slowly, Connor pushed back his bathrobe sleeve, and Canna had him make a fist while she tapped at the bend in his arm. "Here we go," she murmured, and deftly inserted a needle.

Having had my blood drawn, I knew it wouldn't take much, and in less than a minute, Connor was holding a wad of gauze on the wound while Canna busied herself with the black object—a portable analyzer, she'd explained. "This will show me what you've got in your system," she told Connor. "Any potions I don't know about, drugs, things of that ilk, but it'll also give me your numbers for blood sugar and protein, show me whether you've got an elevated immune response, all that fun business."

"And species," he murmured.

"That, too, but stats first." As the machine began to process his sample, Canna said, "Not today, but if I were you, I'd get a full physical done."

"I get annual physicals," said Connor. "Ever since I started in law enforcement. I've got a clean bill of health to this point."

She folded her arms. "Just how thorough an examination are we talking? Bloodwork's one thing…"

"It's more than just a finger stick," he protested.

"All right. I'd still feel better if you got checked out here," said Canna. "There's a research team working with the rest of the East Branchers, and from what I've heard, they've seen a cluster of interesting issues."

Connor grunted. "And that's what inbreeding will do for you. You're talking about the extra fingers and stuff, right?"

"I've got a heart defect," I offered.

He frowned at me. "Really?"

"I'm just saying it wouldn't be a bad idea," Canna interjected, "and if you *did* have a problem that your physicals haven't caught yet, we can start treatment before it worsens."

"Well, whatever you might find, I've got about another sixty years if I'm lucky, so unless you can treat a human lifespan…"

"Not directly," she allowed, "but we might be able to keep you healthy for more of those years."

Jane patted Connor's back, and he grunted and sipped his coffee.

After about fifteen minutes, the machine beeped to signal the end of its cycle, then began to print its report. Connor tensed as Canna began scanning the results, then asked, "And?"

"Your numbers are good so far," she replied, reading. "Nothing here strikes me as concerning…"

He waited a moment longer while the printing finished, then cleared his throat. "So…got some elf in the mix?"

She looked up and cocked an eyebrow. "Seventy-seven percent."

"Human?"

"Elf. You're a little better than three-quarters."

His eyes widened, and as he began to slowly rub his face, he muttered, "Holy shit."

"That's the highest yet," I said, glancing from my stunned cousin to Canna. "I'm only seventy-three percent."

She nodded. "And there's no match in the database, as expected."

But Connor had turned to Jane. "What the fuck?" he whispered. "Janie, I…I…"

"It's okay," she said gently, taking his hands as he sputtered. "It's all right, Con. You're the same man you were an hour ago, right?"

"I…I guess so, but I just thought I'd be *lower*—"

"You're talented," Diriem interrupted. "Jane's seen it, and I had a word with Yacovi—he's impressed by how quickly you've intuited. I'd have been shocked if you were on the lower end."

"And this is all the more reason to get a full workup," said Canna, drawing Connor's attention back. "Since you *are* high, you might have more than sixty years ahead of you."

Connor laughed incredulously. "Both of my parents are dead. What does that tell you?"

She shrugged. "Not much, really. Remind me, your parents weren't talented, were they?"

"No…"

"And no cifyent?"

He shook his head. "No, they were pretty normal."

"So, what that suggests to me is that you're higher-percentage elven than either of them, possibly quite a bit higher."

"And you've had some long-lived people at East Branch," Jane cut in. "Think about Mary Amos all those years back. She was only half-blooded, and she lived, what, a hundred thirty years?"

"Okay, that's one outlier two centuries ago," said Connor. "I don't know of anyone like her in recent memory, and neither of my parents made it to sixty-five. Besides," he continued, glancing around the table, "I look my age, yeah? This is thirty-one."

Canna squinted, considering. "Hard to say. I'm certainly no expert in human aging patterns, but at your age, it'd be difficult to be certain. Ask me in another ten or twenty years, but right now?"

"I'm not baby-faced."

"You're not decrepit, either," said Jane.

"And again, you could get more answers with a full physical," Canna told him. "If you *do* have some inherent longevity, then that's an issue for which you need to plan."

Connor chuckled. "Don't retire in my sixties, you mean?"

"Well, that, and depending on how long you're predicted to live and whether you're going to age slowly, you'll need to leave Georgia eventually, just like Yacovi will."

He groaned, then finished his coffee as he mulled over that information. "Look," he said once he'd drained his mug, "I hear you, Canna, and I appreciate that you're trying to watch out for me, but right now, that's all back-burner stuff. The priority is East Branch—I can deal with myself later."

"That's fair," she replied, and Diriem nodded. "As I said, I don't see any emergency in your bloodwork—I'd just like to keep you around, and I'm sure Jane's with me on that one."

He turned to Jane, who nodded emphatically.

"Firebug," murmured Connor, "you ain't going to want me around when I'm pushing ninety."

"Shut up," said Jane, and kissed him. "You're not the boss of me."

"No, but once I'm wrinkly and lose my hair—"

"*Con.* Stop. East Branch first, right?"

"Right," he mumbled.

"And in the meantime, I'm not going anywhere," she

said. "So there. You're stuck with your arsonist girlfriend."

That pulled a little smile from him, and he kissed her again before he turned back to Canna. "Okay, Doc. I survived the language potion, so how soon am I going to be fluent?"

She squinted at the ceiling. "You took it on Sunday, so about three days ago…I'd say at least another three or four days."

"That long?"

"It takes time, but once it kicks in, it's permanent," she replied. "Try to be patient."

Frustrated, Connor looked at Diriem and asked, "What do I do in the meantime? I can go home—"

"Absolutely not," he said, shaking his head. "If you're out there and Ivari is still looking, you'll have almost no defense. Stay here—it's not as if I'm pressed for space."

His mouth tightened. "I'm not exactly good at sitting on my ass."

"That *is* a skill," Diriem said dryly, "but I'm confident that you can manage for a few days while your brain unscrambles itself and I make the arrangements with the Forum. And…I suppose it wouldn't be an undue hardship for Jane to work remotely a bit longer, eh? Or Maebe will be here for the duration of her suspension," he continued, "so perhaps you could keep her out of trouble."

Connor cocked his head and grinned at me, then cracked his knuckles. "Could do."

"Tell you what," said Jane, "I know for a fact that Rose has a board game collection upstairs. Y'all two could kill at least a few hours with Monopoly."

"What's Monopoly?" I asked.

An evil gleam flashed in my cousin's eyes. "You'll find out, mitta."

# CHAPTER 12

And I did. All through that long week, I received an introduction to the games Connor knew well from childhood, thanks to Rose's wide selection: dice games, card games, checkers, a brief foray into chess (I couldn't keep the pieces straight), and yes, Monopoly, at which Connor particularly excelled. Even with Jane, Rose, and Yven joining in, he dominated, mercilessly bankrupting us one by one.

"Remember, Willow," warned Jane as she sold her last house back to the bank, "I know where you sleep."

Vague threats aside, the week came as an unexpected respite for me—and for Connor and me both, forced to the sidelines for a moment, it gave us a chance to take stock and grieve. With the initial shock of my losses fading to a more manageable ache, I found myself able to think of my parents without immediately tearing up. I couldn't *dwell* on them, not yet, but I didn't feel like my chest was cracking open every time my mind drifted toward my memories of the home I'd never see again. Being away from North Lake and my cousins' angry silence certainly didn't hurt. As for Connor, who'd remained outwardly stoic but for the breakdown I hadn't been meant to overhear, I caught him misting up a few times, but it was during the games he and I played alone that he processed all the death. Between turns, he'd casually mention stories from East Branch, some familiar to me, some not, and we'd reminisce together. Sometimes, there was laughter. Other times, I bit back tears as my throat constricted, and from the twitching in Connor's face, I could tell he was doing likewise.

For me, at least, it was a comfort to know that *someone* kin to me didn't hold me fully responsible for the slaughter. As Connor had always lived away from the community, he'd never been my closest cousin, but in those quiet days at Diriem's, we bonded in our shared grief and guilt and worry for the future.

On Monday, Diriem came home with the news we'd been awaiting: the Forum would take up the matter of East Branch on Wednesday morning. By then, Connor's potion had finished its work, and though his Pactish was far more accented than Jane's was, he could get by. While I'd been before the Forum, Connor and I agreed that he should be the one to speak, not only because he was older but because he understood the law enforcement situation better than I did.

Though my suspension technically ended at eight on Wednesday morning, I opted to take a few extra hours off to attend the session as well—if nothing else, I figured I might offer Connor moral support from the audience.

Tabitha, Jane's friend in Ragged Gap, had reported nothing out of the ordinary around Connor's house all week, but we still had no clue whether Ivari was staying close, looking for the four in DOL custody. But even Diriem, who was taking precautions, agreed that a five-minute trip back would be unlikely to result in tragedy, so Annie came by on Tuesday night to run Connor home. Jane had packed well for him, but he wanted his dress uniform, which lived in a garment bag on the back of his bedroom door. Unlike his usual work clothes, this uniform included a coat, and he seemed to stand a little straighter when he wore it. While he polished his shoes, Rose pulled me back into her enormous walk-in closet for wardrobing assistance, as I'd yet to acquire my own formal robes. The turquoise one I'd borrowed from her during the summer was still appropriate, she decided, and a few of the pieces I'd bought with Keyne were nice enough to work beneath it.

"Why don't you just keep that one?" Rose said as I modeled for her. "It suits you, Maebe, and...well." She glanced back at her rack of robes and snorted. "Lord knows I'm not hurting for them."

"They're pretty," I said, trying to surreptitiously make mine swish.

She grinned. "That was a team effort. When I signed on with DPP, Canna took me shopping, Yven tagged along, and then Pop got wind of the trip and sent Keyne after us to superintend and pay. That woman's got a good eye and no problem with spending money. I came home with five robes the first day," she said, shaking her head. "Enjoy that one, seriously."

Connor looked out of place the next morning as we gathered to leave, the only one in a dark suit, but Jane just muttered a wrinkle out of his shirt and took his hand as we walked to her car. The three of us would drive together, and Rose and Yven, having taking leave from work, would meet us there. Diriem had explained that he'd come separately with a group from DOI but told us we'd have an escort. "Look for Teolm," he'd said to Jane and me. "He'll be in the lobby past security, and he knows the arrangements."

We left with plenty of time to navigate the portals from Viratta to Beukal. Having been driven through the internal system a few times by then, I wasn't taken aback by the large holes in space, each ringed with flashing lights and hanging behind a barrier arm. Connor had been warned, but he leaned forward in the front passenger seat as Jane navigated us into an inbound lane, peering through the windshield for a better look. "They *are* like toll booths," he marveled. "Where do you pay?"

"My truck's marked," Jane explained. "It's like having E-ZPass, and one perk of the job is that the agency covers my portal fees. The external portals are more involved," she said as she inched forward in line. "One through at a time, no matter the portal used, and there's an inspection in Beukal, but the only portal attendants here are in case of malfunction."

"So, what you're telling me is that no one's going to be asking questions?"

"Not if you keep your head down and your mouth shut, babe," she teased. "Seriously, my ride's registered through DOI. No one looks too closely at our vehicles."

"Convenient."

"I know, right?"

As Connor quietly took it all in, Jane drove us through the hole, which opened into the much larger portal building in the capital. At that time of the morning, eight of the ten lanes were inbound, and she carefully joined the traffic outflow toward the city. "This may take a minute," she said, slowly merging between two black SUVs. "Rush hour *sucks*. Beukal apartments are relatively expensive, but since you get to avoid this mess…"

"Are you looking?"

Even I could hear that the question was more than a straightforward query.

Jane reached over to squeeze Connor's hand. "Nope. I've got a bed at DOI, and that's all I need here."

"Eventually…" he said, his voice drifting off.

"*If* that day comes, and I'm not making those plans just yet, then I'm getting a place for two. Yeah?"

He grunted softly. "You don't have to worry about me, Janie."

"Bullshit. If I relocate, it'll be with you."

"I appreciate that, and you know I love you, but you can do better than me."

"Well, I love *you*, so tough," she replied.

"Seriously, you've got to have better options than 'inbred mostly elf.'"

Jane snickered but kept her grip on Connor. "Let me be the judge of that, eh?"

Eventually, we cleared the portal building and headed

downtown toward District 1, where the Forum met. When the domed limestone building came into view, Jane slowed, then parked in the adjacent lot and turned off the engine. "You're going to do great," she told Connor. "Maebe and I will be watching, so if you get nervous, just look for us."

He reached inside his collar and tugged it slightly looser. "Think it's going to fill up?"

"It might, but I haven't yet seen a crowd as bad as the one for Dad's trial, so take a deep breath. Now, you're almost certainly going to have support from the Hunt," she continued, "and they're an easy group to pick out from the dais. If you find the sorcerers, look for Mirrik Voln—black ponytail, kind of young. He's a nice guy. The trolls are pretty easygoing, from what I've seen. Their spokesman is usually Foggy Lake—look for the big guy with the rusty complexion. He always wears enamel caps on his tusks."

"But Diriem is...*not* on the Forum?"

"Not currently," said Jane. "Neither is Teolm. You've got...let me see..." She paused, squinting at the roof of the truck, then said, "There's Cirral ti'Pon, Hemar ti'Dir, and Arana ti'Ansha."

"Ti'Ansha...Yven's family?" Connor asked.

"Distantly, he says. Theirs is a cousin branch, so that's not really a card you can play. But you'll be fine," she insisted. "I have faith in you, Con."

"That *might* be misplaced."

"Doubt it." She leaned over to kiss him, then opened her door. "Come on, let's meet Teolm."

"And who is this Teolm, again?" he asked as we joined her.

"Teolm ti'Cren. One of Rose's great-uncles. He's helping Diriem with the East Branch situation because his family's one of the southern Halls that evacuated."

"Uh-huh," Connor mumbled.

"He's got a jewelry store," I offered.

"That's the family business," said Jane. "He's actually a

botanist by trade—another floramancer like Dad."

Jane led us up the stairs, beneath the covered colonnade, and through the bronze doors, then flashed her badge to the elf manning the security booth. "They're with me," she told him in Pactish, pointing to Connor and me. "Should be on the guest list."

He pulled out a tablet computer and tapped at the screen. "Names?"

"Amos and Willow."

After a moment's search, he nodded and motioned us on, though not without a second look at Connor.

I spotted Teolm standing near an information kiosk and waved, and he reciprocated. Like Diriem, Teolm had the typical thin elven build, but he was a full head shorter, a small, dark-haired man with crinkling brown eyes and a boyish face. His eggplant-colored robe fell perfectly above his shoes, and I suspected it had cost a fair bit more than mine.

"Good morning," he said as we joined him. "Agent Fortune—"

"Trainee," Jane replied, clasping his proffered hand. "You remember Maebe, of course…"

"Naturally, and I'm so sorry to hear the news about East Branch," he said, taking my hand in turn. "Diriem gave me the details." Releasing me, he looked up at Connor and smiled tightly. "Which must make you Chief Willow."

"Connor," he said, shaking Teolm's hand.

"Teolm, and my condolences to you as well, young man. Shall we?"

Following Teolm toward the main meeting hall, I walked close enough to the others to catch Connor whisper to Jane in English, "How old is he?"

"I mean, he's younger than Diriem," she whispered back, "but that ain't saying much."

As I'd been in the meeting hall, I knew about the stained glass ceiling, which was lit to throw rainbows on the floor, but I suppose Jane hadn't mentioned it to Connor, as he stopped in his tracks to take it all in: the light coming from the high ceiling, the tapestries on the walls, the thick green carpets on the three aisles that sloped down to the dais, the two levels of balconies ringing the circular portion of the room, which was shaped like a thick pie wedge with the point cut off. Teolm glanced back and motioned us onward. "This way," he said, and pointed to a cluster of chairs at the foot of the dais. "We've got front-row seats."

"You're coming up there with me?" Connor asked.

"Only if necessary. I'm just ushering," he replied with a grin over his shoulder. "You'll be fine—there's never been a fatality in this building, or so I'm told."

Teolm escorted us to the waiting chairs, and as we took our seats, I turned around to search the room for familiar faces. I found no one at first, just a few reporters with cameras on the lower balcony, but then I spotted Annie two sections over from them. She saw me looking her way and lifted a hand. While Annie seemed underdressed for the occasion in a long-sleeved black T-shirt and pants, the people sitting around her were similarly attired—agents, I figured—so I supposed she wouldn't get in trouble. Directly across the aisle from her group, I found Yven and Rose...and a few seats down, sitting with several people I didn't know, was Diriem, who appeared to be deep in conversation with a brown-haired man in a gray robe. From that distance, I couldn't make out many details, but his ears were noticeable enough to peg him as an elf...and then recognition hit: Pateme ti'Tam, the DPP director.

By then, strangers in the balconies had begun to take notice of our group, but Connor kept his focus straight ahead. Superficially, he appeared to be calm enough, but his jittery knee betrayed him, and Jane kept her hand locked on his.

Shortly before nine, the representatives and their assistants began filing in, filling the chairs and mats behind us.

Looking back, I spotted the Hunt's section, and Wylan, seated at the desk in the middle, nodded in greeting. Some of the other representatives weren't as punctual, however, and as usual, the proceedings didn't commence until about ten minutes past the hour, when the Overseer took her seat at the desk to the lefthand side of the dais. Ostensibly a neutral party, Ketling Tiramae was a gray-skinned nymph who wore her dark hair in a rather severe bun, and as she smoothed her robe and surveyed the room, the murmurings quieted. A quick rap of her gavel silenced the rest, and after a gesture from her assistant, a sorcerer in the front row, she spoke with her voice magically amplified.

"Good morning," she began, scanning the floor seats. "On this the twenty-eighth day of September in the four hundred eighty-fifth year of the Pact, I call this meeting of the Pact Forum to order."

"Wait," I heard Connor whisper to Jane, "they use our months?"

"It was convenient," she whispered back.

Meanwhile, the screen hanging behind Ketling turned on, giving those in the back of the room a better view of her face. "Since no committee has asked for dedicated time, today's will be a general session," she said. After briefly consulting with the secretary, who sat at a desk near her assistant, she glanced at her computer and cleared her throat. "First on the agenda, the Forum has been asked to consider an issue brought by Representatives Voln and...um...the Hunter?" she asked, cocking an eyebrow as she looked toward Wylan. "If I'm not mistaken, this is the first we've seen from you."

Wylan rose. "I've been observing, Madam Overseer. But this matter is important to me, and Mirrik was gracious enough to handle the paperwork."

The other representatives chuckled, and even Ketling smiled. "A true favor," she said. "Well, gentlemen, the podium is yours."

"We're just the facilitators," said Mirrik, going to his

feet as well. "Actually, we have a visitor today. The Forum recalls the quasi-elven community in Georgia, yes?" he asked, looking around the room.

A rumble of voices answered *that*.

"In short, they've been attacked," Mirrik continued. "And, uh…well, we thought it best if someone more familiar with the situation could explain."

Teolm nudged Connor, who stood and looked at Ketling. Noticing him, she nodded and beckoned him onto the dais, and he quickly made his way up the steps. "Good morning," she said as he pulled his hat from beneath his arm and put it on the podium. "Who might you be?"

"Good morning, ma'am," Connor replied, his voice steady enough to disguise his nerves, as the sorcerer down front amplified him as well. "I'm Connor Willow with the Whitford Police Department."

"Whitford…"

"It's the town right next to East Branch—the community, I mean," he said with an awkward shrug. "Probably should have brought a map…"

"Don't worry about it," she soothed. "Tell us what happened."

He hesitated briefly, presumably putting his thoughts in order, then gripped the podium and looked out at the room. "I'm going to go ahead and ask your forgiveness," he said, "since I've only been speaking this language about…oh, three days, and turns out that potion does *nothing* to help your accent."

I heard a few of the people behind me chortle knowingly.

"As I said," he continued, "I'm Connor Willow. I'm from Whitford, but my family are all from East Branch. Parents moved to town," he offered. "And since I've got a job that, to this point, has helped pay East Branch's bills, I've stayed back in Georgia instead of coming over here. Until now."

He paused and swallowed hard, his bobbing Adam's apple huge on the screen behind him.

"Twelve days ago, East Branch was attacked after nightfall. In brief, the community was burned to the ground, and everyone on the property was murdered. We're talking folks from grandparents all the way down to a seven-year-old kid." After giving the murmurs a few seconds to quiet, Connor gestured toward our row and said, "While they were being massacred, I was house-sitting two towns over with Maebe here. We're damn lucky that the house we were watching belongs to a licensed grower with a tough lock on his brew room, since four elves broke in, planning to snatch us."

"Who?" called a voice from the elves' section of the floor.

Ketling zeroed in on the speaker. "Representative ti'Dir?"

He stood and nodded to her, then quickly focused on Connor. "Who are you accusing?"

"None of your constituents, sir. Hang on, I wrote them down," he muttered, digging in his pants pocket, then extracted a folded list and reviewed the names. "All right. I actually interviewed Naculta ti'Pul, and he was forthcoming at the time. I don't know if that's changed…"

From the first balcony, Kabno called, "He's assisting us."

"Great, thank you, ma'am. Per ti'Pul, the others were his older brother, Danirri ti'Ammaas, plus Pean ti'Elta and Tella ti'Fin. All of them were born in New York. They're still in custody, right?" he called toward Kabno, shading his eyes to better see the diminutive chief.

"*Oh*, yes," she replied.

Representative ti'Dir frowned. "How…"

"They broke into the brew room to find us," said Connor, "and the Hunt was nice enough to save our hides and pick those four up. Anyway, by the time Maebe and I had been evacuated, the killing was underway at East Branch.

We got a brief call from Maebe's mother to warn us, and I phoned it in, but there was nothing we could do but wait for the forest fire to die down. So, here's the situation," he said, looking around the room. "Thanks to ti'Pul, I've got a list of individuals involved, and sitting at the top of the pile is Ivari ti'Ammaas. Twelve plus the four here. I don't know where they are now, but what I *do* know is that I can't bring them to justice on my own."

He paused for the space of a long breath, then said, "Your team at DOL has already informed me that this is a jurisdictional nightmare. It's bad from my perspective as well. I'm the chief of the Whitford PD, but we're a tiny department. Whitford's a hamlet. Even if I wanted to try, I just don't have the manpower to bring in twelve elves. Now, technically, I *can't* try," he continued, "at least not by the normal routes, as the sheriff has jurisdiction. East Branch is county land, not part of Whitford. We all play nicely, but for obvious reasons, the sheriff's not going to let me get within a mile of his investigation. And I can't just stop by and tell him that the best suspects are *elves*, because frankly, while my colleagues may believe in sasquatch, they all gave up on elves around the time they stopped believing in Santa Claus."

I heard some confused murmurings behind us, and Connor let them subside before he resumed. "Even if they didn't take me to get my head examined, there's no way the sheriff's team can bring ti'Ammaas's crew in. I've got nothing but respect for the deputies—they're a fine bunch and qualified shooters—but you can't put a handful of guys with guns up against freaking *magic*. Bottom line, even if I were able to pull in every cop in north Georgia, I doubt we'd be able to get our suspects using anything less than lethal force."

The mutterings were louder that time, but Connor waited them out.

"We've been pretty self-reliant at East Branch for a long time," he told the representatives. "Haven't had a choice in the matter. But much as it pains me to admit it, I can't handle this case on my own. *I* sure as hell don't have the training to tackle ti'Ammaas, and functionally, I've got no backup. That's why I'm here today. Twenty-eight people are dead, and they deserve justice. Is there anything you can do to help?"

"Question," said a female voice, and I turned as a platinum blonde sorcerer in a bright pink robe stood from her desk. "What *are* you, anyway?"

Connor didn't flinch. "About three-quarters elf, as it turns out, ma'am."

"And the rest?"

"Human," he said simply. "Didn't think that would come as a surprise to anyone here."

"I see. And these dead of yours...also human?"

Beside me, Jane gritted her teeth, and tiny flames danced above her arms for a split-second before she drew in her power.

"Presumably mixed," Connor told the representative. "None of them were ever tested, but all of the East Branchers here are better than sixty–forty elven–human, so make of that what you will."

"Mm. Assuming, then, for the sake of argument that your dead are comparable...how is this our problem?"

"I hate that woman," Jane muttered to me as the representatives talked over each other.

"Who is she?" I asked.

"Elm Carinar. My grandfather got her onto the Forum, and she's been following in his footsteps."

By then, the Overseer was rapping her gavel for order, and the voices died down. "Representative Carinar, was there anything else you wished to say?" she asked.

Elm folded her arms. "Only that I don't see how this matter is of interest to us. If the southern Halls are cleaning up their mess, then so be it."

"Excuse me, did you just say their *mess*?" Connor snapped, glaring down at her.

"And how would you describe it?" she retorted. "Perhaps someone should translate—that accent is almost incomprehensible."

Though Connor reddened, he held himself in check. "I'm doing my best, ma'am."

"Indeed." Glancing at her colleagues, she said, "You know how I felt about bringing the half-breeds into the Pactlands in the first place. Now they want more? We're to fight their battles for them, are we?" she said, and laughed harshly. "Take up arms against elves on behalf of dead humans? They're short-lived, anyway—where's the real harm?"

At that, Mirrik jumped to his feet to cut her off. "This is *everyone's* problem," he said, raising his voice over the hubbub. "I asked Laws for details, and their best information shows that this attack was brutal and unprovoked."

"Ti'Ammaas has been lying to his people," Connor added. "Telling them we're threatening to expose them. He killed half my family based on nothing at all."

"So you say," Elm retorted. "We haven't heard the other side, have we? And if Laws has incarcerated these people without cause—"

It took Ketling a moment to restore quiet, and she shot Elm a warning scowl before looking toward DOL's contingent in the balcony. "Director? Any rebuttal to that?"

"We have cause," Kabno immediately answered. "The four in our custody were caught inside a restricted area, and the one who picked the lock has confessed everything and is cooperating."

"Seems a bit pretextual, doesn't it?" said Elm.

"With all due respect to the representative," said the director, "the counselors disagree."

"*Your* counselors," she shot back. "I'm sure I could find any number here who aren't beholden to you—"

"That's enough," Ketling barked. "Representative Carinar, you've made your point clear. Representative Voln, was there something you wished to say?"

"Yes, Madam Overseer," said Mirrik as Elm sat with a displeased grunt. "To do nothing—to take such a narrow view of this incident—would be unwise. We're looking at an unknown actor. With the exception of a *very* few of us, no one in the Pactlands has had dealings with ti'Ammaas, and certainly not in the last centuries. But if his reaction to learning of his descendants was to kill them…" Mirrik shook his head. "That's his *blood*. I can't imagine that he'd have any more concern for those unrelated to him. Now, maybe he's happy out there," he continued, slowly turning to address the room. "Perhaps he's comfortable with the life he's built. But what if he isn't? He knows now that the Pactlands has endured. I have a difficult time imagining him petitioning for admission, don't you? Kings don't beg."

"You can't seriously be suggesting that ti'Ammaas would *attack* us," Elm scoffed, standing again. "How would he get through the portals? And even if he did, what's a handful of elves, anyway?"

The elven representatives bristled at that, but Connor spoke before they could protest. "It's not a handful, ma'am. More than a hundred, per ti'Pul. And unlike those of us from East Branch, our more northerly…*cousins*, let's say, are full-blooded. Some of them are probably pretty old, too."

"But all of this is speculation," said Elm, "and you're asking us to take up your claim *now* against a party who's done us no harm. Besides, whatever you say you may be, you're all legally human. Who gives a damn if you live or die?"

That time, Ketling's repeated calls for order fell on deaf ears. As the representatives argued, I noticed two of the trolls slip into the aisle by the Hunt's group, blocking Wylan's view of the sorcerers' spat. While I couldn't hear what they were saying, Wylan clearly had his dander up, and the larger of the trolls—Foggy Lake, I assumed—gripped Wylan's shoulder and shook his head.

As for me, I could feel my power roiling beneath my skin as I silently fumed. Though I knew my family was considered inferior by many in the Pactlands—hell, school was proof enough of *that*—the blatant comments hurt all the same. My mom and dad were good people. My grandparents were good people. They weren't perfect, sure, but they didn't *hurt* anyone, and they didn't deserve their fate...

And then, from the balcony, came a shouted, "*Hey!*"

I looked up to find Annie standing on her bench, her voice presumably having been amplified by the pissed-looking blonde elf in black to her right. "You people can argue about this all you like," Annie snapped, "but if you're too cowardly to commit, then *I'm* in for East Branch."

"You have no authority—" Elm began.

"I know *all* too well what happens when rogue talents are left unchecked," Annie yelled back at her. "People die. My friends *died*. And now East Branch has been obliterated because there's an asshole with talent running around out there and no one can stop him."

"I mean, a bullet to the brain..." said Connor.

"Okay, short of lethal methods," Annie allowed. "Look, I get it. In a perfect world, there would be no need for the Pactlands, but humans make terrible neighbors. But from where I'm standing, we've got two problems. One, ti'Ammaas is going to feel empowered because there's no way in hell that the local cops are going to nab him for...what, twenty-odd counts of murder? Two, he's going to want to retaliate once he figures out where his missing minions are. Laws has *two* of his kids in custody. And you really think your portals are going to defend you?" She laughed and shook her head. "Please. The portals are only a shield until you have money, and then they turn into a sieve."

"The Hunt rides with you," said Wylan, wheeling around to face his wife. "Politics be damned."

As the rest of the Huntsmen clapped, Jane jumped on-to her chair. "And I'm in. Going to need a leave of absence, boss," she called up to Diriem in the balcony.

Before he could answer that, the blonde beside Annie joined her on the bench. "Want another pyro?" Glancing toward Kabno, she added, "Vacation requested, ma'am."

Finally, with a bellowed, "*Enough!*" and a series of gavel blows hard enough to hammer nails, Ketling regained control of the room. "Obviously, this can't be decided today. All in favor of taking up the issue in the morning?" A ruffled majority raised their hands, and Ketling looked at Connor. "Thank you for coming, young man. You're free to leave."

# CHAPTER 13

**T**he drive back to North Lake was quiet.

"You did well," Jane told Connor in the parking lot. "Elm Carinar is a raging bitch, but this isn't over yet."

Beyond that, however, none of us had much to say as we made our way out to District 6. I could guess what was on my cousin's mind, and though I shared his sentiments, the thought that made my stomach knot was that my return to school was growing closer by the minute. As I saw the gray stone building come into view, my pulse quickened, and despite my admonitions to myself, my palms began to sweat.

"Here we are," said Jane, pulling up by the front steps, and parked the truck. "Maebe, hon, are you going to be okay, or do you want us to walk you in?" she asked, turning around to the back seat. Something in my expression must have given her pause, as she said, "Or not. If you're not ready, you don't have to go back."

Connor turned as well and gave me a long look. "It's all right, mitta," he murmured. "You don't have to do this."

"What's my alternative? And I'm the one who wanted an education, right?" I said bitterly, grabbing my purse.

Jane met me as I slid out of the truck. "Diriem won't mind," she said, taking my hand. "And if he did for some reason, then Annie would welcome you. You have options," she insisted.

But I was eighteen and grown, and this mess was my fault, so I feigned a brave face and shook my head. "I'll be fine," I said, then went around to the other door to retrieve the duffel bag Rose had given me.

I didn't look back as I headed up the stairs, afraid that I'd falter if I saw Connor and Jane watching me go, though I took a deep breath before I opened the front doors. Walking past the offices, I saw Ms. Mafatta eating a pastry in the staff breakroom and nodded curtly, then hurried on before she could swallow and stop me.

The dorm was quiet when I let myself in, and my room seemed to have been untouched over the last week. I hung up my new clothes and changed out of my robe, which was far too nice for class, then gathered my books and went out to my morning tutorial.

Sage looked around when the door squeaked open and waved. "Maebe, hi! You're back!"

"Oh—hello, there," said our teacher, pausing at the board. "I didn't think we'd see you until tomorrow."

"Had an appointment," I mumbled, taking a seat beside Sage, who nudged her book closer to show me where we were. As for the others, Heidi acknowledged me with the barest dip of her chin, while David continued to pretend I was invisible.


The dorm parents were warm as ever and welcomed me back, making no mention of why I'd disappeared, but my cousins had yet to defrost after our week apart. I kept to my room when not in class, and I wasn't surprised to find myself eating dinner alone that night. But halfway through my salad, a shadow fell across my tray, and I dropped my fork in alarm.

"Sorry, didn't mean to startle you," said Swift Eagle, settling in on the other side of the table with a dish of pudding the size of a soup bowl. "Is this seat taken?"

"Uh...no, help yourself," I replied as my heart hammered its warning against my ribs. "Hi." I glanced around the dining hall, which was beginning to empty. "Where's the rest of the team?"

"Way too many of us have tests on Friday to be social," she said, digging in. "I don't mean to bother you—just wanted you to know that Ainnet has been *very* quiet of late."

"How's her nose?"

"Bandaged. She'll be fine," said Swift Eagle with a dismissive wave of her spoon. "Little princess should see some of the injuries *we* get. But she's avoided the East Branchers entirely. Stays far clear of their table, and so do her friends. Looks like you finally got through to her, eh?"

"I guess, but..." I hesitated, then decided that I'd ask forgiveness later if it came to that. "Between us?"

"Sure, I can keep a secret."

"The only reason I'm still here is that Diriem talked down Lady ti'Har."

She laughed. "Wait, Ainnet went to the head of her Hall? Over a fistfight?"

"Gave her a sob story, too," I said. "But I didn't tell you any of this."

"Of course not," she replied with a wink, then scooped up another spoonful. "Not that I get a vote, but I think your suspension was unfair."

"Thanks. But hey, if she's leaving us alone, then I guess it was worth it."

"That's the spirit," she replied, toasting me with her spoon before she ate. "So, any interest in melee? We'll have spring tryouts."

"Ooh...thank you, but I don't even know the rules..."

"Eh, those can be taught. I like your spunk," she said, and eyed my salad. "Though I might suggest putting some protein on those vegetables if you want to play."


**I** went to bed that night without a word to any of my cousins. Lying alone in the darkness of my room with the door firmly shut, I listened as our wing of the dorm quieted down and tried to sleep. Part of me wanted to call Jane or

Connor, just to hear a friendly voice, but I knew it had been a long day for them, and I didn't want to be a downer.

So, I rolled over and pulled the covers to my chin, and I slept.

But my dreams were unquiet, and I found myself back in Ivari's burning office, caught in the middle of the blaze of my own making. He'd escaped somehow, and when I looked for Jane or Annie or the others, I discovered I was alone. Maybe they'd fled; maybe they'd never been there to begin with in my mind's twisted recollection of that day. In any case, I was on my own, and the flames were licking ever closer, a shrinking circle trapping me where I stood. I could smell the choking smoke…

I bolted awake, gasping, but the smell lingered…and if anything, it was stronger.

Footsteps ran past my room, and I scrambled out of bed to investigate. Only once I'd flung the door open did I hear the warning cry: "*Fire!*"

It was harder to breathe in the hall, and the smoke stung my eyes. Crouching, I hurried toward the exit to the rest of the dorm, but flames and a knot of my cousins blocked my path. The folks on my side were the younger ones without parents—Zoe, Peter, and David Black, the Amos twins, Heidi and David Amos, and Hannah Church. They backed away from the fire in their nightclothes and bare feet, the older ones pulling the younger toward the temporary shelter behind us, but we were trapped. Our hall dead-ended, and the only escape was a leap from four stories up.

I started to panic. My phone was in my room—I could call Annie, and she might rescue us, but what about the others? How big was the fire? What about the other rooms, the couples with kids? Were they trapped, too?

The last of East Branch was about to burn alive, and it was my fault…

Had I been thinking clearly, I'd have called Annie and

begged Wylan to come, but my focus had narrowed to my immediate surroundings: the growing heat, the thick air that singed my nostrils, the sweat rolling down my spine.

And then, in the midst of the crackling and crying and my racing thoughts, my power surged, straining for release. I wasn't a pyromancer—I didn't have the skill to talk to the flames directly—but fire needed air.

I could dance with it.

"Behind me!" I yelled at the others, shoving my way forward, and squinted through watering eyes at the inferno in my path. Calling upon every lesson Violet had taught me in the last weeks, I channeled my will and shoved against the fire with the force of a hurricane blast. The flames bent away from me, and I hit them again, trying to blow out the nearest and push free an opening.

It might have been simpler, a distant part of me mused as I drove the fire before us, to suck the air from the room and snuff out the conflagration. But doing so would have required me to remove the air from our entire wing, and even if I could accomplish such a feat, I couldn't risk leaving my cousins to suffocate. So, on I plodded, straining against the fire like a plow through sunbaked soil. My nightshirt dripped from the heat and my exertion, and my lungs and eyes alike burned.

Finally, I struggled to the end of the hallway, only to find that the largest common room was engulfed—and the halls that branched beyond it were blocked by fire. Turning briefly to my coughing cousins, I ordered, "Outside, now! Go!"

The little ones didn't waste time and made a break for it, but Heidi hung back. "What can I do?" she asked. "I…I don't even know where to find a bucket…"

"Just go," I said. "I've got this."

Still, she hesitated. "Mitta—"

"*Go*," I insisted. "Get help!"

As Heidi turned and fled, I felt a sharp burn on my arm and yanked it back. With only a few weeks of lessons under my belt, I was far from a truly competent aeromancer, and Heidi had distracted me enough to make me lose focus on the unforgiving fire. My bare skin was angry red where the flames had licked it, but pain and fear fueled my redoubled efforts. I summoned the wind from every corner of the building, fanning the fire toward me and into the common room. Step by agonizing step, I pushed it away from the other halls, though I didn't dare to look back when I heard the smoke-choked coughs of my escaping cousins behind me.

As I pressed into the common room, the cornered fire seemed to burn hotter, roaring as it raced over the wooden ceiling beams. The window casing was already gone, the glass missing, and the cold night air fed the blaze. By then, I was shaking, the center of an unholy cyclone of wind and flame, and my control was beginning to fail. I twitched with each quick burn to my arms, my legs, my shoulders, but I paid them only enough mind to make sure the fire went out—I couldn't afford to tend to my injuries when I was surrounded by flame and smoke.

Then the ceiling started to crack in warning. I threw a gust of wind over my head, desperately trying to keep the burning debris in place, but I knew I wouldn't be able to hold it long.

Could I run? Was it safe? Had my cousins and our dorm parents made it out? But what about the rooms above and below ours? Had anyone warned those students of the danger? And if I left, the fire would advance again and take everything we had…

But I was exhausted, and my skin *hurt*…

"Oh, heavens, child," came a female voice behind me, and I felt more than saw a pulse of power strum through the fire. My circling winds turned to smoky clouds as the flames retreated and died.

A pyromancer. She had to be a pyro…

More footsteps pounded on the floor, and the woman at my back called, "Ceiling's unstable! She's holding it—"

"On it," said a deeper voice. "Let go, youngling."

That was all the convincing I needed. The wind calmed as I fell to my knees, panting and hacking, an acrid taste coating my mouth. By the time I pulled myself together enough to turn around, four dorm parents had gathered. I recognized only Dalm, who was working with another sorcerer to stabilize the weak ceiling. A third sorcerer stood back with a nymph. Judging by the nymph's pale coloration, they were air-aligned, which meant the sorcerer had to have been the pyromancer who'd come to my rescue. As she smothered the last of the glowing embers, the nymph circulated the air around us—and with much finer precision than I'd employed—driving the smoke out the window.

I tried to stand, but the pyromancer said, *"Don't move*, girl. You stay where you are."

"I…I didn't do this—" I began.

"You're burned, baby. Don't make it worse."

She was right, and as my adrenaline ebbed, pain rose to take its place. When a healer finally arrived, I didn't resist as she shot a full syringe into my shoulder, and seconds later, I passed out.

**I** awoke in a strange room with pale sea-green walls, buried beneath cool white sheets, and blinked away the gumminess in my eyes to see Connor sitting beside me. "Hey, no, none of that," he said as I started to sit up. "Be still, mitta."

"Where…" I croaked.

"You're at a hospital in District 3," he murmured. "Your school had you taken to the closer one, but this place has the best burn unit in the city, so you were transferred early this morning."

"Burn?"

"Yeah, burn," he said wearily. "I don't know how they classify burns here, but you're nice and swaddled, and they've been giving you healing potions by IV."

Following his eyes, I glanced at my left arm and discovered the taped-down tube protruding from it. Above and below my elbow, my arm was wrapped with white bandages. "I'm not hurting," I said.

"Probably because they've *also* been shooting you full of painkillers. Keeping you comfortable," he explained. "Now, the good news is that you're not going to need skin grafts, and any scarring should be minimal—"

"*Scarring?*" I interrupted.

Connor stared at me. "Maebe, hon, you were burned in two dozen places. What were you thinking?"

"I couldn't let everyone else die!"

"Why not run for help?"

"The other halls were blocked," I told him. "I didn't know how far the fire went, and if we'd lost anyone else…"

My eyes filmed, and Connor carefully smoothed my hair from my face—my *bandaged* face, I noticed, sensing the tug of adhesive on my cheek. "We didn't lose anyone, and you did one hell of a job," he said, "but next time, leave the firefighting to the pros, eh?"

I reached for him, and Connor clasped my hand. "Been here long?" I asked. "Sorry I'm not better company."

"Since about three this morning. They got you out of there, and once you were stable, someone thought to reach out to Diriem. Jane drove me over. She went to the office around lunchtime, but between you and me, I don't think this is going to be her most productive day."

"Wait—how long have I been out?"

Connor glanced at his watch. "Well…the fire probably started somewhere around one, and it's a bit after three now, so a little better than twelve hours."

I lay there for a moment, letting that sink in. Half a day missing…

"Is the building okay?" I asked. "I tried to control the fire, but it burned along the ceiling…"

"Last I heard, it was saved," said Connor. "There's damage, of course, but it's intact. And everyone got out, so you did good, kid."

Some of the tension in my chest began to relax. "Any idea how the fire started?"

He grimaced. "Me? No, aside from the fact that this is pretty clearly arson. No one's given me the rundown yet, but they're confident of that much. All I know for sure is that Laws and DOI are working on it. Diriem wants the perp *now*."

I laughed to myself. "Guess he didn't see this one coming, either, did he?"

"Well…not every detail."

Sobering, I frowned at Connor. "What do you mean?"

He flashed a tight smile that didn't reach his eyes. "After the call came, he woke Jane and me to fill us in. So, we're half awake and freaking out, and Jane asked him how he missed something like *this*. He said he didn't—per Oz the Great and Powerful, he was fuzzy on the specifics, but he knew you needed to be back at North Lake. That it was, and I quote, 'vitally important' that you return. See, Janie called him after we dropped you off yesterday and suggested that you needed more time away, but he was adamant that you stay at school."

"He knew the place was going to catch fire?"

"I mean, he swore he didn't know it was going to be a *fire*, but maybe that's because I'd thrown him up against the wall and grabbed him by the neck."

"*Connor!*"

"What?" he replied, shrugging. "I don't give two shits who he is—no one makes pawns out of my family without full disclosure. Dude can be as mysterious as he likes when someone else's life is on the line."

"Did you hurt him?" I asked.

"Eh, probably just his pride. Think I startled him more than anything. Anyway, Janie's nominally working today, so I'm keeping an eye on you for now."

"I'm fine," I protested. "I mean, medicated, I guess, but I'm okay. You don't have to stick around."

"I want to," said Connor, and released my hand to pull the blankets back over me. "Someone needs to watch out for you, Maebe. I swear, as soon as I see our cousins again, I'm going to give them a *big* piece of my mind for leaving you like that."

"I told them to get out—"

"The little ones, sure, but Peter and Kyle at least should have stuck around to help. Sons of bitches," he muttered. "But don't worry about them for now. You just focus on feeling better, okay? I'm not going anywhere."

"Unless Diriem has you kicked out of the Pactlands," I replied, grinning at him.

He smiled back at me. "He knows I have Annie's number, so good luck with that."

As Connor finished tucking me in, carefully working around my IV, I asked, "What did the Forum decide? Did they tell you anything?"

"No vote yet," he said, settling back in his chair. "The fire last night put folks on edge, and now your friend's dad, what's his name…"

"Mirrik Voln?"

"Yeah, him. He's raising a stink because that's *his* kid's school that burned. Priorities," he added with a smirk. "Probably a good thing that Sage doesn't board, yeah?"

I grunted in agreement.

"But I did get an update from home," Connor continued. "Mark called in the GBI. Lord knows he needed to. Twenty-eight victims burned beyond recognition and a fire that *miraculously* didn't take out the whole county—"

"What's that?"

"Oh, GBI? Uh…reinforcements from the state. Investigators with more money, more personnel, and better tech."

"They're not going to be able to catch a dozen elves, though," I pointed out.

"No, but they might get a lead on whatever cars Ivari's people used. It's a long shot," he admitted. "Hard to spit in north Georgia without hitting an out-of-town car in the fall. Of course, I can't tell them that the perps probably have New York plates, but maybe they'll figure it out on their own." He sighed and rubbed his chin, which he hadn't bothered to shave that day. "Our informant wasn't quite sure of their cabins' location, which doesn't help. If I knew where they were based, I could plot probable driving routes to East Branch, and I might be able to suggest some security cameras to pull. But since the compound didn't have its own security system, we're blind about what went down."

"Except the farseers."

"I'm talking about the folks in Georgia. Can't exactly bring in a farsighted *elf* as a consultant. I tell you what," he said, "things were a hell of a lot simpler a year ago."

"Before Jane?"

He nodded, then hastily added, "Not that I'd do things differently. That woman's the best thing that ever happened to me, mitta. It's just…"

"A lot."

"Yeah."

Connor fell silent for a moment, and I asked, "Did Diriem tell you that East Branch was doomed? Even if we hadn't gone to Ivari?"

"He mentioned it. Doesn't help with all the guilt, but…it's something, I guess." He leaned back in his chair and held my gaze for a time, then cleared his throat. "Did you ever hear about the time your dad went fishing with my dad and me?"

"No…"

He chuckled. "So, I was maybe five, and Dad brought me out to East Branch for the day to teach me to fish, and some of the men decided to make an outing of it. Ed and Peter, Justin and Kyle, your grandpa and dad, and a few others. Well, I was a little kid, and your dad was, like, thirteen or fourteen, so naturally, he was cool and didn't want much to do with me."

I smiled at the thought.

"Long story short, I got really excited about casting, and I'd been trying to get close to James all morning, so I ended up hooking him in the hand. Freak shot. He *cried*," said Connor, laughing at the memory. "And then *I* cried, and when all was said and done, Dad took me to Dairy Queen."

"He never mentioned *anything* about that," I said.

"No surprise there."

I hesitated before asking, "Do you have any more stories about my dad? Or my mom?"

Connor nodded. "Sure, mitta," he said softly. "Get comfy."


**S**hortly after an aide brought my dinner tray that night—plus one for Connor, who'd been a fixture in my room all day—Jane called with an update.

"Two elves," she said, her voice distorted by the phone's speaker. "Ganti's sure of it, and the rest of his folks back him up."

As she explained it, North Lake had security cameras around the property, one of which had caught a rowboat approaching the beach in the middle of the night. While the boat wasn't the sort of craft to require registration, the camera had picked up a decent shot of one of the two occupants' faces, and Ganti and the backward-oriented farseers had gone to work. The faces were masks—nothing unusual there—but they hadn't been worn long, and the farseers were able to follow the masks' owners back in time until they revealed their true features. With that accomplished, they'd independently taken their findings to DOI's in-house team of sketch artists, and the descriptions of the two men they'd given had been too similar to discount. Portraits in hand, Diriem had called in Rose, who, though employed by DPP, was available for interagency loans. As her farsight showed her current events, Rose tracked the two men to work and stayed with them for a couple of hours, pulling together enough detail to allow the analysts at DOI to find their homes and send Laws to bring them in.

"They're low-level portal attendants," Jane told us. "Both work out at Kelomb."

"Where the heck is *that*?" Connor asked, leaning toward the phone, which he held between us.

"Rose says it's close to New Orleans."

"Huh. Party town?"

"No. Hall ti'Cren's mansion is out that way, but there's not much else of interest. Farmland," said Jane, and yawned. "Sorry, long day."

"I feel that, Firebug," he replied, "but at least we've got TV here."

"Yeah, yeah. Keep the volume low and let Maebe sleep."

Connor winked at me. "Yessum. Get some rest—I'll bunk here in the party suite."

"Uh-huh," she said dubiously. "Maebe, you keep an eye on him, got it?"

Jane and Connor said their goodbyes, and after she hung up, he turned his attention to his dinner tray. "So...looks like pasta," he said, lifting the lid over the plate. "Any idea why it's green?"

"Vegetables mixed in?" I guessed.

"Let's hope that's all it is. Bon appétit." He swirled up a forkful and took a tentative bite. "Not terrible...not great, either, but I've had worse..."

A knock at the door cut him off, and he got up to open it. "More of the good stuff?" he joked, obviously expecting one of the nurses with a fresh IV bag of potion for me.

Instead, Diriem stood outside the room, arms folded over his casual sweater—a turtleneck, I noticed, and wondered if Connor had left bruises. "Feeling better?" he asked, arching a brow at my cousin.

Connor stood his ground. "Kid's alive and doped. That's progress."

Diriem glanced past him and nodded at me. "Good. Do you suppose you and I might share a confined space without resorting to violence?"

He grunted. "What'd you have in mind?"

"Kabno says our suspects are inbound. I take it Jane's briefed you."

That wasn't a question.

"Yeah…"

"Well, Kabno's invited you to sit in on the interviews, considering that this could be germane to the East Branch fire investigation. I told her I'd pass along the offer."

"Appreciated, but I'm not leaving Maebe."

"I'm fine," I said, pushing aside my dinner. "Go, Connor. Who's going to hurt me in a *hospital*?"

The two men shared a long look.

"I've seen nothing about harm coming to her here," Diriem murmured.

"Not good enough," said Connor.

"Very well. In that case, Maebe can come with us."

"Uh…*no*. Have you seen her injuries? Because I—"

"She's been on healing potions all day, yes? And painkillers?" Looking at me again, Diriem asked, "How about it? Feel up to a drive?"

I floundered, briefly taken aback, then lifted my arm. "I'm kind of attached."

"That can be rectified. And you know you want to be there," he said to Connor. "Come on, we'll get her a pain potion for the road."

"They just brought dinner," said Connor. "She hasn't eaten much all day."

Diriem cut his eyes to the tray and grimaced. "Unless you're dying for some high-fiber pasta, we can do better."

Again, the two eyed each other in silence for a moment.

"I'm not apologizing," Connor told Diriem.

"I know."

"All right, then." Turning to me, he asked, "Want to go for a ride?"

Thus it was that ten minutes later, against the on-duty healer's advice, I walked out of the hospital in my yellow institutional pajamas and Connor's jacket, barefoot and carrying a vial of brown liquid that I'd been assured would dull my pain for a few hours. "I've got more at the house," Diriem told me as I gingerly buckled up. "And I *know* Laws has a stash. We can keep you comfortable."

"What's in that stuff, anyway?" asked Connor, sliding into the front passenger seat.

"A number of plants you wouldn't recognize," Diriem replied, hitting the ignition. "Yacovi could give you the full ingredient list. Now, if you were to get a proper education…"

"Don't start that shit right now, bub."

Diriem let it go, but when I met his eyes in the rearview mirror, a tiny smile flickered on his face and vanished before Connor could see.

# CHAPTER 14

"**Y**ou know," said Connor, clutching the door handle as Diriem wove through the downtown traffic, "you don't actually have to drive it like you stole it."

"Heh. I like that one," he replied, swerving past a delivery truck. "I'll need to remember that…"

"Seriously, if you don't have lights and sirens on this thing—"

"We're fine. Try not to soil yourself." Not taking his eyes from the road, he said, "Kabno wants to brief you before the interrogation begins. I think her plan is to slot you in."

"*Me?*"

"You've impressed her, especially considering your youth. Plus, you're something of a wild card."

"Meaning?"

"Laws has a good team," said Diriem, driving far too close to the sidewalk for my taste as he maneuvered. "Solid. They train their detectives well, and their interrogation methods are usually satisfactory. You haven't had that training, yet you had incredible luck with the ti'Pul boy. If I know Kabno, she's intrigued."

"Shoot," Connor muttered, "I don't do anything special. I wing it."

"Be that as it may, she's giving you another crack at this, so let's hope your luck holds. Personally, I agree with Pateme—you're too close to this case—but Laws isn't my agency, is it?"

A few minutes later, Diriem whipped into the DOL

parking garage, then headed for a reserved place near the bank of elevators. A black-clothed sorcerer approached as we climbed out, and Diriem hailed him with a wave. "You're our escort?"

"Yes, sir," he replied. "Though I was told to expect two…"

"It's three now," he said, and the escort didn't argue as he led us onto an elevator.

Giving me a once-over as we rose, the sorcerer quietly said, "Miss, do you need some shoes?"

"Please," I mumbled.

"And, uh…are those hospital—"

"If you could find something more substantial for her, that would be appreciated," Diriem interrupted, shutting down the questioning before it could ramp up.

We rode to the sixth floor, where Connor had previously interrogated our would-be kidnapper, and our escort led us to a windowless conference room set only with a long table, a handful of chairs, and a well-used coffeemaker in the corner. As we entered, Kabno, who'd taken a seat atop the table for want of a gnome-proportioned chair, glanced up and frowned. "What's Maebe doing here?" she asked. "I thought she was on the burn ward."

"Yes, ma'am," I said, hugging Connor's jacket more tightly around me. "We, uh…we left in a hurry."

"Couldn't have one without the other," Diriem explained.

"I see," she murmured, though her expression suggested deep misgivings. "Maebe, are you hurting?"

"A little," I admitted. "They sent me with a potion—"

"Drink it now before the last one wears off. I'm calling Canna Nerin," she said, hopping down from the table, "and as for the rest of you, brief Willow here."

The assembled were a mixed bunch: a male sorcerer, a female troll—judging by her skirt, at least—and a brown-skinned nymph of predictably indeterminate gender. They waited until the door closed behind the departing director, and then the troll motioned Connor closer. "You're the kid from outside, I presume," she said.

He extended a hand. "Connor Willow, Whitford Police."

"Apple Blossoms," she replied, her hand swallowing his as she gripped it. "Arson unit. That's Matti Chela, and this is Devva Hevannid," she continued, cocking her head toward the sorcerer and nymph in turn, "also in my unit. I understand you're connected to the elves in the basement."

Connor made a face. "And what a lovely crew they are. Who're the assholes on deck tonight?"

Snickering, Devva said, "Portal attendants, and more proof that we need to fire everyone at the Portal Authority and start over, but no one asks *my* opinion."

"Crooked bunch?"

The nymph paused to consider that—I supposed the translation wasn't exact—then nodded. "Let's just say their hiring standards are low."

"The ones on the internal portals aren't usually our biggest problem," Matti offered. "The external team, now...if you have enough money, you can get just about anything or any*one* in or out. Half my probationary cases were portal misuse, and that was fifty years ago."

"If you get him going about the attendants," Apple Blossoms interrupted, "we'll be here until morning. Now," she said as Matti mouthed an apology, "the two on the schedule are also elves. We've got them masked at North Lake—"

"Yeah, I heard that much from DOI," said Connor. "What do you know about them other than their employment?"

She looked at Devva, who pulled out their computer. "In room 615 is Talivol ti'Gata," they began. "Age two hundred seventeen. Single, no children. He's been on the portals for about a century, and aside from some minor vandalism as a youth, his record is clean. In room 627 is

Nugera ti'Van. He's a little younger—one hundred eighty-six—married, two children, one underage. Joined up on the portals around the time that ti'Gata did, but his record is spotless."

Connor nodded. "So, how do you go from a clean slate to arson?"

"Well," Devva replied, "in my experience, the right financial incentive can do wonders."

"And then there's my girlfriend," said Connor, chuckling, "who's got a bad habit of running off cretins by setting their houses on fire."

Matti laughed. "And with you in law enforcement?"

"Hey, vigilante arson brought us together, so I can't entirely fault her. All right," he said, rubbing a hand over his face in thought. "Obviously, you folks know the terrain a hell of a lot better than I do, so how can I help?"

"I want you in with Matti on ti'Van," said Apple Blossoms. "Devva and I will take ti'Gata, and once the director comes back, we'll start the show."

"Then I'll follow your lead," Connor said to the sorcerer. "Anyone have a notepad I could borrow?"

As Apple Blossoms and Matti stepped out to double-check the recording equipment for their interrogation rooms, Connor turned to Diriem and murmured, "What else do I need to know?"

Diriem arched an eyebrow. "You're asking me?"

"I'm not expecting prognostication. Do you know our suspects?"

One corner of his mouth quirked. "It may surprise you that I'm not familiar with every elf in the Pactlands."

"You know a shit ton more of them than I do," Connor said, then hesitated and added a quiet, "Please."

"Full truth, I don't know either of your suspects," Diriem replied. "There's no reason that I would. Different agencies, they're not upper management...and we run in rather different social circles."

My cousin frowned. "Explain."

"If I said, 'New Halls,' would you know what I meant?"

"Nope..." he began, then caught himself. "Hang on...Ganti mentioned something about that once. When Janie and I were out west..."

"Did he?"

"You may have been on the phone. That night's a little fuzzy."

Diriem allowed it with a muttered, "Mm. In brief, there was a time before the Pactlands when the Halls were actual fortifications. Those families who controlled them were the nobility, more or less, but within those fortifications lived groups of untitled people. They worked for us, farmed, helped defend us, and in turn, they had the protection of the Hall. Once we fled here, those untitled ones came together and decided they wanted Halls of their own. So, now we have the old Halls, the ones that preceded the Pact, and the new Halls like ti'Van and ti'Gata."

"Let me guess," said Connor, "new Halls don't get invited to the good parties?"

Though Diriem looked a little pained, he didn't deny it. "There's also a fair bit of money still concentrated in the old Halls. I'm not suggesting that everyone in the new Halls is destitute by any means, but the odds are better of finding individuals there with less...generational wealth, shall we say?"

"Uh-huh."

"If one were looking for a person perhaps susceptible to a bribe..." He shrugged. "Unfortunately, that's the best I can give you. I've seen nothing about these two, but Ganti's positive they're your culprits."

Connor gave Diriem a long look. "That would be Ganti *ti'Van*?"

"Best past-oriented farseer I've ever met," Diriem replied. "Without question. I trust his judgment."

"But he's still one of the little people, right? Like us?"

Diriem quietly sighed but held his temper. "Your family line runs to Hall ti'Ammaas. If you want to talk about aristocrats—"

"I am *solidly* middle-class," Connor interjected. "Public schools, community college, blue-collar job. Only reason I've got a decent house is because my parents up and died on me."

"What do you want me to say?"

"I don't know. But the longer I stick around here, the more—"

"You're not going to tell me with a straight face that yours is a perfect meritocracy, are you?" Diriem interrupted.

"No, but—"

To my relief, Kabno returned, cutting their discussion short before they could get truly testy. "Clothes are on the way for you," she told me, "and our healer says you're to keep pain *and* healing potions going down every four hours. She also said to tell you that you should be in a hospital bed right now, but since you're not, limit movement, keep hydrated, and do *not* pick at your bandages. Got all of that?"

"Yes, ma'am," I replied.

"Good. Come observe with me. Diriem, want to do me a favor and monitor 615?"

"As you like," he replied, then offered Connor a curt, "Good luck," and slipped out of the room.

Kabno glanced at Devva, who'd been quietly working on their computer in her absence. "Something I missed?"

"Kid was wading into class politics with Director ti'Dana," they replied without looking up.

She groaned. "Not tonight, *please*. Go on down the hall, Willow. We'll be watching."


The suspect Connor had been tasked with interrogating, Nugera ti'Van, was handsome enough in a twitchy sort of way. He was platinum blond like Yven, but he wore his hair long and plaited back, and he fiddled with the end of his braid as Matti asked him some general questions about his identity, address, and employment. But as the investigator proceeded to more pointed questions about the previous night, Nugera insisted he knew nothing. He was home, his wife would vouch for him, and he knew nothing about fires at schools in Beukal.

After nearly an hour with no progress, Matti rose, announcing he needed a cup of coffee. The others declined, and Matti saw himself out, leaving Connor and Nugera alone in the small room, facing each other across a narrow wooden table. A moment of awkward silence passed between them, and then Connor folded his hands on the tabletop. "So, confession time," he said almost conversationally. "I'm not with Laws."

Nugera's eyebrows, so pale they were nearly invisible against his skin, climbed. "You're with the Portal Authority?"

"Heh, no. Whitford Police Department. That's Whitford, Georgia," he explained when Nugera regarded him bemusedly. "Outside."

The elf jerked backward in his chair, then seemed to realize that Connor was sitting between him and the door—and more importantly, that the dampening potion someone had shot into his arm had eliminated his advantage. Collecting himself, he eyed Connor cautiously and asked, "Um...how, um...who..."

"Have you heard of East Branch?"

He nodded. "That's the place where the half-breeds live..." he began, then let that thought go as the pieces fell into place. "You...you're one of them?"

"Yeah. I figured the accent would be a giveaway. Don't hear Pactish drawled too often, do you?"

Nugera chuckled weakly. "No, I can't say that I do. Not to be rude, but what are you doing here?"

"Observing. This isn't my case," Connor replied. "Obviously, Beukal's *way* outside my jurisdiction. But about two weeks ago, someone set fire to East Branch. Destroyed the whole community."

"That's...very unfortunate."

"Well, I might have chalked it up to a cooking fire or a lightning strike but for the fact that everyone on the property was murdered around the time the fire was set. I was actually on the phone with one of them when she was shot."

My guts clenched, recalling my mother's panicked call, and as a breeze began to blow through my hair, Kabno reached over and squeezed my knee.

"I...I'm so sorry," said Nugera, a sliver of horror peeking through his cracking façade. "Heavens, that's..."

"More than half my family died," Connor continued in the same strangely calm tone. "All of the survivors except me are in school at North Lake. They live together in the dorm, see? So, when someone set the school on fire in the middle of the night..." He grimaced. "Once is a tragedy, twice is a pattern. I'm trying to figure out whether the people responsible for the North Lake arson are connected to the ones who wiped out East Branch."

Nugera said nothing, but he gnawed his lower lip.

"See, I just can't fathom who would want all of us dead," my cousin fibbed. "I lost a baby cousin at East Branch—he was only seven, and *God*, the photos are horrible—but a lot of those folks at home were older, you know, our parents and grandparents. The ones at North Lake...I mean, no one there is older than thirty-five, and some of them are parents to toddlers. Couple of two-year-olds living there."

Silence fell and stretched as the two men looked at each other, and Nugera broke first. "Were they hurt?" he murmured. "The younglings?"

"They made it out," said Connor. "I understand they were treated for smoke inhalation, and they may have lost some of their possessions, but they're alive. One of my cousins was able to push back the fire, give them an exit.

She's burned pretty badly, poor kid. The folks at the hospital put her on a schedule of pain potions." He sighed, then stood and headed for the door. "Man, I wish I knew *why*. Who gives a kill order on a bunch of children? Anyway, I'm having second thoughts about coffee—it's been a long day. Can I get you some? Glass of water?"

"Wait."

Connor froze, hand on the doorknob. "Sorry?"

"I…wait, please," he said, hunching into himself. "Uh…"

Nugera struggled, hemming and hawing, and Connor locked the door and took his seat. "It's all right," he soothed. "Something on your mind?"

The elf nodded slowly.

"In my neck of the woods, we say that confession's good for the soul. Don't know how you feel about that— hell, I don't know the first damn thing about elven theology," he said with a self-deprecating laugh—"but I always feel better once the weight's off. Because it weighs on you, doesn't it?"

"Yes," Nugera whispered.

"What do you want to tell me?"

He hesitated, but after a long pause, his wall finally broke. "I didn't know what we were supposed to do. Talivol was the contact person."

"That's it," Kabno murmured, staring at the window between our rooms. "*That's* it, don't lose him…"

"Let's back up," said Connor, opening his pen. "Walk me through this. Who's Talivol?"

"Talivol ti'Gata. We work together. Laws arrested him, too—I heard him being brought in when they were processing me tonight."

"Uh-huh," he muttered, and began making notes. "He's a friend of yours?"

"I've always thought so. Talivol…sometimes, he walks a little close to the edge, if you know what I mean, but he's been good to me."

"I'm following," Connor replied. "Was it his idea to set North Lake on fire?"

"No," said Nugera. "We were hired."

"Hired?" he echoed. "By whom?"

"I don't know…I can only tell you what Talivol told me. He's the one who dealt with them. Talivol just came to me a few days ago and asked if I wanted to make some easy money. He had an opportunity…"

"Are things a little tight?" Connor asked, rubbing his fingers together.

"Not particularly. My wife and I make decent money, more than enough to support our family. But my son, our older child…" Again, Nugera floundered before blurting, "He's in love with a woman *far* too high for him."

Connor winced in sympathy. "You know, my girl-friend's way out of my league—"

"She's mainline ti'Dir," he said, his face twisting. "A very nice young lady, we have no problem with her. But she's accustomed to a certain *standard*, see, and my boy can't give her that. Not as an entry-level banker. So, my wife and I have been supporting him, giving him what we can spare, but I'm no match for Lord ti'Dir, and we've got our little girl coming up to think about…"

"You wanted to help your boy."

He nodded miserably. "I just want him to be happy. Like I said, Talivol came to me earlier this week. He…he said he'd been contacted by a ti'Cren—someone from Silver's organization."

My blood chilled. Was *Teolm* behind the fire?

Connor paused in his notes and glanced up at Nugera, perplexed. "Sorry, I don't know who Silver is…"

"Old Lord ti'Cren," Nugera explained. "He was dealing in black-market potions and worse on the side. I heard rumors that a full quarter of the attendants on the external portals were working with him before he was arrested. Guess the organization is still carrying on without him, or maybe he's directing things from the penal farm, because one of their people offered Talivol a job."

"Okay." He resumed writing again. "This ti'Cren contact, was it Teolm? He's short, brown hair—"

Nugera shook his head. "Oh, definitely not. Teolm ti'Cren heads that Hall now because he *wasn't* working for his father."

"*Ah*. Good to know."

"You really are from outside, aren't you?"

Connor smirked. "Want to talk about the Gottis?"

"The who?"

"Exactly. So, if it wasn't Teolm, who approached Talivol? And what was the job offer?"

"I don't know which ti'Cren it was," Nugera replied, sounding almost apologetic. "There are quite a few of them, and if Talivol knew the messenger's true name, he didn't tell me. In any case, the ti'Cren was masked."

"Masked?" Connor repeated.

"Uh...you know, using a little magic to change your appearance—"

"Oh, yeah, I'm aware of *that*. But how was the ti'Cren masked?"

"He looked like a sorcerer. Put on a weird fake accent, too—completing the disguise, I suppose. The average sorcerer never gets an Elvish accent right—"

"Weird how?" Connor interrupted.

All Nugera could do was shrug. "Difficult to describe, but it sounded laughably odd. Almost unintelligible at times."

"You met him, then?"

"Once. Talivol brought me to him the night before the...the job," he mumbled. "For instructions. He gave Talivol money and said we'd have the rest on completion."

He grunted. "So, what was the job?"

"Neither of them told me," Nugera insisted. "Talivol just said it was simple, and he wanted to bring me in because he knew I could use it. I thought we'd be delivering messages or not logging a portal crossing or some such, but yesterday afternoon, he told me we'd be going to Beu-kal after dark. I didn't know the plan until we were halfway across the lake."

Connor hèld the miserable elf's gaze. "And you went along with it?"

"I…I thought we were sending a warning. No one said anything about babies…"

As my cousin finished taking notes, I said, "Laws can catch the ti'Cren, right? If DOI finds the meeting and trails him until he takes his face off…"

"Perhaps, perhaps not," Kabno replied. "A number of the ti'Crens are accustomed to taking the blinding potion for privacy, *especially* the ones involved in Silver's enter-prise. It's possible that the farseers won't be able to see him at all…*if* he's even a ti'Cren. That business with the fake accent bothers me."

A thought hit me like a thunderclap. "What if it's not fake?"

"Come again?"

"You heard the ti'Pul guy, right? The one Connor in-terviewed? They're all from New York."

Kabno frowned. "Connor seemed to have no trouble understanding him."

"Because they spoke English together. The New York bunch speaks *High* Elvish," I said. "Diriem said it's an old-er version of what the elves here speak, and not all of the words are the same. So, take that, maybe put a New York accent with it…"

"Damn it," she muttered, and rose. "Stay here. I'm go-ing to retrieve Connor."

Soon, Kabno returned to our viewing room with Con-nor and Matti, who'd extended his coffee break to watch a video feed of both interrogations from another room on the floor. "Ti'Gata hasn't cracked yet," Matti reported. "And I didn't mean to abandon you, kid—I just didn't want to interrupt."

Connor waved him off. "Not my first rodeo, but

thanks. What's up?" he asked Kabno. "Ti'Van and I are getting somewhere."

"Maebe had an idea," she replied, and nodded to me.

"What if the guy who hired them is one of Ivari's people?" I said, hoping Connor wouldn't start laughing at me. "Think about it: a stranger with a weird accent, masked as a sorcerer—"

"And sorcerers look human," he finished. "If you've never been outside and don't recognize an American accent—"

"Not just American. They only speak High Elvish, remember?"

He smiled and pointed at me. "There it is. Good catch, mitta. So, what would you suggest?" he asked, turning to Kabno. "If you want to bring up ti'Pul…"

"Why don't you show your suspect pictures from Rush and Sons?" I blurted.

All three looked at me that time. "What pictures?" Connor asked.

"From their…what's it called, website? They've got pictures of employees all over it. Annie might still have printouts from our trip there."

"Hold that thought." Pulling out his phone, he asked, "Can I get online from…huh. Okay, that works…"

"That's a phone from outside, yes?" said Kabno. "You can't access out local net with that—not without some modifications—but yes, you should be able to pick up a signal."

"I'm in." He tapped briefly, then showed me the screen. "This is the company, right? That's our boy?"

Ivari's masked face smiled back at me—a handsome man in a dark suit with barely graying brown hair and the greenish-brown eyes I knew far too well. "That's him," I muttered.

"Let's see what else is lurking in About Us…and *jackpot*," he said, his smile turning almost predatory. "Ooh, look at all the pretty corporate headshots…excuse me," he said, and hurried out of the room without waiting for leave.

Kabno, Matti, and I watched through the window as Connor returned to the interrogation room, phone in hand. "Sorry about that," he said to Nugera. "I've got a few pictures I'd like you to look at, see if you recognize anyone. Would you mind?"

"Um…sure," he replied, resigned. "On that?"

"Yeah. Just scroll down the page and see if anything pops out at you," said Connor, handing over his phone.

Nugera took his time, considering the pictures of besuited men and women, then sat up a little straighter. "That's him," he said, flipping the phone back to Connor. "The one with the green scarf."

"The tie, you mean?" Connor looked at the image. "You're sure?"

"Absolutely. Either him or someone wearing the same mask."

"Well, taking the simpler approach, that means our supposed ti'Cren is Harry Cedar, Communications Manager at Rush and Sons."

"What's that?" Nugera asked.

"That would be the firm in Manhattan that my ancestors founded. Looks like your contact didn't tell you the truth," said Connor, "since that group has kept to themselves for the last few centuries. Whoever this Harry Cedar really is, I doubt he's a ti'Cren."

By the time Connor had obtained a signed statement from Nugera, Diriem had joined us in the viewing room. "He's good," he murmured as the guards outside the door prepared to take Nugera back to the holding cells. "No luck yet with ti'Gata."

"Ti'Van's given us enough to take them both down," said Kabno. "But that's not the biggest issue tonight."

"No?"

She shook her head as he sat. "They were hired to set the school on fire, and their contact claimed to be part of

Silver's organization. Turns out he's one of Ivari's."

Diriem blew out a long breath. "Question one. How'd he get in?"

"Precisely. Question two is his true identity. Ti'Van identified him in a picture, but that's obviously listed with a fake name."

"Question three," said Diriem. "How does Ivari know about Silver, much less how to recruit here?"

Kabno held his stare. "You think Inade's wrapped up in this?"

"I don't know, but a visit might be prudent."

At that, Connor walked in and handed the statement to Kabno. "All yours, ma'am. I need five minutes with ti'Pul."

"Doable," she replied. "In person or via phone?"

"Call him if you want. This won't take long."

In truth, it took about ten minutes to get Culta ti'Pul into a secure room for the phone call, and the rest of us gathered around the speaker as a guard confirmed he was present. "Hey, it's Connor Willow," my cousin began, slipping into English. "Sorry to bother you after hours."

"It's no bother," said Culta. "Either this or television, and I can't understand the programs, so…what's up?"

"Harry Cedar. Know the name?"

"Sure. Heads Comms at the firm. He's the PR guy."

"Who is he really?"

Culta chuckled. "I mean…he *is* the PR chief, but you want his true name?"

"Yup."

"Hemell ti'Vanil," he said without hesitation. "He's a little younger than me."

"So…he's not one of the original seventeen?" Connor asked.

"No. His parents are—Hudo ti'Vanil and Penti ti'Jan—but Hemell's native-born. Should something happen to his father, he's the heir to what's left of Hall ti'Vanil, if that matters to you. Came with us to Georgia two weeks back."

"Got it." Leaning closer to the phone, he asked, "Does the name 'Silver' mean anything to you? Or...what was it?"

"Inade ti'Cren," Diriem offered.

"Yeah, him," said Connor. "Ring any bells?"

After a moment's silence, Culta said, "Silver, no. I've heard of Hall ti'Cren, but only historically."

"What about 'Silver'?" asked Diriem, repeating the name in Pactish.

"No, never. But look, I told you I'm on the periphery of the firm. All I do is maintain the website. If your guy's come to see Father or Hemell, I wouldn't know unless they deigned to tell me."

"Thanks," Connor replied, then quietly asked Kabno in Pactish, "Is anyone going to give those four language potions, or what?"

She shrugged. "I have my doubts that the other three would take it, but if ti'Pul wants one, we could do that."

"Hey, Culta?" Connor said. "You there?"

"Hard to go anywhere with guards on the door, man."

"Do you want a language potion? You might puke your guts out for a couple days, but it'll let you understand the TV."

"Huh. You're offering?"

"The director's here, and she says you can have it if you want it."

Culta paused, then said, "That might not be a bad idea. I can handle a little puke. And, uh...thanks."

As Connor hung up, he asked, "What's the next step?"

"I suggest we sleep on it tonight," said Kabno. "Give the farseers a few hours off before we drag them in again. In the morning, we'll have a word with Inade. You're welcome to come," she added, patting Connor's arm. "Frankly, I think you should."

"Appreciate that. And, uh...I hate to ask, but is there a couch or something here I can crash on?"

Kabno's brow knit. "Couches, cots, absolutely. We

have space. But I thought you were staying with him," she said, cocking her head toward Diriem.

The two men regarded each other awkwardly, and Diriem spoke first. "If you'd rather camp here, I certainly understand, but I'd appreciate it if you spent another night in Viratta. There's a matter we should discuss...and I'll have you back here tomorrow whenever Kabno wants to set off."

Though Connor's eyes narrowed, he nodded. "All right, then. If you insist."

Kabno looked back and forth between them, but as neither volunteered more, she shrugged and moved on. "I'm going to 615 to relieve Apple Blossoms and Devva," she said, heading toward the door. "Matti, would you please escort our guests out?"

# CHAPTER 15

For the second time that night, I eased myself into the back of Diriem's Mercedes, moving as carefully as I could against the leather seat. Despite the potions in my system, my skin was tight and sore to the touch, and all I really wanted was to slide between sheets and stop moving.

To my relief, Diriem drove at a reasonable speed, making his way through the Thursday-night quiet of District 2's blocks of largely empty office buildings toward the internal portals. Connor sat beside him up front, silent and, if his eyes were any indication, exhausted.

We'd pulled up at a traffic light when Connor, tired enough to slip back into English, said, "Well?"

Diriem didn't answer him until we were moving again. "I owe you two an apology."

"Oh?" he replied, clearly unconvinced.

"Yes. Not for everything, but…"

After he fell silent, Connor said, "I'm listening."

We'd covered another two blocks before Diriem spoke. "I'm not sorry for sending Maebe back to school. That was the right choice, no matter what you may think of it."

Connor sputtered, then jutted one hand toward the back seat. "Have you *seen* her? That kid is covered in bandages because—"

"She's alive, and so are your other cousins. Had I handled matters differently, we'd have had a rather different outcome." With a soft sigh, he stopped at another red light and leaned his arm against the window. "Farsight is as much a curse as it is a talent. Past orientation isn't so bad, and Rosie seems to have adjusted to her gift, but for those of us on the future side, the *strong* ones, about one in three eventually commits suicide. I'm not telling you this as a ploy for sympathy," he continued, "but by way of explanation. We have a code of ethics we live by. It's ancient, far older than the Pactlands, though we've certainly codified the old rules. The one that matters here is that we must set aside our own concerns and guide events toward the most beneficial outcome."

"Play God, in other words," said Connor.

"It might seem that way," Diriem allowed, "but if we're gods, we're pitiful examples. It's one thing to say you need to choose the best path forward, but when five people have different views on what's best and no one has all the facts…" Again, he sighed, then started with the blue light. "We try. For all of our failings, we try. It's a charge we take seriously, you understand. So…almost inevitably, at some point, we're confronted by a situation involving people close to us. Friends, family, colleagues. The best way forward involves them in some way, often to their detriment, but *we can't warn them.* We can't interfere based on selfish desires to protect people we care about." With a weak, mirthless chuckle, he said, "I sat back and let my son kill himself, but Caradin knew what was coming. He was a farseer, too. But neither of us warned his daughter about the car accident that would kill her and her husband. It would have been easy enough to avoid, and I'm sure Rosie would have preferred to have her parents alive," he said bitterly, "but we'd run the variables, and the only way that didn't end with *Rosie* dying and Inade continuing to get away with his crimes was to say nothing. So, I didn't warn her. I walked out of my granddaughter's life when her father died, and I never spoke to her again."

"*Fuck*," Connor muttered. "That's—"

"Cruel? Psychopathic? Monstrous? I've heard it all. There's truth in it. And because this is the sort of calculus we make, farseers are…not popular people. We're respected, perhaps a little feared, but not the sort with hundreds of friends because anyone who knows what we do also knows that we'll let them walk off a cliff without a word of warning if the greater good demands it."

"You've got friends," I pointed out.

Diriem nodded. "I do, but very few of the people in my orbit are what I would truly consider friends. We tend to cling to our own kind because we're the only ones who really understand, so..." He slowed for a motorcycle to pass, then said, "Connor, you mentioned Ganti tonight. No, I don't generally socialize with him in formal situations because for good or ill, there's still a hierarchy among the Halls, and we don't tend to receive invitations to the same events. But I'd consider him more of a friend than virtually any of my so-called peers."

The portal building appeared on the horizon, glowing in the darkness, and Diriem made his approach. "All of this is to tell you that I knew Maebe was going into danger by returning, and I wouldn't have done things differently."

"Right," Connor snapped, "because the best possible outcome is Maebe covered in burns."

"Actually, yes."

"The fuck did you—"

"If she hadn't returned," he said over Connor's rising voice, "the rest of your family would have died. The specifics were hazy, but *that* was abundantly clear in every vision I had."

That shut Connor up for the moment, but I wasn't satisfied. "You could have warned me," I said from behind him.

"If I had, you probably wouldn't have survived the fire."

"Huh?"

"Your talent is strengthening, but it's still underdeveloped, as is your control. Ganti said that what you managed was nearly miraculous, and the only reason you were able to pull it off was because fear fueled you. Had you been warned to expect it…"

"I wouldn't have been so panicked," I finished.

"But you could have done *something*," Connor protested. "Put security on the school, warn the staff—"

"Farsight seldom means perfect clarity," said Diriem, "especially when events are close at hand and the outcome is flexible. I didn't know it would be arson, and I couldn't have named the precise date, but every option I explored ended in death unless Maebe returned unaware of the danger. So, yes, I allowed her to walk into potential peril, but that was only to save the rest of your kin."

The car fell quiet while Diriem got in line at the portal building, aiming for the lane at the far end for Viratta. Finally, Connor said, "You know, if you'd mentioned half of this sooner, I might not have tried to choke you quite so hard."

"You're not the first to express your displeasure by physical means," Diriem replied, and pointedly tugged at his turtleneck with one finger. "Also, you should know that had you held on much longer, I'd have thrown you down the hall and probably broken a few bones, so…fair warning, hmm?"

Connor snorted. "Was that meant to be the apology?"

"No. Hold on, let me do this…"

Once we'd passed through the portal and Diriem had driven out into the quiet of Viratta, he said, "I don't apologize for what I did in not warning Maebe, but I *do* apologize for how it was perceived."

"What do you mean?" I asked.

"Well…you've not had the warmest of receptions here," he said, his voice low, "and the Forum's continued reluctance to offer Connor help must make certain attitudes rather apparent. This notion that you're lacking in some respects."

"You'd noticed, huh?" Connor said.

"That, and you brought up Hall standing earlier tonight, and…" He paused, choosing his words. "I didn't keep my mouth shut because I think your lives aren't important, that you're 'little people' to be sacrificed as needed. Quite the contrary. If I gave you that impression, I'm sorry."

"So," said Connor, "what you're telling us is that the assholery is an equal-opportunity feature?"

"Absolutely. Also, Maebe, I've got plenty of pain potions at home, and if those don't let you sleep, how about a sedative?"

"Thanks," I murmured.

"Of course."

We'd nearly reached the long driveway up to the mansion when Connor said, "I still think you're a dick for not warning Maebe."

"That's fair," Diriem replied. "But I *did* have reasons, and the rest of your family survived—"

"I ain't blessing this, man."

"Agree to disagree?"

Connor huffed. "Fine."

The winding pathway glowed blue ahead of the car as we drove up to the house. "Incidentally," said Diriem, "I wouldn't be surprised if Kabno offered you a job, Connor. She's impressed."

"Is that meant to be forewarning?"

"No, that's common sense and experience. But if you're looking for something larger than Whitford…"

"I made a commitment to Whitford," Connor replied.

"And I appreciate that. She will as well. Still…don't be shocked if she comes recruiting," he said, and tapped the button to open the massive garage door.

With a grunt, Connor said, "I'm nothing special."

"Again, agree to disagree…but that's a matter for daylight. Let's get Maebe to bed."

And that, at least, I could heartily agree with.


Kabno seemed surprised when I walked into the DOL

lobby with Connor and Diriem the next morning. "Mae-be?" she asked, briskly striding our way. "I thought you'd be in *bed*, girl."

The last was said with a stern glance up at Diriem, whose face betrayed nothing.

"They tried," I replied. "I'm fine."

The look she gave me insisted that she knew a lie when she heard one, but she didn't order me out the door. In truth, Connor and Jane had checked on me all night, keeping me well drugged and comfortable enough to sleep. Jane had helped me change my bandages that morning, and while my skin was still angry and raw in places, I could see the potions' progress in the healing at the burns' edges. Clean, fed, and nicely numbed, I'd refused to be left behind—and since I was the one who'd actually been injured, the others didn't fight me.

Besides, as the only clothing I had at the moment was the black T-shirt and pants I'd been loaned from the DOL storage rooms the night before, I was appropriately dressed for the trip out to the penal farm. Kabno nearly matched me, Diriem had gone casual, and when Teolm arrived a few minutes later, he was sporting a long-sleeved gray T-shirt stained in six places and a pair of similarly ruined jeans. "What?" he asked as the directors gave him a once-over. "It's *clean*. There's nothing reactive on these."

Only Connor had put effort into his attire, and while he'd opted for his ordinary uniform instead of the dress version, he looked far more presentable than Teolm did.

With five of us on the trip, Teolm bummed a ride with Kabno, whose massive SUV included a fold-down stepladder to get her into the modified driver's seat. She led our short convoy out of the garage and into the overcast morning, then straight toward the internal portals.

Inade ti'Cren was housed at the penal farm near Cavimet, a little town roughly in the middle of nowhere, and so it took us several rounds of increasingly more remote portals to make it out. As we drove through the rolling countryside, I saw that most of the wide fields had been harvested and left to rest for the coming winter—all but a few cornfields and a plot of sprawling green vines. Noticing those, Connor asked, "Pumpkin patch?"

"They're good for eating," Diriem replied. "You sound surprised."

"They seem small for this late in the season…"

"Because those are food, not decoration. The massive ones you produce aren't nearly as palatable. *Why* you waste the resources on growing those, I'll never understand," Diriem muttered.

"Clearly, someone has never carved a pumpkin."

"Because it's pointless."

"Who hurt you?" Connor retorted, then spotted the shimmering air between the road and a wide patch of fields up ahead. "Whoa. What's that?"

"That," said Diriem, "is the boundary fence of Cavimet Farm. Slightly prettier than barbed wire, yes?"

"And probably more effective, I'm guessing. What happens if you run into it?"

"Think 'high-voltage shock.' There's an access road," he added before Connor could protest. "I wasn't planning to kill us all today."

Kabno pulled up to the guard shack at the perimeter first and was quickly waved through a widening hole in the fence, as were we. I spotted a few brown-clothed inmates picking corn, then another group shaking apples down in a small orchard.

"Those guys have all been dosed with the dampening potion, right?" Connor murmured, eyeing the workers as we drove past.

"Naturally. But in case of a riot, be aware that there's no way to, say, dampen a headbutt from a faun," Diriem reminded him. "Don't get sloppy in here."

"Are riots common?"

"No."

"Are you *anticipating* one?" he pressed.

"No."

"Would you tell us if you were?"

Diriem didn't even look away from the road. "Possibly."

As on our previous visit, we parked in a remote lot and were ferried to the gray stone central building via glorified golf cart. Our driver, a faun, gave Connor an appraising look but kept his mouth shut, and Connor volunteered nothing but his thanks for the lift. As before, Kabno led us past the offices to the visitation room, but this time, there were two black-clothed sorcerers on duty outside, one sitting with a computer and the other standing with a thick baton hanging at her hip.

"Ma'am," said the standing guard, nodding to Kabno. "The inmate is waiting and under guard within."

"Thank you, Officer," she replied. "Has he been difficult of late?"

"No, ma'am," she replied, "but in light of the recent arson…Superintendent's orders."

The director smiled up at her. "I see word's flown from Beukal."

"Not to me, ma'am, but—"

"Oh, no need to explain. I know how the gossip lines run." With that, she pushed open the door to the visitation room, and the rest of us followed.

The room was no homier on my repeat visit, still windowless and illuminated with overhead lights so strong that they almost made me squint. Sitting at one of the round tables was Inade, who appeared much as he had over the summer: brown ponytail, a few days' worth of brown stubble, and a deep tan from his time in the fields. Only his uniform had changed, the shirt having been swapped for one with long sleeves due to the cooler weather. Two more guards stood against the walls, outwardly relaxed but attentive. That they were a troll and a centaur was no great shock to me, considering the influence the ti'Cren name apparently still wielded among the elven set.

Seeing us, Inade sighed and planted his chin on his fist. "To what do I owe the pleasure *this* time?"

"Good morning to you, too, Father," said Teolm, pulling out a chair.

"Nice of you to dress up."

"I've worn worse to the office," he replied, and smiled as Inade scowled. "You remember Maebe, don't you?"

Inade eyed me and snorted. "The half-breed ti'Ammaas girl? Back for more, youngling? And who're you?" he asked, glancing up at Connor. "Or *what* are you, I suppose I should be asking."

Connor cut his eyes to Kabno, who replied with the faintest of nods. "Good morning, sir," he said, taking the chair directly in front of Inade, who watched with a faint smirk. "My name is Connor Willow. I'm the chief of police for the town of Whitford."

"Willow," he echoed, then chuckled low in his throat. "That wouldn't have any relation to ti'Catama, would it?"

"You speak English?"

"It's useful on occasion, and you didn't answer my question."

Connor shrugged. "Yes, I'm descended from that Hall…and ti'Ammaas, ti'Pul…what others?" he asked, looking up at Diriem.

"All of the survivors," he replied, taking a chair at the next table over with Kabno. "You and Maebe both."

"Voila," Connor told Inade. "But we're not here about my pedigree—"

"Are you masked?" he interrupted.

He gritted his teeth but kept his cool. "No. I had plastic surgery for the cifyent."

Inade tutted. "Wanted to look like *them* that badly?"

"Well, I was an infant, so I didn't get a say in the matter. If you're finished, mind if I ask a few questions?"

He looked at the silent directors, then back at Connor. "Laws is outsourcing now…Chief, was it?" he asked with more than a hint of mockery.

Connor didn't take the bait. "No, actually, this is a co-operative endeavor. Multi-agency situation, you understand. See, I've got an investigation in Georgia that appears to involve some folks here, and they claim to be working with you."

That got Inade's attention. "*Me?*" he said, and looked past Connor at Kabno. "Whatever you think this is, I have nothing to do with it. My record here is clean. If you—"

"Whoa, now, hold on," said Connor, motioning him down. "Why don't I tell you what's going on, and maybe you can fill in some gaps for me."

He sat back and folded his arms, a look of deep suspicion on his face. "Start talking."

I suspected that Connor knew exactly what he was doing when he pulled a small notebook from his pocket and took a moment to flip through it.

"Two weeks ago tonight," he began, "a little more than half of my extended family was murdered. The forensics I've seen show that all were shot, though it's difficult to say *what* shot them, as the bodies and the entire community were badly burned. Not a lot of damaged tissue to work with, see?"

A muscle in Inade's jaw twitched, but he didn't respond.

"While that was happening, four individuals broke into a house where Maebe and I were staying two towns over. We didn't see them, but all four were speaking High Elvish, so you do the math."

"Ivari's people," said Inade. "There's no one in my organization who would use that language. It's uncommon here."

"Well, you're right that they're Ivari's crew, since all four are currently in DOL's custody, and one's decided that their odds are better as a witness for the prosecution."

His thick eyebrows drew together. "On what grounds is Laws—"

"The house they broke into belongs to a grower."

"*Oh*," he muttered, followed by a quiet, "Idiots," in High Elvish.

"Could have made a cleaner job of it," Connor concurred. "Anyway, very early yesterday morning, two guys set Maebe's school on fire, and they managed to hit the wing where the *rest* of my family was sleeping. That's why the poor kid here is all bandaged."

"I'd wondered," said Inade, staring at the wrapping on my cheek, then frowned. "Is that one of *my* pendants?"

"It's Maebe's now," Teolm cut in, "seeing as you have no use for it."

He grunted. "You know, girl, you *could* mask your injuries. Look less freakish."

"Didn't feel like it," I muttered, staring back at him.

"Then why is that pendant being wasted on you?"

"Give her a break," his son snapped. "She held back the fire *by herself*, with about six weeks of training, and I know she's still hurting."

He waved off Teolm's protestations and focused on Connor. "So, where do I fit into this mess of yours?"

Connor made a point of glancing through his notes again. "DOI and Laws found the culprits, and one of them started talking last night. Both are portal attendants, and I understand that you have a nasty little habit of putting those folks on your payroll."

Inade smirked. "That's it?"

"Not quite. See, the explanation I heard from our suspect is that a ti'Cren hired them to torch the school."

"And you think I authorized this?"

"Well, since Teolm here is more interested in plants than in organized *fucking* crime…"

"I had no hand in this." He cleared his throat, then asked, "Who was the ti'Cren, anyway?"

"That's the fun part," said Connor, leaning closer to him. "Evidence suggests that the supposed ti'Cren is actually a ti'Vanil. One of the younger ones, I mean. Doesn't look like he changed his mask from the one he uses day to day, and since our suspect said he was difficult to understand at times—"

"High Elvish," Inade finished.

"Uh-huh. Plus whatever accent he's picked up in Manhattan in the last couple of centuries. So, tell me," he said, "how did one of Ivari's guys get into the Pactlands, and why was he using *your* name?"

Inade looked to his stone-faced son, then turned back to Connor. "I have no idea. Honestly, I'll swear by whatever you like. This was nothing of my doing, and if someone's passing himself off as a ti'Cren, take it up with Teolm—I know nothing of this."

Connor nodded. "And if Laws were to pull your phone records?"

"There's nothing in them. Those calls are recorded, anyway—if I were trying to work from here, I'd be a fool to use those lines."

"Mm. So, you're telling us that if those nice folks over there were to flip your cell," he said, pointing to the silent guards, "they wouldn't find a bonus phone hiding in the mattress?"

"Absolutely not."

"Okay." He paged through his notebook once more, then said, "Well, that's a start. Guess the next step is to figure out who's trying to cash checks on your account, so, uh…." He pushed back his chair. "Thank you for your time."

"You believe me, yes?" Inade demanded.

Connor paused and stared down at him. "Should I?"

"I don't want to be stuck in this hell any longer than I have to be," he replied, agitated. "Whatever happened outside and at that school of yours, it has nothing to do with me."

"I'll take that into consideration," said Connor. "Anything else you can think of that might help?"

Inade looked back at him for a long moment, then

murmured, "You have his eyes, you know."

"Whose?"

"Deriap ti'Catama's. Dark with thick lashes…they seemed almost girlish, as I recall."

My cousin shrugged. "Lucky me, then."

"I suppose you're not too fond of him, seeing as he's trying to kill you."

At that, Connor chuckled. "Deriap? Nah."

"He's been dead for better than two centuries," Diriem offered, "at least to hear Ivari tell it. Deriap's the only one of them who wanted to go back for the children they abandoned, and Ivari couldn't have that."

Inade smirked. "So…*this* is the best of Hall ti'Catama, then? Chief here? A country boy playing cop?"

Before Diriem could answer that, Connor said, "You're right, I'm not overly impressive. But unlike you, bub, I get to walk out of here, so…" He grinned impishly. "You take care, now."

Connor started for the exit, and I hastily got up from the table to follow him. Before we reached the door, Inade called, "He won't stop until he kills you."

I stiffened, and Connor glanced back. "Ivari?"

"He's stubborn. Tenacious. And if *that* girl can claim Hall ti'Ammaas, then he'll wipe you out. I guarantee it."

"You sound so heartbroken at the thought," said Connor, crossing his arms.

"I mean, I pity him. Bad enough that there's a half-breed with a claim to my Hall—how many does Ivari have, again?"

"Could be as many as twenty-two, none of whom have done a damn thing to him."

Considering the state in which I'd left Ivari's office, I thought that wasn't entirely accurate, but I held my tongue.

"You exist," said Inade. "That's insult enough."

"None of us asked to be born," I said.

"Then you have nothing to lose if he rectifies the situation."

Connor turned to Teolm, who seemed poised to protest, and muttered, "Damn, dude, you grew up with that
shit?"

He grunted as he stood. "You see why I don't visit?
Goodbye, Father," he said, glancing down at Inade. "Try
to be a good boy, won't you?"

Inade's response was in Low Elvish, the sort of idio-
matic phrase that translated poorly but was without a
doubt profane.

"Lovely. I'll tell Rose you said hi," Teolm added, and
swept out of the room.


**N**ot until we were driving through the boundary fence did
it truly hit me that with my granddad and dad gone, I was
next in line to Ivari for Hall ti'Ammaas—and that fact was
reason enough for him to kill everyone I loved.

Sitting in the back of Diriem's car, I started to tear up
but tried to hide it. Unfortunately, I couldn't subtly sniffle,
and Connor turned around to check on me. "Mitta?" he
asked, brow knitting. "You okay?"

"Fine," I lied.

"Inade blusters because that's the best he can do," said
Diriem. "Don't let him bother you."

"Yeah," said Connor, "guys like that are all talk and—"

Diriem's ringing phone interrupted him, and Connor
gestured toward the console.

The call was coming from Kabno, who spoke over the
low hum of her SUV's engine and the road noise. "My
analyst just called me," she announced. "Connor, you've
got decent instincts."

"How so?" he asked.

"Well, before we left today, I asked for an examination
of the prison phone records."

"Ooh," said Connor with a little smile, "did someone
lie to my face?"

"Not quite. Inade was telling the truth—his calls are

clean. But I also had his incarcerated *children's* calls pulled, and apparently, there have been some questionable conversations between his son Jomin and Jomin's wife."

"I should have known better than to trust Dania," Teolm muttered over the line.

"It's nothing blatant," Kabno continued, "but my people think some of these calls have the hallmarks of coded communications. So, how do we want to play this? Shall we pay Jomin a visit?"

"Where is he?" Diriem asked.

"Eonu," said Teolm. "Last I heard, at least."

Connor frowned and whispered, "Where's that?"

"Minnesota, but also *several* portals from here," Diriem whispered back, then raised his voice to speak to the other vehicle. "I've got a better idea. Let me call Ganti."

"Is he up to this?" asked Kabno. "I know the farseers had quite the rush yesterday…"

"Such is the job," he replied. "I'll call him. Surely he's conscious by now."

After he hung up, Diriem quickly dialed another number. Three rings later, a groggy male voice croaked in Low Elvish, "Boss?"

"I'm inbound from Cavimet," said Diriem. "Want to guess who's with me?"

I heard a brief silence from the other end, and then Ganti said, "Please tell me you didn't break anyone out."

"Nah, it's just Maebe and me," said Connor, slipping into English. "What's up?"

He groaned. "Connor, don't make me translate before my coffee brews, eh?"

Switching to Low Elvish, he said, "Rise and shine. Want to spy on some ti'Crens?"

That seemed to make him perk. "*Which* ti'Crens? And how far back are we talking? Anyone working for Inade was protected until their arrest."

"Caffeinate," said Diriem. "I'll send you the details once we reach the office."

Ganti hesitated, then asked, "Should I expect this to be an all-day affair?"

"I...would wear something comfortable, were I you."

And though Ganti didn't complain, his weary grunt told me he knew *exactly* what that meant.

# CHAPTER 16

**A**round six-thirty that night, as I lounged in front of one of Diriem's televisions in a pair of pajamas I'd borrowed from Jane, Ganti called. Diriem, who'd been watching with one eye while he read through a stack of reports, took the call on speaker, and the rest of our crew—Connor, Jane, and Rose and Yven, who'd come in from work and promptly changed into ratty sweats—muted the program and leaned closer for the update.

"I've been all over Jomin and Dania," Ganti said, sounding only marginally less exhausted than he'd been that morning. "Think you're going to like this—"

"Have you eaten?" Diriem interrupted.

"Uh…no, I kind of forgot. You know how that goes."

"Come out, fill me in over dinner."

"Oh, no," Ganti quickly replied, "there's no need. I can find something at home, and—"

"Please. I mean, correct me if I'm wrong, but I assume that whatever you're planning to tell me will mean a weekend investigation. Surely we have time for one decent meal before alerting Kabno."

The agent laughed softly. "If you're sure…thanks. My pantry's looking bare."

"We'll hold dinner," Diriem assured him. "Come on."

About half an hour later—Friday night traffic at the portals was always a little slow, Jane told me—the doorbell rang. Yven flipped off the television, and from the foyer, I heard Ganti's voice echo back: "Hi, Scel. How's it going?"

We found the two of them by the front door, Scel impeccably dressed as always in a conservative charcoal robe and Ganti in frayed jeans and a loose burgundy Henley, his blond hair pulled back in a slightly cockeyed ponytail that left his ears on full display—pointed like mine but not at all floppy, I noted with a flash of envy. "Sorry, boss," Ganti said as Diriem appeared at the back of our pack. "Probably should have dressed for dinner…"

"Look around," said Rose, who'd traded her formal robe for a fuzzy bathrobe over yoga pants. "This is casual Friday."

"Yeah, but you live here," he pointed out, then nodded to Jane. "And you've practically taken up residence of late, or so I hear. *Someone's* been working remotely."

"Hey, I've got my hands full with these two," she said, gripping Connor's and my shoulders. "Got the okay from on high."

"She did," Diriem confirmed, grinning, and gestured toward the hallway leading to the dining room. "Shall we take this somewhere more comfortable?"

Ganti sidled closer to Connor as we followed Diriem. "I understand you figured yourself out, hmm?"

"Just a blood test," Connor replied. Having traded his uniform for sweatpants and a T-shirt, he looked far more comfortable than he'd been that morning.

"He's still a little screwy," said Jane, and pecked Connor's cheek.

Connor turned to her with a teasing smile. "I mean, I'd have to be crazy to—"

"*Watch it*, Con," she snapped, but her expression mirrored his playful look, and I trusted all was well between them.

The long table had been set for seven that night—Scel and the rest of the house staff had their own dining area, Rose had quietly explained, though they also tended to eat whatever Ranarma prepared for the family—and as we settled in, Ganti's gaze drifted across the platters of fruit, cheese, and tiny pastries set out as a first course. "What are those?" he asked, pointing to the pastries.

"Those," said Rose, "are a little something I used to whip up, only Ranarma's are prettier. Puff pastry, brie, and raspberry jam."

His brow knit. "Brie?"

"It's a mild cheese, and because those are baked, it's nice and gooey."

That was all the persuasion he required, and with one bite, a look of bliss crossed his face. "Oh. *Oh*, those are good..."

Diriem slid the platter closer to him. "Eat. You're starving."

"You're not wrong," he said through a mouthful of cheese. "Wow, I could make a meal off of these...hey, Ranarma!" he called toward the cracked door into the kitchen. "I love you!"

"Tell me something I didn't know!" Ranarma yelled back. "And don't ruin your appetite!"

Once Ganti had eaten enough to lose the look of manic hunger in his eyes, he accepted a glass of red wine from Yven and drank deeply. "Right," he said. "Feeling more normal."

"Excellent," said Diriem. "While Ranarma's finishing the steaks, why don't you tell us what you saw?"

He sniffed. "Is that what I'm smelling?"

"It's the rub," said Rose. "Good stuff."

"I need you to guilt-feed me more often, boss," Ganti joked, but he sobered as he collected his thoughts. "I did take notes, and my pad's out in the car, but in brief, Dania's your real problem."

Connor shifted his chair closer and grabbed a bunch of grapes. "Did she have anything to do with the fire at North Lake?"

Incredulous laughter answered that. "*So* much. But let me back up." He sipped his wine again, then put the glass aside, leaned back in his chair, and stared at the ceiling. "Dania ti'Lir. Decently high Hall, closer to Lord ti'Lir than many. I did some records searching before I plunged in, so let me see if I can remember the dates…she was born in the mid-seventeenth century, married Jomin in her forties, and started having children almost immediately. They've got seven at the moment, and since Jomin's going to be incarcerated for a long time to come, I don't anticipate number eight in the near future."

"Did she work for Inade?" Connor asked.

"No, but she didn't ask too many questions about what her husband or his father were doing. Dania…she had a good thing going on, and she's not a woman of deep scruples, from what I've seen. *Really* liked being a daughter-in-law of Lord ti'Cren, and since we all know how Inade feels about his eldest, Dania reaped the benefits of being married to the next child in line."

"Gossipy bitch," Rose muttered in English.

Ganti glanced her way and smirked. "How do you really feel about your great-aunt?"

"She's my great-uncle's wife, and that's it," Rose retorted. "Not that I have an abundance of warm fuzzies for Jomin, mind you."

"Understandable. Anyway, Dania has not taken the Hall's scandal well. Teolm didn't throw her out when Jomin was convicted, but her social life is a shadow of what it once was—and believe me, I watched," he added, glancing at Diriem. "Jomin used the blinding spell all those years, but no one bothered to protect his *wife*."

"She wasn't involved in Inade's business," Diriem pointed out.

"Still sloppy," said Connor. "Mafia wives need protection, too."

Ganti nodded. "My thought exactly. But since she's unprotected, she's an open book to me, which is good news for this investigation. Now, I said that Teolm didn't make Dania leave the mansion, but that's all he's doing—she has a roof and meals but no allowance anymore. That woman hasn't held a job outside the home in centuries, and she's been burning through her and Jomin's savings."

"They do have a little boy," said Rose. "He's four or five, I think."

"Yeah, but younglings don't need bespoke embroidered robes. Dania hasn't taken to the notion of limiting her unnecessary spending," said Ganti, "and now she's coming to the realization that the money *will* run out. Teolm has made clear to her that there will be no more allowance. But instead of…I don't know, applying for a job like a normal person, she decided that facilitating murder-for-hire was a more lucrative prospect."

"Go on," Diriem murmured, swirling his wine.

"Back in the summer, when you and Teolm took Maebe to the Forum and the existence of East Branch came out, Dania heard about it and paid attention—especially the bit about how Ivari and his followers had done well for themselves in finance. She and Jomin discussed it, and at Jomin's suggestion, she contacted some of Inade's intelligence-gathering sources to find Ivari. It wasn't that difficult, considering how poorly his people disguise their Halls with their assumed names."

"It's not a problem outside if no one around you speaks Elvish," said Connor. "Or hell, believes in elves."

"You know," said Ganti, pausing for a drink, "I'm almost wounded by your general disbelief outside."

"Well, you folks did leave…"

"*Fled*, you mean?"

"Later," Diriem interrupted. "So, Dania made contact with Ivari?"

With a grunt, Ganti said, "In early August. I don't think she met with *him* directly—I believe she spoke with underlings—but I can't be sure because they're all protected. Based on her half of the conversations, she offered up Silver's organization to help Ivari eradicate the problem of his half-breed descendants. Ivari must have decided that they could handle the ones outside on their own, but his people made a deal with Dania to help them take care of the ones in the Pactlands."

"I'm guessing she never mentioned that Silver's in prison and the org has splintered," said Rose.

"Must have slipped her mind," he replied, his mouth quirking. "And before anyone asks, no, she doesn't have legitimate portal credentials."

Connor grimaced. "I'm starting to think Devva and Matti were right about firing all those clowns and hiring a fresh batch."

Ganti chuckled low in his throat. "Matti Chela at Laws? Yeah, he's had his share of fun with the Portal Authority. Anyway, Dania obviously paid her way out, and she used one of Silver's people to take care of her out there—*multiple* times. At least she wasn't fool enough to try to navigate on her own with zero training. She doesn't even speak the language."

I thought of Nugera and the almost unintelligible mystery "ti'Cren," then tried to imagine Dania and one of my elder kin fumbling and signing through a conversation in two varieties of Elvish. "Guessing her handler did a lot of the talking at Rush and Sons, yeah?" I asked.

"Exactly," said Ganti. "And he wasn't protected, either. I've got information on him for Laws," he added to Diriem. "Anyway, that's August. Two weeks ago was the East Branch fire. Three days after that, Dania's handler got a message and left for New York. He returned with someone protected and a suitcase full of precious metals."

"Payment," Connor muttered.

"And an operative. Do we have an ID on him? Her?"

"Hemell ti'Vanil," my cousin replied. "Oversees PR for the firm."

"Plus odd jobs, I suppose," said Ganti, and sipped his drink. "He stayed with the handler far away from the ti'Cren mansion. The plan was for Dania to find people to do the job—"

"Patsies," muttered Jane.

"Uh-huh. The operative would pose as a ti'Cren, both

to make him seem legitimate to whomever Dania found and to give him a chance to see the arsonists for himself and call off the operation if he didn't think they were up to the task. He must have been convinced, since Dania's guy took him home on the night of the North Lake fire."

"And the suitcase?" Yven asked from down the table.

Smiling, Ganti said, "If someone were to call Teolm right now and strongly suggest that he take a look under Dania's bed, he might find a suitcase full of murder-for-hire money."

"*Don't*," said Diriem as Rose pulled her phone from her robe pocket. "Let Laws handle this."

"Teolm would want to know," she protested.

"Cornered people do desperate things, and I'd rather he not end up in a hospital. Excellent botanist, not a great fighter."

"So, what's the next step?" asked Connor, looking from Ganti to Diriem. "His findings are admissible evidence, right?"

"Once he's under oath," Diriem replied.

"Damn," Connor said under his breath. "Is that all Laws needs for a warrant?"

"Sure, it could suffice, but the best practice is always to have corroborating evidence. Laws pulled Jomin's phone calls from the penal farm, but between that and Ganti's findings, I think they have a sufficient basis to pull Dania's phone records as well. Do you know what number she used?" he asked Ganti.

"She only has one phone. Amateur," he replied, shrugging.

"And I sincerely doubt it's protected." Rising, Diriem said, "Excuse me for a moment—I should relay this to Kabno."

"What about dinner?" Rose asked. "Sit down, Pop, it can wait."

He smiled slyly back at her. "This will only take a minute, just long enough to tell Kabno to have her people pull Dania's calls and start looking at the numbers. Let her make her own findings before we talk again. And as that should occupy Laws for a few hours, we can have Friday night in peace. Save me a steak, eh?" he said, and stepped out of the room.

We might have had a relaxing night—Ganti, at least, drove home with a full belly to sleep off the day's work—but the data analysis team at DOL wasn't so lucky. Kabno called Diriem shortly before six Saturday morning with an update: between their findings and Ganti's, she had more than enough to haul in Dania for questioning. "You might want to warn Teolm," she apparently told him. "I'd rather if we didn't have to break down the door."

She needn't have worried, as when the agents showed up, they found Teolm waiting outside the mansion, flanked by the two burliest members of the house staff. Rose, who watched it go down live via farsight, laughed as she gave us the recap. "He opened the door for them and offered them coffee," she said, her voice slightly dreamlike as her eyes darted behind her closed eyelids. "Teolm, buddy, this isn't a social event."

"*Is* there an etiquette for letting in the cops?" Jane mused.

Connor grunted. "A general lack of sudden moves is appreciated. Refreshments are optional."

Thanks to her rambunctious little boy, Dania was awake when Teolm led the agents to her suite, but she was still in her nightclothes and severely displeased to be barged in upon. Laws didn't care. Within five minutes— and with a female agent watching her—she'd thrown on pants and a sweater, she'd masked her hair and face into presentability, and Teolm had taken her son down the hall to his aunt Meala, a teacher who'd married Kilch, Teolm's other criminal brother. Protesting her grave mistreatment, Dania was marched from the mansion while Apple Blossoms, the detective in charge, left a copy of the arrest paperwork with Teolm as the homeowner.

"And Teolm just gave her a latte for the road. Unbelievable," said Rose.

While Kabno wasn't thrilled by the reminder that Rose could peek in on her operations, considering the circumstances, she authorized Rose to watch remotely as Dania was interrogated. "She's so pissed," Rose reported from her couch as Apple Blossoms prepared to go in. "They gave her a shot of the dampening potion in the van, and now her hair's all messy again."

"How bad is it?" Jane asked.

She sucked her teeth. "Not quite 'walk of shame,' but it ain't pretty."

That Rose had reverted to narrating in her native tongue was unsurprising, Yven had explained when I'd quietly asked. "She's working to hold her focus, and that takes enormous concentration. That she can talk at all while she's like that is surprising—not all farseers can, as it so happens. If this is easier for her, I'm certainly not complaining."

Thus, when Kabno called again around ten, she didn't have to tell us why she was peeved. "Connor, do you want to try?" she asked, only half joking.

"Don't want to ruin my streak, ma'am," he replied. "Dania's not cracking yet."

"Maybe a few hours in the cells will change her mind," the director muttered. "Miserable way to spend the weekend."

Given what Rose had relayed, Dania would be sitting for a while. Apple Blossoms had been frank with her, going over Ganti's findings and her phone records. When she'd played back some of Dania's calls with Jomin, Dania had tried to blame everything on her husband...but that had only lasted until the detective confronted her with her phone log, which listed a striking selection of 212 numbers. Dania had tried to pass those off as belonging to friends, but Apple Blossoms wasn't stupid—Pactlands phone numbers were sixteen digits long, and all of the suspicious ones were far too short. Finally realizing how much evidence Laws already had against her, Dania had done the wise thing and stopped talking—frustrating to Laws but understandable.

With their primary suspect locked away, Laws turned their attention Saturday afternoon to Dania's handler, Yinkin ti'Mal. A distant cousin to the main ti'Mal line, Yinkin had been moving up in the ranks until Inade's sudden downfall, but he'd been smart enough to keep his legitimate job. The agents found him in the tattoo parlor where he rented space just as he was preparing to start a full-back piece on a customer, and they'd hustled him out before the poor woman had time to put her shirt on.

Back at the tower, Yinkin had listened when Apple Blossoms laid out the case against Dania and presented the evidence of his involvement. "Your phone's protected," she'd told him, handing him a sheaf of papers, "but Dania's isn't. Now, unless you'd like to convince me that she's deeply interested in some ink…"

Perhaps Yinkin would have held out had he still been in Inade's employ—those who'd given information about the previous Lord ti'Cren had a way of dying in custody, Yven had told me—but Dania had Yinkin's loyalty only as long as there was payment involved, and she'd been remarkably slow about splitting the proceeds from the job. Seeing no chance of compensation and a long sentence ahead unless he took quick action, Yinkin started talking—and as Rose described their conversation, it became clear to me just how good at his job Ganti was.

Thus it was that night that Kabno and Diriem got on a conference call with Mirrik Voln, Wylan, and a select few other Forum representatives to offer an update. "We've got a blatant conspiracy between Pactlanders and Ivari's people to murder children," Kabno concluded. "I've got a farseer, phone records, portal cameras, and a confession, not to mention enough gold and silver bars to send me on a *lovely* vacation. So, what are you going to do about it?"

Listening in from Diriem's office, I glanced at Connor, who grimly watched the phone lying on the desk as if it might jump up and attack him.

After a long pause, Wylan asked, "Do you want to strike tonight? We'll saddle up—"

"Wait, *wait*," Mirrik interrupted. "I want them, too, but let's try to be somewhat legal about this."

"*Oh?*" muttered Wylan in a tone that alarmed me on a deep, instinctual level.

If Mirrik noticed, he didn't let on. "Give me a few hours before you do something rash. I'll call a session for tomorrow morning."

"And if you don't get results?"

"If this fails, I'll damn well ride with you," Mirrik snapped. "But we need to *try*. I'll call the Overseer and set it for ten. If someone could arrange a presentation of your findings—"

"We'll see you then," Kabno told him.

As Diriem hung up, he glanced at us and winced. "Looks like I'm going to owe Ganti a makeup weekend."


Under ordinary circumstances, the Forum's offices were open only during weekdays, and the full body might meet once a week, if that. But members could call for emergency meetings if the need was sufficiently great, and since Mirrik wasn't the only representative with a connection to North Lake, the Forum was spooked enough to come in on Sunday morning.

"Thank you, Madam Overseer," said Mirrik once Ketling Tiramae ceded the floor. He stood at his desk below the dais, robed and neatly groomed, but the camera projecting his face on the large screen revealed the dark circles under his eyes. "We have a problem," he said, slowly turning to address his colleagues, a few of whom were already nodding. "I'll turn this over to Laws and DOI in a moment, but to save you the suspense, the fire at North Lake this week was the handiwork of two men who thought they'd been hired by Silver...or what's left of his gang, I guess. In truth, they were retained by Dania ti'Lir— that would be Inade ti'Cren's *daughter-in-law*—on behalf of Ivari ti'Ammaas, who sent one of his agents here to ensure that East Branch dies. *Here*," he stressed. "He wasn't content to murder his descendants outside. Instead, he paid ti'Lir a hefty sum to help him murder children. And I do mean children," said Mirrik, stooping slightly to pick up a notepad from his desk. "The eldest of the East Branch survivors is thirty-four. The youngest—his son, incidentally—isn't quite two years old."

He paused for a moment, letting the rumbles subside, then located our group in the first balcony and pointed at me. "If not for that young lady up there, who's still recovering from her burns, they would probably all have died—and not just them. There are student dormitories above, below, and around the East Branch section. Thankfully, the fire was contained, and none of the other students or staff were injured beyond smoke inhalation. The building is being repaired as we sit here. They got lucky—*this time*. I'm no farseer," he allowed, "but I anticipate another attempt. If ti'Ammaas is willing to let toddlers burn in their beds, then what's stopping him from trying again, given the opportunity?

"Now," he continued, "I can imagine what some of you are thinking: why should we care what happens to the East Branch children?"

Personally, I thought he showed remarkable restraint in not staring at Elm Carinar while he delivered that line.

"We should care because it's the decent thing to do," said Mirrik. "Because these children are here, in school, and should be safe. Because they have nowhere else to go now that ti'Ammaas has destroyed their home. Because, whatever else they may be, they're partly elven—and for that reason alone, I believe there should be a path to citizenship for them, though that's a matter for another day. But if those reasons aren't enough"—and there, he cut his eyes to Elm—"then my colleagues would be wise to consider the number of their constituents with children at North Lake."

"Or," said Elm, "we could do the wiser thing and throw the half-breeds out."

"Right," Mirrik replied, nodding, "we throw them out with the clothes they can carry. Ti'Ammaas burned down their community, so they have nowhere to live. They have no money, no food, no employment, and winter is on its way."

"Let the humans care for their own," she retorted.

Mirrik started to counter that, but Connor stood and called down, "If I may?"

"You're out of turn," Elm snapped, but Ketling raised a hand and looked up at him.

"You have something to add…Chief?" she asked.

"Yes, ma'am…oh, uh, thanks, Janie," he muttered as she whispered the spell to amplify his voice. "The representative suggests that there are sufficient community resources around East Branch to support my cousins. This shows a staggering lack of understanding of the situation."

Though Elm reddened, a stern look from Ketling kept her quiet.

"East Branch has been self-sufficient for its entire existence," said Connor. "It's on county land, but it has no services—no paved roads, no power, no water, nothing like that. Kids born in the community don't go to public schools. Basically, East Branch has been an entity unto itself for centuries, and the folks who live around it don't quite know what to make of it. Mostly, it's the butt of jokes—and I've heard more than my share. There's a popular conception that the place is…well, *was* inhabited by inbred dirt farmers, and honestly, that's not far off. If twenty-two of us just show up out of nowhere, there'll be questions. Where the hell were we when the community burned? *Who* are we? I mean, aside from me, none of my kin have documentation, ID cards, driver's licenses. They don't *exist* on paper. And once some well-meaning souls get their first glimpse of the *slight* cifvent issue with virtually all of us..." He shrugged. "No one's going to suggest elves, naturally, but there'll be doctors poking around to get to the bottom of the weirdness. Journalists. Curiosity-seekers. So, what we're looking at is a group with no resources, none of the education or documentation needed to find work or a place to live, and a bunch of tabloid pieces—because hey, who doesn't want to talk about inbreeding in Appalachia? Maybe some of the area churches will take pity and offer food. Maybe we'll be split up into homeless shelters—and good luck finding facilities that'll take whole families. I've got a place, but I sure can't house everyone. I realize you've been generous in letting us in and putting us up at North Lake, and I know we don't have any right to ask for more. But if you throw my family out, they're going to suffer. That's all there is to it."

With a nod to the Overseer, he sat down, and Mirrik stepped in before Elm could resume. "Putting aside all questions of decency to a group of newly orphaned younglings, the fact remains that ti'Ammaas attacked us. Here, on *our* soil, with no consideration for collateral damage. This cannot be tolerated."

"May I be heard?" came Kabno's amplified voice from farther down the bench.

Ketling picked her out of the crowd, and when Mirrik nodded, she replied, "Director Erenani?"

"There's an additional wrinkle the Forum should consider," she said, stepping onto her seat to be better seen below. "Four of ti'Ammaas's people are currently in our custody, including two of his children. Even if you were to expel the East Branchers today, I'm confident that he or his operatives would return to the Pactlands to extract our prisoners."

"Or Laws could release them," Elm interjected.

"With all due respect," said Kabno, her voice dripping with scorn, "I'm not in the habit of releasing individuals caught breaking into restricted areas just because it's politically *easier*. And since those four had every intention of kidnapping *them*," she continued, pointing to Connor and me, "and delivering them to ti'Ammaas, I'm particularly disinclined to give them a free pass. So, no, Representative, they will not be released prematurely, and they will go before a tribunal."

As Kabno took her seat, Mirrik said, "So that the Forum need not act on my word alone, agents from DOL and DOI are here to offer testimony as to their findings."

Over the next half hour, Ganti was put under oath to relate what he'd seen, an agent from Laws quickly walked the Forum through the relevant phone records, and Apple Blossoms testified as to her interrogation of Yinkin, who had not only given up Dania but had also confirmed the names of the elves hired to set the fire. When they finished, Mirrik waited for acknowledgement from Ketling, then said, "You've heard the evidence, and this was only the abbreviated version. I propose that Special Forces be activated to retrieve ti'Ammaas and his associates so that they may also face justice. And with that, I cede the floor."

Confused whispers broke out across the room, and the Overseer rapped her gavel. "For the benefit of our newer members…and the media," she added, glancing at the balcony, "the Special Forces team is comprised of select individuals within DOL, DOI, and DPP. It's tasked with neutralizing external threats, and if memory serves, I don't believe it's been activated in more than a century. Still, I believe this is a situation that would qualify under the rules, so if the Forum is inclined to take a vote, I'll allow it."

The motion was swiftly made and seconded, and a considerable majority of the representatives agreed with Mirrik's proposal.

"The measure passes," said Ketling. "And with Special

Forces having been activated, the next task is to choose a leader. As a refresher, Special Forces answers to the Forum, not to any one of its agencies, and so the customary practice is to select a representative to direct its actions during the designated period. Do we have any nominees?"

One of the gnomes raised his hand, and Ketling acknowledged him. "Look," he said, tugging down his robe as he stood, "this is a find-and-retrieve mission, yes?" Pointing to the Hunt's section, he continued, "There are only three of us here who regularly leave the Pactlands, and Wylan's already salivating. Give it to him."

Coordination, I mused, was a beautiful thing, as the rest of Mirrik's supporters fell in line. And as no representative was keen to fight the Hunter, Wylan got the job.

Peering up into the balcony, he asked, "Is Pateme here?"

"No," Kabno called down.

"Ah. Well, would one of you please let him know that we'll be meeting at three? You might want to inform your people."

"Meeting *where*?" Diriem asked.

At that, Wylan spread his hands. "I've got plenty of room…"

"And I've got a multipurpose space that doesn't necessitate figuring out transportation to the Hunt's little hideaway," said Kabno. "See you there."

As I followed the directors out of the balcony, I heard Kabno ask, "How many of his brothers do you suppose he'll draft into this operation?"

Diriem chuckled. "Oh…all of them?"

"That's what I was afraid of," she muttered. "Even Morial, do you think?"

He shrugged. "I haven't looked into it, but I wouldn't be surprised. Why?"

"Just thinking about how I should explain to my people that we don't ask why the sports guy, who's *totally* a troll and in no way a Huntsman with an identity crisis, is riding with the Hunt."

Stooping slightly, Diriem patted her shoulder. "One problem at a time, hmm?"

# CHAPTER 17

**I** wanted to be in on that afternoon's meeting. If anyone had a bone to pick with Ivari, it was me. Unfortunately, as Connor pointed out, I was an injured eighteen-year-old civilian who needed to be in bed, recovering from her burns, before Canna tied me down for my own good. Thus, I was left in my room at the mansion to sulk and continue recuperating while Diriem gave my cousin a lift to the DOL tower.

But even if I wasn't invited to the planning session, at least one involved party saw no need to keep me in the dark.

"Hey!" said Annie, cracking open my bedroom door after a rapid double knock. "Maebe? Feel like company?"

I sat up and eagerly welcomed her in, and she closed the door behind her before bringing me a canvas sack. "What's that?" I asked.

"This," she said, extracting a small jar with a flourish, "is the single best skin cream I've ever used. My dermatologist recommended it after I basically tried to take my skin off, and it does wonders. Gentle, hydrating, all that good stuff. You're going to want to stay on whatever healing potions they're giving you," she said, handing me the jar, "but trust me on this. It'll help with the scarring, too."

"Thanks," I said, but frowned up at her. "What happened to *your* skin?"

"Oof." Taking a seat on the side of my bed, she said, "I used to be human, yeah? Got dosed with a highly unstable, experimental potion in secret, and that's how I ended up stuck here for a while. The problem with the shit I took is that it affected every other potion and magical object I used—some good, some bad, some *ugly*. You know Keef ti'Mal's sister, Fellora?"

"I mean, we haven't met…"

"Sure, sure. Anyway, back in the weird days, Fell got in some trouble, and I went on a rescue mission to find her. Under ordinary circumstances, there aren't any side effects to scent neutralizer or invisibility jewelry, but coupled with the crap in my system…" She winced at the memory. "Horrible blistering, especially where I carried Fell. *And* renal failure, but that's beside the point. Use the cream. Oh, and I brought you this, too," she added, pulling a pint of frozen yogurt from the bag. "Good old Ben and Jerry might not be able to cure what ails you, but their products don't hurt."

Taking the dessert from her, I glanced at the label and smiled to see English. "You went outside for this?"

"Between us girls," she replied, lowering her voice, "there's plenty of decent ice cream in the Pactlands, but I've yet to find anything that scratches the Half Baked itch. Enjoy, hon. And while you get started on that," she said, handing me a plastic spoon from her bag of tricks, "do you want the skinny from the Special Forces meeting?"

I grinned, and as I shoveled down bites of cookie dough and brownie batter, Annie gave me the recap.

The Special Forces team was heavy on the elves and sorcerers. "It makes sense," she explained. "They're designed to handle problems outside, right? Sorcerers don't need to mask, elves can do it on their own steam—"

Well, *most* elves.

"—and both can deal with a broad spectrum of magical attacks," she concluded. "The team's got a handful of nymphs, too, plus some gnomes—surprisingly strong and excellent at camouflage—and more trolls than I'd have imagined. But since the objective here is to corner and bring in a group of elves, some of whom are older than dirt, they're leaning hard on the magically adept side of the group."

Augmenting the designated members of the Special Forces team was the Wild Hunt: Wylan, Annie, and Wylan's forty-six brothers. "The agency folk are a *teensy* bit twitchy about this, and I can't blame them," said Annie, "but if you want a targeted strike, why not use the guys who can get in and out in the blink of an eye?"

"They all wanted to participate?" I asked.

She laughed softly. "The boys like a challenge. Even Morial showed up."

"Who's that?"

Annie hesitated. "Can you keep a secret?"

I nodded.

"Ever seen Moonless Night on TV? He comes to schools pretty often."

Even with my brief stay in the Pactlands, I recognized *that* name. Keef had been beside herself when Moonless Night showed up for a rowing meet, and she'd shown me the recorded segment from the news. Channel 1's sports chief was a gray-skinned troll nearly eight feet tall with an orange stripe of hair, a sonorous bass, an encyclopedic knowledge of a century's worth of athletic events, and a soft spot for junior athletes.

"Yeah, I've seen him," I replied, puzzled by the question. "Why?"

"His real name is Morial. One of Wylan's brothers."

"Wait, the *troll?*"

"It's all a mask. Oh, he's not hurting anyone—he loves his job," she hastily added as my eyes widened. "For various reasons, he's been operating under that persona for most of his life, and Wylan is disinclined to order him back to the lodge. I mean, he has a standing *invitation*, but it's not generally a summons. This time, considering the quarry…I think he's intrigued."

"So, Special Forces knows that he's—"

"*No*, they do not. He showed up today as Morial, not

Moonless Night, and no one but the directors are the wiser. And us, naturally."

In theory, the plan was simple: get to Manhattan, storm Rush and Sons, grab as many elves as they could, and get out. The details, however, seemed to give Wylan heartburn.

"I know the way, and he doesn't," Annie told me. "He might be able to get folks to the building by using photos, but I've been up inside it, and I can get us past security. The faster we're in, the less time Ivari has to call for backup, and hopefully, the fewer the casualties."

But whereas Wylan was virtually indestructible, Annie didn't have the same protection, and the last thing he wanted to do was put his wife in front of a trapped and desperate elf. Unfortunately for him, Annie was both stubborn and right about her need to participate, and he'd reluctantly agreed to her part in the plan on the condition that once they arrived, she'd hold back and play lookout.

"I mean, I can't be *too* upset with him," she confessed. "The guys have, at the very least, decades of experience on me when it comes to combat. Most of them have been fighting for centuries. That doesn't mean Wylan gets a free pass to bench me," she added with a little smirk, "but I'm not sending him to the couch, either."

The other hiccup in the plan was a problem of identification: beyond what they could glean from the pictures on the Rush and Sons website, all of which were masks, no one in the Special Forces group knew what their targets looked like. Per Culta ti'Pul, the group's living quarters were below the building, but Special Forces had to assume that anyone coming above ground would be masked. After all, the firm *did* employ humans. The question, then, was who to grab.

It was Connor who'd thought of a potential workaround. "Diriem gave him High Elvish," said Annie as I worked through a chunk of batter the size of a walnut, "so if he starts hearing people around us use it, he'll know.

Also, if *he* starts shouting at them and gets responses, they'll give themselves away. It's not a perfect solution, but all things considered…" She shrugged. "We don't have a better option."

Finally swallowing, I mulled that over. "But a lot of them had nothing to do with East Branch or the fire at school. Only sixteen went to Georgia, and Laws has four already."

"Believe me, I know," Annie replied. "This has been *heavily* discussed. But unless we want to get into a firefight with a pack of elves, the thought is that we grab as many as we can and sort them out in Beukal." With a grimace, she said, "Not ideal, but if it means we don't get shot, I can live with it."

Thus, it was settled. Special Forces—plus Connor and the entire Hunt—would assemble at DOL again Monday morning at quarter of eight in order to hit Rush and Sons before business hours. With any luck, they'd have their targets out the door before anyone on the street was the wiser.

"Don't you worry, hon," said Annie as she gathered her bag and stood. "By this time tomorrow, with any luck, we'll have the bastards. So, get some rest, and don't forget to give that cream a try," she added, and disappeared.

I saw Connor off the next morning. Sporting a borrowed long-sleeved black T-shirt and pants from Laws' stash in lieu of his uniforms, he was quiet at breakfast, almost pre-occupied. I couldn't blame him. While I was sure that Connor had trained with guns, the little training in magic he'd had came from either the barebones basics taught at East Branch or whatever he'd picked up from Jane and her father. If he was nervous about the prospect of trying to defend himself against, say, fireballs…well, he had every right to be.

Jane, who *could* legitimately throw fire, had offered to

help, but she hadn't been invited to come along. "This isn't to insult you," I'd overheard Diriem tell her Sunday night when he and Connor returned. "The team already has two pyros and a fire nymph, and you are still *very* green. Besides, it took considerable work to convince Wylan to bring Connor on top of Annie," he'd added. "I can't imagine him agreeing to a third volunteer."

So, Jane had stayed back at the mansion that morning to keep an eye on me, and after a goodbye noticeably longer than usual, Connor had checked his gun and followed Diriem to the garage.

Having had no communication with North Lake since early Thursday morning, I didn't know what assignments I'd missed—and anyway, my books had been left behind in the chaos of the fire evacuation. Unable to play catchup, I watched TV while Jane sat on the couch beside me with her computer, reviewing her own lessons. "I've skipped a few of my tutoring sessions over the last two weeks," she told me, making a face. "Probably a good thing that the boss is on board with it, yeah?"

I kept sneaking glances at Jane's computer screen, checking the time and imagining what was happening in New York. Catching me in the act a little after nine-thirty, Jane squeezed my hand and said, "They'll be fine. Con's going to call as soon as they're back—"

Her thought ended abruptly as we heard Annie yell, "Anyone here?"

Jumping off the couch, we ran to the foyer to find her scowling. "What happened?" Jane demanded. "Is everyone okay?"

"We're fine," Annie replied, though she didn't seem overly pleased with this development. "Place was empty."

"*What?*"

"Yeah," she muttered. "We hit the exec wing, and it looked like they'd abandoned ship in a hurry. Computers gone, drawers left open, papers on the floor. When we made it down to the lobby, we saw that someone had put a sign on the door—bullshit about being closed for building repairs."

"What about the living quarters?" I asked.

"Oh, we found *those*," said Annie. "Broke right on in. Same story—no signs of life, valuables taken, everything else a mess. Which means—"

"There's a mole on the Forum," Jane finished. "Or in Special Forces."

"Yep. And while we try to find the leak, Ivari's in the wind." She shook her head, glowering into space. "Son of a *bitch*."

I stood there, stunned and trying to take it all in, but Jane was quicker to react. "What's the plan?"

"As far as I know, Laws and DOI are pulling phone records. Kabno is *pissed*," she said, "and for a woman who looks about as threatening as a kindergartener, she's kind of scary when she's furious. Not going to lie."

"Appreciate the update," said Jane, giving Annie a quick hug. "And I'm glad you're okay. Maebe, you're on your own, babe," she said, heading back toward the sitting room. "I've got to get downtown."

"Wait, where you are going?" I asked, looking from Annie to my departing babysitter.

"I may not be ready for the strike team, but I can look at fucking phone records," she replied, not even slowing. "If you see Con before I do, tell him I've gone to the office."

As Jane hurried away, I glanced at Annie, who grunted. "My chief gave me the rest of the day off," she said. "So, uh...do you like Yahtzee?"

To decrease unauthorized snooping into confidential government business, Forum representatives were given the protection of the blinding spell, which left them invisible and inaudible to farsight. Rose said that focusing on someone thus protected left her feeling like she was walking through a blizzard, and if she came across a protected person while focusing on someone else, they were nothing more than a white splotch. The spell was complicated, however: pulling it off involved a sorcerer and an elf working in tandem, and the target also had to drink the blinding potion, which was expensive and difficult to brew. And for all of that, protection only lasted about three months, making it a costly *and* time-consuming undertaking.

Perhaps this was why the Forum didn't extend the same protection to the aides, who were wide open to remote surveillance from DOI. But even if they had been protected, there wasn't a damn thing the blinding spell could have done to hide their phone records.

"There's a central office that handles telecommunications here," Jane explained when she returned to the mansion that night, exhausted and ravenous. "All *legitimate* phone lines go through them. You can buy burners and sneak them onto the network for the right price, but that ain't cheap."

The phone office had balked when Laws and DOI made an emergency request for the work and personal records of every Forum employee for the last three weeks, but the Overseer had authorized the release, and the agents had spent the afternoon digging for suspicious calls and texts. Some employees were easy enough to eliminate—most people made repeated calls only to a handful of other numbers, such as their spouse and nearest colleagues, and nothing raised alarms. Some made calls to non-Pactlands numbers, which required greater scrutiny, including searches of public records outside for details and interrogation. One representative *really* liked a particular pizzeria and admitted to slipping out on unofficial business for a large supreme and garlic bread. Another had a son who did fieldwork for DOI and had both of his boy's numbers saved in his phone, which he used interchangeably, much to the young agent's chagrin.

"And then there's the rep who will remain nameless,"

Jane continued with a smirk, "who's fond of a few 900 numbers."

Connor snorted. "Do I want to know?"

"What are those?" I asked.

They shared a look. I suppose Jane lost, as she said, "Uh…phone sex, hon."

"*Huh?*"

"Tell you later, but it's nothing you should be doing on a government line."

Fortunately for the investigative team, the mole wasn't exactly among the best and brightest. The agent in the office beside Jane's discovered a personal phone record with a New York number, and when he ran the local calls, he realized that the phone had also communicated with Dania ti'Lir's. Cross-checking the records against Dania's revealed that the New York number *also* appeared in Dania's history. Within half an hour, the phone's owner—an elf, one of Hemar ti'Dir's aides—had been arrested at his apartment and hauled in for a *pointed* conversation.

He wasn't exactly a hardened criminal, as the mere threat of getting the farseers involved was enough to make him crack. According to Jane, who'd been allowed to watch from a viewing room for training purposes, he was crying five minutes into the interrogation, as he knew damn well that his career was toast. Dania had paid him well—enough for a new car, as it turned out—and had given him Ivari's number in case he learned anything interesting on the job. The vote to activate Special Forces had barely finished on Sunday morning when he slipped into the bathroom to make a quiet call to Ivari, warning him of the raid to come.

But Ivari was craftier than Dania's amateurs could ever hope to be, and there was no sign of the phone he'd been using. DOI had tapped into cell towers all around New York City and several hundred miles up and down the coast, but the phone had vanished. "He's either turned it off or destroyed it," Jane told us, "but in either case, it's useless to us right now."

"Are there any leads yes?" Connor asked her.

She shook her head. "Not at the moment. But he'll sur-face—he has to," she insisted. "We've got people trying to find his bank accounts and credit cards. Whatever he's up to, he'll have to make a withdrawal eventually."

Despite her upbeat tone, her positivity sounded forced, and judging by the tension in my cousin's face, Connor wasn't buying it.

I went to bed early that evening, and though my burns felt quite a bit better, my mind was a mess.

Ivari was supposed to be in DOL custody. Instead, he was on the run—and someone as wealthy as he was could be anywhere. Worse still, he'd found people within the Pactlands willing to help him, and who was to say that Da-nia, her handler, and the Forum aide were the only ones taking his money? For all we knew, Ivari had a backup team in case Dania failed him, people he might be mobiliz-ing even then. And unless DOI got wind of them, they'd never be the wiser, as Ivari was impossible to track via far-sight.

It's tough to sleep when you're afraid that someone might come after your family in the middle of the night, and you're not there to help.

And they *were* my family, even if they hated me. If they never forgave me for inadvertently setting off the chain of events that led to our parents' slaughter, if they never spoke to me again, if they pretended I was dead until the day I actually dropped...they and Connor were all I had left. Connor was safe with me at the mansion, but what about the other twenty? Were they still at North Lake? Were they under guard? Had Ivari bought his way through the school's security, mediocre though it was, in order to kill the last East Branchers in their beds?

We had to find him. *Now.*

And I knew the way.

**D**iriem looked up from his computer when I stepped into his office in my hospital pajamas and borrowed bathrobe, guts roiling and palms sweating. "Maebe? Are you ill?"

"No, sir," I replied, trying to keep my voice steady despite my anxiety. "Do you know where Ivari is?"

He hesitated, then said, "Not specifically."

"What do you know?" When Diriem didn't answer, I huffed a sigh and asked, "What can you tell me?"

Again, he was slow to respond. "I suspect he's not in the Pactlands, but as to where he may be? That's a blank."

"If you can't see him, how do you know he's not here?"

"Snatches of farsight suggestive of a raid. The landscape seems foreign, but there's nothing of substance I can use to pinpoint it. I'm sorry," he said, shaking his head, "but I'm little better than blind when it comes to Ivari."

"What about my cousins?" I asked. "Are they safe?"

Diriem's expression turned pained. "I haven't seen a direct threat, but…"

"That's not a guarantee," I finished.

"Correct. And after last week, I wouldn't want to make assumptions."

This was it. I knew what I had to do, even if the deep part of my mind that remembered pain screamed at me to keep my fool mouth shut and run.

For East Branch. Always for East Branch.

"You need to get some of that bloodline potion," I told him. "Use me again. I can find him."

Diriem's eyebrows rose. "Absolutely not. You're still injured—"

"I'm better. I know what that potion's like, and I can handle it. I can tough it out. You saw me do it last time."

"Maebe—"

"This is my fault," I insisted, speaking over him.

"Okay? It's my fault. And no matter what you and Connor and Jane say, it's going to *stay* my fault. So, let me make it better. My family's not safe as long as he's out there."

"Maebe," Diriem murmured, "finding him won't bring East Branch back."

"No, but it'd be something! Please," I begged, "you've got to let me try. I could fix...*some* of this..."

By then, he'd risen and headed across the room to join me, and he lifted my chin when I scowled in frustration at the ornate rug. "You're hurt, little one."

"The burns are healing—"

"And your heart? What about that?"

I stiffened. "How did you—"

"Know? Teolm and I were informed of the research healers' initial findings. Received a formal report and everything. I told them not to give us anything further unless it was an emergency—you're entitled to your privacy," he said—"but I did notice your weakened heart."

Stepping back from Diriem, I folded my arms and glared up at him. "I could have been born with it for all anyone knows. There's no proof that the bloodline potion did that to me, and I can handle another round. Come on, I haven't collapsed in physical education."

"Yet." He stared me down for a moment, then said, "Connor could be the anchor. He has virtually the same bloodline you do."

"Except I've done it before, and I know what to expect. Connor hasn't, and more importantly, you need him functional," I countered. "Connor's the cop, right? He's got training—he can help in ways that I can't. Hell, he even got better control of his touch," I muttered. "Connor needs to be ready to move. If I end up in bed for a few more days, where's the loss?"

"Maebe, I'm not worried about you ending up in *bed*," said Diriem. "I don't want you hospitalized again, or worse."

"What'll happen if I take it?"

He hesitated, then said, "I…don't know. I haven't seen any flashes about that—"

"But you *do* think we'll find Ivari outside. *How* do we find him?" I pressed. "How better than the bloodline potion? We could get him, like, tomorrow!"

"Child—"

"We could stop him before he kills the rest of my family."

The two of us stood there in silence as the wall clock ticked, me practically hugging myself over my bathrobe and Diriem wrestling with my suggestion.

Finally, and hoping I wasn't about to make matters infinitely worse, I asked, "If you could've stopped him from killing your parents, wouldn't you have?"

He released a long sigh, then turned and headed for the leather sofa. As he sank down, I joined him. "Did you know it was coming? Their deaths?" I murmured.

"Yes," he said, his voice barely louder than a whisper. "Not the precise date, not every detail, but…yes." His hands clenched in his lap, the fingers turning pale as he balled them into tight fists. "I hate that man for sending the assassins, but in a way, I'm just as guilty. Didn't warn them, see?" he said with a bitter little smile. "Because if they had lived, the alternative would have been worse for us all. You want to talk about *fault*, Maebe? I've carried that burden for a long time."

"But they knew, too, right? If they were farseers…or one of them…"

"Neither. My grandfather was the last before me. Perhaps he knew how his son would die," said Diriem. "I've been there, and it's…well, I wouldn't wish it on Ivari," he muttered. "But at least my boy was farsighted, and we both knew what was coming. If my grandfather knew, I suspect he took it to his grave. Also an assassination," he added, "by the lord of a Hall that no longer exists. Father saw to *that*." His fists relaxed a degree but didn't open. "Can you imagine knowing the identity of the person who will take your family from you, but not only can you not stop him, you also can't eradicate his line?"

As part of that line, I sat still and waited while Diriem stewed.

"I wanted to go after him, desperately," he continued. "Good children avenge their parents, yes? But I saw the possible outcomes if I tried. The number of soldiers we'd lose on both sides. And because fate is cruel, I knew that the best path forward was the one in which that faithless *animal* lived. Couldn't tell you exactly why, but...I knew." Meeting my eyes, he said, "It might have been because of East Branch, for all I know now."

I took a second, choosing my words, then said, "He took my parents, too. And my grandparents. Aunts, uncles, cousins...and he'll take more if he's not stopped. So, help me, Diriem. I can find him if you'll give me the potion. Let's *get* him."

For the space of a slow breath, we watched each other's face work.

"I can't guarantee your safety," he told me.

"I'll risk it."

And though he didn't seem happy about it, he said, "Very well. Tomorrow morning."

# CHAPTER 18

Canna didn't waste any time with pleasantries when she arrived a little after eight Tuesday. "Do you have a death wish?" she demanded of me. "Because I saw what happened to you the last time you anchored a bloodline trace, Maebe, and you were healthy then."

"I'll be okay," I replied, though I knew that was an empty reassurance. Yes, I felt better by the day, but that was because I was still guzzling healing potions.

"Uh-huh," she said dubiously. "Well, let's be clear that if you do this, it's *firmly* against medical advice, and my presence here doesn't mean I condone this plan." Glaring at Diriem, she added, "Going the farsight route would probably be a lot less painful."

"And if I could use it to find Ivari, I'd do so," he retorted. "But he's shielded, and so are the rest of his people. We're useless."

Though obviously still displeased, she followed us to the same sitting room we'd used the first time I took the bloodline potion—a fact that was doing nothing for my nerves. I'd unconsciously avoided the space since I'd been back in Diriem's house, and now, seeing Teolm waiting in there with Jane and the bottle of dark green liquid placed on the end table beside them, I was more confident than ever in my decision to skip breakfast. My host might have been able to remove puke from the carpet with a few gestures, but I still hated to be sick like that.

Kelra Epannae, the potions professor who'd walked us through the process back in the summer, hadn't been invited out for round two. "I know what I'm doing this time," Diriem had explained to me, "and Teolm should as well. Besides, don't you think we're going to have enough disapproving participants without her?"

He was right on that front. Annie, Rose, and Connor had joined the festivities, and while none of the women seemed happy, my cousin was tense and watchful, as if he were deciding whether the time had yet arrived to throw punches.

On the table beside the bloodline potion lay a vial containing the antidote, which Canna drew up into a syringe as soon as she'd unpacked her bag. "Here's the deal," she announced, looking around the room. "If Maebe tells me to hit her, she's getting the shot. If one of you two tells me to hit her," she continued, pointing at Teolm and Diriem, "then she's getting the shot. And if I believe she's had enough, then she's *damn* well getting the shot. So, work quickly while I monitor the patient, hmm?"

"Understood," said Diriem, and turned to Teolm. "Like before. Ready?"

While the two of them gesticulated in tandem, beginning to sweat with the effort needed to set up the spell, Canna ushered me to a nearby couch. "Lie down," she ordered. "Connor, come here, will you?"

He hurried to my side, his face taut. "What do you need?"

"Your job is to sit here," said Canna, pulling over a chair with a muttered command, "and look after Maebe. I'll be watching," she quickly added, "but if you could hold her hand and keep her from rolling onto the floor, that would be helpful."

"Sure." He took a seat, and I tried to smile for him…but considering his expression, he wasn't fooled.

After another few minutes, I heard Diriem say, "We're on."

Sitting up, I looked over and saw the familiar—and now somewhat anxiety-provoking—visualization of a globe. With my few weeks of school, I still couldn't name all the continents and features—gently rippling lakes, jagged mountains, wide green plains, massive seas—but I *did* recognize the projection of the outside world, which was progress from the summer. "I'm ready," I said.

Jane passed me the potion bottle, and before I could think about it too hard, I chugged the liquid. It certainly wasn't the worst potion I'd tasted, kind of like chocolate-covered pumpkin, but I knew what was coming next, and I stretched out as I began to flush. "It's working."

"Last chance," said Diriem as my skin reddened like I'd stood too long beneath the scalding dormitory shower.

I closed my eyes and gripped Connor's hand. "Try to hurry, okay?"

"Of course. Rosie, Annie, Jane, gather around," he directed. "Annie, your computer's in order?"

"Map's open and waiting," she replied. "Let's roll."

"All right. Maebe, brace yourself."

Before I could answer him, pain burst over me, and my back arched off the cushions as I screamed.

"*Maebe!*" Connor cried. "Oh, my God, you're hurting her—"

"Hold her down," I heard Canna say, then felt an arm land across my stomach, pushing me back toward the couch. But above those sensations, blaring along my nerves like a siren in my ears, was the inescapable pain, and experience had done nothing to lessen it. My body felt like it was on fire, like my blood had turned to lava and was burning me from the inside out, and my patches of new skin seemed to shriek with the memory of flames.

I could do this. For East Branch...

For Mom. For Dad. For the rest of my lost family, the charred corpses scattered around the ashes of our home...

For the cousins who hated me, whose lives I'd upended, whose safety depended on my strength now...

"Zoom," I heard Jane order over my wailing. "We need more."

The pain spiked, and Connor pressed me down as I tried to rise off the couch again. "Got it?" he asked, panting.

"Not yet," Jane muttered. "Okay, that's Lake Superior to the right, that's the edge of the Great Lakes, so we're in—"

"Minnesota," Annie finished. "I think. Might have crossed the border into Canada…"

I could tell each time the image narrowed in by the increasing agony of my personal hell. Sucking air into my lungs sent ripples of pain through my throat, the only sounds I could make were screeches, and even the tears that had been squeezed from my eyes felt like they were burning my face. Deep in my chest, my heart thundered like I'd been sprinting for miles, pumping the fire through my veins.

As if in the distance, I heard Annie say, "Lake Vermillion. That's Minnesota. Someone get a picture of that, they're on a fucking island—"

"How many islands *are* there?" Rose asked.

"Too goddamn many! Camera, now!"

"We can get closer," Teolm began, but Canna, bless her, intervened.

"Got it?" she snapped from above me as I writhed beneath Connor's arm, clutching his hand like I was trying to break his bones.

"Got it," said Rose.

"Yeah, we're good," Jane added. "Hit her."

And suddenly, the pain receded, the fire extinguished by a cooling rush that washed through me from a spot in my right shoulder. I groaned and went limp, drenched in sweat and tears, breathing in little sobs, and finally released my death grip on Connor.

Something soft landed atop me, and a hand smoothed my soaked hair from my face. "It's over, baby," Canna murmured. "You did so well. Keep your eyes closed. Are you feeling sick?"

"Queasy," I managed.

She rolled me onto my side and rubbed my back. "Slow breaths, dear, that's the way. If something needs to come up, let it. Connor, you're in the splash zone."

He'd barely scooted away when my guts roiled and vomit rushed forth. Canna braced me as I threw up over the side of the couch, and as I spat the acid from my mouth, I heard her say, "Someone get a glass of water, please."

By the time my stomach calmed, the requested water had appeared, and Canna coaxed it down me in little sips. Finally, I looked up and saw that the projection had vanished...and that everyone was watching me. "Uh...sorry," I croaked.

Teolm twitched a few fingers, and the evidence disappeared. "Believe me, I've cleaned up worse in the greenhouse. Feeling better?"

"Ugh." I drank again, then waited, but the nausea had passed. "Where are they?"

"Only spot on the map was in northern Minnesota," said Annie, who was staring at her computer. "Lake Vermillion. Big tourist area for fishing. Looks like there's tons of islands in the lake. They're on one of them—well, that, or they've got an underwater base, which I kind of doubt. Give me a few hours to see what I can dig up, and I'll try to narrow it."

Politeness suggested that I should offer to help her, but exhaustion won out. I put my glass on the rug and staggered to my feet, and Connor rushed in to catch me as I started to fall. "Think I'd better lie down," I said.

"Uh, *yeah*," said Connor. "Hold still."

Before I knew what he was up to, he'd grabbed me and swung me around his shoulders, grunting as he took my weight. "What are they feeding you at school, bricks?" he asked, and started toward the door.

"Put me down, I can walk," I weakly protested— though that was almost certainly untrue—but my cousin didn't listen. I managed to hold on until he carried me up to my room, but I was unconscious as soon as my body landed on the rumpled sheets.

The light outside my window had shifted toward late afternoon when I came around. Groaning, I started to push back the blankets, but a hand to my shoulder stopped me. "Easy, mitta," Connor soothed. "There's no rush...unless you're about to be sick—"

"No, just...gotta pee," I muttered, and he released me. By the time I'd sat up, he'd come around the bed, and he escorted me to the bathroom a few feet away with an arm around my waist. "I'm fine," I said.

"You're wobbly. Hold on to the counter," he replied, and closed the door behind me.

Crossing the bathroom was a trial. My body ached, and my heart raced with the mild exertion. I had to stop by the sink while a wave of dizziness washed over me on my way out, and Connor was waiting to escort me back to bed.

"All right," he said once he'd tucked me in again, and reached for the tray of tiny potion bottles on the table by the window. "Healing potion first, and then Canna left you some for pain. I *think* I've got these straight..."

"Healing is the burgundy one."

"Or maybe not," he mumbled. "And painkiller is—"

"The light green bottle."

"Thanks." He grabbed them both and handed them over. "How do they taste?"

"Surprisingly good," I said, and quickly downed both. "Could I have some water, please?"

Connor filled a glass at the bathroom tap and brought it to me. "Canna's coming back tonight to check on you," he said as I drank. "And she's bringing one of the folks who've been examining y'all at school."

"The research healers?"

"Yeah, them. They've got baselines on you, so that'll

give Canna an idea of how badly you were hurt today." He waited while I finished the glass, then took it from me to refill it. "You're crazy, you know?"

"How else were we going to find Ivari?" I called after him.

"Time and patience?"

When he returned from the bathroom, I said, "That's just more time for him to figure out a weakness here. Thanks." I drank deeply, willing my thundering heart to slow. "Please tell me they found a trace."

"Oh, better than that." Taking a seat on the bed beside me, Connor grinned. "Annie's *good*. Did you know she was a private investigator before she came here?"

I nodded. "Still not quite sure what that means..."

"Well, importantly, she's damn good at records research. Guess what she found?"

"Something on one of the islands?"

"Yep. There are hundreds of the damn things, by the way. Most of them aren't privately owned, but there's a members-only fishing club on one of them. It's not a big island, maybe eight acres, and there's a substantial lodge structure there. Looks kind of like a rustic hotel," he said, and smirked. "Thanks, satellite photography."

"And she thinks it's Ivari's?" I asked.

Connor chuckled. "She found the articles of incorporation for the company that owns the fishing club. Seems like the place was founded by one Irving Rush IV. I understand our current Irving Rush is the sixth of his name, but—"

"That's him. *Has* to be."

"That's what everyone thinks. So, Special Forces is going to raid the place late tonight and see what they can get. Annie says the photos are enough for her and Wylan to hit the target...and where do you think you're going?" he asked as I started to throw back the covers again.

"Minnesota."

"Absolutely not. I've been benched, too," Connor said,

giving me a hard look until I stopped struggling to get up. "*You're* on bedrest. Doc's orders."

I glared back at him. "Canna's not the boss of me."

"No, but—"

"I *want* this, Connor," I insisted. "I want Ivari."

"As do I," he said. "You want blood, and I get that—believe me, mitta, I'm with you. But this isn't the sort of operation for a kid."

"I'm not a child!"

"You're not trained in snatch-and-grab tactics, either. I actually know how to break down a door and clear a house, and *I'm* not invited. This isn't personal. But hey," he said, gripping my shoulder, "you got them there, Mae-be. You found Ivari. And having seen what *that* process entails…well, you did good. *Real* good. You should be damn proud of yourself."

"I made this mess to begin with," I mumbled. "If I haven't told you yet, I'm so sorry for—"

"You don't owe me an apology," he said firmly, cutting me short. "There's blame to share for East Branch, and I'm just as guilty as you are."

He fell silent, and after a moment, I ventured, "What if they never speak to us again?"

"Our cousins?" I nodded, and Connor grunted. "That's up to them. If they don't, then we'll be each other's family, yeah?"

"Yeah," I murmured.

"And by the way, I want you to know that you're not stuck here," he continued. "If it's too much, if school is miserable…once things are safe again, you're welcome to come home with me. We'll figure something out."

I chuckled. "Not sure if Jane would be thrilled about that."

"She'd understand. Besides, she's still got her own place," Connor pointed out. "So, if you need somewhere to land, I've got you covered."

When I leaned forward and hugged him, he held me

tightly and patted my back. "It's going to be okay, Maebe," he whispered. "One way or another, we're going to make it okay again."

As promised, Canna returned just before dinnertime with one of the research healers, who gave me and my pajamas a disapproving once-over as he set up his computer. "You know," he said as Canna primed my arm for another blood draw, "there are far simpler ways to kill yourself than anchoring a damn bloodline trace."

"Except I'm still breathing, right?" I replied.

"Yes, but your lungs aren't my first concern."

My bloodwork came back as expected: an obscene amount of healing and painkilling potions, plus proteins indicative of inflammation—a sign of tissue damage, Canna explained as she parsed the results from her machine. "Your body's rebuilding itself. That's a good sign," she said. "I'd be concerned if we *didn't* have a little inflammation right now."

But my cardiac scans were less reassuring. The research healer used a combination of a wand-like device attached to his computer and a spell to create a visualization of my heart, and he frowned as the image came into focus, slowly spinning on the screen. "Here's your inflammation," he said to Canna. "Look at that."

She hissed as she took a peek. "Oh, little girl, that's…"

"How bad is it?" I asked.

The two healers shared a look, and the researcher took the lead. "Definite damage. Even if you had some congenital weakness, two rounds of bloodline potion have done a number on your heart."

"Can you fix it?"

He winced. "Not directly—not unless we start talking about transplants, and I don't believe you're there yet. So, here's the plan. You'll have monthly scans for the foreseeable future. We need to know whether any of the damage is being repaired. Healing potions for now. I suppose I can have some prescribed from the hospital supply, but there'll be a review hearing if I call in the quantity you need."

My brow furrowed. "Review hearing?"

"Healing potions aren't cheap, youngling. The hospital will make them available if they're medically necessary, but we'll need to convince the review board of that—"

"I can get them," Diriem interrupted, and I turned to find him loitering in the doorway of the sitting room the healers had commandeered with his arms folded, observing. "Prescribe what you think you can request, and I'll make up the difference."

"She'll need them almost daily for the next few months," the researcher cautioned.

"Fine. What else?"

"No strenuous physical activity," he said, glancing back at me. "That means no sports, not even jogging. Keep your heart calm and slow, and let's see how it recovers."

"Basically," said Canna, "you can sit in class, you can do your homework, and you can watch TV. This is one step up from bed rest."

As much as I chafed at the decree, I didn't argue with them. Just walking around the mansion made my heart race, and I didn't want to think about what a long run would do to me. "But you *do* think I'll get better, right?" I asked, looking at both healers.

The fact that they didn't hurry to reassure me made my overtaxed heart pound.

"I'm hopeful," the researcher finally replied. "You're young, you're relatively healthy, and perhaps whatever elven genes you have will make a difference—longevity is, after all, largely an incredible degree of tissue repair. But I make no guarantees, and you'll need to be careful for now."

As they packed up, I promised I'd behave, and Scel escorted them to the door while Diriem and I headed for the dining room and the smell of Ranarma's vegetable soup and fresh bread. "This isn't a death sentence, you know," he murmured. "It's a setback."

"Will I recover?"

He hesitated, then said, "I'm afraid I can't answer that."

"Aw, come *on*…"

"I have my reasons. But for the time being, no more bloodline traces for you, understood?"

I sighed. "You're being difficult."

"Patience, Maebe," Diriem replied, and pushed open the dining room door.


**D**espite the potions in my system, I slept poorly that night, but even if I'd been dead to the world, I've have awakened when Annie arrived.

Loud, rapid pounding on my door pulled me from half-formed dreams. "Hey!" Annie yelled in the hallway. "Y'all up? We got them!"

Five minutes later, Jane, Connor, Diriem, and I clustered with Rose and Yven in their apartment's den, surrounded by Yven's potted orchids. Rose had thrown on the tea kettle, it being two in the morning, but Annie, dressed all in black and *wired*, took pulls from a bottle of beer and paced as she spoke. "Sons of bitches never saw it coming," she said in rapid English, almost tripping over herself in her haste to get it out. "Most of them were asleep when we got there, and the two watching TV didn't notice us in time. Let ourselves into the house and bombed the hell out of the place with knock-out. Like walking through orange pea-soup fog. *Great* stuff. Assholes were unconscious before they knew what hit them."

Seeing my bemusement, Jane interrupted. "Knock-out potion. It's used for riot control."

"Yeah, it comes in these little bottles, and you shatter them, and *boom*, cloud," said Annie. "Super effective."

"Worked on *you*," Rose teased on her way to calm the shrieking kettle.

"Don't remind me. Anyway, we cleared the place. Neutralized every one of them and dragged the whole bunch back to Laws to get sorted out." With a little laugh, she added, "The boys were disappointed that it was so easy. They were hoping for a real fight, but once the prey's, like, *unconscious*..."

"Takes all the fun out of it, I'm sure," Diriem said. "The whole Hunt went?"

"Even Morial," said Annie. "He couldn't very well have stayed back and let his girlfriend have all the fun."

Yven coughed. "No, I suppose that wouldn't work. She'd never let him hear the end of it."

That time, Rose came to my rescue. "He's seeing Annie's chief, Gentle Breeze," she explained, poking her head out of the kitchen.

"I'd say they make a cute couple," Yven added, "but I'm afraid she might hurt me if she learned I'd called her *cute*."

Recalling the green-skinned, razor-tusked troll in her floral blouse, I silently agreed.

"You took *everyone* into custody?" asked Diriem, drawing the conversation back on track.

"Yep," said Annie, and sipped her beer. "Tough to get an ID on anyone when they're all unconscious and we don't have any clue what the targets look like."

He frowned in thought. "How many?"

"Hundred and nine."

"*Jesus*," Connor muttered, though he sounded impressed.

"There's even some babies in the mix," Annie said. "Kids. Figuring out who goes with whom might take some doing, but that's Laws' problem now."

"What about Ivari?" I asked.

She nodded. "*Oh*, yes. That's one face I remembered. Sleeping like a baby when I left him in a cell."

Connor slumped back on the couch, visibly relieved. "Kabno should try getting help from ti'Pul. Surely he doesn't want the rest of his pack sitting in jail while Laws tries to decide who was behind the fires."

"The *fire*," Diriem quietly reminded him. "Remember, we have no jurisdiction to punish them for East Branch. But yes, I think Laws would be wise to ask their cooperating witness for assistance."

As Rose brought in a teapot and a selection of cups on a wooden tray, Connor quietly asked, "Are we ever going to get justice? We've got twenty-eight dead…"

"I wish we could," said Diriem, "but you understand, yes?"

Connor sighed. "Yeah. Well," he said, glancing at Jane, "in that case, I guess it's about time for me to go home."

Diriem's brow knit. "You needn't leave so soon—"

"Ivari's in custody, and I've got responsibilities," he replied. "Thanks for putting me up for this long—and y'all," he said, nodding to Annie, who tilted her bottle in acknowledgement—"but this ain't getting it done. If nothing else, I need to go home in case the folks investigating at East Branch have questions. Someone's got to be the next of kin."

As Connor helped himself to the tea, Diriem said, "Keep your schedule flexible, if you will."

"Any particular reason?"

"Trials move quickly around here," he replied, "and while I don't know what Laws has planned, I'd be surprised if they didn't start with Ivari. Both of you will presumably be needed as witnesses," he said, pointing to Connor and me.

"Why me?" asked Connor. "I wasn't at North Lake."

"No, but…" He paused, then said, "While Laws can't prosecute Ivari for East Branch, the counselors *can* use his actions there as evidence to show motive for the arson here. It's not ideal, I know, but even if there's no proper justice for East Branch, you can tell their story."

When Connor looked at me, I held his stare for a moment, and then he slowly nodded.

It wasn't what we wanted for our family—it wasn't *fair*—but it was better than allowing East Branch to disappear without a word.

"Y'all know how to reach me," Connor said, and poured his tea. "Just call."

# CHAPTER 19

To my relief, Connor didn't leave immediately in the morning—or rather, once the sun was up. No one had slept much after Annie's visit, and Diriem had departed for the office before Ranarma had breakfast on the table, considering how much work the farseers had ahead of them with Laws' new guests. Rose and Yven had headed into Beukal at their usual time, leaving Jane, Connor, and me to figure out our next steps.

Canna had reluctantly cleared me to return to school during her latest house call, and though I wasn't feeling entirely like myself, I was bored of lying in bed. While the idea of facing my angry cousins again left me a little queasy, I knew I couldn't avoid that forever—not unless I planned to run away and never return. So, I gathered my few things that morning, the clothes I'd been given from Laws' stash and my hospital pajamas and the bits and pieces Rose had told me to keep, and I packed them into a borrowed tote bag for the trip back to see what had become of my other few worldly possessions.

When I stepped into the hall, I found Jane and Connor waiting with their luggage, and I followed them downstairs. "Not going to lie," said Connor, "I'm going to miss that bed. How much do you think that mattress cost, anyway?"

"More than mine," Jane replied. "There might be magic involved."

"And that's his *guest* room?"

She glanced at him, eyebrow raised. "Look around, babe. He's *loaded*."

"Yeah, I gathered that, but..." He grunted. "You're not going to get in trouble for chauffeuring, are you? I could ask Annie for a lift."

"Seeing as I'm not farsighted, this is probably where I'm going to be most useful today. And the boss approved," she added, then lifted a hand when Scel stepped into the foyer. "We're off," she called. "Out of your hair. Thanks for putting up with the mess."

He smiled. "It's no trouble. Drive safely, now."

The three of us headed into Diriem's massive garage, then loaded into Jane's truck for the trip to North Lake. While Jane and Connor chatted during the drive, I sat quietly on the rear bench, watching the grasslands roll by and trying to call the mountains of home to my mind's eye.

I could go back, I mused. Tell Jane I was done and run away with my cousin...

But what was there to go back to? My home was gone, and I suspected that short of a miracle, we'd never have a chance to rebuild. I had neither the skills nor the funds to make it on my own in Whitford, and while I could do a little magic, that wasn't going to get me far. On the other hand, Connor *had* offered me a room...

No.

As much as I longed to run, *no*.

I'd started us down this road, and I owed it to East Branch to continue—to do *something* to prove that our loss wasn't in vain. I needed to stay the course, make up the many classes I'd missed of late, and learn how to survive outside the community's protective fence.

Even if my stomach flopped at the thought of seeing my kin again.

Not to mention Ainnet.

All too soon, Jane parked in front of the school, but as I started to get out, she and Connor joined me. "You don't have to come in," I hastily told them. "I'll stop by the office and see where they've moved us—"

Connor squeezed my shoulder and steered me toward

the steps, and so I led the way inside.

Once through the main doors, Jane took charge, marching into the principal's office with barely a knock on the wall to announce herself. "Good morning," she said crisply. "I'm returning Maebe Amos. Where should we take her things?"

Ms. Mafatta, who'd been sitting on a mat behind her desk, rose and took us in. "And you are…"

"Jane Fortune. DOI," she added. "The director knows she's here."

Her gaze shifted to Connor as her long tail swished. "Your…colleague?"

"Boyfriend," he corrected her, "and kin to all of the East Branch folks. Where are they?"

"Their dormitory has been repaired, so Maebe's room should be ready for her…wait, where are you going?" she demanded as we turned to leave.

"Going to escort her upstairs," Connor replied. "Is there a problem?"

"I'm afraid I can't allow that. You're not her guardi-an—"

"*You* let my baby cousin be attacked by that brat for weeks," he snapped. "Maebe's still healing up, and I don't want her getting jumped, see? So, *I* will take her back to her room and make sure she's okay before we leave her here. Understood?"

"I assure you," said Ms. Mafatta, "Ainnet is in class—"

"Don't care," he interrupted, and walked out. "All right, mitta, which way?"

Smiling to myself, I showed Connor and Jane up to our dormitory—which, to my surprise, appeared to be just as it had been before the fire. Not even the smell of smoke lingered. I checked my room and found that someone had been through to clean it, as the bed was made and there was no trace of ash on my desk. My computer started when I opened it, and I nodded to my chaperones. "Looks like everything's in order. I, um…I should probably get to class…"

"Not so fast," said Connor. "Where is everyone? Peter, Kyle, Monica?"

"They're in the group above mine. I know where they meet."

"Great. I'd like a word with them before we go."

Grabbing my books, I led them out of the dorms toward our tutorial rooms. Passing mine, I paused outside a closed wooden door and whispered, "In there. Want me to—"

"I've got it," he murmured, then knocked twice and let himself in without waiting.

The seven of our cousins in the eldest group were seated in a rough semicircle around the board and their tutor, a middle-aged sorcerer in a pretty purple robe who watched bemusedly as Connor entered. "Uh…good morning," she said. "Can I help you?"

"Sorry to interrupt, ma'am," he said. "Just need a minute of their time."

Justin, who was sitting closest to the door, glared at us. "What do *y'all* want?" he asked, switching to English.

"Don't start with me," said Connor, and while I couldn't see the look on his face, something in his expression made Justin's bravado falter. The only one of us left who was older than Connor was Peter, and sometimes, age carried weight. "Thought y'all'd want to know that Ivari and the rest of his bunch are in custody."

"*How?*" Uncle Kyle asked incredulously. "Y'all got him?"

"No, it was a group from Laws and DOI and…like, dozens of antlered guys. Grabbed them for the fire here."

My uncle's eyes narrowed. "Did he set—"

"Not directly, but he paid for it. Still wants us all dead. Anyway, the folks here can't go after him for East Branch, but he's going to be prosecuted for arson, at least. Attempted murder if we're lucky. Someone may be stopping by to get witness statements from y'all, so don't be surprised." Squeezing my shoulder, he added, "The only reason they were able to find him so quickly is because of Maebe, and she's on restricted activity for the foreseeable future now because of heart damage, so, you know, you could try not being absolute assholes to her."

They turned to me, assessing.

"What happened to *you*?" Uncle Kyle finally asked.

"The same potion Ivari used to find East Branch," I replied. "It's...pretty rough."

"And she took it on top of all those lovely burns she's been nursing since the fire," said Connor. "Remember that? The one none of you helped her fight?"

Uncle Kyle looked chagrined, but Peter began to flush as he protested, "It was chaos! We had to get the kids out—"

"You didn't go back, did you? Leave the little ones with Monica and grab a damn bucket?"

"That's not fair," said Monica as her husband sputtered. "We've lost *so* much—"

"So, it would've been acceptable to lose Maebe, too?" As Connor's grip on me tightened, he continued, "I'm just trying to gauge whether it's safe to leave her here. None of y'all lifted a finger with what's her name—"

"Ainnet," I mumbled.

"*Her.* And look, I get that you're angry with us. We're *all* mourning right now, okay? But can we try to be adults about this?"

In response, Amy pointed at me. "I lost my big sister," she snapped. "My parents. My uncle and aunt and their spouses...my nephew..."

"And I'm sorry," I blurted. "I'm *really* sorry—"

"But it doesn't matter what Maebe did," Connor interrupted. "Or what I did. East Branch was on its deathbed, one way or another."

Justin grunted. "You can't say that. We were fine—"

"We were *broke*," Peter interjected, eyeing Connor, "but that could have been fixed."

"Debatable," said Connor, "but I'm not talking about money. Diriem saw the alternative if we hadn't been exposed."

He folded his arms. "Which was?"

"Shootout with law enforcement. County, maybe. Presumably not my department. But there'd have been a raid on East Branch, and no one inside would have cooperated and come out quietly."

The others stared at him for a moment, considering that, until Peter took the lead again. "How many would have died?"

"That's unclear," Connor admitted, "and now there's no way to know. Might have been some of y'all. Might have been the little ones." He let that sink in briefly, then sighed and released me. "You're upset, and I get that, but we were screwed either way. *Y'all* made the choice to come here, and you survived. You wouldn't have had that option if not for Maebe."

They stared back at us in silence.

"It sucks," said Connor. "No way around that. And I swear to y'all that I'll do anything I can to see that Ivari's buried under the fucking jail for what he did. But are you going to keep treating Maebe like a goddamned pariah?"

The others traded glances, and I held my breath until Peter announced the consensus: "You can stay, mitta."

It wasn't exactly a welcome, and I suspected that it'd be a long time, if ever, before my cousins warmed to me again, but it was a start.

"Thanks," I said, then nodded at Connor and Jane. "I'm going to go to class now. See y'all later."

"Hold on," said Connor, "we haven't talked to your bunch yet—"

"We'll handle it tonight," Uncle Kyle assured him. "You going home?"

He sighed. "Yeah. Got work to do in Whitford. Is there anything y'all need?"

"I mean, if there's any part of East Branch that can be

saved…"

"I'll take a look as soon as the sheriff lets me on the property," Connor promised.

"What about our family?" Laurel asked. "The bodies?"

"I believe they're still with the coroner. Once they're released, what would y'all like me to do with them?"

"If you can," said Peter, "put them in the cemetery. Maybe the outsiders will let us keep that much, eh?"

Connor made no promises, I noticed, but at least our cousins weren't cursing his name as he left.

Sage welcomed me back and offered to help me catch up on my missed work, and Heidi was, if not enthusiastic at my return, at least willing to smile and say hello. Her brother David was another matter, but I simply ignored him and hoped for the best.

I wasn't invited to the dorm meeting that night—or *meetings*, rather, as I heard feet sneak by my closed door all evening—but Heidi was considerably warmer in the morning, and David actually asked how badly I was burned. I turned my back to him and pulled up my shirt, giving him a fair view of my healing scars without risking indecency, and he whistled low. "Peter said you're out of physical education for the rest of the year," he remarked as I straightened my clothing.

"Yeah. Medical excuse."

"That's got to be boring."

I shrugged. "Extra study time, and I need it."

He let the matter drop, but when I struggled to follow along with the morning's lecture, he sighed and passed me a page of handwritten notes—and frankly, that was good enough for me.

I sat with Sage at the far end of the East Branch tables that day at lunch, trying to focus on our conversation and ignore the stares I could feel from Ainnet's group two tables over. Finally, I turned to glare back at them, and the girls suddenly discovered a deep interest in their trays. As for Ainnet, who appeared none the worse for her injuries, she held my gaze for a moment but made no move to bother me. In fact, she avoided me in our few shared classes that day, and I suspected that *someone* had received a talking-to from Lady ti'Har.

Over the next two weeks, as I worked to make up for lost time, I kept my head down and tried not to draw attention to myself. Slowly, the mood in the common rooms began to thaw when I was around, and while I was clearly no one's favorite cousin that fall, the others would at least acknowledge my presence.

I was also grateful to be back in private tutoring with Violet, who knew how to nudge me just to the edge of losing control. After a few sessions, she pulled in a pyromancer, explaining, "I don't want you to be overly traumatized by the dorm *incident*, so we're going to learn some strategies for controlling fire."

"I thought I did all right," I said, eyeing the pyromancer as my heart raced.

"You did very well," Violet soothed, "but I'd rather you know these techniques through training rather than try to intuit them on the fly. And I'll be right here," she added, patting my back. "You won't be burned again today, youngling."

I didn't realize how much fear I carried until I started sweating and found myself staring down a small blaze with a dry mouth and tunnel vision. Slowly, Violet coaxed me through my panic, showing me how to protect myself and manage the fire without fanning it out of control, and while I wasn't a pro by the end of the afternoon, I hadn't thrown up—a win.

My biggest disappointment of that strange October was having to tell Swift Eagle that I probably wouldn't be able to try out for melee in the spring. "My heart's not in great shape," I explained to her one night at dinner, when she stopped by my table to say hello. "I'm not even allowed to run right now, and I'm on, like, *all* the potions, so I doubt I'll be cleared to play."

"Sorry to hear that," she replied, eyeing me as she stabbed at one of her thick porkchops. "What happened, the fire?"

"Uh...no, I took another bloodline potion, and—"

"*Another* one?" Her eyebrows shot toward her dark mohawk. "Are you trying to kill yourself, girl?"

"Desperation," I muttered, and poked at my salad.

"Huh. Well, in that case," she said, leaning toward me, dinner forgotten, "I need details."

Late that month, I received a call from an unknown Pactlands number and blew my door closed to take it in private. "Hello?" I said, settling onto my bed.

"Hi, is this Maebe Amos?" asked a woman's voice.

"Yes, ma'am."

"I'm Cennis Paf from Laws. We met briefly..."

One of the counselors, I recalled—the centaur. "Uh...yes, I remember you. Hi."

"Is this a good time?"

"Sure. What's going on?"

She chuckled briefly. "Well, a *lot*, but as far as you're concerned...congratulations, you're on our witness list."

Cennis explained that Ivari would be going to trial on October 31. "I imagine this will take two days," she said, "and we want you and Connor to testify against him."

"What does that entail?" I asked.

"You'll sit in the witness seat at the tribunal, and either my partner, Remari, or I will ask you questions—we'll guide you through what we need you to talk about. Then Ivari's counsel will have a chance to ask you questions."

"Will he be there? Ivari?"

"It's encouraged. If he's disruptive or declines to be present, we'll go on without him, but odds are he'll be sitting there. Is that going to be a problem?"

I forced myself to say, "No, ma'am," though my guts roiled.

The counselors didn't want to shove me into the seat without preparation, so Cennis arranged to pick me up the following morning. "There's nothing to fear," she insisted. "We're on your side, little one."

"Is Connor coming, too?"

"He'll be prepped tomorrow night," said Cennis. "Scheduling issues, you know? But we'll walk you through this—you're not going into the tribunal alone, Maebe."

The following morning, after asking Heidi to tell our instructors where I was, I sat on the front steps of the school and waited, willing my injured heart to slow. Just before eight, a blue ivan turned down the driveway and came to a stop. The doors were unusual, I thought, about twice as long as car doors normally were…but then the driver's door opened, and Cennis carefully stepped out, her hooves gently clicking on the pavement. In lieu of a robe, she wore a sensible green knit twinset and a pair of coordinating leg warmers on her front legs, which slouched like oversized socks. "Morning!" she called, giving me a little wave. "Ready to go?"

The interior of the van was bizarre, empty of seats but for a bench in the rear. Between it and the front were two rows of raised mats. "Make yourself comfortable," said Cennis, settling in on the mat behind the wheel. She reached behind herself to strap a seatbelt over her back, then clipped a pair of dangling belts in from the front, forming a sort of harness. Black webbing extended between the hanging belts from her chest to her waist—protection, I supposed, to prevent her from going through the windshield. She tucked three of her legs beneath her, keeping one free to work the pedals. "Buckled in?" she asked, checking over her shoulder.

"Yes, ma'am…"

"Good. Sorry to send you all the way back there," she said as she started to drive, "but my ride's not great for bipeds. I had the back bench added when my boys were little and wanted to bring their friends over."

"You have kids?" I asked, trying to make conversation so as to ignore my nerves.

"Mm-hmm. Twin sons," she said proudly. "They're about your age, I think—seventeen. Too big to ride with Mom anymore if they can at all help it."

"At least they still have you, right?"

Cennis's shoulders stiffened. "Oh...oh, heavens, I'm sorry. That was insensitive—"

"No, no," I quickly said, "I just meant they're lucky, that's all."

We drove on in silence until we hit the capital's inbound morning traffic.

"Were you and your mother, uh...close?" Cennis asked. "If you don't want to talk about it—"

"It's okay," I replied. "Um...yeah. It was just Mom and Dad and me. Never had a sibling."

"Good parents?"

"Yeah. They...they tried. They wanted the best for me."

"I'm sure they're proud of you," she said, pulling up to a red light.

My mother's screams rang in my ears, but I managed, "I guess they were."

Again, Cennis went quiet for a moment, then asked, "Do your people have any thoughts about an afterlife?"

"Come again?"

"What do you believe happens after death?"

"Oh," I mumbled. "Um...I don't know, really. My parents never talked much about it. Guess I'll find out soon enough, huh?" I added with a weak laugh.

"Tell me to stop if you don't want to talk," said Cennis, "but for my people...most of us believe in a life following this one. Or an existence, I suppose I should say. The Eternal Fields. You get to run forever with all the ones who've come before, and you never tire." She hesitated, then added, "Or that's what they say, anyway. I've never known anyone to sneak a peek and report back, but…I don't know, I've always found it rather comforting."

"That sounds nice," I said.

"Well…if it exists for us, then surely there's something comparable for you. And if I were your mother, and I knew half of what you'd done of late, I'd be very proud indeed."

"Thank you," I replied as my throat tightened, and I coughed to clear it. "So, um…what am I testifying about?"

Fortunately, Cennis went along with the change in topic. "We'll go through everything in detail once we get to the office, but broad picture, you'll be talking about East Branch, what happened this summer with Ivari, what happened to you and Connor the night East Branch was destroyed, and then the fire at the school. And we'll probably get into your bloodline potion experiences to explain how we got Ivari into custody. Those are the main topic areas."

"That's a lot," I murmured.

"It'll go by faster than you imagine. Unlike this traffic," she muttered, bracing her elbow against the window. "I'm starting to think I should have brought snacks for the ride."


Witness preparation was much more involved than I'd imagined. It wasn't as simple as answering the counselors' questions—and Cennis and Remari had *plenty* of those. We painstakingly went through their topic areas, often pausing for one or both of them to take notes. While Cennis would be questioning me at trial, Remari would be paying attention for questions her partner had missed, so both wanted to be fully apprised of my answers before we got in there.

After we covered practically everything I could remember of the last five months, we did a run-through with me sitting across the room and Cennis talking to me from behind a scuffed wooden podium. Every few questions, she or Remari would make suggestions: give a shorter answer, stay on topic, expand upon a particular facet, don't be nervous. After I flailed my way through one question three times, Remari called a break and let me calm down. "You're doing well," she said as I chugged a glass of water. "I know it's a lot, dear. The important thing is that you tell the truth—we can work with whatever that may be."

"I'm not lying," I insisted when I came up for air.

"Oh, I'm not accusing you of anything," she quickly amended. "But…has Cennis mentioned the spell?"

I eyed the other counselor, who was checking messages on her computer further down the table. "No, ma'am…"

"It's nothing to worry about," said Remari. "When you testify, you'll swear to tell the truth, but then you'll be ensorcelled for the duration of your testimony. It won't affect you at all unless you knowingly lie," she explained. "If you say the wrong thing and don't realize it's a mistake, the spell won't react—it responds only to intentional untruths."

"What does it do?" I mumbled, liking witness prep less by the moment.

"You'll experience discomfort, often in your hands first. It's like a burning sensation, and it gets worse the longer you go without correcting the lie."

Having had more than enough of burning flesh lately, I must have seemed a little freaked by this news, as Remari said, "You're going to be *fine*. That's why we're practicing now."

By early afternoon, I was comfortable with my testimony and familiar with the general order of questions, and I was feeling better about the situation until Cennis cracked her knuckles and said, "Let's try cross-examination."

What followed was miserable. Until Remari called a halt for dinner, Cennis grilled me on every facet of my story. Just what *had* happened at Ivari's office, anyway? Hadn't I wanted to hurt him? Didn't I want to hurt him now? Wasn't it convenient that I was somehow outside the Pactlands yet far from East Branch when the fire out there started? How had I gotten outside, anyway? Surely not through legal channels, right? If I didn't respect Pact law over something as serious as portal security, then how could I be trusted to be telling the full truth about my dealings with Ivari? East Branch had been desperate for money, had it not? The survivors still were, weren't we?

And then my favorite topic: my family.

"I *really* don't mean to upset you," said Cennis, taking a few knees beside my chair as I blew my nose and struggled to stop crying. "Little one, I'm not trying to make matters worse—I just don't want you to be surprised if Ivari's counsel start probing."

"He's got a deent team," Remari added. "I respect them, and they usually keep things civil, but considering this case, they may be a bit desperate."

I sniffled and wiped my eyes. "You think you've got a good chance?"

The counselors looked at each other, and both nodded. "Confessions, corroborating evidence, farseers, witnesses like you and Connor," said Cennis. "We've got a decent shot, especially if we can offer the evidence about what happened last summer to show his motive."

Remari grunted. "And his team knows it, so they may get dirty. I wouldn't be shocked if they try to focus on your, uh...*situation* in East Branch."

Cennis's line of questions had made that tactic clear: what was the harm in Ivari eliminating rogue quasi-humans? We were minimally talented, untrained, inbred, physically defective, and too impoverished to take care of ourselves, meaning we were a threat to the safety of the Pactlands. In his twisted way, hadn't Ivari done everyone a favor?

And though her increasingly pointed inquiries had left me in tears, they'd also tested my restraint of my talent, which kept whispering its offer to blow Cennis out the window.

"Question," I said, balling my tissue in my fist. "What happens if I get upset and, say, start a tornado in there?"

The counselors traded glances, and Remari asked, "Is that a legitimate concern?"

"Possibly?"

"Huh," she muttered. "Um…well, we can take breaks if things get too intense, but, uh…"

"Try not to make a tornado, eh?" said Cennis. "Maybe, um…maybe you could work on some deep-breathing exercises over the next few days."

I smiled weakly and promised that I'd look into that, but I didn't know how much good it would do me once I saw Ivari again.

*Had I known before now that they lingered, I'd have corrected the problem.*

His mocking green-brown eyes appeared again in my mind, and I forced them away as a sourceless breeze rippled against my skin.

For East Branch, I could manage.

I had to.

# CHAPTER 20

Not until Sunday afternoon did the counselors inform me that I'd be their first witness.

"We've been thinking it over," Remari said as I sat in my bedroom, clutching my phone and trying not to hyperventilate. "Considered a few different strategies, but it makes sense to begin with someone who can describe the worst part of the crime."

They would, she added, be calling me at least twice, bringing me back later when they got to the attack on East Branch. "I'd love to put you in the chair once and have it over with," she told me apologetically, "but we need to stick to the actual offense and get the elements established before we backtrack to his earlier deeds."

Thus it was that I found myself sitting in a small, windowless waiting room on the top floor of the Tribunal building early Monday morning, hoping I wouldn't throw up all over the robe Rose had given me. My only companion was a trainee counselor named Tilla Poum, a young faun of forty who'd been shadowing Cennis for months to learn the ropes. Short and pudgy, with a mop of dark, curly hair, prominent horns, and a pair of ruby stud earrings, Tilla kept up more than his half of the conversation as he chatted with me. "Our team are pros," he said, adjusting his black robe as he crossed his goatish ankles. "Seriously, I would *not* want to face those two in a tribunal. And with our judge…" He chuckled almost nervously.

I frowned. "What's wrong with the judge?"

"Oh, nothing, but she's tough. Did Cennis not tell

you?" I shook my head, and he shrugged. "Few things on her mind, I suppose. We got Caganni."

"Caganni…"

"Just Caganni," said Tilla. "Sirens don't use surnames."

While I'd heard of sirens, I'd yet to encounter one. Next to the Hunt, they were the least populous of the Pact member races. I'd heard that one had tried to kill Rose and Yven, but I hadn't pressed them for details of their encounter. All I knew from my reading was that sirens could live about five hundred years, they were amphibious and equally comfortable in fresh and salt water, and they could hypnotize their victims by singing—the better to lure them in for an easy meal. And since sirens weren't exactly picky eaters, there had been a bit of friction when they signed the Pact, as well as a firm condition that they not prey on their fellow citizens.

Perhaps sensing my growing unease, Tilla said, "Really, she's very nice when she's not overseeing a tribunal. I interned with her after graduation."

"What if she starts singing?" I asked.

In response, he patted my arm. "She wouldn't. The only time she's ever done it was when a witness tried to jump down and stab the defendant, and she sang to bring the tribunal back to order…and to give security a chance to disarm the witness," he said. "But that was, say, fifty years ago. The real problem is for the counselors—she's the type to jump in and ask questions, and she'll ruin your planned witness list if she gets interested enough. Caganni's not going to hurt you, if that's what you're worried about."

Honestly, I was worried about many things, from the annoying twinges in my bladder to the possibility that I might release a hurricane under cross-examination, but I forced a wan smile for Tilla.

I'd have preferred to hang out with Connor or Jane, but that wasn't an option. Witnesses were meant to be kept apart from each other and the tribunal until they testified so that they didn't compare notes. While Jane wasn't testifying, her relationship with Connor meant that the counselors didn't feel great about letting her keep me company, so Tilla had been tasked with babysitting me until I was called. Since Cennis had picked me up around seven that morning, I'd assumed my wait would be brief once the tribunal began, but it was nearly lunchtime when she and Remari stopped by to check on us.

"Motions," Remari said wearily, rubbing her forehead as she leaned against the wall. "*So* many. I get it, but…ugh."

"Motions?" I echoed.

"Matters for the judge to consider before we begin," Cennis offered. "Whether certain evidence will be admissible, whether we can discuss East Branch—"

"Whether we can try Ivari," Remari interjected.

"Why couldn't you?" I replied.

Cennis snorted. "His counselors argued that he's a foreign head of state and therefore ineligible for prosecution."

"How'd that go over?" asked Tilla.

"Well," she said, grinning at him, "Caganni asked what territory he controls. They tried to argue that he's in exile, but she wasn't convinced. Ivari hasn't had a state to lead since the time of the Pact, and while he claims control of land now, they had to admit that he pays taxes to another government. So…yeah, we're going forward today."

"*Are* we?"

"Patience," she replied. "Come downstairs with me to get some food. Remari, why don't you take a break with Maebe?"

They returned soon with lunch to share, but I was too anxious to do more than pick at my sandwich. About twenty minutes later, a soft bell chimed from a speaker on the wall, and the counselors hastily packed up the leavings and brushed the crumbs from their robes. "That's us," said Remari. "Stay here, Maebe. We'll give our opening remarks, and then you'll be called in. We've been assigned to the big room. Tilla will escort you," she added before I could ask where I was supposed to go—which, considering that I'd seen little of the Tribunal building beyond the waiting room and the bathroom, was a solid plan.

Tilla tried to keep me distracted, but by the time I was called, I was a nervous wreck. "Hey, look at me," he said, squeezing my hands. "You're safe. Nothing's going to hurt you in there. Ivari can't—he's on neutralizer, and if he tries anything, he'll be taken out. Just tell the truth and try to relax. And, uh…can you control that breeze?"

I hadn't even noticed that my hair was waving in an indoor wind, and I called my power back into me with a muttered apology.

"Don't worry," he said, then released me to open the door. "Did I mention that I fainted at my first tribunal? All of those mock tribunals I did as a student, and what happened? Got flustered, locked my knees, and down I went…which you will *not* do," he hastily added, "since you'll be sitting. Come on, let's get this over with, eh?"

Not exactly reassured, I followed the black-robed faun through a pair of wide double doors and into the tribunal.

To me, at least, the room was massive, a two-story space topped with a skylight-pocked dome. We walked down the center aisle between two sets of a dozen curving benches, and once we'd cleared the balcony, I glanced up to see extra seating above us—plus a handful of cameras positioned along the railing, recording the proceedings below. About two-thirds of the way to the front of the room was a stone divider carved to look like trees and mountains, which separated the audience from the action. Beyond it were a pair of tables, each covered with a black cloth, set to either side. Like the benches, they curved to harmonize with the lines of the room. Behind the one on the left sat the counselors from Laws, Remari in a wooden chair and Cennis on a mat, while the one on the right had three occupants: two nymphs in expensive robes and Ivari, who wore a dark suit and stared off into space as if the proceedings were beneath him.

Averting my eyes from them, I looked up to the high stone table, which was carved like the room divider. The woman seated at the center wore a rich blue robe decorated only with gold braiding at the cuffs and collar. She was gray in complexion, with black eyes and long white hair partially bound back from her face, exposing her tiny ears. A chair had been placed to either side of her; a sorcerer waited behind a computer in the seat to the left, but the one on the right was empty.

My seat, I assumed.

As I paused at the divider with Tilla, I caught the judge's eyes, and she gave me a small, brief smile. "Your witness?" she asked Laws' table.

Cennis stood and nodded. "Honored Caganni, the Division of Laws presents Maebe Amos."

At that, Ivari finally shot me a contemptuous glance. He was unmasked, a youthful man with short, neat blond hair, a decent tan, and the eyes that had haunted my nightmares for the last few months. I didn't know where he'd found the suit—perhaps Laws had released someone to fetch it for him—but it fit him beautifully, evidently a piece of custom tailoring. The left cuff of his coat had ridden up enough to expose a heavy gold wristwatch, and while I was certainly no expert in such, I assumed the metal was the real deal.

He looked away again with a quiet, disdainful sniff.

"You may approach, Ms. Amos," said the judge, and gestured toward the empty chair. "Watch the step, now, don't trip."

Leaving Tilla behind, I hurried between the tables and up to the chair. As I sat, fighting back the power that strained to break free, Caganni leaned toward me and murmured, "First time, dear?"

"Yes, ma'am," I managed.

"It's all right. Why don't you pour yourself some water?" she suggested, cutting her eyes to the pitcher and stack of short glasses between us. "I always get thirsty during these things."

I did as she said, but I was so focused on avoiding a spill before all of the watching eyes that I didn't notice the sorcerer from the other chair coming around to stand in front of me. "Do you swear to give truthful testimony?" he asked.

I clutched my glass and said, "Yes, sir."

"Very good." He winked, then murmured under his breath, and suddenly, a brilliant blue light flashed around me. "It only lasts until you're dismissed," he whispered. "Don't worry."

Easy for him to say. I sipped my water and tried to keep my legs from bouncing as Cennis rose and straightened her notes on the table. "Good afternoon," she said, holding my stare.

"Good afternoon," I murmured.

"What's your name?"

I swallowed hard, willing my voice to strengthen. "Maebe Amos."

"And how old are you?"

"Eighteen."

"Where are you in school?" Cennis asked, her gaze steady and almost calming.

"North Lake," I replied. "I'm a boarding student."

"You live too far away to make the commute?"

"Yes, ma'am. I'm from East Branch," I explained. "It wouldn't be practical."

She nodded. "And where is East Branch?"

I called to mind the map Jane had shown me months before. "Northeastern Georgia. We're about an hour from the Central portal."

"Outside, you mean?"

"Yes, ma'am."

She waited until the soft rumblings in the audience faded. "Do you attend school here alone?"

"No, ma'am. It's me and, uh…hang on, I want to get this right," I muttered, frantically counting my kin.

"There's twenty-one of us who came over for school, but only nineteen are students. The two youngest are toddlers, and they came with their parents."

"All from East Branch?"

"Yes. We're all family. Most are my cousins, but my uncle's in there, too."

Cennis cocked her head. "He must be fairly young."

"Eleven years or so younger than my mother. But, you know, human lifespans, so…" I shrugged. "I guess we're all pretty scrunched up by your reckoning."

"I see," she said, and glanced at her papers. "Maebe, were you at school on the night of September 28?"

I paused. "Do you mean September 28 into September 29, or—"

"Yes, exactly."

"Then yes," I replied, nodding. "I was there."

While Cennis and Remari knew *precisely* why I wasn't there the night before, none of us saw the need to mention my suspension.

"Do you recall anything unusual happening that night?"

I closed my eyes and took a deep breath, willing the memory of the roaring fire and choking smoke to subside. "Yes, ma'am."

"And what was that?"

"In the middle of the night—I don't know exactly when, but it was dark out—I woke up, and our part of the dormitory was on fire."

"Small fire? Large fire?"

"It was based in our big common room," I said, seeing the flames again. "All along the ceiling and walls. We've got a few communal spaces, but all of the hallways that lead to our rooms come off of that main room. You walk into our wing, and it's right in front of you," I added, and wished I had a photo.

"How did you know there was a fire?" asked Cennis.

"I smelled smoke and heard yelling, and when I came out of my room, the end of the hall close to the common room was blocked. Burning," I said. "And we're on the fourth floor, so jumping out the windows wouldn't have ended well."

"No, I can imagine that," she replied. "How did you escape?"

"I...wasn't really planning anything," I confessed. "Too scared. But I'm an aeromancer—not a good one, not really trained, but it's *something*. I was able to blow the fire away from us, and that let the folks on my hall get out."

Cutting my eyes to the defense's table, I saw that even Ivari was watching me now—probably figuring out how to attack us better the next time, with my luck.

"So, you ran?" Cennis asked.

I shook my head. "No, ma'am. I'm the only aeromancer in the group, and the other halls were blocked, too, so I stayed to try to control the fire. Everyone got out eventually."

"Why not run and find a pyromancer? Surely there's one on faculty, yes?"

"Like I said, I wasn't thinking too clearly, and it was working...but a pyro came eventually, and an air nymph, and a couple of sorcerers who kept the ceiling from collapsing."

Her voice softened. "Were you hurt?"

"Yes, ma'am. Burned in a bunch of places, but I'm much better now."

"That's commendable, young lady," the judge interjected. "Fighting a fire as an *aeromancer*..." She grimaced. "I imagine most would have fled."

"Well, we'd just lost half our family, ma'am," I murmured, "and I didn't want to lose anyone else—"

"Defense objects," said one of the nymphs by Ivari. "Honored Caganni, this is the sort of irrelevant, prejudicial information we've asked the tribunal to prohibit—"

"And I recall denying your motion," she replied. "But I've interrupted Laws. Ms. Paf, do you have further questions for the witness?"

"Not at this time, Honored Caganni," said Cennis, "though we intend to recall her later in the proceedings."

"As you like. Defense, your witness."

The nymph who'd objected stood and smoothed his— her? their?—robe. "Ms. Amos, I don't believe we've met. I'm Periga Ularru."

Male, then, and considering his dark brown skin and striking blue ponytail, probably an earth nymph. "I'd say it's nice to meet you, but with the spell on me…"

He chuckled, and I heard the judge snicker to my right. "Fair enough," he said. "This is your first tribunal, I take it."

"Yes, sir."

"Since the tribunal has denied our motion to limit the discussion of certain facts," he continued with a faint smile, "I'd like to ask you about your acquaintance with our client."

"Objection," said Cennis. "Honored Caganni, we haven't presented that evidence yet."

"I realize that," said the judge, "but I'll allow it. Answer the question, Ms. Amos."

I nodded, my stomach clenching.

"You *have* met Lord ti'Ammaas, have you not?" Periga asked again.

"Yes, sir."

"When?"

"Uh…that would have been back in June," I said, trying to pinpoint the date. "I don't remember exactly *when*, but it was June. Could be in the last week or two of the month."

He consulted his notes. "If I said June 23, would you dispute that?"

"No, sir. That sounds about right."

"Mm." Again, he shuffled the papers before him, then looked up and stared at me. "You set my client's office on fire, did you not?"

"I…it was an accident—"

"Yes or no. Did you set Lord ti'Ammaas's office on fire?"

"Yes," I admitted, gripping the edge of my chair.

"I see. Now, how long have you been blackmailing my client, Ms. Amos?"

"*Objection!*" Cennis cried. "Honored Caganni—"

The judge lifted a hand to silence her protestation and turned to me. "Answer him, please."

I hesitated, as this wasn't a line of questioning we'd practiced. "I'm sorry," I said, "but what do you mean by 'blackmail'?"

Again, Periga barely smiled, though I imagined I caught a flash of triumph in his pale eyes. "Is the term unfamiliar to you, youngling?"

A few observers laughed.

"Well, let me explain," said Periga. "How long have you been threatening to expose Lord ti'Ammaas and his people, and how much have you demanded for your silence?"

Frowning down at him, I said, "I haven't done any of that."

"Is that so? Interesting."

I waited in my seat, sipping water, as Periga riffled through a notebook, then a binder. After a long moment, he glanced up at me again, smirking. "The pain you're feeling will go away once you tell the truth, Ms. Amos."

"I'm not in pain," I replied.

"No?"

"No, sir."

He lowered his notebook and held my stare, but when I hadn't so much as flinched after another minute, his confidence faltered. "It will worsen, you know. Whatever you're feeling now will only increase until you come clean."

"And I'm telling you, sir, that I haven't lied. I know what burning feels like," I added. "Nothing I want to go through again, so I'm really trying to be careful, here."

By then, Periga's smirk had vanished, and he looked across the room at Cennis, who arched an eyebrow.

"Honored Caganni," he said, "might we have a word with our client?"

As the tribunal went into recess, I watched Ivari walk out with his counselors, who hustled him through a side door and let it slam behind them. Cennis and Remari likewise left the room, leaving me at the high table beside Caganni.

"You know," she murmured, leaning closer, "when I was training to be a counselor, my instructors stressed the importance of trusting one's client. It was only once I began working that my more experienced peers explained the need to trust but *verify*."

Though her expression remained a careful blank, I noticed a twinkle in her black eyes.

"Have you noticed those people sitting on the defense side...oh, about two rows back?" she continued, glancing out at the audience. "Strange crowd. Not a robe among them, so I suspect they're acquainted with Lord ti'Ammaas."

Following her gaze, I noticed the cluster of besuited elves, who were animatedly whispering to each other. "I'm afraid I don't know them, ma'am," I replied. "Haven't seen most with their masks off."

"No, I don't suppose you would have outside the Pactlands. More water?" she asked, lifting the pitcher.

As I sipped my refill and the judge turned to her computer, I considered Ivari's agitated supporters below. He'd told them I was blackmailing him, that I was threatening to go public with their existence unless he gave me half the firm's assets...but I'd denied it, and the spell knew I was telling the truth. Had any of the ones out there been among those who murdered my family and burned down East Branch?

Were they realizing they might have made a mistake?

When the tribunal resumed, Cennis and Remari looked collected, but the mood wasn't nearly as pleasant at the other table. Ivari was red-faced, while his counselors kept their eyes fixed on the high table, ignoring their client. I'd have paid dearly to eavesdrop on their conversation during the break, as Ivari either somehow believed his lies wouldn't be discovered or just didn't care.

"Mr. Ularru, your witness," said the judge.

He stood and cleared his throat. "The defense is finished with this witness, Honored Caganni."

Cennis also rose. "May Ms. Amos be excused for now? We'll keep her isolated—"

"Not so fast," said Caganni, and turned to me, folding her hands atop the table. "I have questions."

I didn't suppose the counselors could stop her. After all, she wasn't going to grant objections against herself.

"Yes, ma'am?" I said.

"Ms. Amos, what's the nature of your relationship to the defendant?"

I glanced at Ivari, who sat at the table, squeezing a pen, then looked back at Caganni. "We've only met once before today. Technically, we're kin, but he doesn't claim us."

"By 'us,' you mean…"

"Folks from East Branch, sorry."

"Mm." She nodded. "You two are…cousins?"

"He's my ancestor. I don't remember how many generations back offhand, but it's a lot. I, uh…I'm descended from three of his kids."

I knew I wasn't imagining the rumble of voices from the elves in the audience.

"*Three*?" Caganni echoed, surprised.

"Yes, ma'am. East Branch…our families are close, if you know what I mean."

Her mouth tightened. "I…believe I do, but why don't you spell it out for me?"

A flush began to creep up the back of my neck. "So,

um, our community records say—"

"Objection," called Periga. "What records? We've received no records."

The judge cocked her head in query, and I explained, "There was an old book. Births, deaths, marriages, all that sort of stuff. Most was in English, but the first few pages were written by one of his daughters," I said, pointing to Ivari, "and she wrote in High Elvish. Talked all about where they came from and how they got to Georgia."

"Do you have a copy of these records?"

"Just a copy," I replied. "The original was at East Branch when it burned."

"And to be clear," said Remari, "we sent a copy to the defense."

Ivari gripped Periga's arm and pulled him down to mutter at him, and Periga straightened to address the judge. "We do have that, Honored Caganni, but we would prefer if this book were not discussed. It's...*distressing* to our client and irrelevant—"

Caganni's laughter cut him short. "Irrelevant? Really, that's the best you can do?"

"There's nothing in there pertaining to North Lake," he said stiffly.

"Perhaps not, but if it explains why your client might have cause to set the school on fire, then I'd say it's rather relevant." Looking back at me, she asked, "Have you read this book, Ms. Amos?"

"Not the whole thing," I replied, "but the history in the front, yes."

"What reason do you have to believe that the narrative is accurate?"

I paused, mulling over the question. "Well...as I said, it's written in High Elvish. No one at East Branch could read it, and we had no idea what it said until Lord ti'Dana took a look."

"He went outside, did he?" she asked with a slight smile.

"Considering my genes, he seemed concerned that there was a mixed elven community out there. Most of us have at least a little talent, and there's a lot of cifyent."

She frowned. "Which is?"

"Just a moment." I gripped my pendant to disengage my mask and watched the judge's eyes widen as my ears flopped over. "This. One case would be weird, but a whole community…"

"I…yes. Heavens," she murmured, and waited until I'd fixed my mask again to resume. "Do you have any other reason to believe the book is accurate?"

"Yes, ma'am." I hesitated long enough to sneak a peek at Ivari, who was quietly fuming as he sat beside his counselors. "The book said that there were eighteen elves from the old southern kingdom who survived when it fell. Those were half the founders of East Branch—they intermarried with a group of humans."

"Objection," Periga tried again, but the judge silenced him with a shake of her head.

"The survivors and their children were the ones who settled East Branch," I continued. "The book said there was a bad winter, and all the elves sneaked off to die. Mary—the one who wrote this down—thought they did it to make sure there was enough food for their children and grandchildren. But the book lists their names, and their children's names, and on down over the last few centuries."

"That doesn't suggest accuracy to me," said Caganni.

"Maybe not by itself, but then I took a bloodline potion, and—"

"You did *what?*"

Shrinking in my seat a little, I said, "I wanted to see if there were any other communities like ours out there. I'd just learned about the Pactlands and how much magic could really do, and…East Branch was pretty poor, and we didn't go to real school, but then folks were saying we might be able to go to school *here*, and if there were any other distant cousins out there—"

"Wait," she said, holding up her hands. "You took a bloodline potion on the chance that you'd find oth-er...what, quasi-elves?"

"Yes, ma'am."

"Who was foolish enough to give you *that*?" she de-manded.

I winced. "Do you really want to know, ma'am?"

"Let me guess: someone from DOI?"

"Yes, ma'am."

She grunted. "Go on. Did you find another communi-ty?"

"No—it led us straight to our ancestors," I replied, and cut my eyes to Ivari. "He goes by Irving Rush out there," I added, then gave the Pactish translation of his surname. "And ti'Ammaas means—"

"'Of rushes,'" Caganni finished.

"Yes, ma'am. He's not the only person in that group who uses a fake name that's close to his real one. So...anyway, that's why I think the start of our community records are accurate, or at least as accurate as Mary could make them. After that, it's just a list of dates. No reason to make those up. And, uh...like I was saying, our families are all close. The children from those eighteen stuck to-gether and didn't marry outside the community, so that's why I'm related to *him* in a few ways."

Cennis climbed to her feet again. "If the tribunal would find it helpful, Laws has compiled a comprehensive family tree for East Branch based on those records."

The judge rubbed her chin. "*How* comprehensive, Ms. Paf?"

In reply, she patted a thick stack of paper on the table. "Folded for transportation. We were going to introduce this later, but if you'd like to see it now..."

"Perhaps tonight," she replied. "Answer me this, if you can offhand. Of those East Branch children at North Lake, how many are descended from the defendant?"

She didn't hesitate. "All of them, Honored Caganni."

Across the room, Ivari groaned.

"And it might interest both the tribunal and the defendant," she continued, "to know that Ms. Amos is his next heir."

"Truly?" Caganni asked, glancing from Cennis back to me. "That's curious—"

"*Lies.*"

I looked out to find Ivari on his feet, ignoring his hapless counselors' attempts to pull him back into his chair. Crimson-cheeked and fuming, he glared at me, his hands fisting at his sides.

"That's enough," the judge snapped. "You're out of order, sir. Counselors, if you could please control your client—"

"*That* is nothing of mine," Ivari continued, ignoring her. Apparently, he'd been given a potion for Pactish during his time in custody, though even I could hear the strangeness in his accent. "That...*vermin*," he spat, "has no claim on me—"

"Three bloodline potions suggest otherwise," I retorted.

The judge's head whipped toward me. "*Three?*"

"Laws needed help finding him in a hurry..."

"Your agency put her through that?" she demanded of Remari and Cennis, who'd preemptively stood. "She's a *baby*! What do you mean by doing that?"

"Honored Caganni—" Remari began, but I interjected.

"It's not their fault, ma'am," I said, and Caganni turned to me once more, frowning. "My idea, actually. Laws was just told where to look."

"And the third?"

I thumbed one hand toward Ivari. "That's how he found me in September."

"We have a witness who'll testify to such," said Cennis. "If the tribunal would like to hear from him now—"

"No, no," Caganni muttered, rubbing her head. "Everyone...*sit.* Ms. Amos, I'm not sure I want to know, but *why* would you take a second bloodline potion? Has no one explained the risks to you?"

"I know about them," I said quietly. "The healers in my life aren't happy with me."

"Then why? Could one of your kin not have assisted?"

"They...could have, yes, ma'am. But..." I paused and took a deep breath, willing the warning tightness in my throat to subside. "I'm the one who brought Ivari into our lives to begin with, see? It's my fault. So, I should be the one to do it."

Still furious, Ivari jumped to his feet again. "You little wretch, you'll address me——"

"*Shut up,*" I barked, and he twitched as if I'd slapped him. Pushing myself from my chair, I stared down at him. "Just *stop*, okay? I'm sorry. I'm sorry about what happened to your office—I swear to you, I didn't go in there meaning to set a fire. And I'm *really* sorry that you lost your family," I continued as my voice quavered. "But why'd you have to take mine?"

"Ms. Amos," said Caganni.

In that moment, tribunal forgotten, I had eyes only for Ivari. "We just needed help," I told him. "If you didn't want to, fine. But East Branch is gone now." My straining voice finally cracked as my vision blurred. "We've got *nothing*. We're homeless, and everyone here lost their families. Are you happy, huh? Just had to kill some farmers who never hurt you?"

"Ms. Amos, please sit down," the judge tried again.

"You *orphaned* me," I told Ivari, tears spilling down my cheeks. "The last thing I heard from my mother was her begging and screaming, and I will never, *ever*, forget what that sounded like."

He gazed back at me, silent and stone-faced.

"'Correcting the problem'—isn't that what you called it?" I asked. "Getting rid of us? Because heaven forbid anyone know you married a human woman once."

Ivari reached into his pants pocket, and as he withdrew it, something glinted in his hand.

I've heard it said that in periods of great stress or panic, time can seem to slow. It almost stopped for me then, those few seconds in which Ivari ran around the table, sprinted for the high table, and hurled the knife.

*How'd he get that in here?* one part of my brain absently wondered as the blade arced toward me. Had one of his people slipped it to him? Had it been hidden in his suit?

Fortunately for me, instinct didn't need input from my distracted mind. I threw up my hands in front of me, and as my unleashed power coursed through them, a blast of wind caught the knife and sent it careening onto the stone floor.

And in that nearly frozen moment, I *just* had time to register Ivari's dismay and smile at him before one of the security officers, who happened to be a *very* large troll, body-slammed him to the ground.

# CHAPTER 21

The rest of that first day of the tribunal was conducted without the defendant present, as attempting to stab witnesses was frowned upon.

I pulled myself together during the break, drying my face and trying to stop trembling. Tilla ran down to the Tribunal's on-site healer and returned with a blanket, and I huddled beneath it in the waiting room, rocking in my chair and hoping I wouldn't puke as my surge of adrenaline ebbed.

Cennis was coaxing water down me when someone knocked, and Remari opened the door to find the judge and two security officers in the corridor. "How is she?" Caganni asked.

"Shaken," Remari replied.

Since my hair was blowing around me and I was having to cling to the blanket to keep it from sailing off, that seemed like a fair assessment.

Caganni took a long, appraising look at me, then grunted and glanced at Remari. "I believe I'm beginning to see why your colleagues have been trying to so fervently to keep certain evidence out."

"Could be, ma'am," she replied.

With a grunt, the judge sank into the chair beside mine and patted my shoulder. "Are you going to be able to testify, Ms. Amos, or should I tell these counselors to rearrange the schedule?"

Straining, I drew my power back into me, and my mussed hair flopped down. "I'll, um...I'll do my best."

"How're you feeling?"

"Not great," I said, still unable to lie.

"I'd imagine. Well, that was some quick thinking back there, and you seem unharmed, so…five more minutes?" she asked, looking at the counselors.

By the time we resumed, I'd run a brush through my tangles and altered my mask in the bathroom mirror to hide some of the puffiness under my eyes, and I took my seat with a nod to the judge. Once I'd made myself comfortable and poured a fresh cup of water, she said, "I keep hearing references to a fire in the defendant's office. What happened?"

I looked out at the audience, the cameras in the balcony and the knot of uneasy elves on the floor, then cleared my throat and resumed.

At the counselors' strong suggestion, I didn't go back to school that night.

"Holy *shit*, kid," said Rose, settling in beside me on the couch in her private quarters. Two mugs of hot chocolate sat on the coffee table, both laced with liquor and slightly too warm to drink. With Caganni's permission, Diriem had brought me home with him, and since I wasn't supposed to talk to Connor or Jane yet, Rose had swooped in to keep me company. "I saw the clips at work. Can't believe she kept grilling you after the knife incident."

I shrugged. "At least I don't have to come back. She covered *everything*—East Branch, my blood test, Yacovi's house, all of us left here. I feel bad for the counselors," I said, chuckling. "We practiced what I was going to say, and then the judge upended everything."

"Who are they calling tomorrow? I know Pop's on the list…"

Tucking my legs beneath Rose's afghan, I said, "I don't think the judge is very happy with him. She knows about the bloodline potion."

"Yeah, well, he's a big boy," she replied. "Don't worry about that."

I sighed as I leaned against the couch cushion. "Didn't think I'd be back here so soon. I don't mean to keep dropping in—"

"You're fine, hon. Pop's not hurting for beds, believe me."

"Yeah, but…" I struggled, then settled for a weak, "You know?"

"I get it," Rose murmured. "Everything's weird and unsettled, and you're feeling like a burden. You're *not*," she said as I nodded emphatically. "And you're safe here tonight, so drink that," she ordered, pointing to our mugs, "and let's get you to bed. I bet you'll drop as soon as your head hits the pillow."

Uncurling enough to reach the coffee table, I grabbed my mug and took a small sip, then frowned at it, surprised. "Mint?"

"Peppermint schnapps. That'll cure what ails you," she said, and clinked her mug against mine. "I've got a bottle of Chambord, too, but frankly, I think the mint works better."

Ignorant of most alcoholic beverages beyond moonshine, I just smiled and drank.

On Tuesday morning, I returned to the tribunal in Monday's robe and found a seat in the audience beside Devva Hevannid and Matti Chela, who claimed they'd come to offer moral support for Apple Blossoms when she testified. I wasn't sure I believed that, given the number of black-clothed agents sitting around the room, but since the pair of investigators didn't mind sharing their bench, I didn't ask too many questions.

Ivari was back, but he sat with his shoulders slumped and his hands cuffed in his lap. His counselors began the day by offering an apology to the tribunal for the previous afternoon's "disruption," which they blamed on Ivari's trauma. "Ms. Amos is a living reminder of a...*difficult* time for Lord ti'Ammaas," said Periga. "It's unfortunate that he snapped yesterday, but that won't happen again."

"I should hope it doesn't," Caganni replied, "as I've already permitted Laws to add one assault charge to this proceeding. I would hate to see more."

As the morning progressed, it seemed that the judge might get her wish. Laws began with Ms. Mafatta to discuss the damage done to the school and to confirm the names of the affected students—including those who lived above and below our group—then brought up Apple Blossoms to walk through the investigation. When she finished, Ganti took his turn, explaining DOI's end of the investigation...though he had to admit that the agency had outsourced locating the would-be hitmen to DPP's lone farseer. Remari offered to bring Rose in if necessary, but Caganni declined and allowed the testimony to proceed. Diriem briefly covered what Ganti couldn't, and then Nugera ti'Van, quiet and remorseful, was sworn in to confirm the farseers' findings.

Last to testify before the lunch break was Dania ti'Lir, who, faced with talkative co-conspirators and staring down the barrel of a lengthy sentence, had decided her odds would be better if she cooperated with Laws. Sitting stiffly, clearly unhappy to be in the witness seat, Dania confessed to everything: seeking out Ivari, hiring the portal attendants, and orchestrating the fire.

Once Dania was released, Tilla came to find me and brought me into a witness room, where the two counselors were sitting with Connor and Jane. "Hey, mitta," said Connor, rising to hug me as Tilla headed back out in search of sandwiches. "Heard you had quite a time yesterday."

"Not something I want to do again," I replied, and released him before I could wrinkle his dress uniform. "But they've got Ivari handcuffed today, so maybe you'll have an easier time of it."

"Let's hope so," said Cennis, pushing a chair aside to make room for herself on the carpet. "Now, here's the plan. Since our testimony went *far* out of the expected order yesterday, we only have Connor and Naculta left. Naculta will be first—I want to put Ivari in Georgia before you go over the aftermath," she said, looking at my cousin. "And that'll be our case. I haven't seen any witness list from the other side, and unless Ivari changes his mind, I doubt they'll present a defense."

"Probably still hoping for a jurisdictional win," Remari grumbled.

"Seeing as Caganni shut that down yesterday, they can keep hoping," her partner replied. "But here's the thing," she said to Connor. "We have enough evidence right now to support a conviction for North Lake. We don't *need* to go any further. Everything that you and Naculta would present would go only to motive. So, considering what happened to Maebe yesterday, if you don't want to testify—"

"I want to," he insisted. "No question. This is as close as our family will probably ever come to getting their day in court, and I owe it to them."

"That's fine. Just, uh…be prepared. Ivari's not exactly delighted to be here."

Connor shrugged. "Won't be the first defendant I've pissed off."

The phrase didn't translate perfectly into Pactish, but the counselors seemed to catch his meaning.

We ate in that room—I had a far better appetite that day with my testimony behind me—and then I returned to the tribunal to watch.

Culta was brought in flanked by a pair of sorcerers, and given the angry whispers from the elves across the room, it wasn't difficult to see why. Unlike his father, he wore a zipped navy sweater over dark pants, and he barely spared Ivari a glance as he walked up to the witness seat.

"Traitor," Ivari stage-whispered in High Elvish as he passed.

"Monster," Culta replied in kind, not looking back.

Once he was sworn and ensorcelled, Remari began her questioning. "Your name?"

"Naculta ti'Pul," he said calmly, focusing on her.

"What's your relationship to the defendant, Mr. ti'Pul?"

"I'm his son."

"Not anymore," Ivari muttered.

Ignoring him, Culta added, "His second *living* son. I'm the third of seven children."

"You have deceased siblings?" Remari asked.

He nodded. "Several from my parents' first marriages. They were all killed by 1540 or so. And several more from my parents' second marriages, who are also long dead. I'm in the third batch."

"Let's focus on the second marriages," she said, folding her arms. "Are those the ones that led to the East Branch settlement?"

"Objection," Periga tried. "Honored Caganni, this isn't necessary to their case! All it's doing is provoking our client—"

"Goes to motive," Remari interrupted. "Why the defendant would decide to murder a group of children. The ones he *didn't* catch outside."

Periga briefly consulted with his partner, then said, "We can stipulate that Lord ti'Ammaas was...involved in an incident outside. There's no need to delve into the details."

"Your stipulation is appreciated, but I'm overruling your objection," said Caganni. "Proceed, Ms. Houn."

Working methodically, Remari pulled the whole story from Culta: Ivari's claims of blackmail, the drive down to Georgia, the bloodline potion to find East Branch, and then his trip to Yacovi's house with his brother and the others to find Connor and me. Finally, she said, "You were arrested for breaking into Mr. Hewt's home and his brew room, correct?"

"Yes," replied Culta.

"Have you made a deal with our agency?"

He nodded. "A recommendation of dismissal of the charges for my testimony against my father and everyone else involved in the East Branch trip."

She glanced over her notes. "Mr. ti'Pul, you realize that the penalty for the break-in is no more than ten years, correct? The only real damage was to the lock."

"So I was told."

"Yet you're testifying against your *father* to avoid a reasonably brief incarceration?"

Culta didn't flinch. "If someone really had been blackmailing us and was threatening to expose us, then I might be okay with what happened. I *thought* we were just grabbing two people so Father could talk some sense into them. But there was never any blackmail, and I..." He turned away, covered his mouth, and briefly closed his eyes. "I saw pictures from the scene. What was left of a little boy whose only failing was sharing blood with my father. And I...no," he said, shaking his head. "I didn't agree to kill anyone, especially not children. He deserves what he gets," he added, finally looking at Ivari. "And if Mr. Hewt's here today, I'm sorry about your brew room."

Yacovi wasn't there—he'd offered to come along for Connor's sake, but since he had a big brew on the schedule, Connor and Jane had insisted he stay home.

The cross-examination was brief, given Culta's blatant disgust for his father, and then Tilla hurried into the hall to find Connor. As he did, I noticed Teolm slip into the room—wearing a robe instead of his usual grungy greenhouse clothes—and take a seat midway down the aisle.

My cousin walked in with his head high, and Jane took the spot I'd saved beside me on my bench. Ivari watched Connor as he passed, but he made no sudden moves, and Connor was prepared for testimony without an outcry from the defense table.

As planned, Cennis questioned him. "What's your name?"

"Connor Willow."

She gave him a once-over. "Not to be rude, but I don't recognize that uniform."

"I'm the chief of police of Whitford, Georgia."

*That* got the room's attention, at least judging by the whisperings from the watching elves.

"Any connection to East Branch?" Cennis asked.

He nodded. "My parents were from the community. I was raised in the neighboring town, but they claim me."

"Kin to Maebe Amos?"

"Several times over. We're cousins, but please don't ask me to get more specific than that."

She patted the folded East Branch family tree. "Understood, Chief. I'm showing you a document from one of our agency healers," she said, approaching him with a piece of paper. "Do you recognize this?"

He glanced at it and nodded. "Yes. My genetic report. Canna Nerin ran it back in September."

"That's as you remember it?"

"Yes, ma'am."

Cennis presented it to Caganni, who accepted it and read it over before giving Connor a curious look. "Better than three quarters, young man?"

"That's what they tell me," said Connor.

"You don't look it…but of course, neither does the ti'Dana girl."

He tapped one ear. "Reconstructive surgery. I'm another cifyent case."

"I see. Go ahead, Ms. Paf."

With Cennis's guidance, Connor echoed what I'd said the day before about our terrifying night at Yacovi's house, albeit with one hitch. "Sorry, I have a question," Caganni interrupted. "What *were* you and Ms. Amos doing at Mr. Hewt's home, anyway?"

"I was house-sitting for him," Connor replied, "and

Maebe was having a hard time at school, so she came home for the weekend. Well, it was supposed to be for the weekend…"

"And this is a service law enforcement provides in Whitford?"

He chuckled softly. "No, ma'am. In any case, he lives in the next town over. Mr. Hewt…" He paused, then said, "I'm dating his daughter. We've gotten pretty well acquainted—"

"His daughter?" she echoed.

"Yes, ma'am. Jane."

The room began to murmur again, and that time, I caught voices from the balcony as well. Jane gripped my hand but sat still as Caganni motioned for the noise to subside.

Turning back to Connor, she asked, "You don't have citizenship here, do you?"

"I don't. But Jane and I got together back when you people were still wringing your hands over her being half human, so…" He shrugged. "She got her citizenship in February. Still keeps me around for some reason."

Caganni's voice softened. "I don't mean to bring up a difficult subject, but has anyone discussed with you the issues that arise when—"

"The death draught? I'm aware," he said, his tone taking on an edge. "If it comes to that, I'll step back. Janie's not killing herself on my account."

"I…do understand that you two are in an unfortunate position," the judge replied slowly. "Is there any path to citizenship for you? I suppose you'd require acknowledgement, but—"

"If I may be heard?" came a voice from behind me, and I turned to see Teolm standing in the aisle.

Caganni squinted into the room, then motioned him closer. "You are…"

"This is Lord ti'Cren, Honored Caganni," said Cennis. "Who was *not* on our witness list…"

"It was suggested to me that I show up," said Teolm as he approached the high table. "I think I see why. Afternoon, Connor."

"Teolm," my cousin replied with a nod.

"Don't mean to cause a scene," he continued, "but just so no one gets a crazy idea about chasing after Jane with the draught, there *is* a potential work-around. Lord ti'Dana asked me to co-sponsor, if you will, the East Branch group at North Lake. It wasn't a matter of sharing fiscal responsibility—we share blood," he explained, gesturing to Connor.

The judge frowned. "How so?"

"My grandfather was Joril ti'Ammaas…his cousin," he said, pointing over his shoulder at Ivari. "They shared grandparents. So, if the Forum can't find a way to grant the East Branch survivors citizenship on their own, they could enter through Hall ti'Cren."

"That's a *very* distant connection," she mused, and turned to Cennis. "How many generations did you say had lived at East Branch?"

"Distant, yes," said Teolm, "but my understanding is that they all descend from Lord ti'Ammaas, so there *is* a kinship tie to my Hall through my grandfather. Granted, it's a stretch," he allowed, "but if it's necessary…"

"Thanks, man," Connor murmured in English.

"Of course," Teolm replied, following his lead. "Look, I know the shit my great-niece went through with Yven, so if this saves any trouble…"

"I mean, we've already made one cross-country drive to avoid the draught," said Connor, laughing weakly. "Don't think I won't do it again."

Finally, Jane's hold on my hand began to relax.

"Thank you, Lord ti'Cren," said Caganni. "That is, of course, a matter for another day, but…I suppose that does explain why you were able to access a secure DPP facility," she said, turning to Connor.

He nodded as Teolm started back to his seat. "Since

Maebe and I would probably be dead today if Yacovi hadn't given me emergency access, I hope DPP doesn't hold it against him."

"Mm. Ms. Paf, I apologize," she said, turning to Laws' table. "Would you like to take over?"

Cennis smiled briefly, then quickly sobered as she resumed. "Chief Willow, when you and Ms. Amos were being...*sought* at Mr. Hewt's house, do you know what was occurring at East Branch?"

Connor paused before answering her. "I don't know the precise sequence of events, but I can tell you what I observed."

And he did. My mother's panicked call, his desperate drive out to the community, Wylan's fire assistance—he had an excellent memory for that night, and Jane wrapped her arm around me as he recounted it.

"How many casualties were there?" Cennis finally asked him.

"To the best of my knowledge, twenty-eight fatalities. That's how many bodies were recovered, and that's how many people were living on the property at the time."

Cennis nodded. "You say you're answering to the best of your knowledge. Why is that?"

"Because," said Connor, "I haven't been part of the investigation. I've read the reports and reviewed the evidence, but only because my colleagues keep slipping things to me."

"Why are you not involved?"

"The easiest answer is that it's not my jurisdiction," said Connor. "I cover Whitford, but East Branch is on county land—it's unincorporated. That means the sheriff has authority. Now, folks from the local police departments pitched in that night, and the sheriff's called in help from state agencies, but I've specifically been kept off the case in any official capacity because everyone knows that was my family."

"But you *have* seen evidence?" Cennis prodded.

Connor nodded. "The sheriff's a friend, and my people have been quietly keeping me in the loop. We all have an understanding: I can't be on the case, but they're not going to leave me in the dark."

She reached under Laws' table and grabbed a stuffed cardboard box with English printed all over it. "Do you recognize this, Chief?"

"Yes, ma'am."

"And what is it?"

"A copy of everything I've been given about the East Branch investigation from my people, plus whatever Laws...*borrowed* on their own, which I've also reviewed. I don't know precisely what channels you used to raid our files."

Glancing across the room at the defense, Cennis said, "You received your copy electronically."

"We did," said Periga, "but nothing was translated."

"Original versions," she replied sweetly.

I could just make out Cennis's tail flick below her full-body black robe.

Turning back to Connor, Cennis asked, "Are you familiar with the type of documents in this box?"

"I am," he replied. "I've liaised with the sheriff and with other agencies around the area, so I'm comfortable with this sort of evidence."

"And what, in general, is in here?"

"Incident reports," he began, counting off on his fingers, "autopsy reports, scene photographs, reports from the fire investigator, some witness statements...that should cover it. I also included the paperwork about the property. As far as anyone there knows, I'm the next of kin, and since I've been making property tax payments for a few years, I probably stand to inherit East Branch. The lawyers are doing their thing," he added, spreading his hands. "No one at East Branch had government identification, and there were certainly no wills, so I've been looking after the place of late. Buried our dead, at least."

Cennis looked up at the judge. "Honored Caganni, I believe that the witness is sufficiently familiar with these documents to be questioned about them."

"He didn't make them," Periga countered. "He's not even a proper custodian for them, is he?"

"No, I'm not the custodian of any of these," said Connor. "But they're the type of records I know well, and they fit the facts of the case as I've been told. The best person to speak to the investigation would be Mark Cain, our sheriff, but since he's about as human as they come, I'm guessing you'd prefer not to get him involved."

Caganni thought for a moment, then said, "Under the circumstances, I'll allow it, with the understanding that the witness did not create…any of these documents?"

"A few of them, ma'am," said Connor. "Photographs."

"All right. Proceed."

"Thank you," said Cennis, with a nod to the judge. "We'll need the projector."

Caganni's assistant brought one to their table, a slim, flat device slightly larger than a piece of paper that connected to Remari's computer. While they set up, two security officers wheeled large screens into position at the far sides of the room, giving the audience a view of the exhibits as well.

With that accomplished, Remari put the first photo in the stack onto the projector. My heart clenched when I saw the screen: a view of East Branch taken from near the wooden meeting house, showing the old building, the handmade picnic tables in the grass outside, the tall pines and hardwoods around it, and the mountains in the distance. I'd stood at the end of the rutted dirt road to capture it with my new phone, building a collection of shots of home for when I'd miss it.

"What are we looking at?" Cennis asked.

"That's the meeting house at East Branch," said Connor. "Sort of the center of community life. Place to store important documents—the deed to the land, the record book, things of that nature."

"When was this photograph taken?"

He screwed up his face. "Well, Maebe took that right before she started school here, so...late June, first of July. I don't know the precise date."

"This summer, yes?"

"Exactly."

When the picture changed, I groaned before I could stop myself.

I could tell the scene was the same only by the position of the mountains. The meeting hall was nothing but ash and a few burned timbers, while the remaining trees around it were charred skeletons, blackened and dead. Smoke still rose in the morning light, though everything appeared to be soaked.

"And this?" Cennis asked.

"That," said Connor, "is an evidence photo taken by one of my officers on the morning after the fire. Same view as before."

"Total loss?"

"Yes, ma'am. The sheriff let me come in a couple weeks ago to look for personal belongings—this was after his team and the fire investigator finished—but I didn't get much more than a few scraps of paper and some melted bits of metal and plastic. The fire burned *hot*."

"Was the investigation able to establish a cause?" asked Cennis.

"No. There were no signs of accelerant, and the whole conflagration was the result of multiple fires," said Connor. "It's been ruled arson, but no suspect has been identified."

For the next hour, Cennis meticulously went through scene photos and reports with Connor, showing the extent of the damage and detailing the fruitless investigation. "It's unfortunate," he said as she wrapped up that portion of his testimony. "I'm the one guy in the county with an inkling as to who's responsible, and I can't touch the case."

"And how do you know who's responsible?" Cennis asked.

"Admittedly, it's a circumstantial deduction. However, the participants were protected from farsight, we had devastating fires out of nowhere without the slightest indication as to what could have naturally started them...and then there's Naculta ti'Pul. I took his confession. All that, and there's one asshole in the universe I know of who would have wanted a bunch of poor farmers dead and would have had the means to get in undetected, avoid farsight, and kill everyone with freaking magic."

"Objection to the characterization of the defendant—" Periga began.

"Excuse me," Connor muttered to the judge.

She let it slide and waved the peeved counselor back into his seat.

Cennis then turned to the stack of autopsy reports. "Chief Willow, I'd like to go through the deceased with you. Have you reviewed the information from the coroner?"

"Yes, ma'am," he replied. "Every bit of it."

"I realize the victims are members of your extended family, and I don't mean to cause distress—"

"I'm prepared. Where would you like to begin?"

She slid a picture onto the projector. "Could you identify these people, please?"

"Sure," said Connor. "Those are Peter and Delia Amos and their youngest, Joseph."

Cennis's head cocked. "*Amos*. Are they direct kin to Maebe?"

"No, ma'am. Peter..." He paused, grimacing as he thought. "I know they're cousins, but I can't be more specific than that."

"Would the family tree help you?"

"*Please*."

She and Remari carefully unfolded it, and with a quick mutter from the sorcerer beside the judge, the lowest few generations appeared on the screen. "Do you see them on here?" Cennis asked.

The judge passed Connor a laser pointer, and he identified them. "Right there. Peter Amos, Delia Smith, and their kids. The twins go to school here, but Peter and Delia decided that Joseph was too young to leave home."

"Just a moment—you gave Delia a different surname."

"In our region, it's traditional for a wife to take her husband's name," he explained. "That's always been the practice at East Branch. Delia was born a Smith, but as you see on that chart, both of her grandmothers were Amoses. The families at East Branch are *very* close," he muttered.

Cennis switched the view on the screen back to the picture of my cousins. "When was this taken?"

"Right before Maebe left for school. Photos were rare at East Branch, and she was given a phone with a camera, so this was a novelty."

"I see. How old were these three, do you know?"

"Joseph was six or seven—I don't recall his birthdate offhand," said Connor. "Peter was eight years my senior, so...thirty-eight or thirty-nine. Delia was a few years younger than Peter...I'm sorry, but I don't have exact numbers. Maybe thirty-five."

She nodded and removed the photo. "I'm going to switch to Joseph's autopsy report now. Before I begin, do you know precisely which reports refer to his parents?"

"No. The bodies were burned beyond recognition. In fact, the only one the coroner was able to identify was Joseph, and that was by process of elimination."

"What does that mean?"

"Well," said Connor, "the other victims were adults. Joseph was the only child still on the property, so the lone child skeleton had to be his. I was able to give the coroner a list of the residents, but for most of the bodies, the best he could do was sex, maybe an age range."

"And was the condition of Joseph's body typical for

the deceased?"

He nodded, his mouth tight. "Yes, ma'am."

Cennis picked up another photograph, then said, "If anyone in the room has a weak stomach, you might want to look away."

I wish I had, and upon seeing what remained of my little cousin, I understood why Culta had thrown up. Instead, I buried my face against Jane, hearing gasps and disgusted mutterings from the other spectators.

For the next few minutes, Connor testified about Joseph, including the odd holes found in the pieces of his skull. "The coroner couldn't tell whether he was alive when he started burning," he concluded in an oddly flat tone. "Not enough soft tissue left to determine whether he died from his head injuries, smoke inhalation, or the fire."

"Thank you," said Cennis, and paused, giving Connor a closer look. "Do you need a break, Chief?"

"I'm...capable of continuing," he replied. Judging by his expression, telling her he was fine probably would have triggered the spell.

Mercifully, Cennis replaced the autopsy photos with another family photo, and Connor identified the dead one by one. Mason Black and Iris Smith. My parents. Gregory Amos and Candice Black. Uncle Joel, Mom and Uncle Kyle's brother. Then the elders of the generation before.

Finally, Cennis showed him one last picture: my paternal grandparents. "And who are they?" she asked.

"On the left, that's Veronica Amos, born Veronica Tine," Connor replied. "Her mother was an Amos, too," he added, pointing to the family tree draped over the counselors' table. "On the right is her husband, Walter Amos. Until September, he was the defendant's next heir."

From the audience, I could see Ivari shifting in agitation.

"Why do you believe that?" Cennis asked.

"Back in June, uh...Lord ti'Dana used a spell, I guess, to take a look at Maebe's and my ancestry from the record book. Walter was the firstborn of the firstborn to procreate up the Amos line, all the way back to Henry Amos. He was Ivari's second son, but the eldest never had children—"

"Shut your damn mouth, you little worm!" Ivari yelled, jumping out of his seat. Periga's partner grabbed his arm and tugged, and Ivari wheeled on him with a murderous expression. Had he not been handcuffed, he probably would have taken a swing at the counselor.

"Counsel—" Caganni began, but her warning went unfinished as Connor stood and glared back at Ivari.

"The *fuck* did you just say to me?" he demanded in English.

"You know nothing," Ivari spat, switching languages with him. "You *are* nothing. That trash was nothing of mine—"

"That *trash* was a good man," Connor retorted, coming around the high table, then marched toward Ivari. "A hard worker who loved his family. How fucking *dare* you. You're not worth the dirt on his boots."

The security officers began to close in, but neither my cousin nor Ivari seemed to notice.

"I will not be lectured to by a damn animal," said Ivari, ignoring his counselor's urging to sit. "Know your place and shut your—"

"*Sit down*," Connor growled, slamming his palms on the defense table, and the hapless counselor finally managed to yank Ivari into his chair. Leaning over him as both counselors pressed him into his seat, my cousin's expression as close to murderous as I'd ever seen it, Connor said, "I'll be damned if I take orders from a fucking piece of New York shit like you, old man. You're *pathetic*. And you'd better be fucking glad I ain't a pyro, or else you'd get it as good as you gave at East Branch." With that, he grabbed Ivari's lapels and yanked him up, throwing off the counselors with the force of his tug. "Try to touch my family again, and I'll kill you myself."

That was as far as he got before security intervened. When the troll's massive hands landed on his shoulders, Connor released Ivari and retreated, though he was red-faced and almost panting.

Caganni called a break, and as the troll hurried Connor from the room, Jane and I ran out to intercept them. By the time we reached them, the officer was standing guard outside the witness room, Remari and Cennis were inside, and my cousin was bent over in a chair, head in his hands, sobbing.

"I'm sorry," Cennis said, kneeling beside him. "Young-ling, I'm so sorry…"

"I thought I could handle it," he managed between gasping breaths. "In prep—"

"You did well."

"Finally seeing that smug bastard…he didn't even *flinch*, did you notice?" said Connor. "When you put up Joseph's autopsy photos, he didn't *care*. That little guy was just a baby…"

"Honey," said Jane, slipping past the security officer ahead of me, and my cousin glanced up, eyes streaming. "Con, sweetheart, I'm here."

He hugged her like his life depended on it, his face contorting as he tried to stop himself from crying, and Jane murmured reassurance over his mumbled apologies. "It's okay," she said, rubbing his back. "It's going to be okay…"

I stepped deeper into the room at the sound of approaching footsteps, and then the officer moved aside to admit Caganni and her own detail. She stood there for a moment, taking in the scene, then sighed and folded her arms over her robe. "Too much, eh?"

He raised his head from Jane's shoulder and hastily wiped away what he could with his hand. "I'm really sorry, ma'am. I—"

"You're not the first to lose control in one of my tribunals. Thank you for not punching the defendant," she said dryly. "You've given solid testimony thus far—I'd hate for you to have to continue with a knot on your head."

He looked past her at the officer on the door, who flashed a brief, almost sympathetic smile.

"You're not throwing me out?" Connor asked the judge.

"Consider this your formal warning. I wouldn't ordinarily be so lenient, but in light of what Laws asked you to do today…" Her eyes narrowed as she looked at the counselors. "I believe the human agents were wise to keep him off this case."

"We didn't have a better witness," said Remari.

"And I understand that, but those are pictures I'd rather forget, and the poor boy isn't even my kin." Turning back to Connor, she said, "Ten minutes. Wash your face, hmm? And will this conclude Laws' case?"

"I'm finished with him," said Cennis. "We'll rest once he's excused."

"Great. I doubt that the defense will have much to ask, considering that little display." She started to leave, then looked back at Connor. "Mind your manners, now. Your part in this mess is almost finished."

# CHAPTER 22

As Connor had had one hell of an afternoon, he accepted the invitation when Diriem sent Jane a message inviting the three of us to spend the night.

"Thanks," said Connor when Diriem met us in the foyer. "For sending Teolm, I mean."

One side of his mouth rose in a little grin. "Thought that might be helpful. See, Oz the Great and Powerful isn't entirely useless, right?"

"Yeah, yeah," Connor muttered, but smiled back at him. "Sometimes."

I hadn't realized the extent of the media coverage of Ivari's trial until I saw the cameras in the tribunal, and hearing it rehashed on the news that night as we sat around the television in one of Diriem's dens was bizarre. While the reporters touched on the victims at East Branch, the clip they played was of Connor and Ivari, complete with censored subtitles.

"Getting your fifteen minutes of fame," Jane teased Connor as he closed his eyes and groaned.

"I look like a lunatic," he muttered, further loosening his tie.

"It's not that bad," said Diriem.

Connor gave him an incredulous stare. "Come *on*, man. I lost it in there."

"Granted, but let's just say that I've witnessed my share of tribunals, and that little display doesn't crack the top ten."

The video ended, and one of the presenters at the desk,

a dark-haired elf with blindingly white and rather sharp teeth, turned to the reporter and tutted. "It's truly sad what's become of storied Hall ti'Ammaas," he said. "Considering the history of the Hall, for its lines to have run to…what, inbred half-bloods living in squalor? Such a shame—"

"They're *survivors*," came a deep voice from off camera, and the view panned to the sports desk, where Moonless Night sat in a burgundy robe, scowling around his tusks at his colleague. "I don't know what notes *you* read, Oalit, but my takeaway was that ti'Ammaas and the rest of his cohort abandoned their children in the wilderness. They weren't fully talented, they had physical defects—no wonder they didn't integrate with the humans around them. But their community survived."

"That's true," Oalit allowed, "but—"

"And you heard the Amos girl yesterday, right? She's taken the bloodline potion *twice*. That child's not even twenty! Who cares what she is? That's *tough*."

The reporter nodded as Oalit started to flush. "Well…yes," he said.

"And heavens, she's an aeromancer, isn't she? That trick with the knife—I mean, how much training can she have had? Weeks? A few months' worth?" Moonless Night snorted. "Be fair, now."

I smiled to myself as the chastised elf continued with the next story, then glanced at Diriem, who was chuckling. "What?" I asked.

"You know he helped bring Ivari's people in, yes?"

"And I'm guessing that nice anchor has no clue," said Jane.

"*No*, I would think not," Diriem replied. "If anyone at Channel 1 knows that the sports chief is a Huntsman, it's certainly not the pretty boy on the desk."

Connor grunted. "Bets as to whether Oalit is masked?"

"Keep your money," said Diriem. "I saw him when he started."

"Yeah? How bad?"

"I doubt his own mother would recognize him if he weren't on television every weeknight." With that, he gestured at the screen until it went black, then turned to Connor. "Get some rest. You'll want to be fresh for the tribunal in the morning."

My cousin frowned in suspicion. "Was that a warning?"

"No, that's common sense," Diriem replied. "You're exhausted. Sleep."

Connor stared into the distance for a moment as if contemplating a thorny problem, then muttered, "Yeah, you're not wrong. Night," and stumbled off toward the staircase.

**B**y Wednesday morning, I was tiring of my robe, but Scel muttered away the wrinkles on my way out the door, and I didn't complain.

I sat in my seat from Tuesday beside Jane, who'd sandwiched herself between Connor and me. Apple Blossoms and her crew took the end of the row, blocking us from the clump of agitated elves on the defense's side. I watched as Kabno and Diriem slipped in, taking spots in the balcony...and then, with about five minutes before the hour, the rear doors opened to admit Ms. Mafatta, who escorted the rest of my kin.

"Hey," I whispered as they grabbed seats on the benches behind us.

"Hey yourself," Uncle Kyle whispered back. "Nice job with that knife, kiddo."

I smiled. "Panic and luck."

"Yeah, well, it worked. And you," he said, squeezing Connor's shoulder. "Didn't your mama ever wash your mouth out with soap?"

"Shove it," Connor replied, grinning. "Good to see y'all."

"Good to be here," said Laurel, who'd grabbed a seat

beside her husband. "Y'all did well."

It wasn't full forgiveness, I knew, but it was something, and Connor murmured his thanks.

Soon, the counselors walked in, and just after Ivari was escorted into the room—handcuffed again, I noticed—Caganni took her seat at the high table. She paused, giving the cameras in the balcony a chance to adjust, then cleared her throat. "Good morning. We're here today for final arguments and the verdict. Let me hear from the Division of Laws."

I listened as Remari summarized their case, and then as Periga took his turn for the defense. After about an hour, when both sides had made their best cases, Caganni called a ten-minute break.

"This is it," said Apple Blossoms as the judge walked out. "She'll rule when she returns."

Though the troll's smile seemed encouraging, I shifted in my seat, impatient for the verdict but dreading Caganni's reappearance. If this didn't go our way...if she wasn't convinced...

As I fidgeted, Jane hugged me from the side and whispered, "Breathe, Maebe. No tornadoes today, all right?"

I tried, but I was a nervous wreck by the time Caganni returned to the tribunal. She situated herself, looked over her computer, then said, "Rise, Mr. ti'Ammaas."

At his counselors' prodding, Ivari did so, standing alone to face her with his cuffed hands in front of him.

"I am *appalled*, sir," Caganni began, "and I've presided over more tribunals than I care to remember. The evidence put before me shows that you abandoned your children and practically forgot about them until your distant granddaughter showed up and asked for help—and for what? To purchase food? Make repairs? Keep the home they settled with you? You could have simply said no," she continued. "All questions of morality aside, that would have been your right. But instead, you *attacked* that child, then used the evidence of her untrained self-defense to concoct a story that she and her kin were poised to reveal your true identity. And that story, far-fetched though it seems to me as an outside observer, was sufficiently convincing to not only lead your people to murder twenty-eight of your innocent descendants and burn their settlement to the ground, but then to attempt to murder the remaining children. *Children*," she repeated. "We can quibble about the age of majority here and outside the Pactlands, but there were unquestionably children in that building when the men you paid set it on fire. Toddlers. Children under ten. Teenagers. And that's only within the East Branch group—I shudder to think about the other students in that building who could have been burned alive if Ms. Amos hadn't risked her own safety to hold the fire at bay."

She paused, letting the echo of her words fade.

"But as your counselors have been so fond of reminding me of late, you're not on trial for anything but the fire at North Lake. For that, at least, I find you guilty of arson and of twenty-one counts of attempted murder. Let's not forget Monday's outburst while we're at it—you threw a knife at a *child*," she said, shaking her head. "Whether you like it or not, your own blood. Think about that."

Glancing out at us, Caganni said, "Your victims are here today, Mr. ti'Ammaas—the survivors, that is. I wish I could do more for them. They deserve the sort of justice that I cannot give them, and frankly, I doubt they'll ever receive it. But I sincerely hope they take a measure of solace in what I *can* give them." Turning back to the defense table, she said, "I sentence you to one hundred years of incarceration on a penal farm. You'll labor for the good of society, and perhaps you'll have time to reflect upon your decisions. I hope you're a better man at the end of your sentence, though I'd be lying if I said I was counting on it."

"You can't keep me here!" Ivari yelled back at her. "You have no authority—"

"Agree to disagree," said Caganni. "And I'm fining you five hundred thousand marks per victim—all twenty-two."

"Five hundred…" he sputtered.

"Honored Caganni," said Periga, quickly standing, "you mean twenty-one, correct?"

"Twenty-two, Mr. Ularru. The fine is for the victims' pain, suffering, trauma, and loss—and having witnessed Chief Willow's testimony yesterday, I believe he's suffered as well."

"How much is that?" I whispered to Jane.

"About half a million bucks. *Each*," she whispered back to me.

I wasn't sure my brain could comprehend a sum that large, and considering Connor's stunned expression, I suspected he was in the same boat. But as Ivari's counselors began to protest, Connor shook his head and leaned toward me. "Don't get your hopes up, mitta. We'll never see a dime."

"Why not?" I asked.

"How's she going to enforce that? She's got Ivari, but she can't touch his bank account from here."

Though that was a sobering disappointment, I smiled to see Ivari dragged out of the room by two trolls, kicking and shouting curses at the judge.

After Caganni closed the proceedings, Remari and Cennis came down to speak to us. "It's a good result," said Cennis. "A reasonable sentence, too, so I doubt he'll find any traction if he tries to get the Forum to reverse it."

"Thank you both," said Connor, and shook the counselors' hands. "Much appreciated."

Remari nodded. "Of course. I'm sorry we couldn't do more."

"So…what happens now?" I asked.

"Now?" She shared a look with Cennis and faintly smirked. "Well, we won't be seeing dear old Ivari for a while, and if I know the director, she'll make sure that he's placed far away from Inade ti'Cren, just in case those two get any ideas. After that?"

Cennis cracked her knuckles. "Got a few more tribunals lined up, don't we?"

"Are you going to need Maebe and me again?" Connor asked.

"Hopefully not. We should be able to use your testimony from last time—Caganni has all of the related cases, so that'll be fun for the defense counselors."

"Who will probably be beating down our door...oh, after lunch," said Remari. "Which I think we've earned. I'm hungry."

"We'll keep you informed," Cennis promised as the first of the reporters reached the ground floor and headed toward us. "But for now, you should hurry out of here unless you just want to see yourself on the news. Apple Blossoms, Devva, Matti, would you mind giving our victims an escort?"


I returned to school that evening after dinner, feeling better about being back in my dorm room than I had in weeks, and slept like the dead.

My cousins seemed more at peace the next morning as we gathered for breakfast—if not ecstatic, then closer to content. They made room for me at the table, and even David was unusually civil.

When we joined up with the rest of our age cohort, the folks in my class swarmed me with questions, much to the art teacher's chagrin. The tribunal had been on TV, after all, and they'd seen me swat down a knife attack. How'd I do it? Was I scared? What was it like to be unable to lie without pain? Did Caganni ever try to sing?

I answered them as best as I could while we got down to work, but more questions popped up over the days that followed, to the point that I seldom had lunch in peace. I wasn't exactly *popular*, but I was apparently interesting.

"Oh, people watched the recaps from the tribunal,"

Violet told me during one of our tutorials when I broached the issue. "Old Halls long thought dead, murder, conspiracy—it was good fodder, I'll say. But they're not just coming to you because of that."

"No?" I asked through gritted teeth, struggling to keep a whirlwind under control as it encircled me.

"You know that Moonless Night talked about you, don't you? I mean, forget the fact that you saved the dorm and quite a few lives—*Moonless Night* complimented you, and you aren't even an athlete. That doesn't happen every day…and watch your left flank, you're getting sloppy."

As I tightened my grip to avoid disaster, I made a mental note to send my thanks through Annie the next time I saw her. If nothing else, my former tormentors were keeping their distance, and I was mighty grateful for that.

**T**wo weeks after Ivari was ignominiously shipped off, Cennis called me after dinner. "Hi, dear," she said as I sank onto my rumpled bed and pushed my books aside. "Busy?"

"No, ma'am," I replied, gripping my phone. "Is everything, uh…okay?"

She chuckled. "Don't worry. I think you'll be pleased."

In the days after Ivari's conviction, the other defendants' counselors had come running to Laws to work out deals. Talivol ti'Gata, the portal attendant who'd refused to talk, had bargained for a century of imprisonment like Ivari on twenty-one counts of attempted murder and arson. His remorseful partner, Nugera ti'Van, who'd testified, received only fifty years. Dania ti'Lir also received fifty years for her part in the conspiracy, as did Hemell ti'Vanil, meaning that Rush and Sons would be in need of a new PR director. Jomin ti'Cren, Dania's husband and Teolm's younger brother, had another five years tacked onto his sentence for helping Dania get the plan off the ground.

That left only the four who'd broken into Yacovi's

house. "Three went home today," Cennis told me. "We worked out an exchange with Ivari's wife: once she sent his fine, we'd release them without charges. She came through."

"How'd she find marks in New York?" I asked.

"Oh, she didn't, but precious metals work well. So, with that said, each of you is now half a million marks wealthier, but we've got the money in an agency account right now. We'll set up individual bank accounts for all of you, but, uh…" She paused, then huffed a little sigh. "I don't mean to sound rude, but you're not accustomed to handling large sums of money. The director wants to attach Lord ti'Dana and Lord ti'Cren to the accounts until you're a bit more fiscally savvy. They'll know how to safely invest for you while you're in school, and once you're ready, the money will be waiting."

"That's probably not a bad idea," I concurred.

"You don't suppose the others will be insulted?" asked Cennis.

I thought of Peter and the rest of my older kin—and of Conner, who surely knew better than any of us how banks worked—and grunted. "I think they'll come around. But you said only three went home…"

"Correct. Danirri ti'Ammaas, Pean ti'Elta, and Tella ti'Fin. Their families wanted them back."

"What about Culta?"

Cennis hissed. "Mr. ti'Pul is…not a popular fellow right now, shall we say. It was tough to get a read on that bunch while they were here, but the ones back home have made it clear that he's not welcome."

"So…is he staying?" I asked.

"We're working on that, and on all of you, too," she said. "Caganni can be a force of nature when she makes up her mind, and she's been rather vocal about working out a solution to give you citizenship."

"Hall ti'Cren?"

"Beyond that. I don't know all that's gone on at the

Tribunal building this week, but I *do* know she's been behind closed doors with several other judges and a number of representatives, so be patient, Maebe."

When I hung up, I hurried into the main common room to begin sharing the news. The money was a nice surprise—with that much on hand, I imagined we'd never have a hungry winter again—but my older cousins especially were keener than I'd anticipated to explore citizenship options.

"I like it here," said Monica, and Peter, his arm around her, nodded. "School's useful, the roof doesn't leak, I don't worry that the kids aren't going to get enough to eat…"

"And what do have waiting back in Georgia, anyway?" said Uncle Kyle. "Unless we want to rebuild East Branch."

"Yeah, and do what with it?" asked Amy. "The fields are worn out, there's nowhere to live and no tools, I'm sure the livestock are dead or gone, and then there's…well." She reached up and flicked one of her floppy ears. "This place ain't home, exactly, but I don't have to worry about someone seeing me with my headband off. And if Winston has the touch, then he'll be able to grow up learning how to use it right. Winston and Toby, Eugene, little David, Eleanor…things'll be so much easier for them."

"So, what's the plan?" Peter asked me. "Teolm's adopting us?"

"Cennis didn't think so," I replied, "but you know as much as I do."

He snorted. "Don't you have a farseer or two in that phone of yours, mitta?"

"They're a quiet bunch."

"Uh-huh," he muttered, and rolled his eyes. "Well, have a seat. Going to watch TV, or were you planning to hide in your room all night?"

I spent the rest of the evening sitting around with my cousins, saying little but grateful to be somewhat back in the fold.

Sure, I woke from a nightmare around two the next morning, having dreamed of my mother's burning, eternally screaming corpse, and barely made it to the bathroom before I was sick...but small progress was better than nothing.

And as had become usual, while I clutched the cold toilet and panted, I whispered my apologies to the ones I'd doomed.

Late the following Wednesday afternoon, our dorm parents piled us into two vans for the trip to the Tribunal building. I didn't know what to expect—Cennis had been thin on details when she called me about our appointment—but I'd thrown on my robe, just in case. The rest of my cousins made do with sweaters or long-sleeved dresses, as November was drawing to a close and a true chill was setting in with the dwindling daylight.

Caganni's assistant met us in the lobby and ushered us upstairs to the domed room where Ivari had faced justice. As I headed down the aisle, I thought of how different the room seemed when it was nearly empty—no cameras, no muttering elves in the audience—and then I noticed the long table set up just in front of the stone divider, behind which three chairs had been placed. Apparently, no one would be at the high table that day.

Looking around for a sign as to where I was supposed to land, I spotted Jane and Connor near the front, waving to get my attention, and hurried to join them. "Hey," I said, sliding onto their bench. "Didn't know if you'd make it."

Connor grunted. "My people have racked up *so* much overtime in the last couple of months, but...you know, you get the summons, you come." Giving me a scrutinizing look, he picked a fuzzball off his sweater and said, "Thought this was supposed to be casual..."

"You're fine," Jane assured him. "And do you *really* want to be in your dress uniform for dinner?"

He shuddered. "That seems dangerous."

"Annie gave us a lift," Jane explained, leaning past Connor to fill me in, "and she's invited us up for dinner with the boys tonight. It's not a true evening with the Hunt unless someone ends up under the table, so…you know, wish us luck."

A few minutes after the last elevator load of my cousins trickled in, Caganni appeared from a side door, along with a massive, violet-skinned troll and, to my surprise, Mirrik Voln. The three of them smiled at us in our awkward clump down front and took their seats, and Caganni's assistant returned carrying her computer. "Oh, thank you," she told him, opening it. "Now, it looks like we're almost all here…*ah*," she said as the rear door opened again. "There you are. Right on time."

"Just left a meeting," said Diriem, who seemed polished as ever in a deep green robe as he swept down the aisle.

Behind him jogged Teolm, who…well, he looked like he'd had a *day*. His jeans and shirt were stained with bright red streaks, and his short hair was badly mussed.

Mirrik watched with concern as they drew near. "Uh…is everything all right at Dashom Brothers, or should we be alarmed?"

"Apologies," said Teolm with a weary sigh. "Let's just say pollination isn't for the faint of heart."

"In *November*?"

"That's the beauty of greenhouses," he replied, then seemed to notice the state of his clothes, winced, and gestured himself clean. "Sorry about that," he said as he ran a smoothing hand over his hair. "No disrespect intended, I assure you—"

"You're fine, youngling," the troll rumbled, poorly hiding a smile. "Take a seat. Breathe."

I still didn't know how old Teolm really was, but the

white-haired troll had to be practically ancient. They could see eight hundred years, I'd read, and the one beside Caganni was surely drawing close.

As Teolm collapsed onto a bench, Caganni turned toward my group. "We didn't have an opportunity to be introduced properly the last time you were here. I'm Caganni…and I suppose it's obvious what I do," she added, grinning as some of my cousins chuckled. "To my right is one of my fellow judges, The Scent of the Smoke of the Home Fire, who's been here…how many years, now?"

"Too many," the troll rumbled.

"Fair," she replied. "I worked for Smoke when I was starting out," she added to us, almost conspiratorially, "so let's not run the numbers. And to my left is Representative Voln, but I assume he's familiar to at least some of you."

He glanced at the row where I sat with Connor and Jane, and his eyebrows waggled.

"Thank you all for coming," Caganni continued. "For what little it's worth, you have my sincere condolences for your losses, and I hope you can take a measure of comfort in the fact that some of the parties responsible will be enjoying Laws' hospitality for years to come."

"And the funds," Smoke reminded her.

"Yes, those came through. Director Erenani informs me that your accounts should be finalized by the end of the week," she told us. "One of the challenges Laws has faced in completing that is working around the tiny matter that you don't legally exist here…*yet*. We've been seeking a solution with the Forum," she said, nodding to Mirrik, "and I'm pleased to tell you that we've agreed upon a route to citizenship for you—if you want it."

Many of my cousins looked to Peter, who sat with little Eleanor on his lap while Monica held squirming Tobias. "Yes, ma'am," he said simply. "Thank you."

"Glad to hear it." Caganni pushed her computer aside and folded her hands on the table. "Here's what we've decided. At the time of the Pact, the southern Halls were invited to join us. Few did"—she glanced at Teolm—"but the invitation was extended to all. While your ancestors declined," she said to us, "your families have evidently suffered for it. Our solution, then, is to reestablish the southern Halls here."

Connor raised a finger to draw her attention. "Just to clarify, ma'am, you're proposing to set up a system here whereby, say, Ivari would have—"

"He'll have nothing," said Caganni. "The old heads of those Halls rejected us. We've reviewed East Branch's records and determined their next heirs, and we'd like to set you up as such. Some of you will be lords and ladies in your own right...though given this group's youth, we'd like for Hall ti'Cren and Hall ti'Dana to assist for a time. At least until you're of majority."

We turned in our seats, gauging each other's reactions, and again, Peter spoke for us: "That'd be all right, I think."

"Excellent. And what say you, gentlemen?" she asked, turning to Teolm and Diriem.

"Whatever needs to be done," Teolm replied as Diriem nodded. "We'll continue to support them."

"That's what I was hoping you'd say. Now, obviously," she said, looking back at us, "your Halls will be tiny for now. It isn't as though we can compel your kinfolk outside to join us...though I believe that ti'Pul will have a subordinate member, yes?"

"He's staying," said Smoke, looking to Diriem. "DOI suggests that it wouldn't be safe for him to return, considering family sentiment."

"Then I suppose we'll see whether he can stay out of trouble," said Caganni.

That took care of Culta, then. I wondered how he'd feel about this arrangement, but that wasn't my problem.

"Now," Caganni murmured, sliding her computer closer once more and squinting at the screen, "we made assignments based on the old Hall inheritance laws—eldest of the eldest—but as it happens, under that scheme, some of you would inherit multiple Halls."

"The lower one would typically pass to a younger sibling in that instance," Diriem offered.

"Believe me," Mirrik interjected, "I've spent more time in the last week with Hall inheritance rules than I ever imagined I'd need to."

Diriem smirked. "Try working out those disputes on your own. Using patchy records, I should add."

"Yeah, yeah," he said with a good-natured wave.

"Our point," said Caganni, drawing the discussion back on track, "is that we feel this is the most accurate distribution of Halls. So, let's see…" She looked at the screen and smiled. "Well, I imagine this is no surprise. Despite the sheer number of Amoses in your family, Maebe Amos heads ti'Ammaas."

Jane leaned around Connor and poked my knee. "Lady ti'Ammaas," she whispered. "Not too shabby, kid."

"Moving on—and we're using the order of prominence, based on what's known of the southern kingdom," she added—"Connor Willow has the clear claim to ti'Catama."

He seemed momentarily startled, then concerned. "I appreciate that, I really do," said Connor, "but I've got responsibilities in Whitford—"

"We'll work it out," Caganni assured him. "Let's see…ti'Pul goes to Heidi Amos. Is she here?"

Heidi raised her hand. "Um…what about that other guy?"

"Naculta? He answers to you now," she replied. Leaving Heidi to consider this development, she said, "Next is ti'Tola, and that goes to David Amos."

He sat up a little straighter, frowning at the judge. "Sorry, but my sister…you just assigned her…"

"That's the reality of the situation, I'm afraid," replied Caganni. "Ordinarily, children are given one of their parents' Halls, but because the family lines here are so interconnected and there are fifteen Halls represented, we're getting a little creative." She glanced at Diriem, who nodded. "You agree?"

"I've seen sibling splits," he replied. "Look at Hall ti'Cren—if Teolm's mother and her mother were to die, one of his siblings would inherit Hall ti'Tam."

"That would be Jomin," Teolm muttered, "assuming he's been released from custody by then. If not him, then his son."

Satisfied, David relaxed on the bench, and Caganni continued. "After tiTola is ti'Elta, and that goes to Marshall Amos."

The three siblings shared a look, and Marshall, only fourteen, flashed a thumbs-up at his sister and brother.

Caganni chuckled. "Ti'Non goes to Zoe Black. Is she...ah, thank you," she said as my younger cousin raised her hand. "Very good. And Peter Black, that's your brother, yes?"

"Here," he said, lifting a hand in turn.

"Excellent. Yours is ti'Fin."

I glanced at the senior Peter, Uncle Kyle, and the other older cousins, none of whom but Connor had yet received Halls, and tried to read their expressions. Concern? Frustration?

"Ti'Gen goes to David Black," said Caganni, "who is...hmm. Rather young," she murmured as the seven-year-old stood on his bench to be seen, "but I suspect you'll have assistance, dear. Moving along, we have ti'Merin, and that falls to Sebastian Amos."

I glanced at the twins. Sebastian, thirteen, was the elder only by a few minutes, but if that was enough to make a difference...

"Then we have ti'Vanil," Caganni continued, "which goes to Stephanie Amos."

The pair grinned at each other.

"A few more," said the judge. "Is Amy Smith present?"

At last, another of the older cousins. Amy raised her hand and said, "Smith's my maiden name. I'm Amy

Church these days."

"Perhaps not for long," said Caganni. "You inherit ti'Gol."

"All right." She hoisted Winston, who was fidgeting as badly as Tobias was. "What about my son?"

"He can have either parent's Hall," Diriem interjected. "His father is…"

"Me. Paul Church," he said, waving to catch Diriem's eye.

Caganni consulted her computer. "Paul…ah, there you are. A little out of order, but you inherit ti'Nallo."

"Huh," he mumbled. "So…our son…"

"Traditionally," said Diriem, "for children, preference is given to the higher parental Hall unless one of the parents is in line to inherit, in which case he or she would get preference. For a situation like yours, the usual procedure is to split the children. The eldest is the heir to the higher Hall—here, ti'Gol—and the next one would inherit ti'Nallo."

"But in the meantime, or if there's never another child," said Caganni, "Hannah Church is also a member of ti'Nallo."

"Finally," joked Paul, "you're keeping siblings together."

"Trust us, this wasn't simple," said Smoke, and turned to Caganni. "How many more?"

"Three Halls, plus other assignments," she replied. "Ti'Jan falls between ti'Gol and ti'Nallo, and that belongs to…Peter Smith?"

I cut my eyes toward him in time to see his relief.

"Ti'Un goes to Kyle Smith," said Caganni—my uncle seemed surprised—"and last is ti'Fer, which falls to Monica Church."

She and Peter nodded at each other, each still holding one of their children. Eleanor, I assumed, would get ti'Jan from her father, while Tobias would get ti'Fer from his mother.

Caganni scanned her list once more. "And now we have the other assignments. Laurel Amos?"

My older cousin raised her hand. "Yes, ma'am?"

"You're in ti'Ammaas. Unless and until Maebe has children, you're her heir."

I looked back at Laurel, ten years my senior, and she flashed me an evil grin that I sincerely hoped was her way of teasing.

"Justin Church?" said Caganni, and nodded when he identified himself. "Thank you. You're in ti'Fer. The heir to that Hall is currently one of your sister's children, but—"

"No hard feelings," he interrupted, shaking his head.

"Thanks. And…that's it," she said, closing her computer. "Let me welcome you to the Pactlands," she said as the men flanking her nodded. "The titles are official, so feel free to use them. If you prefer your current name—and I do understand that—you needn't adopt the other, but that's your option."

"Again," said Mirrik, "your accounts will be finalized soon. If I may make a suggestion?"

We waited, watching him expectantly, and Peter motioned him on.

"Stay at North Lake for now," Mirrik continued. "If nothing else, housing and food won't come out of your savings. I realize that some of you are almost at graduation age, but considering your late start, you might want to stay a few years longer. The school has no problem with that, and delaying your graduation will give you the skills you'll need to find work."

Peter, who at thirty-four would be the first of us to the finish line, didn't argue with him. Then again, Monica was four years his junior, Eleanor was already in class, and Tobias was coming up behind her. Small as it was, occasionally as painful as it was, we had a community in the dorm, and after losing East Branch, no one seemed eager to move away.

The meeting wrapped up quickly thereafter, and as my cousins gathered their things to return to school, Jane tugged my sleeve. "Stick around, okay?" she murmured. "Haven't seen you in a bit, hon. I'll drive you back."

I agreed, told our dorm parents the plan, and waited while the others filed out, leaving Jane, Connor, and me with the two judges, Mirrik, Teolm, and Diriem.

Mirrik waited until the door closed, then gave Connor a little smile. "You're going to be an odd case, aren't you?"

"I'm not saying I don't appreciate all of this—I do," Connor replied. "But you need to understand that I've got commitments out there, and among those is making sure that East Branch doesn't get turned into a parking lot."

"Which was made clear to the Forum during our discussions last week," said Mirrik, shooting a knowing glance at Diriem.

Connor looked over at Diriem's poker face and muttered, "*Again?*"

Smoke grunted. "Get used to it, boy."

"Here's what we thought," said Mirrik. "You'll have unrestricted portal credentials, Connor—officially managed by DOI, but that's just on paper. If you need to be out there for now, we won't try to stop you. I mean, it's obvious that you know how to blend," he added, one corner of his mouth twitching. "Now, I *do* have concerns about the New York group..."

"And we can't watch them," Diriem added. "They're protected from farsight, remember."

"Right," said Mirrik, focusing on Connor. "I don't like the thought of you out there on your own, son. They know where to find you."

Connor nodded slowly. "I get that, but I can't spend the rest of my life in hiding."

"Would you consider training, at least? Something more formal than those lessons I *know* Mr. Hewt hasn't been giving to someone legally human?"

"I have no idea what you're talking about," said Jane,

grinning.

"I'm sure."

"Look," Diriem interjected, "Connor, I realize you've got a...*complicated* schedule, but can you carve out time? For your own sake? The better you learn to manage your abilities, the lower the chance of accidental use."

Connor frowned. "I've got things under wraps—"

"You're in a potentially stressful position, and I have *seen* you upset. Come to DOI," he offered. "I can set you up with Jane's tutors. Even if it's once a week, it'll do you good."

"And give me peace of mind in case your unfriendlier kinfolk come calling again," Mirrik added.

"It's actually pretty interesting," Jane murmured. "Besides, you know Annie wouldn't mind picking you up."

Connor gave her a long look, and she smiled.

"All right, fine," he said with a sigh. "If it'll make everyone happy."

As we started gathering our things, Connor paused and pointed to Mirrik. "Question."

"Sure," said the representative.

"No one's going to come after Jane with the draught now, right? We're good?"

At that, Caganni softly laughed. "You're legal, Lord ti'Catama. Whatever else happens is between the two of you."

My cousin still seemed bothered as we headed out of the room, and Teolm jogged up beside us. "It becomes less weird," he whispered.

"What's that?" Connor whispered back.

"The title. I've only had mine about two and a half years. It's...*bizarre* at first, but you adjust," he replied, and patted Connor on the back. "Be careful out there, Chief."

Once the three of us had piled into Jane's truck, she started the engine but remained parked. "Y'all okay?" she asked, mercifully slipping into English.

Connor leaned back against his seat and groaned. "Holy *shit*, Firebug. What've we gotten into now?"

"A question I keep asking myself," she said, and leaned over to kiss his cheek. "Welcome to the madhouse, Con. I'm sure Wylan will open more than enough bottles of booze tonight." Turning around, she added, "And welcome to *you*, little miss Lady ti'Ammaas. So, where am I going? Back to North Lake? Out to the Edolis so your cousin here can find a mountaintop suitable for a primal scream?"

"I'd settle for a beer," Connor muttered.

I sat there for a moment, my head still whirling, and finally realized that for the first time in months, I felt *safe*. Not like I had at home once, before I knew what lay beyond the fence of East Branch, but...I had a place to stay. An education ahead of me. More money than I'd ever imagined.

A family, diminished though it was, that was speaking to me again.

While I still felt the ache of our loss like the empty socket of a rotted tooth, I recognized also in my emotional muddle the stirrings of hope.

This was far from perfect. We'd lost our home and half our kin, only some of the people responsible would ever be punished, my heart was still injured, and I had absolutely *zero* idea what being the lady of a Hall entailed...but maybe this could be all right.

"I'd better get back to school," I told Jane. "Lot of work ahead of me."

"You've got it, hon," she replied, and drove off through the late-fall twilight as the last of the sunset glinted over Beukal.

# ACKNOWLEDGEMENTS

Hello again, dear reader! Thank you for coming along on the ride thus far. I do hope you've enjoyed and that you'll return for the conclusion of Maebe's trilogy.

Writing is often a solitary endeavor, but writer friends make everything better. My sincere thanks go to the Novel Chicks for keeping me around. Adam Domby somehow finds the time to give me his generous feedback, for which I remain so grateful.

And yes, here's to you, Mom and Dad.

# ABOUT THE AUTHOR

When not writing fiction, Ash Fitzsimmons is an appellate
attorney and an unrepentant car singer.

Find her online:
www.ashfitzsimmons.com